Under Ground

Under Ground

A Novel

Michael Daly

LITTLE, BROWN AND COMPANY
BOSTON NEW YORK TORONTO LONDON

First Edition

The characters and events in this book are fictitious.
Any similarity to real persons, living or dead,
is coincidental and not intended by the author.

Library of Congress Cataloging-in-Publication Data

Daly, Michael.
Under ground: a novel / Michael Daly.—1st ed.
p. cm.
ISBN 0-316-21709-3
I. Title. II. Title: Under ground.
PS3554.A454U53 1995
813′.54—dc20 94-48453

10 9 8 7 6 5 4 3 2 1

MV-NY

Published simultaneously in Canada
by Little, Brown & Company (Canada) Limited

Printed in the United States of America

For Mary Daly
“Not lost, but gone
before . . .”

I

One

THE DEAD AIR stirred and Jack Swann gazed across the deserted mezzanine to the stairs leading down to the platform. Another train was arriving and it was pushing the hot staleness before it. He felt the tunnel's breath and he listened to the rumble grow steadily louder.

"It should be over by now," Swann said.

Swann was addressing Police Officer Barney Fredricks, who was his partner. Fredricks was tall and thin, Swann of medium height and more than average girth. Fredricks wore dark blue slacks and a powder blue polo shirt; Swann, denims and a green shirt. They remained indistinguishable by the measure that held them both to be civil servants of the transit cop variety. This Independence Day of 1986 saw them working plainclothes in the Times Square subway station while the whole city seemed to be down at the harbor's edge.

"I don't know," Fredricks said. "They say it's supposed to be the biggest one ever."

The rumbling stopped. Swann kept his eyes on the stairwell until even the slowest passenger would have ascended from the platform. Another train had come in empty.

"Anyway, what's it matter?" Fredricks asked.

A younger Swann would have taken the remark as proof of the difference between himself and officers such as Fredricks. The Swann of this night was thirty-six years old, and one small sign of his youth's passing was that he was not so quick to decide that Fredricks was wrong. He went back to surveying the underground mezzanine with its steel columns and grimy concrete floor.

The overhead fluorescent lighting was the same day or night, but on this particular evening his assigned realm seemed all the more gloomy for being deserted. He felt his heart thump from one uneventful moment to another, and he had the general sense of slowly cooking in his own circumstance.

"What time is it?" Swann asked.

"You got a watch," Fredricks said.

Swann had never worn a watch as a civilian, but the Patrol Guide deemed a working timepiece to be as much a part of an officer's equipment as handcuffs and a revolver. He glanced at his watch and saw that it was not quite as late as he had imagined.

"And forget about going for meal early," Fredricks said.

Fredricks assumed that someone so stout as Swann must be forever hungry, though this was not the case almost half the time. Swann had, in fact, hardly thought about food since assuming his post four hours before.

He did so now only at the mention of meal period. He was contemplating a double pastrami sandwich with Russian dressing when he once more felt the breath of an approaching train.

He had his eyes back on the stairwell as the squeal of brakes came from the tracks below. Another train brought only a momentary break in the silence, and he fell to wondering if he would rather have a double cheeseburger with Russian dressing.

The next train's arrival was followed by a scuffling on the steps, and Swann saw the first citizens returning from the harbor. People of every description herded shoulder to shoulder up to the mezzanine, their faces offering no hint that they had joined the President himself in marking the Statue of Liberty's hundredth birthday. They had just witnessed what had been billed as the biggest fireworks display in American history. They showed only a desire to leave the dank and dirty subway.

Not one of the many citizens paid the slightest attention to Swann, but that would only have added to the drama had the chance arisen for him to leap to their rescue. Their hero would seem to have materialized out of nowhere.

The problem was that for all the public's fears the underground was not that dangerous a place. The whole vast system with its millions of riders reported an average of thirty-five crimes a day.

Still, even one crime was a lot if you happened to be the victim, and enough of a real threat existed to maintain both the public's dread and Swann's vigilance. He remained watchful as a second and a third and a fourth train discharged passengers. The closest thing he saw to a crime came when a man dropped a candy wrapper.

A littering collar was not what Swann had in mind, and his vigilance might have faltered had his adolescence not been such perfect training for a job that consisted mainly of standing around watching other people do things. He had only to do what he had done as a fatso all through high school, and he found that working the subway was in some ways much easier. The underground had no In crowd.

Swann glanced at Fredricks, who had been the type in high school who played football and felt up the girl with the big tits. Fredricks had not easily adjusted to the life of a transit cop, and he had long since ceased to look for anything other than an easy collar when he was in need of a little overtime. He now had the profoundly vacant look that comes over cops of all agencies who do not want to make an arrest that will land them in court on a holiday. He had told Swann he was planning a Liberty Weekend barbecue for the following afternoon.

Another train brought more shuffling, and among the first faces to rise from the concrete was that of a raven-haired woman with huge blue eyes. More of her appeared with each ascending step, her long neck followed by her full breasts followed by her rounded hips. The hem of her black dress clung to a rising thigh and a knee flashed bare.

Swann heard a grunt and he looked over to see that Fredricks had snapped alert. Swann returned his attention to the woman, feeling himself taken over by what he did indeed share with his partner.

"Nice," Fredricks said.

Swann could only agree. He was married and he had a daughter who gave him great joy, but that did not keep him from swelling with desire as unthinking as had filled him in high school. A fatso still had the same yearnings as the coolest of quarterbacks.

"Oh," Swann said.

"Oh, yeah," Fredricks said.

Swann watched the woman give a turnstile a little bump with her hips, and the single metallic clank came to him as though it were the only noise in the crowded station. She passed on to the street and he was left standing as if the bustle around him were silence. He felt a trickle of sweat race down between the two meaty slabs of his back.

"Oh, shit," Swann said.

The next train brought a group of teenagers who stepped with immaculate sneakers onto the grimy mezzanine. They were black and they wore neatly pressed clothes in the latest street fashion and each carried an extra jacket or shirt of the previous season's styles. These were "throwaways," to be donned just before a robbery and discarded immediately afterward.

The smooth young faces looked puzzled by the rush hour crowd on a Saturday evening, and Swann decided that this posse was unaware of the great celebration of Lady Liberty's centenary. They must have thought that this was just another night for the posses of the outer boroughs to go robbing in midtown Manhattan.

Swann shifted his weight from foot to foot and watched the youngsters head for the street. They were not bothering to look about for either cops or victims. Even fledgling criminals knew that the fear of the underground was so pervasive that nobody with real money was likely to take a train at night. And no crook traveled all the way in to Manhattan to rob somebody who could not even afford a cab.

On they went through the turnstiles, no doubt off to stalk some unfortunate victim or, in their parlance, "vic." Swann was still enough unlike Fredricks that he pictured himself shadowing them through midtown, poised to intercede when they struck. The reality of being a transit cop was such that he could follow them only with his eyes as they trooped up the steps leading beyond his official jurisdiction.

After a few more trains, the crowds began to dwindle. Swann watched another posse start across the mezzanine and were this in fact just another Saturday night he would have continued to stand his post.

All week, he had been hearing talk that Liberty Weekend had fallen at a time when America had returned to glory, when Vietnam had become only an error in strategy, when patriotism was again fashionable and the economy was booming proof that the country's destiny was indeed divine. Tonight was supposed to be historic, and he was having more trouble than usual simply staying put.

Besides, he decided that what he really craved was a cheese omelette and sausages. He guessed the teenagers would be turning uptown, which meant he could trail them for a few blocks on the way to the nearest diner.

"Officer Fredricks, let's take the air," Swann said.

Fredricks checked his watch.

"We still got forty minutes," Fredricks said.

Swann found he was also more impatient than usual with Fredricks. He pulled the tiny knob at the side of his own watch and twirled it between thumb and forefinger until the hour and minute hands stood at the start of the meal period set by their sergeant. This half hour was the one time a transit cop was allowed to venture into the street.

"Your watch must be slow," Swann said.

Swann's ample middle prowed through the turnstile and he reached the eighteen littered steps just as the teenagers hit the street. He lumbered on up to see that he had guessed right. They were indeed heading uptown.

"What, it's gonna kill you to stay in the hole a few more minutes?" Fredricks asked.

Swann stepped from his official domain and turned the corner to trail the teenagers up Broadway.

"What do we do if he sees us?" Fredricks asked.

"What would the sergeant be doing up here?" Swann asked. "He's with the transit police. He's supposed to stay in the subway."

Swann felt a crosstown breeze and caught a whiff of marijuana and tasted the diesel exhaust of a passing bus. He heard a child's laugh and a drunk's slurred shout and the blare of a portable radio. He saw couples in evening clothes and out-of-towners in leisure suits and kids in street attire and derelicts in castoffs, and he did not for an instant lose sight of the dozen heads bobbing together beneath the lights of Times Square.

"One reason he might be up here is to look for us," Fredricks said.

"We'll say we were looking for him," Swann said.

Swann watched the teenagers' springing step deepen to a loose-jointed roll. Every citizen who veered from their path, each pair of eyes that dropped to the sidewalk, all the small but unmistakable signs of fear, proved that as far as the teenagers were concerned this was indeed a night like any other. The President might have been aboard a mighty warship down at the harbor and a million people might have stood at the water's edge to join him in celebrating the nation's glory. The fear of young black skin still ruled the street.

"Why would we be looking for him up here?" Fredricks asked.

Swann saw the teenagers slow. They had been shown only fright by those who had money and position and power. They seemed now itchy to become the very specter that had gotten the fear going.

"We figured he might be looking for us," Swann said.

The back of Swann's neck prickled as he watched the teenagers match their step to that of an elderly woman who was edging along, her purse slung over her shoulder. He tugged once on Fredricks's sleeve.

"What?" Fredricks asked.

Fredricks only then realized that Swann was not just after food.

"Hey, how're we gonna explain a collar up here?" Fredricks asked.

"We'll say they were robbing somebody," Swann said.

Swann scooted ahead, knowing Fredricks would come along. He had halved the lead to fifteen feet when the teenagers began to look about for police.

Swann lowered his eyes and eased to a casual stroll. He felt a surge under his ribs as he now did all he could to escape notice. He looked up to see that the teenagers were pulling on their throwaways.

The woman crossed the street and appeared to focus all her attention on mounting the far curb without falling. She did not sense danger even as two of the teenagers stepped ahead of her and prepared to make the block. The others eased up from behind, and one of them cocked his right arm for the snatch, taking a final glance over his shoulder.

Swann lowered his eyes again. He fixed his gaze on the snatcher's feet, and all the rest of Times Square fell away. Everything in him poised for the instant that those immaculate white sneakers would flash into motion.

"Five-O!"

One of the posse had called out a street term for police taken from the name of a television show. The sneakers broke stride and Swann looked up to see the snatcher peel away without making the hit. The woman tottered on into the rosy glow cast by the Coca-Cola sign at the top of the square.

"Thank God," Fredricks said.

Swann gazed about, sure that the posse had "made" neither him nor Fredricks. He spotted a gray Dodge cruising down Broadway a touch slower than the traffic. The three passengers were plainclothes officers of the city police.

Here were cops who worked up in the street and drove cars with sirens and radios, who would dismiss him as a "cave cop." They rode past, slouched in their superior copness, oblivious to the robbery they had interrupted, their eyes dulled with the same holiday vacancy as the partner whose grumbling again reached his ear.

"You had enough?" Fredricks asked.

Swann looked over to see that the teenagers had suspended their hunt to get their picture taken by a sidewalk photographer. They were laughing and clowning like kids on a class trip as they squeezed together before a backdrop emblazoned with dollar signs and the words GO BIG OR STAY HOME.

"Where we ought to go is back," Fredricks said.

"Back where?" Swann asked.

"The fucking *subway,*" Fredricks said.

The near hit had left Swann all the more hungry.

"What're you, nuts?" Swann said. "We still got twenty minutes of meal."

The waitress at the Parthenon Coffee Shop wore a black polyester uniform. She had dyed red hair and penciled eyebrows. She was nearly as fat as Swann.

"Sausage is a dollar thirty-five extra," the waitress said.

"That's okay," Swann said.

"I just wanted you to know," the waitress said. "One check or two?"

"One," Swann said.

"Two," Fredricks said.

Fredricks ordered only coffee, to which he added four packets of artificial sweetener. Swann took his black, sipping with pursed lips as he studied the people who passed along the sidewalk outside. The well-dressed citizens were all strangers. Nearly every street person was familiar.

"You didn't see enough freaking people tonight?" Fredricks asked. "I mean, it's not like we could have at least took a table at the back. We got to make sure the sergeant sees us."

Swann held up his watch.

"Relax," Swann said. "We got another fifteen minutes."

The omelette arrived. Swann forked in a mouthful and placed his elbows on either side of the plate as he chewed and swallowed.

"Fuck," Fredricks said.

Swann saw that Fredricks had spilled coffee down the front of his shirt. Fredricks reached for a napkin and a glass of water. He only succeeded in enlarging the stain.

"I don't think that's working," Swann said.

"Fuck," Fredricks said.

Swann took a genteel sip of his coffee and ate steadily until he was done. He leaned back, his hands pressed against the edge of the table. A calm radiated from his gut and rose in his throat as a sigh. He spoke only when the waitress slapped down the checks.

"The sausages were excellent," Swann said.

Swann left $2 over the tab and stepped from the cool of the Parthenon to the heat of the street. He and his contented belly turned back toward the subway, but he had gone just a half block when his eye chanced upon a group of figures on the other side of Broadway. The posse that had almost pounced on the elderly woman was now trailing a middle-aged executive type who looked as if he had just tottered from some bar.

"You take this side," Swann said.

"Forget it," Fredricks said.

Swann was starting across Broadway when he saw one of the teenagers break from the group and step quickly up to the executive. He had done enough meal-period hunting of posses to know that the moment had come to "size" the vic.

The idea was for the teenager to check the executive's eyes in that first instant a black face appeared before him. A steady gaze would suggest a rare readiness to fight, most likely inspired by the possession of a badge and gun. The more usual response was the faint but unmistakable flicker that signaled fright and weakness.

The next step was to dispel the alarm by making an excuse for the approach. The executive checked his watch, and Swann knew that this teenager had chosen the usual ruse of asking for the time.

The executive lurched on down Broadway as the teenager reported to his fellows. Their visible agitation told Swann that the executive's trousers must have had a good "pocket print," as the outline of folded cash was called. He watched them make their decision without deferring to any particular teenager. He had on other nights noted that the posses were generally not guided by a dominant figure, that no individual could be called a leader or, for that matter, a follower. They were all just going along. They were all just there.

The executive continued down Broadway, the scuffle of his loafers matched by the pad of the dozen pairs of sneakers behind him. Swann followed in his black tie shoes. He took his eyes off the posse just long enough to check that Fredricks was keeping parallel on the other side of the street.

At the corner, the executive again paused for traffic. The teenagers stopped, and the tallest one crouched to pull up his right sock. Swann drifted to the doorway of a souvenir shop and absently spun a postcard carousel. Pictures of the Statue of Liberty squeaked before him.

The executive started across the street. The teenagers were right behind him and Swann stayed right behind them. He drifted toward the curb until he could follow their reflections in the windows of a clothing store favored by the older pimps.

In the glass, Swann saw one of the teenagers look over his shoulder. Swann shifted his gaze across Broadway and saw that Fredricks was moving through the glow of the Coca-Cola sign. The teenager had swung his head back toward the executive by the time Swann returned his eyes to the glass.

At that instant, the reflections of the teenagers became a streak. Swann was already in motion as he looked to see one of the taller ones throw a choke hold. The executive went up on his toes and let out a strangled shout.

* * *

Three great bounds and Swann was there. His left hand shot out to grab the collar of the taller one's plaid throwaway while his right went for the back of the pants. He spoke in a low, firm voice.

"Here I am," Swann said.

The teenager thrust his hips to the left, breaking Swann's grip on his belt. His shoulders dipped down to the right, and he slung the executive to the pavement.

The throwaway stretched taut and then came off in Swann's hand as the teenager catapulted himself straight down Broadway. Swann leaped in pursuit and a burst of adrenaline gave him the exhilarating sensation of being as sleek and lean as the quarry that stayed just out of his grasp.

The teenager bucked to the left and swerved back to the right. Swann kept straight on and pitched himself forward, throwing out both his hands. His fingertips brushed the teenager's back.

The touch ignited something in the teenager, and Swann suddenly found himself a full stride behind, shouting, "*Police!*" The Liberty Weekend crowds parted before them, young women in summer dresses and tourists in Bermuda shorts and sailors in dress whites now all taking notice of Jack Swann. He felt their attention as a physical force that fired him on.

At the end of the next block, Swann began to gasp for air. He had known from the start that he would be good for only a short distance, and he now jolted to a stop, his chest heaving, his legs leaden. He watched the teenager vanish along the shadowy edge of an excavation site.

Swann turned to look back up Broadway. The other teenagers had scattered when he pounced, and he could see neither them nor Fredricks. He saw only streams of pedestrians and fleets of cars that passed gleaming through the blaze of billboards and marquees.

Swann heard brakes squeal and a horn blare. He saw a cab veer across two lanes of traffic to pick up a middle-aged couple. The man was opening the door for the woman when Swann brushed past her and dove in.

"Police officer," Swann said.

The driver stared at the fat man who had landed wheezing on the backseat. Swann had to show his badge before the cab began to speed down Broadway. Night air flowed through the open windows, cooling his face and chest.

Swann could only guess the teenager's path beyond the excavation site. Uptown was out of the question. Downtown meant exposure in the lights of the square. Left entailed crossing Broadway and leaving the cover of the crowded sidewalk.

"Make a right at the next corner," Swann said.

The cab turned onto West Forty-fifth Street and Swann spotted a lone head bobbing in front of several couples in evening dress. The teenager was keeping to the slow pace of the crowd, trying not to draw attention as he made for the dark sanctuary of Eighth Avenue.

"Not too fast," Swann said.

Swann slid low in the backseat. He felt the barrel of his revolver prod his groin and he pulled the weapon from his waistband. He laid it on his lap, his fingers resting lightly on the black rubber grip.

"Very easy now," Swann said.

The driver flicked off the radio, and Swann could hear the tires hiss on the asphalt as the front bumper drew even with the teenager. Swann ducked his head into the shadows below the window.

"Pull over by the theater," Swann said.

Swann's right hand tightened around the revolver grip. His left reached for the door latch.

"Okay," Swann said.

Swann rocked upright and yanked the latch and threw his shoulder into a locked door.

"It sticks sometimes," the driver said.

The lock clicked, and Swann leaped from the cab just as the teenager came alongside. He grabbed the teenager by the shirtfront and slammed him against the white brick wall of the theater.

"Remember me?" Swann said.

The teenager's black, unflinching eyes showed no emotion. He was betrayed by the heart that hammered hard and fast under Swann's open hand.

"If you run, I am going to kill you," Swann said.

Swann made his own face a mask. He seized a fistful of sweated shirt and laid his forearm across the teenager's chest.

"Do you understand me?"

Swann pulled down and to the right, yanking the teenager off balance and whipping him around. The teenager knew he was to throw his hands on the wall. Swann planted his own left hand between the teenager's shoulder blades.

"There," Swann said.

Swann stole a sidelong glance and saw a ring of onlookers.

"Move along, people," Swann said. "There's nothing to see."

The flesh under Swann's left hand began to shift slowly from side to side. He forgot the onlookers and returned his full attention to the teenager.

"Place your hands behind your back," Swann said.

The teenager's splayed fingers trembled on the bricks. Swann took the handcuffs from his belt, and there was a clicking sound as he squeezed open one of the bracelets.

"Now!" Swann said.

The teenager hurled himself off the wall and into a spin. Swann's index finger curled on the smooth steel of the trigger and then froze. He had drawn his revolver to intimidate, but his bluff was being called. He was not about to shoot an unarmed kid.

"Hey," Swann said.

The teenager slapped both hands on the revolver. He was as strong as he was quick.

"No," Swann said.

The handcuffs clattered to the sidewalk, and Swann struggled with both his own hands to hold on to the revolver. He threw back his shoulders, rocking onto his heels. The revolver rose in a quivering arc traced by the tip of his bulk against the teenager's strength.

"Let go," Swann said.

Swann felt his right heel skid, and he was suddenly on his back with the teenager's breath hot on his cheeks. The teenager's eyes were slits. His own eyes widened.

The revolver went slick with the sweat of the grappling hands, and Swann felt the grip twist in his fingers as the barrel began to pivot toward his face. He had his free hand on the cylinder, and he pushed away with all his might. The barrel continued to pivot. The grip kept twisting, catching on his hooked fingertips. It tore free.

* * *

The black hole of the muzzle now loomed huge before Swann's eyes. He clasped both hands around the cylinder in an attempt to freeze the firing mechanism. He felt the steel begin to rotate between his palms.

Swann thrashed his feet and arched his back and strained with his arms. The muzzle jerked a half inch to the left.

The shot was an almost distant popping sound. Orange and blue flame flashed from the muzzle, and a wind more heated than the teenager's breath seared Swann's cheek. The bullet had missed. Swann's voice went high as he screamed.

"He's killing me!"

The barrel jerked back to the right. The hot muzzle brushed Swann's lips.

"Help!"

The cylinder again began to spin in Swann's palms. A spasm of panic charged his arms and he pushed with all his might as a second remote explosion came. The orange and blue flame flashed up and away.

"God! No!"

Swann unthinkingly drew up his right foot and pitched to the left. He was surprised to end up on top, gazing down at the teenager's face. The face clenched and the teenager bucked and Swann was once more on his back. They were cheek to cheek and the revolver was now pressed between them. Their hands grappled blindly.

Then Swann felt the contour of the trigger guard. He wriggled his right index finger and touched the trigger itself. He could not see the revolver. He could neither see nor feel which way the barrel was pointed.

The teenager tugged, and the trigger began to slip away. Swann was losing strength and he knew that whatever chance this was, it was his only one. He held his breath and gazed up over the teenager's shoulder and past the lights of the theater to the black night sky. He curled his finger around the flange of steel.

The teenager's scream seemed louder than the shot. His head rose, his eyes wide, his hands still on the gun, but now pushing it away. He sounded young and frightened as he spoke for the first time.

"I'm shot," the teenager said.

Swann yanked the gun from the teenager's hands and clasped it tightly in his own. He aligned the end of the barrel with a spot just below the teenager's nose.

"Don't," the teenager said.

The finger on the trigger did not move. Swann heaved his hips and the teenager rolled off him. The teenager lay face up as Swann got on one shaking knee. He watched blood seep across the front of the teenager's T-shirt.

"God," the teenager said.

A shout caused Swann to look up. He saw Fredricks stepping over citizens who had thrown themselves to the pavement. Fredricks stopped and pointed his revolver at the teenager's head.

"I'm gonna kill you, motherfucker," Fredricks said.

The teenager raised a hand to his face. His eyelids fluttered and his lips parted in a moan.

"Fredricks, either blow his head off or put your fucking gun away," Swann said.

Fredricks lowered the revolver and turned to Swann.

"You got blood all over you," Fredricks said.

Swann looked down and saw that the teenager's blood was smeared across his chest.

"Are you hurt?" Fredricks asked.

Swann gazed up at Fredricks, who had only the coffee stain over which he had fretted.

"No," Swann said.

"I lost the others," Fredricks said.

Swann stuck his revolver back in his waistband and retrieved his handcuffs. He realized how weak the fight had left him as he strained to flip the teenager over.

"I need help," Swann said.

Fredricks yanked the teenager's shoulder, rolling him onto his stomach. Swann drew the limp arms together and snapped on the handcuffs. He patted the teenager down.

"So, what's the story?" Fredricks asked.

Swann understood that Fredricks was not asking something so

irrelevant as what had actually transpired. He was following an unofficial procedure whereby the officers involved in an incident agree on their story before the first supervisor arrives.

"We were on meal," Swann said.

"What happened then?" Fredricks asked.

Swann had his palms resting on the teenager's back. He felt the teenager's rib cage swell in unison with his own. He heard a wet, whistling sound as the teenager exhaled.

"What happened is what happened," Swann said.

"What did I see?"

"What you saw."

"Whatever you say."

Sirens keened up the block and squad cars began to screech to the curb. Uniformed city cops leaped out wild-eyed, guns drawn, portable radios crackling with a report of shots fired. One cop bowled over a man who was stooping to brush off his trousers.

Swann rose from beside the teenager and held out his badge.

"I'm a police officer," Swann said. "Put your guns away. I'm all right. This is the perp. He's shot."

Black shoes ringed the teenager. Voices jittery with adrenaline rang out.

"Die."

"Die, you fuck."

"Nigger motherfucker. Die."

Swann found himself grabbing one of the cops by the elbow.

"We should get the crowd back," Swann said.

A toe cap dug into the teenager's side. Swann again felt a protective reflex he could not have explained.

"I already shot him," Swann said. "I don't need anybody to kick him."

The ring broke and the black shoes moved toward the onlookers. The voices grew even and assured.

"Let's go, people."

"Get back."

"Move along."

* * *

Swann remained standing beside the teenager as Fredricks went in search of the executive who had been robbed. A uniformed transit cop named Paddy Mannering huffed over, having heard enough on his radio to come running from his post.

"Do we want witnesses, Jack?" Mannering asked.

"Yes, Paddy," Swann said. "We want witnesses."

An ambulance arrived and a burly driver barged through the onlookers, lugging equipment. Behind him came a thin technician who wore wire-rimmed glasses.

Swann knelt beside the teenager, and his trembling fingers struggled to fit the tiny handcuff key into the lock.

A petite pair of black shoes appeared next to Swann, and his fingers were pushed aside by a pair of small hands a shade darker than those of the teenager. These hands were sure and steady and they had the cuffs off in an instant.

"Yours?"

The hands that now held the cuffs out to Swann belonged to a uniformed female transit cop named Coleman. She had worked in his district for the past few months, but he had never paid her much attention beyond a quick initial appraisal that classified her as female, black, and closer to plain than pretty.

"Thanks," Swann said.

Swann took the cuffs, and he found himself being almost gentle as he joined her in turning the teenager over.

"How you doin', pal?" the ambulance driver asked.

"I'm all right," Swann said.

"Can you hear me, pal?" the driver asked.

Swann understood that the driver was talking to the teenager.

"Are you diabetic?" the ambulance technician asked.

"Can you hear me?" the driver asked.

"Are you allergic to anything?" the technician asked.

The teenager worked his lips without speaking. His head lolled back and forth. His muscular arms flailed in an infant's aimless circles.

"Who shot him?" the driver asked.

"I did," Swann said.

The driver shone a penlight in the teenager's right eye.

"Pupils dilated," the driver said. "How many times?"

"Once," Swann said.

The teenager's chest heaved, and Swann again heard the wet, whistling sound. The technician cut away the teenager's T-shirt, and blood glistened crimson on the dark skin. There was a bubbling black hole just below the left nipple.

"I got one here," the technician said.

The technician slapped a piece of aluminum foil over the black hole and the whistling sound stopped. He applied a pressure bandage and ran an IV line into the teenager's left arm.

The driver calmly forced one end of a clear plastic airway down the teenager's throat. An orange bag half the size of a football was attached to the other end, and he began squeezing air into the teenager's lungs.

The technician tugged canvas shock trousers over the teenager's pressed Lee jeans. He was inflating the trousers with a foot pump when Fredricks came back with the executive who had been mugged.

Fredricks recited what cops are taught to ask at a show-up identification.

"Do you recognize anybody and, if so, from where?" Fredricks asked.

The executive rubbed his throat and stared down at a closed-eyed face gone slack save where the lips suckled the plastic airway.

"I know they were black," the executive said.

Coleman and several other uniformed cops helped the ambulance crew place the teenager on a stretcher. The driver strapped a small EKG monitor between the teenager's legs, and Swann kept his eyes on the four-inch gray screen as he trailed the stretcher to the ambulance. The neon green line was still bouncing as the teenager was loaded into the back.

Procedure required an officer to ride with an injured prisoner, and Coleman hopped inside. The doors thumped shut and Swann watched the ambulance roar off into the Liberty Weekend traffic, lights flashing, siren wailing as they would had he been the one on the stretcher.

A hand touched Swann's arm, and he turned to face an aging city sergeant. Swann presented his badge and identification card. He then held out his revolver, butt first. The barrel was warm.

The sergeant broke open the revolver and emptied the cylinder into his hand. He kept the three spent shells, handing back the three live rounds with the revolver.

"These are still good," the sergeant said.

Swann returned the revolver to his waistband empty.

"What happened?" the sergeant asked.

Swann's fingers closed around the three bullets still in his hand. His words came out fast.

"He tried to get my gun and I . . ."

Swann stopped when the uniformed transit cop, Paddy Mannering, took his arm.

"Hold on, Sarge, this officer is hurt and he's going to the hospital," Mannering said. "You can talk to him later."

"I'm okay," Swann said.

"Come on," Mannering said.

The sergeant was left standing there as Mannering led Swann over to a squad car.

"It's always better if you're hurt," Mannering said.

The teenager lay on a steel gurney in the trauma room, his heartbeat now recorded by the larger screen of an EKG monitor mounted on the wall. He was surrounded by people in white and surgical green. Their voices were tense and excited.

"No respiration."

"Dilated pupils."

"He's almost flat."

Swann watched from the doorway as a young man in surgical green got on a footstool and placed both hands just below the teenager's sternum. The young man counted aloud as he pushed.

"*One.*"

"Do we have a rhythm at all?"

"*Two.*"

"Do we have a pulse with this rhythm?"

"*Three.*"

"Can we get some leads in this guy at least?"

"*Four.*"

A nurse with pale blond hair began squeezing a bag of intravenous fluid. A doctor raised a huge syringe primed with a clear liquid.

"*One.*"

"Do we have blood on this guy?"

"*Two.*"

"I got decreased breathing sounds on the right."

"*Three.*"

"Can someone make me up a chest tube?"

"*Four.*"

A doctor sliced a half-inch hole in the teenager's side, and bright red arterial blood exploded from the chest cavity. The geyser sprayed the blond nurse and splashed onto the linoleum.

"*One.*"

"Damn."

"*Two.*"

Overhead, the EKG monitor was buzzing. Swann felt his own heart pound as he watched the light blue line cross the screen without a ripple.

"*Three.*"

"That's it. Let's call it."

The young man got off the footstool. He and the blond nurse and the rest of the trauma team filed silently past Swann and into the hall.

The teenager was left alone and open-eyed on the gurney. His lips were blue around the plastic airway and his skin had turned waxen. The floor below him was spattered with blood and littered with gauze and surgical gloves and an open pair of scissors.

"Mister, excuse."

A janitor pushed a mop bucket into the room and Swann turned back to the hall. He slumped on a yellow plastic chair, his body aching now, the muzzle flash on his cheek starting to sting. His gun hand also hurt, and he saw that he had torn the flesh between the thumb and the forefinger.

Swann absently sucked on his tiny wound, and juices seeped into his dry mouth. He tasted gunpowder and blood and he became conscious of the ticking of the watch strapped to his wrist.

"Want something for that?"

Swann looked up and saw the blond nurse. The front of her white uniform was sprayed with blood.

"You're the officer who was in the shooting, aren't you?" the nurse asked. "One of the uniformed officers said you were hurt."

Swann considered that Mannering was right, that he should have some injury officially recorded. He held up his gun hand. The fingers were still trembling.

"Maybe you could put down I got a cut here," Swann said.

"Do you want something to relax you?" the nurse asked.

"No. Thanks. You got a phone I can use?"

"If it's local."

Swann rose and glanced back through the doorway to Trauma 1. The floor had been swabbed clean and the janitor was cranking the mop through the ringer. The soap water frothed pink.

Nobody answered, but Swann knew his wife, Ellen, would be no other place but home. He let the phone keep ringing.

"*Hello?*"

Ellen's voice was thick with sleep.

"Listen, don't get upset," Swann said.

"Upset? About what?"

"I'm all right. I had to shoot a guy."

"Jackie . . ."

"I'm all right."

Swann caught some movement to his right, and he looked over to see Coleman striding by the nurse's station, her revolver looking huge on her narrow hip, her shield shining big and bright on her chest. She could not have weighed more than ninety-five pounds, but she passed with undeniable authority.

"Did he die?" Ellen asked.

"Yes," Swann said. "He died. He's dead."

Swann noticed for the first time a thin, two-inch braid dangling from under the back of Coleman's hat.

"Well, better him than you," Ellen said.

Swann stood silent, listening to the faint crackle of the telephone wire that stretched between him and Ellen. He watched Coleman continue away and he saw the sergeant who was his immediate supervisor approach. Sergeant Quinn was accompanied by Lieutenant Raymond Gentile of the transit Internal Affairs Division.

"I'll be right with you," Swann said.

"What?" Ellen asked.

"I was talking to somebody," Swann said.

"Where are you?"

"The hospital."

"I thought you were okay."

"I am. I am."

"Jackie."

"Go back to bed."

"I wasn't in bed. I was watching the fireworks. I must have fell asleep."

Swann became aware of the television murmuring in the background.

"I'll talk to you when I see you," Swann said.

Swann hung up and met Lieutenant Gentile's lidded gaze. IAD reviewed all shootings involving transit cops as part of a larger duty to investigate any possible wrongdoing within the department. Cops called IAD "the Dark Side."

"Good evening, Officer Swann," Gentile said.

Gentile was holding a pipe, and he stuck the stem in his mouth as he fixed Swann with a silent stare. Swann might have been intimidated if he had not just killed a youngster who had come very close to killing him. He remained numb.

"Lieu, I don't know if you're supposed to smoke here," Swann said.

At that moment, a pair of city detectives came up carrying a manila envelope and a clear plastic bag containing the teenager's T-shirt. The time had come for the next step of the routine, and Swann followed them out.

Mannering stood by the double doors, saying something that brought a giggle from the blond nurse with the blood-sprayed uniform.

"Thanks, Paddy," Swann said.

The nurse covered her mouth on seeing Swann.

"Anytime, Jackie boy," Mannering said.

The ambulance had left for another job. An unmarked car with a crumpled fender was parked at the curb, and Swann waited while the detectives searched their pockets.

"You got the keys?"

"You got 'em."

"I do?"

"Yeah. No. Wait."

The detective who had spoken last was balding and wore a blue wrinkled suit. He raised his arm and jingled the keys, giving Swann a little nod.

The squadroom at the Midtown North station house swarmed with people from the Precinct Detective Unit and Transit Police District 1 and transit Major Case and Manhattan Detective Task Force and Patrol Borough Midtown North and the Crime Scene Unit and Emergency Service and, with the arrival of Lieutenant Gentile, transit IAD. Telephones rang. Voices called out.

"Who's with the DOA?"

"Call the ME. Make sure we get the bullet."

"Who has the tuna on rye?"

"What's the time of death?"

"Who's making the notifications?"

"We want that cab driver."

"We got ballistics on the other shots?"

"This ain't Sanka."

Nobody was supposed to question Swann until his union-supplied lawyer arrived. He sat beside a gray metal desk where the balding detective upended the manila envelope. The teenager had been carrying a silver house key, a quarter, two nickels, a folded bit of notebook paper, and a Polaroid from when the posse had posed for the street photographer.

Swann pointed at a face to the right of the picture's center.

"That's him," Swann said. "And those are the ones who were with him."

The balding detective mumbled no more than polite interest, as if he were being shown a family snapshot. He had the executive as a complainant, a perpetrator who was not going anywhere, and numerous upstanding witnesses. He did not need to go chasing after all these other young criminals.

"I forgot to ask you," the balding detective said.

Swann looked up.

"You want coffee?" the balding detective asked.

"Thanks," Swann said.

Swann's eyes went back to the Polaroid and the teenager who had been just one of the posse. The teenager was standing with his arms folded across his chest, his head cocked back and to the side. One corner of his mouth was raised toward a smile.

The balding detective brought a Styrofoam cup for Swann and one for himself and then sat down to unfold the bit of notebook paper from the teenager's pocket. Swann craned his neck to see the name Darlene and a telephone number. The handwriting was flourished with a teenage girl's loops and swirls.

"This look like a seven or a nine?" the balding detective asked.

He held out the paper with his thumb on the fourth digit of the telephone number.

"A nine," Swann said.

The balding detective dialed the number and spoke in the tone of somebody who had made many such calls.

"Now try and be calm, Darlene. That was Daryl what?"

The balding detective wrote *Daryl Coombs.*

"Did he tell you how old he was?"

The detective wrote, *16.*

"You wouldn't by any chance know his date of birth, dear? . . . No, it's okay . . . Yes, I'm sure his mother will know."

The balding detective hung up.

"You were right," he said to Swann. "It was a nine. She just met him on the train last week. They were supposed to get together tomorrow night."

A stooped man in pinstripes came up to Swann and introduced himself as David Meltzer, the lawyer retained by the transit cop union. Meltzer's starched white shirt cuff ended in an absent handclasp. His voice had the hollow tone of a man who was going through the motions of serving as a cave counsel.

"I suppose we should talk," Meltzer said.

Swann went into a back room with Meltzer and recounted what had happened. He ended with his heart pounding and his mouth dry. He realized why the teenager must have fought.

"It turns out the kid had a date tomorrow night," Swann said. "I guess he didn't want to get locked up and miss it."

The lawyer grunted and stuck out his lower lip.

"We're fine," the lawyer said.

A young man in a blue blazer came into the room and began by asking Swann his first name.

"Hi, Jack, I'm Mr. Hurston," the young man said.

Hurston was an assistant district attorney, and he had Swann repeat his account before a video camera. The others in the room included the balding detective and Lieutenant Gentile, who silently packed his pipe until everybody else seemed satisfied that the teenager's death was what is known as a "good" shooting.

"There is one matter we have not addressed . . . ," Gentile said.

Gentile paused and held a match to his pipe. He puffed hard and sent up clouds of smoke before pulling the stem from his mouth. He solemnly declared the one sin the department considered Swann had committed in killing the teenager.

"Officer Swann, you were off the system," Gentile said.

Swann sat beyond all emotion. The pipe smoke smelled sickly sweet, like smoldering licorice.

"I told you, I was on meal," Swann said.

"That's what Fredricks told us," Gentile said.

"That's because Fredricks was with me," Swann said.

Gentile smiled.

"There remains the question of time," Gentile said.

Gentile's tone was patronizing, as if Swann was being foolish to lie in the face of uncontestable fact.

"Numerous sources place the shooting right about when you should have been leaving for meal," Gentile said. "Not returning."

Swann gazed at this man who was trying to intimidate him after what had happened. His first clear feeling since the shooting was a flash of resentment that burned to the depth he had been shaken.

"I guess I was wrong . . . ," Swann said.

Gentile began to smile again, now, at what seemed to be an admission.

". . . I thought Fredricks's watch was slow. I guess mine was fast."

Swann looked down at his watch.

"I got three-ten," Swann said. "What do you got?"

"Two-thirty," Gentile said.

"What do you know," Swann said.

Swann reset his watch, steeling his fingers against any tremor that Gentile would read as fear of IAD.

"There."

Gentile puffed some more smoke. He maintained his lidded gaze long enough to communicate that he might not be able to do anything now, but there would come a time when he would demonstrate to Swann that IAD was indeed something to be feared by officers who strayed from the hole.

"Officer Swann, I would recommend you purchase a more accurate timepiece," Gentile said.

Swann went out the green door marked Detectives and in a green door marked Men. He unzipped before an antique four-foot urinal and gazed down over the blood-spattered swell of his belly. He was just able to see the circumcised tip of the extremity he had sometimes heard compared to a gun. That had never seemed so wrong.

Swan pondered this flesh resting between his thumb and first two fingers. He could not have offered even a suitable name.

"Penis" was too anatomical. "Cock" was vulgar. "Prick" was too small. "Hammer" was too large. "Dick" was his father-in-law's name. "Shlong" was not commanding. "Johnson" was the wrong color.

"You know, I don't think your man from IAD likes you."

Swann glanced over his shoulder and saw that the lawyer, Meltzer, had come in.

"Anyway, you're not going to have any problem with the grand jury," Meltzer said.

Swann tucked his bit of flesh back in his jeans.

"Though you might want to wear a suit," Meltzer said. "It never hurts to make a good impression."

Fredricks was waiting outside the men's room with Sergeant Quinn. No IAD men were around, and Quinn seemed about to launch into the predictable tirade when he checked himself. Swann surmised that he must look very forlorn indeed.

"Is there anything I need to say?" Quinn asked.

"No," Swann said.

"You know I'm gonna have to do something?"

"Yes."

Swann followed as Fredricks and Quinn descended to the courtyard and the lone radio car fielded by District 1. They started uptown and a pair of city police cars screamed past, lights and sirens going. The transit car rolled the five blocks up to Columbus Circle, its transit radio silent, the driver yawning.

Sergeant Quinn led the way down into the subway and the underground headquarters of District 1. Swann stopped at the top of the steps, not ready to face a whole command full of cops with their looks and questions and pats on the back.

"Hey," Fredricks said. "Aren't you going to sign out?"

"No," Swann said.

"What's the sergeant gonna say?"

"He's gonna say I was supposed to sign out."

"What do you want me to tell him?"

Swann took a breath and felt his chest swell as he had felt the teenager's chest swell under his palms.

"Tell him I killed somebody and I felt like going home," Swann said.

None of the lines from the Columbus Circle station ran to Queens. Swann as usual ended a tour in the subway by strolling across town to a station where he could catch a direct train home. He started along the southern edge of Central Park and gazed to his right down darkened Broadway. Many of the marquees and electric signs of Times Square were no longer lit at this early morning hour, but the floodlights were still on a billboard across which reclined the 150-foot figure of a nearly nude woman. Her lips were parted with the ecstasy of wearing the latest Calvin Klein underwear.

Swann kept walking and peered over the stone wall on his left. The park lay silent and shadowy. Cast iron lamps shone white between the black silhouettes of the trees, the light turning a faint silver on the grass of the clearings.

Horse hooves clip-clopped on the asphalt ahead and Swann watched a sway-backed nag pull a carriage-for-hire out of the park. A woman's laugh rose from the backseat.

The driver flicked the reins and the nag raised its head and began trotting crosstown. Swann straggled along a row of luxury apartment buildings, listening to the sound of the horse hooves fade. He became aware of the rasp of denim rubbing against denim but felt none of the stinging that would signal his stout thighs were beginning to chafe themselves raw. He had employed his fatso's trick of dumping talcum powder down his denims just before the tour.

That seemed to have been in another time, one that had ended when he pulled the trigger. Each step he now took was a step that easily might not have been. His considerable girth did not make his existence seem any less a matter of whether a gun muzzle had swiveled a half inch one way or another.

Swann had the gun back in his waistband, and his emotions remained in keeping with this insensible instrument of his fate. He was feeling more like a ghost than a transit cop as he neared the Plaza Hotel and its incandescence of white marble and polished brass.

Swann came first to the small, dark opening at the near corner of the building's grand facade. This passageway's true purpose was disguised by a canvas awning that bore the name of an adjoining jewelry store. None of the usual exterior signs marked it as a subway entrance and no doubt many citizens passed by without imagining that below this most elegant hotel was a station as grimy as those beneath the city's most ragged neighborhoods.

The difference was that this was one part of the underground where minorities were actually in the minority. Swann's bosses had applied a theory that a scarcity of black people meant less crime, which translated into fewer arrests. That meant scarce overtime, and there lay the reason this station had long been the punishment post for District 1.

The entrance to the subway line that would take Swann home was another six blocks further on. He continued along the Plaza and he once more came to a four-by-five-foot window that was set a throne's height from the sidewalk. He peered inside expecting to view yet again the elegantly clad figures whose life seemed free of the worries and hazards that ruled his own. He was momentarily startled to see nobody at all.

Swann reminded himself that he was coming off-duty at least four hours later than he usually did after a night tour. The people beyond the plate glass had themselves returned home and he passed three more brass-framed windows without seeing a soul. He saw only a dim, wood-paneled chamber that was no less a realm apart for being empty.

Swann passed on beneath the Plaza's white awning. The brass doors and banisters were polished as bright as cartridge casings. The carpet that ran up the marble steps was the same emerald green as the uniform of the doorman who stood ready even at this hour. His gold-decked shoulders and sleeves made him look more elegant than any cop.

Swann circled the dry fountain at Grand Army Plaza and started down broad, deserted Fifth Avenue. He felt his heart continue to thump into the next instant and the next, and yet he discerned no higher meaning from the fact that Daryl Coombs was dead and Jack Swann was the one whose blood was still coursing. Each beat seemed at once more distinct and less significant.

He reached an intersection and saw the light switch from red to green as it would were he there or not. He crossed the street and descended into the subway. He stood alone on the platform, toeing the yellow caution line at the track's edge. He felt the air stir and he peered into the black muzzle of the tunnel to see an amber glow spread along the twin rails.

The glow slowly intensified to a white blaze, and a pair of headlights appeared. Metal screeched against metal. The platform began to vibrate. Swann took a step back and tensed against the coming roar.

He stepped into a car occupied by a lone dozing derelict. He stood with his back against the far doors.

"Oh," Swann said.

The brakes hissed and the train clanked to a slow roll. The car began to sway as the speed increased. The last lights of the platform fell away, and the window glass became a dark mirror. He beheld the stout, bloodstained figure that was nobody but John J. Swann.

"Oh, baby."

Two

IN THE HOUR BEFORE DAWN, Swann emerged from the subway and shuffled down the hushed streets where he had been raised. The cracked sidewalk pitched along a row of modest frame houses. Sycamore trees arched overhead, blocking all but a few pale beams of the streetlights.

Swann came to Forest Park, and he gazed into the deeper dark of the evergreens where he had passed many afternoons of his childhood. He peered down a path on which he had often scampered to join the neighborhood boys in their favorite game.

The game had been war, and Swann had done battle with an imitation-leather gunbelt cinching his outsized waist. He had lumbered more than crept, and he was killed so often that the rules were amended to allow for resurrection after a count of sixty.

One.

Two.

Three.

Four. Five, six, seven, eight more steps took Swann to the corner and the street where he had returned after being killed again and again in the woods. He kept on another two blocks and turned down this block to a frame house that was distinct from the others primarily because his name was on the mortgage.

Swann went up his stoop as he always did, as he might never have again, and he found himself listening to the thud of his own steps. He then heard the murmur of a television commercial through the open bay window.

"Meow-meow-meow-meow."

Swann squeezed his hand into his pocket and took out his key ring, flipping aside his handcuff key and the key to the Ford whose engine had long since self-destructed. He brought his house key up to the lock and found that his hand was still shaking.

"Meow-meow-meow-meow."

Swann used his other hand to steady the first and managed to unlock the door. He stepped over his daughter's tricycle and crossed the small foyer to the living room.

"Purina Cat Chow is meow-meow-meow-meow."

In the cool flicker of the television, Swann beheld the still form of Ellen sleeping on the sofa. She was on her back with a thin forearm draped across her modest breast. She wore a pink tank top and white panties.

"Meow-meow-meow-meow."

He hit the power switch to the television and the quartet of lip-syncing cats shrank to a pinpoint of light.

"Hi."

Swann turned and saw Ellen sitting up. She stood, and he did not move toward her.

"Hi," Swann said.

The faint light from the street silhouetted Ellen as she drew closer. She was small-boned and slender. Her brown hair fell straight on either side of her shadowed face.

"I wanted to wait up for you," Ellen said.

"I'm okay," Swann said.

Ellen reached over and flicked on the floor lamp. Her features were regular and well proportioned and no more remarkable than his own. She squinted at him, her eyes puffy with sleep.

"What's on your shirt?" Ellen asked.

"Blood," Swann said.

"Yours?"

"No. His."

Ellen touched the muzzle flash burn on Swann's right cheek.

"Your face is red here," Ellen said. "Does it hurt?"

"It's okay."

Swann looked at Ellen and she looked at him.

"I'm okay. I'm gonna look in on the baby."

* * *

Swann saw by the glow of the Donald Duck night-light that his four-year-old daughter, Jenny, was sleeping face up, her mouth slightly parted and both her arms thrown back. He felt himself steady as he watched her small chest rise and fall under the sheet. He was no ghost. He was a father.

The floorboard creaked, and Ellen appeared at his side. Father and mother stood silent over their child as she rolled her head and made a faint dream noise deep in her throat. He reached down and his trembling index finger touched a nose that was a diminutive of his own.

In the hallway, father became husband and mother turned wife. Her whisper came to him as real as all their nights together.

"Come to bed."

Ellen was offering him comfort, to make him feel as if there had been no shooting. His throat was still dry, and his own lowered voice was a rasp.

"In a little while," Swann said.

"Don't I get a kiss?" Ellen asked.

The kiss was unlike that of other nights only because Swann noticed it was no different at all.

The refrigerator stood humming in the dark kitchen. Swann yanked the chrome handle, and the light inside shone on tuna casserole and left-over meat loaf and potato salad and pickles and an economy-sized bottle of Pepsi. He had on other nights sought to quiet what troubled him by stepping away with something in each hand.

Swann closed the refrigerator without reaching inside. He opened the cabinet next to the sink and stared blankly at the instant vegetable soup and peanut butter and marshmallow dessert topping.

Only the hope that food would have its usual narcotic effect caused Swann to take down the Cap'n Crunch cereal. He did not fail to shake the box and gauge how much remained. He decided he could have half a bowl and still leave enough for Jenny's breakfast.

As he sat, Swann again felt the poke of steel in his groin. He put the revolver on the table and reached for the spoon. He raised some cereal to his lips with as steady a hand as he could manage. He chewed and listened to the crunch of Cap'n Crunch, his eyes going from the black shape of the revolver to the watch on his wrist.

Swann saw the red second hand sweep around as it still would if he were the one who had been killed. The minute and hour hands set the time at 5:26 A.M.; a transit radio car would by now have pulled onto the block and a chaplain and maybe Fredricks would have gone up the stoop. They would have heard the television and they would have knocked and waited. They would have knocked again, a little louder, and Ellen would have wakened. She would have dashed into the laundry room for some jeans before she went to the door. The moment she saw who was there, she would have known what had happened.

The watch and the revolver lay by the bathroom sink as Swann peeled his denims down over his talcumed thighs. He pulled his T-shirt over his head and saw that the dark red stain had soaked through to his skin.

Swann stood under the shower with his head bowed and his hands flat against the tiles. The water beat on his shoulders, running down his sides and sluicing between his legs. Steam rose to envelop him as he watched the last traces of the teenager's blood swirl down the drain.

In bed, Swann lay next to Ellen. He felt his pulse thudding hard, but not fast. He felt his chest rise to draw in a breath. He slowly exhaled and breathed in again.

Swann awoke alone and winced into the kitchen in a pair of Jockey shorts. His arms, neck, sides, back, everything hurt.

"Hi, Daddy," Jenny said.

She was at the kitchen table, eating the Cap'n Crunch he had made sure to leave.

"Hi, sweetie," Swann said.

Ellen was also at the table. She had already begun peeling the outer covering from the empty cereal box.

"'Morning, Jack," Ellen said. "You okay?"

"Yes. I'm fine."

"You want eggs?"

"No. Thanks. Do what you're doing."

"Pancakes?"

"I'll just get some coffee."

"Since when aren't you hungry?"

Swann on other mornings might have had eggs *and* pancakes. And maybe home fries.

"I said, I'm okay."

"Okay."

Ellen returned her attention to the empty cereal box. She would discard the cardboard backing and file away the whole outer covering against a future refund or gift offer; one vagary of her life was that she never knew whether she would need a box top or a front panel or a tear strip or a UPC seal or an ingredient panel or a net weight statement. The very coffee cup he now filled had come from a salad dressing firm that demanded not only the neck bands of three bottles, but the cap seals as well.

"It's in the paper," Ellen said.

"What?" Jenny asked.

"It's just something about Daddy at work," Ellen said.

Swann sat down and saw that the morning paper was open to a page toward the back. An item was headed COP KILLS TEEN and in the single paragraph Swann saw his name in print for the first time.

> A transit cop shot and killed an unarmed robbery suspect in the theater district last night, sending dozens of Liberty Weekenders diving for cover. Police said that Officer John Swann fired one shot after the suspect attempted to take the cop's service revolver. The suspect's identity was withheld pending notification of next of kin.

Swann raised his cup to take a sip. Coffee splattered on the newsprint.

"You spilled," Jenny said.

Swann closed the newspaper. The front-page picture was of the Statue of Liberty standing amidst bursting fireworks.

"You sure you don't want something?" Ellen asked.

"Ellen . . ."

"Okay. Okay."

The telephone rang and Swann had the standard transit police response, which was to wait for the spouse to answer. Ellen gave the three standard transit spouse replies to anybody who called from the job.

"He just stepped out."

A pause.

"I have no idea."

A pause.

"I'll tell him if I see him."

Ellen hung up and informed Swann that he was to report to the city police lab at 1300 hours. He glanced at his watch, seeing only the black minute and hour hands.

"I better get going," Swann said.

The street was baking under a gray haze as Swann stepped out into his first day that might not have been. Jenny clunked down the stoop ahead of him on her roller skates and scuttled up the sloping sidewalk. She wheeled about at the top of the block as Ellen emerged from the house in jeans and a tank top.

"Mommy," Jenny said. "Daddy."

Jenny scooted out one foot and then the other. She began rolling downhill toward them.

"Watch me," Jenny said.

Jenny was gaining speed. She leaned a little too far back and she waved her arms to regain her balance. Her long brown hair whipped behind her and she streaked on, fast and fearless.

"Baby, that's too fast," Ellen said.

"Catch me," Jenny said.

Swann snagged a squealing Jenny about the waist. He hoisted her high over his head and gazed up at her laughing face as he felt just how sore his muscles were.

"More!" Jenny said.

Ellen took one of Jenny's hands.

"Come on, baby, we'll walk with Daddy up to the park," Ellen said.

Swann took the other hand, and together he and Ellen pulled Jenny up the street.

At the park, Jenny slipped her hands free and skated up to a blond boy who was playing with a blue-and-red ball.

"Hi, bumphead," Jenny said.

"Hi, yuckface," the blond boy said.

The boy threw the ball at Jenny. He missed, and the ball bounced over to a browned patch of grass where a woman was sunning herself.

Danica Neary, née Cowan, lay on a red beach towel in a faded black halter top and cut-off jeans. Her skin was tanned and oiled. Her lean thighs and flat, bared midsection flexed as she sat up. Her breasts swelled big and buoyant.

"William, be nice," Danica said.

"You too, Jenny," Ellen said.

Danica ran a manicured hand through thick, honey-colored hair that fell in tousled layers to her shoulders. The planes of her cheeks were smooth. Her nose was slender and straight. Her mouth started blade thin at the corners and her whole face might have seemed hard had her lips not puffed full at the center. Today, those lips were glossed burgundy.

"Hi, Ellen," Danica said.

"Hi," Ellen said. "You're getting a nice color."

Danica looked at Swann. Her green eyes had a feline luminescence.

"Hi, Jack," Danica said.

"Danica," Swann said.

Danica had thrice played Mary to Swann's beast at the manger in the grammar school Christmas pageant, and by high school she had grown into such a beauty that the sight of her coming down the hallway had left him transfixed. He had never been more aware of his girth than when she walked past without paying him any more notice than if he had been a wall locker. He had then felt so fat as to be invisible.

Now, two decades later, Swann got that same being-on-a-swing-with-your-eyes-closed feeling in his stomach he experienced each time he saw Danica.

"I saw you in the paper," Danica said.

The cat's green eyes stayed on Swann. He was accustomed to her affecting him like some force of nature. He was not at all prepared for the faint but unmistakable interest he detected in her gaze.

"It must have been terrible," Danica said.

Swann swallowed.

"Yes," Swann said. "It was."

The interest then seemed to pass. Danica glanced from Swann to a watch that he guessed was one of the counterfeit Rolexes that Senegalese street peddlers were hawking in Manhattan for $35.

"I got to run," Danica said.

Danica ran her hand through her hair again, and Swann saw a

white mark on the tanned finger where her wedding ring would have been. He watched her raise a slender leg and slide a bare, tanned foot into a sneaker white enough for a posse. She put on the sneaker's mate and rose before him, standing at almost exactly his height and yet seeming much taller in her magnificence.

"Bye," Danica said.

Danica went off with William, his sneakers no less white. Swann refrained from gazing after her. He stood with his wife and daughter. A grown-up.

"She and her husband got separated," Ellen said. "I hear she moved back with her mother."

Swann said nothing for a moment.

"I better get going, too," Swann said.

As the train rocked under the East River, Swann felt his knees buckle, and he realized he had begun to nod off. He blinked and looked around and shifted his hand on the stainless-steel pole. The car swayed. The wheels clacked underfoot.

In another moment, the heat and motion had Swann's head dipping back down toward sleep. He heard the door at the front of the car rattle open and he snapped awake on seeing four black teenagers file in.

One and then another and then another teenager brushed past Swann, and the fourth was going by when the car jolted into a turn. The teenager's sneakers squeaked as he tried to regain his footing and he reached out to steady himself. His dark hand slapped onto the pole above Swann's.

Then the teenager was gone, passing with the others farther down the train, no doubt to the last car. Swann shifted his eyes to the side windows and beheld his reflection as he had the previous night. He saw no bloodstains, no visible sign that he was at all different.

Swann thought of that interest in Danica's cat's green eyes and through the numbness of the past hours came a shiver such as he had felt in high school. He might have again been a rotund youngster who had to crane his neck to view the newly sprouting hairs around what he had until then been calling his weewee.

* * *

In the ballistics lab, a technician put on goggles and ear protectors and aimed Swann's revolver at a ten-foot tank of water. Swann stood with his index fingers in his ears, watching the hammer ease back and then flash down. He went rigid.

All that came was a faint metallic click, and the technician snapped open the cylinder. He looked from the three empty chambers to Swann.

"Sorry," Swann said.

The technician raised one of his ear protectors.

"What?" the technician asked.

"Sorry," Swann said. "I forgot to reload."

With the cylinder set so a live round was next, the revolver rose again. What had seemed a remote pop the night before was now an explosion that jarred Swann even with his ears plugged. He saw the bullet rip a diagonal track in the water that dissolved into a multitude of tiny bubbles. The bubbles drifted slowly up to the surface, and the spent slug settled to the bottom.

The technician handed Swann the revolver and took up a small aquarium net. The bit of lead came out of the tank wet and shining, the sides etched with delicate markings that would be compared with those on the bit of lead that had killed Daryl Coombs and nearly killed Swann.

"That's it," the technician said.

At the Columbus Circle subway station, Swann disembarked with every other Caucasian in the car. Blacks and Puerto Ricans rode uptown to Harlem and the Bronx, and the Caucasians surged toward the street. Swann ambled alone down a littered passageway to an orange steel door.

On this afternoon, the first person to take notice of Swann's arrival was Marie. She was a short, round retarded woman who had become a sort of mascot to District 1, and she was at her usual spot by the door wearing a baseball cap nobody ever saw her without. She called out over the ringing phones and crackling radios and the rest of the station house din.

"You fly open," Marie said.

Swann stretched his neck and made a show of peering over his belly at the zipper he already knew to be closed. He then looked up to see a broad, nearly toothless smile break across Marie's sooty face.

"Ha, ha," Marie said.

Swann nodded to the desk officer and walked past cops and clerks who were hunched over TP-67 arrest reports and TP-117 incident index reports and TP-95 condition cards and TP-150B court notifications. One clerk was on the phone giving the standard response whenever a female asked for one of the men of the command.

"He's out in the field," the clerk said.

The clerk hung up and called after Swann.

"Swann, you see Mannering back there, tell him his wife just called again," the clerk said.

In the locker room, Mannering was winding cellophane tape around his hand with the sticky side out.

"That was some night last night," Mannering said.

"Yes it was," Swann said.

Mannering proceeded to use the adhesive of the tape to lift the lint and dandruff from his uniform coat. Swann remembered that this was the day of Mannering's interview for admission to the plainclothes anti-crime unit.

"Speaking of which, the guy at the desk said to say your wife called again," Swann said.

"She must be calling to apologize," Mannering said.

Swann stepped before his own gray metal locker and began working the dial on the combination lock.

"Last night, I call and tell her about the shooting and that you're at the hospital," Mannering said. "And I come home this morning and she's changing the baby and I give her a kiss like I always do."

Swann opened the locker and reached into a heap of crumpled papers and soiled laundry. He pushed aside a police hat, a gun belt, a nightstick, and a pair of pants that was rolled up with two shirts.

"All of a sudden she throws this dirty Pamper at me," Mannering said. "And I say, 'What the fuck are you throwing a dirty Pamper at me for?' She says, 'You know exactly why,' and I say, 'If I knew why, why the fuck would I ask?'"

Swann sorted on through a towel, a worn pair of Jockey shorts, a clump of arrest reports, a black shoe, a Lost Property form, the mug shot of a sixteen-year-old robbery suspect, and another pair of Jockey shorts.

"Anyway, it comes out that she thinks she smells something she calls 'musk' on me," Mannering said. "I say, 'Musk? What the fuck is musk?' And she says it's like perfume. And *then* she starts sayin' that I musta been fuckin' some broad. So, I say, 'Great.' I say, 'I got a cop who just had some moo try to *kill* him. And I'm supposed to tell him, 'Gee, too bad you had to shoot that fuckin' moo. I'd love to stick around and make sure you're all right, but I got to get home. Because, if I don't, I'm goin' to get a lot of shit about being out fucking some broad.'"

"You got any bullets?" Swann asked.

"I mean, I really told her," Mannering said. "I gave her all that 'You don't understand, it's real life' shit. She didn't smell no perfume. That nurse don't *wear* no fuckin' perfume."

Swann pushed aside a single sock and a second black shoe and saw a small cardboard carton. He shook the box as he had the Cap'n Crunch.

"Never mind," Swann said.

Swann pulled his revolver from his waistband and popped open the cylinder. The spent shell from the ballistics test joined the jumble in the locker.

"Maybe it was pussy," Mannering said. "Maybe what she smelled was pussy. But you'd think she'd know that."

Swann began slipping a bullet from the box into each empty chamber. One. Two. Three. Four.

"I mean, pussy's pussy, isn't it?" Mannering said.

Swann snapped the cylinder shut. Mannering stepped before a small mirror and hooked on his dark blue regulation clip-on tie.

"How about them white gloves?" Mannering asked.

Swann had said the day before that he would lend Mannering the gloves he had worn to his own interview. He went from feeling as though he was back in high school to wondering how a single day could seem so long ago.

Mannering left with the gloves. Swann still had a few minutes before roll call and he decided to clear away some paperwork. He first completed a firearms discharge report.

Time to aim?:	[ ] Yes [x] No
Bystanders killed?:	[ ] Yes [x] No
Reason for discharging:	[x] Protect self [ ] Protect citizen
	[ ] Accidental [ ] Other

That done, Swann filled out his time card for that period, inscribing in quarter-inch squares the hours he had gone on and off duty over the past two weeks. The last little box was for the previous night, and he reported that he had worked four hours beyond his assigned tour. The reason for this or any other overtime had to be explained with a double-digit code, and he was not certain whether the shooting and its aftermath should be marked a 12, which would signify an arrest, or a 30, which would mean an investigation. He looked up for somebody who might know and he happened to see Coleman crossing the far side of the room.

"*Would you?*"

Swann did not have to turn to know that the voice beside him belonged to Fredricks.

"Hunh?" Fredricks asked. "Would you?"

Swann watched Coleman go on out, her nightstick tucked under her arm, the tiny braid of hair dangling from under the back of her uniform hat.

"Not me," Fredricks said. "Not with *your* dick."

Swann then heard Fredricks utter the phrase that had become the standard description for the young cops who had come on the job since the federal courts threw out the height requirement as discriminatory to women.

"Runts and cunts," Fredricks said.

Swann turned to Fredricks, who seemed an altogether appropriate person to ask about overtime as it pertained to killing somebody.

"If he hadn'ta died, I'd say definitely a twelve," Fredricks said. "But with the perp dead, you can't really call it an arrest, can you? Make it a thirty."

Fredricks belched and put a hand on his stomach.

"Which is about how many frankfurters I musta had at that fucking bar-be-cue."

* * *

At roll call, Swann stood with Fredricks and the rest of the plainclothes officers. Sergeant Quinn offered a reminder.

"Your world ends at the top of the subway steps," Quinn said.

One and then another officer yawned. Quinn went on to announce what Swann expected: Effective immediately, Police Officers Swann and Fredricks were assigned to Post 24, the station under the Plaza Hotel.

Swann joined the others in checking out a portable radio, these required by the Patrol Guide and next to useless underground. He was leaving when he heard somebody call his name, and he looked over to see a uniformed cop walking a handcuffed black man toward the holding pen.

"Hey, hey, Swann," the cop said. "You all right?"

"Sure," Swann said.

Swann then asked a question in keeping with station house etiquette.

"What ya got?"

The cop put a hand on the black man's shoulder to guide him into the empty cell.

"A car payment," the cop said.

The hours necessary to process an arrest could mean a good $150 in overtime for an officer who needed to meet a mortgage installment or pay for a new septic tank or, in this instance, make a car payment. This way of financing the suburban lifestyle was known variously as "collars for dollars" and "trash for cash," and there was a good chance that anybody who brought in a prisoner on a holiday was receiving payment overdue notices at home.

"Looks like I can forget going for that new Cutlass," Fredricks said.

Swann assumed that this remark signaled the start of eight hours of complaining, but hardly another grumble came from Fredricks as they made the journey to their punishment post and its scant promise of trash for cash.

No subway lines crossed from Columbus Circle to the Plaza, and Quinn had forbidden them to simply make the five-minute walk across the bottom of Central Park. They spent twenty minutes catching a downtown IRT and then an uptown BMT, though they might just as well have taken the whole tour to get there. All was quiet when they arrived and remained so through the next four hours.

Still, hardly a mutter came from Fredricks, a mystery solved only when he stepped over to a pay phone. He first called his wife on Long Island, and a great weariness suddenly weighted his voice.

"Honey, I had to make a collar," Fredricks said.

He gave a sigh and a second stock sentence.

"I have no idea when I'll be out of court," he said.

Fredricks then dialed a local number. His voice became instantly vibrant.

"Hey, baby," he said.

Fredricks was speaking to a girlfriend, generically known among transit cops as a "goom," a word derived from the Italian for godmother. Swann gathered from what followed that said goom was not happy with Fredricks because he would be working too late to take her to a Liberty Weekend concert in Central Park.

"Honey, come on, take it easy," Fredricks said. "I was up all last night with a shooting."

Fredricks did not seem to get the response he wanted.

"Fuck you then, cunt," Fredricks said.

The conversation ended there, and Fredricks was left dateless. He had already lied to his wife about making a collar, which meant he could hardly go home, and there seemed to be nothing else to do but actually arrest somebody. He reassumed his post, suddenly alert, but the few citizens who happened past seemed bound for the Liberty Weekend concert, and even the minorities looked decidedly uncriminal.

"Some fucking place you landed me," Fredricks said.

Fredricks was still complaining an hour later, when a dark-skinned derelict appeared from the downtown platform. He seemed dazed and went out the exit gate before deciding that he had gotten off at the wrong station. He turned about and passed back through the gate, technically entering the subway without paying the fare.

Fredricks used the Voice of Command they had all been taught at the academy.

"STOP RIGHT THERE," Fredricks said.

Swann stood with the revolver big and heavy in his waistband.

"Fredricks, don't bother," Swann said.

Swann had no choice but to follow as Fredricks hurried after the derelict.

"I SAID STOP RIGHT THERE!" Fredricks said.

The derelict strolled on toward the downtown platform. Fredricks rushed up and grabbed his arm. The derelict threw off Fredricks's hand.

"I SAID STOP!" Fredricks said.

The derelict turned and slammed an open hand in Fredricks's chest. Fredricks fell back against one of the steel columns that studded the mezzanine.

Swann was now forced to move in. He grabbed the derelict by the lapel and yanked him off balance.

"You are under arrest," Swann said.

Swann spun the derelict around and snapped on the handcuffs. Fredricks stepped up and grabbed the derelict by the hair.

"Nigger motherfucker," Fredricks said.

Swann heard a thump as Fredricks smashed the derelict's face against the steel column.

"He's under control," Swann said. "Just call for a run."

Fredricks raised his portable radio and tried to get the dispatcher. They proved to be in one of the many underground dead spots where the steel and concrete blocked transmissions. The only response was a burst of static.

"Why don't you call 'em by phone," Fredricks said. "I'll watch my friend here."

Fredricks swung the radio and hit the derelict in the face.

"Take it easy," Swann said.

Fredricks looked about.

"What's the matter?" Fredricks said. "Nobody's around."

Fredricks kneed the derelict in the groin and he went down.

"That's the only good thing about this freaking post," Fredricks said.

Fredricks kicked the derelict in the head and prepared to do so again. Swann surprised himself by shoving Fredricks away.

"My cuffs. My collar. Keep your fucking hands off him," Swann said.

Fredricks pointed to the derelict, who lay gurgling on his back.

"This fucking nigger hit me," Fredricks said.

"ENOUGH," Swann said. "GO CALL."

Swann found the Voice of Command could actually work when used on a fellow officer. Fredricks went off, and Swann helped the derelict to his feet and conducted a quick search, gagging on the stink of stale sweat, excrement and ulcerated sores.

The derelict stood with his eyelids swelling and blood seeping from his nose and mouth. He remained expressionless when Fredricks returned. The three of them were silent until two uniformed cops appeared.

Swann took the derelict up the steps and out from beneath the canvas awning that disguised this most unlikely of subway entrances. A jam of limousines had forced the uniformed cops to park a few feet down the block, and Swann had to lead his bloodied prisoner alongside the Plaza. Swann glanced at the first of the brass-rimmed windows and saw that the wood-paneled chamber was once again filled with elegantly clad figures. A man in a gray suit was sitting with a woman in a black dress at a table just beyond the glimmering glass, the two of them staring at the scene on the sidewalk with much the same expression as the people at the shooting the night before.

"Why don't you go in *there* for ice," Fredricks said.

The two uniformed cops laughed and climbed into the front of the radio car while Swann and Fredricks loaded the battered derelict into the back. Swann climbed in after him and took a last look up at the window. The couple had returned to each other's company.

A whoop of the siren and the radio car sped off, just like in the movies, though in the movies the cops do not head with their prisoner for the nearest diner. That happened to be the Parthenon Coffee Shop, and Swann watched from the car as Fredricks brushed past the heavyset waitress on the way to the counter.

Fredricks returned to hand Swann the standard bunch of napkins and cup of ice cubes.

"You want him, you fucking clean him up," Fredricks said.

The radio car rolled slowly uptown as Swann worked on the derelict, daubing with the napkins and pressing with the ice. He once more felt warm blood and melting ice trickle between his fingers.

"Do a good job," Fredricks said. "Or somebody might say we beat this fuck."

Fredricks grabbed the derelict's chin.

"If you say you're hurt and ask to go to the hospital, you're gonna be there twelve fucking hours," Fredricks said. "Keep your mouth shut and you'll make court tonight."

The derelict turned toward Swann and spoke through ballooned lips. His front teeth were stained pink.

"Cigarette," the derelict said.

His eyes were nearly swollen shut. Swann saw only a glistening behind the slitted lids, a wet shine that seemed to be the very thing that had left the eyes of the dying Daryl Coombs.

"Sorry," Swann said.

Swann wiped a trickle of blood from the corner of the derelict's mouth.

"I don't smoke."

An unwritten rule dictated that a disputed collar ultimately belonged to the officer whose cuffs were on the prisoner. Fredricks registered no official protest when Swann told the desk officer at District 1 that he was taking the arrest.

"Anybody hurt?" the desk officer asked.

"No," Fredricks said. "I'm fine."

Fredricks made his unofficial position clear as Swann slid his hands into the derelict's pants pockets.

"Watch out for needles," Fredricks said. "You get that AIDS, nobody's gonna believe you're not a faggot."

Fredricks walked off just as a Hispanic man in handcuffs stumbled through the door. The propelling force was Coleman, and she spoke to her prisoner in a clear, steady tone that seemed to come from self-confidence more than Voice of Command lessons.

"Stay right there, young man," Coleman said.

The lieutenant asked what Coleman had, and she set a large automatic pistol on the front desk. This was not some simple little bit of trash for cash. This was a gun collar, real aggressive police work, enterprising and therefore not at all necessary. The lieutenant had an irritated edge to his voice as he asked the probable cause for the search.

"Only thing a bulge that big could be," Coleman said.

Coleman did not seem bothered that nobody laughed but her. She also did not seem put off by the prospect of searching a male prisoner. She was sticking her hand into the Hispanic man's front pocket when the lieutenant suggested she allow Swann to take over. She spoke to her prisoner.

"Young man, who'd you rather have run their hands all over you, this man here or a fine-looking woman like me?" Coleman asked.

Coleman's prisoner gave a shrug.

"It must be this shade of blue," Coleman said. "I put on this uniform and they all turn into lovers."

Coleman resumed the search.

"Listen, thanks for your help last night," Swann said.

Coleman looked up.

"It was the least I could do," Coleman said.

Coleman's tone had cooled; she had noticed the derelict's face. Swann busied himself with searching his own prisoner, indeed careful about needles. He found instead a small glass tube that was blackened at one end. A new high called crack had hit the streets big that summer, and he had begun to see these pipes on at least half the prisoners.

"Drug collar?" Coleman asked.

Coleman was giving him an opening to offer whatever reasonable explanation he might have for his prisoner's condition. The desk officer answered for him.

"Fare-beat."

Swann met those eyes that had been so steady the night before.

"I guess the fare ain't all that got beat," Coleman said.

Swann finished processing his prisoner and went over to the pay phone. He had to wait for Fredricks, who had called his goom back.

"I'm sorry, honey," Fredricks was saying. "That shooting last night must have left me a little jumpy. I'll be right over."

Fredricks hurried off so excited he neglected to give Swann a dirty look. Swann took up the receiver and dialed Ellen to say he had made a collar. She told Swann that his father had seen the article in the paper and had come by to ask how he was doing.

"I said you were fine, that you just got that little cut and some scrapes," Ellen said.

Swann said nothing. The only sound he heard in the background was the usual murmur of the television, though on this night he heard no shots or squealing tires or canned laughter, just music.

"Hello?" Ellen said. "Hello? Are you there?"

"Yes, I'm here," Swann said.

Swann asked Ellen what she was watching.

"They got on that concert in Central Park," Ellen said. "They said there's a million people."

"How is it?"

"Not bad. But it's not really for me."

A city cop arrived to announce that transportation was ready, and Coleman emerged from the women's locker room. Most uniformed cops changed before going to court in order to sign out from there and save themselves the trip back to the district. Coleman strode over to the holding cell in a black satin jacket with the word GIANTS across the chest and a black leather baseball cap turned sideways. Her tail no longer looked out of place.

"Come on, young man," Coleman said.

Coleman took the Hispanic man by the elbow, and Swann followed up to the street with the derelict. The concert that Ellen had been watching on the television was going on just beyond the dark trees. He heard the orchestra winding up some kind of classical music as he placed the derelict in the back of a dented paddy wagon. The million people applauded, sounding to Swann like a cooling rain as he crowded in the front with Coleman and three sweaty city officers.

"'S up?" Coleman asked.

The three city officers said nothing. The wagon began rolling downtown and the right front tire hit a pothole, the resulting jolt knocking Swann next to Coleman. He eased away and looked over to see that she was staring straight ahead. She was humming, but he could not quite catch the tune over the rattle of the wagon. He could hear even less as the cops began chattering among themselves.

The wagon soon reached Greenwich Village, and the sidewalks began to fill with students in dungarees and punks in black leather. A traffic light ahead turned red, and a gangly young woman in a short white shift strolled in front of the wagon. The other male cops went quiet and Swann might have joined them in gazing after her had this momentary hush not enabled him to make out Coleman's tune.

"Nice ass," one cop said.

"No tits," a second cop said.

The van started up and continued downtown with Coleman humming the snatch of classical music the orchestra had been playing beyond the trees. She repeated it two or three times and then turned it around, drawing it out and speeding it up, making it into a sound all her own.

Behind police headquarters, Swann trailed with the derelict as Coleman led her prisoner to Manhattan Central Booking, also known as Manhattan Central Bank for all the trash that had there been converted into cash. Coleman showed her face in the small window cut into the steel door. That was always enough for Swann or any other white cop to gain entrance, but the door did not buzz open until she held up her shield.

Swann followed, her tail jouncing one procedure ahead of him as he continued on to a large room on the second floor of the courthouse. This was ECAB, Early Case Assessment Bureau, where cops waited to see an assistant district attorney.

Swann saw that Coleman had signed the log with big, looping script that was less of a signature than an autograph. He made his own entry in the space below, his of more basic scale and form, but with a little curlicue at the end.

The room was the same as on any other night; the cigarette haze, the droning television, cops slumped on benches and sprawled on the floor, some sleeping, others sitting slack-faced and bleary-eyed. You could have just been looking for a little overtime or you could have risked your life grabbing some crazed killer; either way you still had to wait long enough so that you felt put in your place.

Swann sat on a bench in the far corner and picked up a discarded newspaper which had the front-page picture of Lady Liberty he had seen that morning. He had found that the best way to pass the wait at

ECAB was to go through the paper from front to back, making himself read every word of stories he would otherwise have barely skimmed.

The result was that each arrest saw him pick up any number of facts he would not have sought to learn, and on this night most of them concerned Liberty Weekend. An item about the statue's refurbishment reported that the old lighthouse lamp in the torch had been replaced by gilded steel hammered into the shape of a flame. The new beacon to the tempest tossed was the flash of spotlights reflected off gold.

Another article informed Swann that twenty-five thousand ships had assembled in the harbor for the fireworks and that this was four times the size of the armada for the Normandy invasion. The president had stood on the deck of the aircraft carrier *John F. Kennedy.* Also present was the U.S.S. *Iowa,* sister to the *Missouri,* which Swann's mother had helped build in the Brooklyn Navy Yard.

Swann read that the chief organizer of Liberty Weekend had entertained aboard a ten-million-dollar yacht. The man was an auto executive who had become famous using billion-dollar government loans to make his company almost competitive with the Japanese. His guests had included corporate raiders and real estate developers and movie actors, several of whom Swann had seen play cops.

The name of the cop with the car payment crackled over the public address system, and Swann looked up to see his fellow officer rise from the floor and shuffle off. Swann then glanced over at Coleman and saw that she was sitting erect, her chin up.

Coleman looked Swann's way, and he dropped his eyes to continue his reading. He eventually came to the small item that reported to the city that he had killed somebody, the single paragraph that seemed to have had a greater effect on Danica Neary, née Cowan, than two decades of his longing.

Swann read on, scanning the classifieds, though he was in the market for neither apartment nor house nor vacation property nor pet nor anything else. He was still waiting for his name to be called when he reached the business section.

To read of high finance was to read of people who traded whole freight trains of commodities they neither saw nor owned, who dealt in stocks they never actually purchased, who bought entire companies with money they did not have. They all seemed to be borrowing, borrowing, borrowing, and then borrowing some more to cover what they owed. Only it was not called borrowing. It was called "leverage," which summoned to Swann's mind his grammar school lessons concerning Archimedes, who said you could move the whole world if only you had a long enough lever.

On this Liberty Weekend, one of the financial writers had taken the occasion to note that the prime borrower was the government itself and that the previous few years had seen America go from being the biggest creditor nation to being the biggest debtor. The writer added that the present administration had borrowed what broke down to $10,000 for every adult in the country. That included the derelict and all those down in the holding cell, the cops in ECAB and John J. Swann himself, who had never possessed such a sum to begin with.

When Coleman's name was called, Swann watched her jump up as if the eight-hour wait had been but a few minutes. He was next, and he crossed the hallway to a row of cubicles. A young assistant district attorney in a seersucker suit began by asking his first name.

"Hi, Jack," the assistant district attorney said. "I'm Mr. Trimingham."

Mr. Trimingham took notes as Swann recounted the events just as they had happened, right up to the first blow Fredricks had thrown.

"Any force used?" Mr. Trimingham asked.

Back at the time of Swann's first arrest, this same question had caused his heart to pound and his face to flush. He now gave the same answer, but he needed no conscious effort at all to compose an expression whose total earnestness had convinced prosecutors and judges and juries and bosses and, on rare occasion, even Ellen. He might not have been happy with Fredricks, but he was not about to side with a suit person who was getting a little trial experience before going on to the big bucks of private practice.

"Only necessary force was used to effect the arrest," Swann said.

On the stairs down from ECAB, Swann got a glimpse of Coleman passing through the courthouse door. He himself then stepped squinting into a bright Sunday, feeling much as he usually did after a night at ECAB. He could not have said which aches lingered from his fight for his life and which were from sitting all night. He itched and probably smelled bad, and his eyes seemed to have sand in them.

One difference was that Swann was still not hungry. He strode right on as he went by the canteen truck parked out front.

Swann passed his parish church as the late mass was letting out, and he saw people coming down the steps in their Sunday clothes. He himself now went only to weddings and funerals and First Communions, but on the night of the shooting he had called upon only the Almighty. So had the teenager. So had a good many others Swann had come upon in moments of terror. People who had not entered a house of worship in decades needed only a gunshot to start shouting out, *Oh God!* or *God help me!* or *Please, God!* or *No, God!* or, like himself, *God! No!* Or, like Daryl Coombs, simply *God!*

Swann arrived home to find Ellen at the kitchen table with the instruments of her present Sabbath ritual: the Sunday paper, a pair of scissors, and a small accordion file.

"I guess you're not gonna feel like going," Ellen said.

Jenny scampered in and threw her arms about one of his thighs. He laid an open hand atop her head and watched Ellen snip precisely along the dotted lines bordering a coupon. A bit of trim fluttered to the table and the promise of fifty cents off on Vim went into the appropriate pocket of the file.

"I can sleep later," Swann said.

Swann trudged into the heat with Ellen on one side and Jenny on the other and the cart rattling empty before him. They soon came to a supermarket that had a banner across the front announcing a Double Coupon Day and bearing the legend LET FREE-DOM RING.

As always, Jenny insisted on pushing the cart, and Swann walked alongside ready to prevent any collisions. Ellen strode ahead, her accordion file tucked under her arm, her steps quick and confident, her eyes scanning from the bottom shelf to the top.

Ellen had explained to Swann that the highest profit items were placed at eye level or in the first aisle, the latter so you encountered them while you still felt flush. The milk was in the most remote corner, so you had to pass whole rows of enticement on the way to the one thing you were most likely to need. Items that were stacked at the end of aisles and marked Sale or Feature of the Week should have been labeled Can't Sell or Taking Up Shelf Space.

The whole store was a scheme to make you succumb to immediate impulse, and here was one circumstance where a plain young woman of Catholic upbringing could triumph. The tricks of a supermarket manager were nothing compared to the works of Satan, and making do without another brand of shampoo was easy for somebody who had been dateless for her junior and senior proms. Ellen's two-ringed hand never faltered in reaching past an enticement to seize a better deal.

Jenny had to bow her head to push the growing mound of bargains that landed in the cart as they went past canned goods and frozen foods and on into household items. Swann lagged behind, seeing nothing at all tempting at eye or any other level. His gaze went from Cheer to Gain to Caress to All to Dash to Aim to Zest to Joy.

The store had the latest in registers, and each time the laser read a price, the machine emitted the same little beep that comes from an EKG machine. This stopped only when the total flashed on the display.

The next sound was of Ellen removing the rubber band that held her file closed. The two-ringed hand flipped nimbly from Baked Goods to Noodles to Snacks and the EKG sounds began again as the cashier entered the various coupons. The impatient noises of the people in line ceased as the cashier announced aloud that Ellen would be paying only $19.28 for $148.07 in groceries.

"All right!" Ellen said.

Ellen waved the four-foot register tape, grinning as if she had just tipped herself $128.79. She and her fellow coupon clippers called themselves "redeemers" and among them she was a champion.

"Very good," Swann said.

Swann understood that he should be happy because she was happy, and yet his smile felt stuck on, like a label reading Delite.

* * *

Swann had been up for more than twenty-four hours, and he felt every minute of it as he performed the manly task of pushing the bargain-laden cart back home. He set the bags on the kitchen table, and Ellen put the register tape up on the refrigerator door, the two totals circled in red ink.

Swann lay down in the living room, and he was awakened in the evening by Jenny landing on his chest. She was in her pajamas, fresh from her bath. She led him down the hall.

Swann sat on one side of her bed while Ellen settled on the other. He was the one to read, as was customary on those nights he was home.

Jenny as usual insisted on turning the pages. She had chosen *Sleeping Beauty,* which he remembered from his own childhood and which contained notions of adventure and romance that were not entirely unlike those he still occasionally entertained. The tale ended as a good number of them do, with beautiful princess married to handsome prince, the two of them headed off to live happily ever after in a castle.

Swann slouched before the television with Ellen. The show of the moment was neither comedy nor drama, but the $6 million "Last Blast" marking the end of Liberty Weekend. The 500 members of the marching band and 234 Jazzercise ladies and 200 square dancers and 75 Elvis impersonators were all singing "America the Beautiful" when Swann rose and announced he was going to bed.

In the bathroom, Swann at first thought that Ellen was soaking a pair of panties in the sink, as she sometimes did when her period came unexpectedly. He then saw that it was his bloodstained T-shirt. He sat on the edge of the tub and brushed his teeth using the spigot.

Swann went in to bed with his mouth tanging of Crest, and he was only easing deeper into the routine as he and Ellen began making love. She ended up straddling him, her head bowed, her hands on his chest, seeming as soothed as he by the marital familiarity of every sensation.

Ellen slid out her arms and sprawled along Swann's length. Her face vanished from sight to press warm against his cheek and pant hot in his ear. Her hair covered his eyes.

Suddenly, Swann pitched his hips and rolled upright. The tickling blindfold fell away, and he gazed down at eyes popped wide.

"What, Jackie?" Ellen asked.

As Ellen began to speak again, Swann pressed his mouth to hers. He entered her once more and began bucking and she stayed with him and soon they were both clawing as they had not in years. She made small, sharp cries that came faster and faster.

"Oh, Jackie," Ellen said.

Ellen began tossing her head from side to side, and Swann worked his face against her straining neck. He drew back and then thrust as deep into her as he could. She froze.

"No," Ellen said.

Ellen thrashed and pushed at Swann's hips with both hands.

"Jackie, *no*."

Ellen pushed again, and Swann landed slick and spurting on her belly.

"Did you make it?" Ellen asked.

Swann rolled onto his back, his chest heaving. Ellen had long since wearied of using a diaphragm and he had never used anything at all.

"Don't worry," Swann said.

Swann heard the mattress creak, and he turned his head to see her reach for a box of tissue she kept by the bed.

"You *want* to make a baby?" Ellen asked.

Swann watched Ellen wipe the semen off his belly and then her own.

"We can't really afford another baby right now," Ellen said.

A smear of the stuff remained on her belly.

"You missed a spot," Swann said.

Three

THE NEXT MORNING, Swann found his single white dress shirt in the back of the bottom dresser drawer. He then went to the closet and pushed aside several dresses that Ellen never seemed to have occasion to wear. He took out the polyester navy pinstripe suit he had worn first at his wedding and later at his mother's wake and funeral.

The suit had since hung unneeded and untouched, but Swann was able to pull up the pants zipper with hardly a wiggle. His waist remained the forty-four inches measured a decade before in the husky section of a discount haberdashery. He had come to accept this measure as constant enough to be his destiny.

Swann stepped before the dresser mirror with the blue-and-white striped tie that the salesman had thrown into the deal. The police uniform ties were all clip-ons, and he was still vainly attempting to remember how to make a knot when Jenny came in. She relayed an inquiry from Ellen as to what he wanted for breakfast, and he worked his tongue. He got a thick, bitter taste.

"Tell her just coffee," Swann said.

Swann pulled the tie tight and saw his latest attempt turn out worse than the first.

"You look like the picture," Jenny said.

Jenny was speaking of the wedding photograph that stood in a silver frame on the dresser. Swann was indeed wearing this same suit, the tie knotted by his father. He considered that this would be the outfit he would be wearing in the coffin had he been the one who was shot.

"Where are you going?" Jenny asked.

Swann pondered how to explain a grand jury. His mind had no more luck than his fingers were having.

"I have to see some people," Swann said. "And I want to look nice."

Swann gave up on the tie and left it hanging around his neck. He felt Jenny watching him as he reached for the revolver on the dresser.

"Why did you kill the nigger?" Jenny asked.

Swann turned from the mirror to Jenny.

"Don't use that word," Swann said.

"I heard Mommy tell Aunt Deirdre on the telephone," Jenny said.

"She was just upset because he tried to hurt me," Swann said.

"Why didn't you just yell at him?"

"I did."

"He didn't listen."

Swann drew in his gut and stuck his revolver in his waistband.

"Are you going to shoot more bad people?" Jenny asked.

"I hope not," Swann said.

"Then why are you taking that?"

Jenny had never asked why he was taking his revolver any more than she had asked why he was taking his house keys. He was going to say *Because that's my job,* but that would have sounded like television. What he did say certainly would have drawn hoots at District 1.

"In case somebody needs help," Swann said.

Ellen was at the kitchen table, prying a seal from a juice bottle cap.

"Look at you," Ellen said.

Swann went to pour himself a cup of coffee.

"You should put something in your stomach," Ellen said. "At least have a doughnut."

"It's okay," Swann said.

"*Jackie,*" Ellen said.

Swann forced down a bite of jelly doughnut and sipped coffee as he watched Ellen drop the cap seal in an envelope.

"You were tossing and turning and making noise all night," she said.

"I musta been dreamin'," Swann said.

"You should sleep with the light on," Jenny said.

Swann and Ellen were smiling when they looked at each other. Swann glanced down at his watch, which reported the correct time, this being the time to go.

"I gotta be at the grand jury," Swann said.

"One more bite before the grand jury," Ellen said.

Swann swallowed another mouthful and rose to leave.

"What about your tie?" Ellen asked.

"I couldn't figure it out," Swann said.

"You used to know."

"I never knew in the first place. My father did it."

"You never told me that."

"So?"

"So, nothing. I thought every guy in the world knew how to tie a tie."

"When am I ever gonna wear a tie?"

"You're wearing one now."

Ellen laughed.

"Or at least you're trying to. You better stop by your father and get him to tie it again."

Ellen's victory at the supermarket had included four boxes of frozen fish sticks for his father. Swann took them along and arrived at his childhood home with melting freezer frost dripping from his fingers.

Joseph Swann was just back from another shift at the post office and sat shirtless in the kitchen. The sink was piled with dirty dishes. The trash bin was overflowing. The once shining floor could have been a piece of subway platform.

"I read the paper," Joseph said. "Sounds like there was nothing you could do."

"No," Swann said. "There wasn't."

"Anyway, you're okay," Joseph said. "That's what matters."

Joseph said this in a way that made clear he understood that Swann might be feeling otherwise. Swann held out the fish sticks from Ellen.

"Ellen's a nice girl," Joseph said.

"Yes," Swann said. "She is."

Joseph opened the refrigerator in which the young Swann had often sought solace. The inside was empty save for some condiments that could have dated back to when his mother, Celeste, was alive. The freezer compartment was half-choked with ice, and Joseph had to cram the dripping boxes in.

"What's with the suit?" Joseph asked.

"I got the grand jury," Swann said. "I thought you could help me with this tie."

Joseph came back, drying his hands on his pants.

"You know, the way things are going, you really ought to learn to do this yourself," Joseph said.

Joseph took Swann before the bathroom mirror and peered over his shoulder as he gave instructions. Their two faces were side by side in the glass, father and son.

"Around, up, around, up, and through," Joseph said.

A Marine Corps knot slid snug against Swann's throat, feeling something of a noose, but also something of an assertion, something ceremonial, proper.

Swann turned from the mirror. Joseph gave a last little tug and looked up, his eyes red as always after a shift of punching three Zip codes a second on the ZMT sorting machine. His error rate at work had lately become such that he had been sent for retraining, and an instructor had said that he needed to bypass the brain and let his fingers act reflexively. The instructor had declared that Thinking Is Counterproductive, which had led to a standing joke.

"So, you staying productive?" Swann asked.

Joseph smiled.

"Always," Joseph said.

Their eyes met and the smile dropped. Joseph seemed to veer close to tears.

"You know, if God forbid something had happened, I would have made sure Ellen and Jenny were taken care of," Joseph said.

Joseph was speaking as someone whose own father had fallen to his death while laboring on the Empire State Building. The rules of the time had dictated that an ironworker's wages stopped the instant his body hit the ground.

"I know you would," Swann said.

Swann said nothing more to Joseph on the subject, but as he went to the subway he considered that the Swanns had advanced considerably in at least one regard. He calculated that his demise would have brought his wife and child more than $1 million in death benefits, which was a considerable sum even by the standards of those people back in the brass-rimmed windows of the Plaza. This was also a much greater sum than he would ever possess in life, and he arrived at the courthouse a man who would have been worth much more dead than he was alive.

On the ninth floor, Swann stepped off the elevator to see the various witnesses arrayed along a long wooden bench. Fredricks offered no greeting, yet Swann still had to resist an almost gravitational impulse to sit beside his partner. He might have settled next to the balding city detective had the man not been holding the clear plastic bag that contained the dead teenager's shirt.

"Hey, how's it going?" the detective asked.

Swann saw that the blood stains had turned the same dark brown as those on his T-shirt.

"Fine," Swann said.

Swann stood against the wall, a few feet from the executive who had been robbed. A voice called from the doorway, and the executive headed in to testify, emerging a few minutes later and brushing by Swann without any sign of recognition. The voice called again.

"Officer Swann?"

Swann rose and polished the toes of his black police shoes on the back of his pants before striding into a large room whose walls were peeling. He took the straight-backed wooden chair beside the stenographer.

The grand jurors sat in leather chairs arranged in three ascending rows like movie theater seats. They appeared to be retirees and housewives and people glad to escape a monotonous job for a few weeks. A man in the center of the top row wore a lime green sports coat and a red tie. He was the foreman, and he instructed Swann to raise his right hand.

As Swann swore to tell the truth, an assistant district attorney climbed to the top row of jurors. He stopped beside the foreman and peered down. Swann found himself noting the expensive-looking charcoal suit, the starched white shirt, and the neatly knotted blue-and-gold striped tie.

The assistant district attorney asked Swann to state his name, shield number, and command. Swann began to answer and heard his words come out faint and high-pitched. He paused and took a breath before he continued.

The assistant district attorney directed Swann's attention to the previous Friday, July 4, and asked if Swann had been in Times Square at approximately 10:50 P.M. Swann said that he had.

"What, if anything, happened?" the assistant district attorney asked.

The stenographer typed silently as Swann spoke. His voice was stronger now, but he experienced something the older cops had told him in the days following his first collar: The truth is harder to tell than a lie. You do not practice the truth a hundred times in front of a mirror. You cannot add just the right amount of inconsistency to make it believable. All you can do is tell what happened, which in this case ended with the struggle for his gun. His voice went faint again as he told of pulling the trigger without knowing which way the barrel was pointed.

"Would you repeat that last part?" the stenographer said.

Swann leaned to the side. He watched the ribbon of white paper pass through the stenographic machine as he spoke.

"I heard the perpetrator scream," Swann said.

Swann turned back to the grand jurors.

"That's how I knew it was him who got shot. And not me."

A female juror in a blue pantsuit raised her hand and whispered something to the assistant district attorney. He relayed the query to Swann.

"Why did you fire when you might have been shot?"

"Because I didn't have any more strength," Swann said.

Swann met the female juror's gaze. He spoke in the tone he had used with Jenny that morning.

"Because I had reached the end," Swann said.

None of the other jurors raised a hand, and Swann was excused. He strode into the hallway as Fredricks was called, and the two of them passed without so much as nodding. They still had to head up to their post, and Swann waited in the hallway.

When Fredricks emerged, he was followed by the assistant district attorney. That meant the grand jury had begun its deliberations, and

Swann decided to wait for the result. He huffed and fidgeted as if he really were in some jeopardy. He jumped when the buzzer signaled that the jurors had reached a decision.

No more than two minutes had passed, and the assistant district attorney ducked inside for only a few seconds. He came out with a pink slip of paper reporting that the grand jury had returned No True Bill, that the killing of Daryl Coombs by John J. Swann had been found justified.

Swann and Fredricks assumed their post under the Plaza. They had no cause to speak to each other until Fredricks uttered the word *meal.* Swann did not bother to check his watch before going with him up to the street.

Fredricks turned left, no doubt toward the Parthenon, the nearest place for ice also being the nearest place a cop would go to eat. He had taken a half-dozen strides before he realized Swann had stopped at the top of the steps. Two more words came.

"The fuck?" Fredricks asked.

"Go ahead," Swann said.

Fredricks stood there. He had gone along with Swann on the night of the shooting only because of the unwritten rule that partners eat together.

"There's something wrong with you," Fredricks said.

Fredricks strode away, leaving Swann to watch the comings and goings of Central Park South. He saw people in taxis and horse-drawn carriages and limousines, the last seeming to be both privately owned and available for hire. He noted that many of the people on foot walked with a particular briskness and that the ones who turned into the Plaza received a touch of the hat and a nod from the doorman.

A gust of air came from the entrance at Swann's back as a train entered the station below, the tunnel breath as stale as that expelled from under Times Square. He thought back to the grand jury and remembered being almost disappointed on hearing the finding. He knew that he would not have welcomed an indictment. He decided he must simply have been feeling that something more should attend the killing of Daryl Coombs and his own near death.

Instead, the buzzer had signaled that Swann was simply to go back to his life. He was reminded of what that entailed when he saw his fellow cave cop Fredricks returning from meal.

Swann went down the steps, and Fredricks came with him.

After three hours that might as well not have been, Swann headed with Fredricks for District 1. Swann expected at least the usual greeting from Marie, but she had apparently taken a day off. Most of his fellow officers made a point of ignoring him, having heard by now that he had interceded on behalf of the derelict. He was heading for the door when he heard a decidedly friendly voice.

"Hey, hey, Jackie boy."

Mannering approached with a big smile and they left the district together.

"I see you got on your grand jury suit," Mannering said. "How'd it go?"

"No problem," Swann said.

"That's what I like to hear," Mannering said.

Swann went down the passageway, and Mannering stayed alongside him, his voice going low.

"Sometimes, a nigger gets shot, they try to make it a race thing," Mannering said.

Mannering raised his voice.

"Know what I mean?"

"I just told them what happened," Swann said.

"That's always scary," Mannering said. "You must be ready for a cocktail."

Swann assumed that Mannering was as usual going to Joey Farrell's Bar. Other cops were sure to be there, and they would no doubt make a point of ignoring him. They would all keep playing "My Way" on the jukebox and everybody would drink Budweiser save for him, who had never liked the taste of alcohol. He would draw stares when he ordered his usual soda water.

"Thanks, but not tonight," Swann said.

"Listen, Jackie," Mannering said. "The word is some knuckle scraper hit Fredricks, and you stepped in to keep him from doin' the right thing."

Swann said nothing.

"I told 'em that wasn't like you, that you must be fucked up over that shootin'. Few days, you'll be the old Jackie boy again. Right?"

Swann and Mannering had reached the bottom of the steps.

"So, how was the interview for plainclothes?" Swann asked.

"They asked the same hypothetical they asked you," Mannering said. "'If a civilian came to you with an allegation of police misconduct, would you ignore that allegation or bring it to the clear light of day?'"

Mannering stood at the top of the steps and laughed.

"I lied, too," Mannering said.

Night had fallen since Swann had last been on the surface. He could still feel the heat of the afternoon.

"You know who was down for the interview was that little jabone with no tits," Mannering said.

Swann concluded that Mannering must be speaking of Coleman.

"Let me tell you, I was down there, waiting for them to call me in, and I'm looking at her and I'm thinking, 'Isn't this some shit?' Here I am up against *that.*"

Mannering put an arm around Swann.

"Plainclothes," Mannering said. "You meet a lot of girls with that uniform, but who fucking needs girls. You know what I mean?"

Swann had no quick response to that.

"You sure you don't want to come along?" Mannering asked. "What else you got to do?"

Swann stood at the center of the city that he had heard described as the hub of modern Western culture and civilization.

"Nothing," Swann said.

"Well, in that case, you better get going," Mannering said.

Swann crossed Broadway on his way along the park, and he was gazing down at the lights of Times Square when he heard a car horn sound behind him. He glanced over his shoulder to see that a posse of teenagers had crossed in front of a turning taxi.

The posse's deliberate step told him that it was on the hunt, and he peered ahead for their prey. He saw no lone woman or businessman in a suit or anybody else.

A breeze gusted up the street and whipped Swann's tie over his shoulder. He smoothed it back down over his chest and belly. His hand went toward his revolver when he heard a rustling behind him.

A gangly teenager with bright dark eyes appeared at Swann's side. The teenager wore red sneakers, creased designer jeans, a green nylon T-shirt. He had a torn blue cotton jacket slung over his shoulder as a throwaway. Four gold teeth flashed as he spoke.

"Mister," the teenager said.

Swann knew without looking that the posse was hanging back, waiting for the teenager's report.

"Mister," the teenager said. "You got the time?"

The bright eyes dropped to study Swann's pockets and then flashed back up. Swann had only to blink and drop his head a quarter inch and the teenager would take this as the sign of an easy victim. The teenager would then signal the others to pounce, and Swann would very likely be forced to shoot at least one of them. Swann would possibly end up killing the teenager who stood before him.

Swann kept his gaze absolutely even.

"I'm not who you think I am," Swann said.

The bright eyes widened.

"I am who you think I am now," Swann said.

The teenager slipped away, and the posse went with him.

Swann continued along Central Park South. The thumping in his chest eased, and the only reminder of the encounter was a dryness in his mouth that persisted as he went by the entrance to the punishment post. He passed the first brass-rimmed window of the Plaza and saw a woman in a black beaded dress. She was accompanied by a man who wore a double-breasted blue suit, a shimmery white shirt, and a red tie. He was raising a tall iced drink.

Swann went on by the second, third and fourth windows. He saw more beautifully dressed people in each. In the last, a young woman in an evening gown sat facing the dim room. Her hair was swept up, her back was bare and luminous.

Swann reached the entrance to the Plaza, the lights shining overhead as he gazed into the darkness before him. He saw only the promise of the subway and another train ride home. He must have slowed.

"Good evening, sir."

The greeting had come from a uniformed doorman. Swann had never been addressed as *sir* by anybody other than a crook seeking to wheedle a favor, and he stood still in the suit and tie that had apparently led to a second misapprehension.

The doorman then moved to turn away, seeming to realize he had made a mistake. Swann heard himself speak.

"Good evening," Swann said.

Swann buttoned his suit coat and started up the carpeted marble steps.

The suit and tie were apparently as convincing to the people in the lobby as to the doorman. Nobody appeared to pay Swann any particular heed as he followed a carpeted passageway to the right and arrived at the doorway of the Oak Bar.

Small lamps with red shades shone warm and faint on the wood-paneled walls. The voices of the people standing at the bar and scattered at the tables were a restrained murmur. Glasses clinked off in the far corner and there was a muffled laugh.

Swann entered and took another six steps up to the bar. He held the smooth, dark wood with both hands, as if to steady himself. He watched the white-jacketed bartender approach.

"Yes?" the bartender asked.

"Soda water," Swann said.

"Lime?"

"Please."

Swann watched the bartender fill a glass with ice and open a six-ounce bottle of the same brand of soda served at Joey Farrell's. The bartender then dropped in a section of lime and set the drink down before Swann.

The bartender ignored the $10 bill Swann tossed out. Swann looked along the bar and saw that nobody else had set out money. He slipped the bill back into his pocket.

With one hand still holding the dark wood of the bar, Swann took a sip of soda water. Some sort of transubstantiation seemed to take place, and his mouth filled with a wonderful, bubbly tang that he had never before experienced. He reasoned that he just might have been thirsty from his encounter with the teenagers, and he took a second sip. The miracle repeated itself.

Swann peered over one shoulder and then the other. Red-jacketed waiters went from table to table with silver-rimmed trays. A cigarette lighter flickered in a bejeweled hand. A champagne cork popped and a female voice rose in excitement.

As he turned back to the bar, Swann glanced at a tall, trim man who stood next to him. The man's suit was also a navy pinstripe, but any similarity with Swann's stopped there. This other one had the deep, rich luster of a much finer material and hung perfectly smooth. It did not appear to strain at so much as a thread as the man lifted his glass and knocked back his whiskey.

"Bill, please," he said.

The bartender produced the check, and the man withdrew a credit card from a thin leather billfold. He was moving to leave when Swann saw that he had forgotten a navy blue box.

"Excuse me," Swann said.

The man kept walking.

"*Hey!*" Swann said.

The man stopped and turned with a surprised expression shared by several other patrons. Swann held up the box, which was embossed with a golden lamb and the words BROOKS BROTHERS in gold script.

"Right," the man said.

He took the package, and his smile flashed white.

"It's been one of those days," he said.

Swann drained the last of his drink and set down the glass. The bartender immediately came over.

"Another?" the bartender asked.

"Bill, please," Swann said.

Swann went down the carpeted marble steps of the Plaza feeling that $4 for a club soda could be a bargain. He hopped the subway with a bounce that was still in his stride when he started up his stoop. His springing excitement sounded hollow on the wood planks as he entered a house he had never before compared to anything fancier than the identical house next door.

Ellen looked up from a talk show and asked how he had fared with the grand jury. Swann said everything had gone fine. He normally would then have settled down before the television with her, but he instead went to the window. He stared out at the street.

"What are you looking at?" Ellen asked.

Swann had never seen carriages or limousines on this street, but he had also never seen that there were *not* carriages and limousines on this street.

"Nothing," Swann said.

"Well, then you might take a look at this," Ellen said.

Ellen held up the most recent late-payment notice from the gas company, the one bill that Swann for some reason tended to neglect in the unending juggle of their finances. He felt all too keenly how much less than $1 million he was worth alive.

"Don't worry," Swann said. "I get paid tomorrow."

"Try and see the gas company does, too," Ellen said. "I don't want to end up having them take out the meter again."

Swann went to bed feeling he had done well not to tell Ellen about his bargain club soda. He awoke at midmorning as she dropped an armload of fresh laundry at the foot of the bed. She was still folding the clothes when he came in from a shower, and she held up the T-shirt he had worn the night of the shooting. He saw that the last traces of blood were gone.

"It came out fine," Ellen said.

The absence of stains did not mean Swann was going to wear that T-shirt. He sought something else in the pile of folded laundry and came upon his permanent-press dress shirt. The material was still warm from the dryer.

"What are you doing?" Ellen asked.

"Getting dressed," Swann said.

Swann began buttoning the shirt, deciding that plainclothes did not mean he necessarily had to dress plain. He reached for the suit he had draped over the top of the dresser the night before.

"Jackie, *what* are you doin'?" Ellen asked.

"Ellen, millions of people go to work every day in a suit," Swann said.

Swann took the tie from the doorknob and turned to the mirror.

"Not anybody *I* know," Ellen said.

"Over, under, around and through," Swann said.

At District 1, the retarded woman, Marie, called out her usual greeting and Swann gave his usual response. He strolled by the front desk, and heads went up one after another from the paperwork. Nobody else spoke until he entered the muster room.

"Whas up?" Coleman asked.

Swann realized that Coleman must have heard what really happened with the derelict. He also understood that he was being addressed with a certain tone of kinship by somebody wearing a bright yellow satin jacket that had silver tassels on the shoulders.

"How ya doin'?" Swann asked.

Coleman continued toward the women's locker room without looking back.

"Who could complain?" Coleman said.

Swann went in to roll call. Sergeant Quinn eyed Swann, clearly wishing there was something in the Patrol Guide prohibiting officers from wearing suits without particular cause. He was able to cite once more the regulation against straying from the subway. He suggested that anybody caught on the surface would be sent back to uniform.

"For some that would mean more than for others," Quinn said.

Swann took a moment to duck into the anti-crime office, where an older cop named Sullivan performed clerical duties pending his retirement. Sullivan was also overweight, though not so much as Swann.

"Let's see, Appleton, Axthelm, Baker . . . ," Sullivan said.

He was making a show of taking his time as he thumbed through the stack of paychecks.

"You'll find it after 'Scumbag' and 'Sullivan,'" Swann said.

Sullivan handed Swann the check.

"And I gave you your first collar," Sullivan said.

Swann had an image of a prisoner kneeling, head bowed, blood dripping on the concrete floor of the place known as "the Room." He stopped the memory right there.

"That's right," Swann said. "You did."

* * *

Swann was just assuming his post when who should ascend from the platform but the bartender who had performed the first miracle of the club soda. He wore a red plaid jacket and looked incapable of any marvels at all as he started up the steps to the street. He stopped halfway and disappeared through a steel door that served as the Plaza's employee entrance.

At meal period, Swann himself went up the steps. He ascended to the street and this time started along the park with Fredricks.

"Don't get excited," Swann said. "I'm just going to the bank."

Swann stood in line with the payday crowd, listening to the row of cash machines emit electronic beeps. His turn came, and he stepped up to slide in his plastic card. He made four little beeps of his own as he punched in his identification code, CAVE. More beeps came as he deposited the $622.47, what he was worth alive for a two-week period after taxes. The computer added it to what remained of the last check, and the screen flashed what the financial pages would term his total liquid assets.

"$683.19."

Swann gazed upon a number that was almost exactly where he had started the previous pay period. He then hit the button next to the words "Get cash." *Beep,* and two new words appeared.

"How much?"

Swann might have had the lowest food bills in the city, but this was the first check of the month, and what the financial pages would term his accounts payable included a mortgage and property tax and house insurance. He also had the gas company to consider, and that would just about clean him out.

Another result of having come so close to death was that he had little difficulty choosing between going to the Oak Bar and letting the gas company wait one more month. He returned to his post with $50, by his calibration five-o dollars, making at least a hint in his pocket.

The bartender was again in his white jacket and at his post. Swann once more felt the cool on his skin and the smooth wood of the bar under his hands.

"Yes, sir," the bartender said.

The miracle of the club soda repeated itself. Swann admired several more elegant suits, noting that one man wore a yellow rose in his lapel.

"Did you pay the gas bill?"

"What did I tell you I would do?"

"I didn't fucking think so."

"Ellen, you want to go out and make money?"

"You want to wash freaking dishes?"

"I don't need this, Ellen."

"I don't, either."

"Then what are you doin'?"

"What am I doin'? What are you doin'?"

"I told you, I don't need this."

A wail came from Jenny's room. Swann and Ellen both looked down the hall.

"I'll go," Swann said.

"No," Ellen said. "I'll go."

Ellen and Swann went down the hall as if they were each the only one going.

Jenny was sitting up in bed.

"I had a bad dream," Jenny said.

Jenny did not have the puffy-eyed look she got when she was roused by a nightmare.

"Let me guess," Swann said. "You were dreaming that Mommy and Daddy were having an argument."

Jenny lowered her eyes.

"Well," Swann said, "do you hear anything now?"

"No," Jenny said.

"That means it's over," Swann said.

Jenny looked to Ellen, who had yet to speak.

"It's okay, baby," Ellen said.

Jenny lay back down and Ellen kissed her cheek.

"'Night, Mommy," Jenny said.

Swann bent to kiss the same cheek.

"'Night, Daddy."

* * *

Swann had the next day off, and the pleasant look he got from Ellen no doubt came because he had appeared in the kitchen doorway wearing denims and a T-shirt. Her expression soured when she saw the suit balled under his arm.

"I'll be back," Swann said.

As he walked along the park, Swann felt the revolver in his waistband slip. A slight adjustment caused the butt to fit snugly, but Swann wondered if his pants were just a touch looser, if he had not lost a little bit of weight. He had no standard against which he could test this suspicion, for the last time he had felt a need to step on a scale had been at his physical for the transit police.

The scuff of sneakers caused Swann to snap his head around, ready to confront a fleeing felon. He instead saw a jogger such as he had often encountered here. This one was a lean, middle-aged man in a torn college T-shirt, faded shorts, and running shoes. The man seemed to float by, streaming sweat, his face showing no strain.

Swann trudged on to the dry cleaner's and for once entered with something that did not have a patch sewn onto the left shoulder.

Swann retrieved the suit that evening and arrived home to smell chicken roasting. The sour taste in his mouth was gone and he was feeling a distinct stirring of appetite when he sat down to dinner.

Still, Swann was not possessed by anything like the craving of times past. And, mindful that he might actually have begun to lose weight, he kept himself to a few bites of chicken.

Ellen eyed him. She seemed more unsettled by this moderation than when he had not eaten at all.

"You want me to make something else?" Ellen asked.

Swann declined, saying the chicken had been perfect.

"Do you have any coupons for soda water?" Swann asked.

The next day, Ellen returned from the store with two liter-sized bottles of Swann's request. He nibbled some leftover chicken for dinner, this time washing it down with club soda that tasted precisely like club soda.

Ellen seemed to make a point of not washing his dress shirt, and Swann did so in the bathroom sink before retiring. He left the house the following morning in his freshly pressed suit.

Swann was on his crosstown walk from the Queens subway to District 1 when he passed a sidewalk florist. He slowed and his eye fell upon the white roses. He had bought white roses for his mother when the cancer was almost done with her.

"Yes, mister?" the florist asked.

Swann's suit might not have been exactly elegant, but he did have enough change to afford the stand's most perfect white rosebud. He noticed for the first time that the buttonhole in his lapel was a fake, and he had the flower pinned over the vestigial loop when he arrived at District 1.

Swann's fellow officers had never been able to refrain from passing remarks when he did something as individual as ordering soda water in a bar. The sight of him reporting for duty in a suit garnished with a flower tested the unspoken stricture against speaking to him. The result was a series of huffs, snorts, and grunts.

One person who did address Swann was the bartender at the Oak Bar that evening. The miracle of the soda water once more repeated itself, as it did at the end of each workday that followed. The soda water at home remained just that, and he restricted his eating to a few bites of chicken or fish.

On his next day off, Swann again dropped his suit at the dry cleaner's. He returned in the late afternoon with the four wadded bills that remained of his $50. He added a dollar of change he had found under the sofa cushions.

"Sorry about the pennies," Swann said.

"Money's money," the dry cleaner said.

In the morning, Swann put on his clean, pressed suit and reached for his revolver as he would no matter what he was wearing. The weapon began to slide down his pants, and he adjusted it only to have it slip again.

The solution was obvious, but as unprecedented as the problem. He had not lost any measurable amount of weight since that brief time in his youth when *vigor* was the word and he answered John F. Kennedy's call for fitness. That had ended with the assassination, and he had still been several thousand jumping jacks away from having to draw in his belt. He now did so a full notch.

II

Four

SWANN HEADED DOWN THE HALL to report to Ellen the result of his diet of near death, homicide, soda water, and the occasional bite of chicken or fish. A knock came at the front door, and he was reaching for the knob when instinct prompted him to peer through the peephole. He saw a man wearing a blue uniform.

Swann tiptoed into the kitchen and saw Jenny drawing at the table. Ellen was washing dishes.

"*Gas man,*" Swann said.

Ellen glared, but she and Jenny remained mute as a second and then a third knock came at the door. Several minutes of silence followed, but Swann raised his index finger to his lips, correctly guessing that the gas man had only been listening for noises inside the house. Another, more insistent series of knocks erupted, and the Swanns stayed silent until they finally heard feet going down the stoop.

"Can I talk now?" Ellen asked.

"Sure," Swann said.

"Good," Ellen said. "PAY THAT FREAKING BILL."

Ellen was clearly not in the mood to discuss Swann's waistline. He instead reminded her that this was payday.

"For the gas company, too," Ellen said.

Swann hurried out of the house as quickly as he could without appearing to hurry out of the house. He had his belt cinched to his new girth as he once more encountered joggers along the park.

At District 1, Swann went directly to his fellow fatso, Sullivan, for his check and what promised to be another hassle.

"All right, what's your secret?" Sullivan asked.

"Excuse me?" Swann said.

Sullivan eyed him.

"Maybe I should cut you more slack," Sullivan said. "You got to be having a hard time."

"I've had easier."

"Believe me, I know what you're going through. I been there."

Swann had not known that Sullivan had been in a shooting.

"And nobody who hasn't been through it has any idea what it's like. Everybody thinks it's nothin'."

"It's not nothin'."

"How're your dreams?"

"I don't know."

"I always dreamed a lot. Hamburgers. Pies. Candy. Fucking devil's food cake."

"Excuse me?"

"Yeah, I'd dream I ate it all. Then I'd dream that I felt bad because I ate it all. Sometimes, I'd wake up and say, 'Did I eat or didn't I eat?' Then I'd realize I didn't and I felt good. Then I'd want to really eat, and I'd feel bad again."

Sullivan paused.

"I never could decide if that made them good dreams or bad dreams," Sullivan said.

"I don't remember mine," Swann said.

"Then you don't got to worry about 'em, good or bad."

Sullivan handed Swann his check.

"Mannering was saying you must be all fucked up over that shooting," Sullivan said. "Maybe I should go out and shoot somebody. You must have dropped ten pounds."

"Yes."

"Jackie . . ."

"Really."

Swann had, in fact, paid the gas bill. He had also stopped by the Oak Bar after work, but he was not about to tell Ellen. Not after the events of the morning. And not after she had spent the day ranging all over Queens in search of a Cabbage Patch doll for Jenny's birthday.

The problem was that Jenny apparently wanted one because everybody else did, and the stores were all sold out.

"I'm ready to pay double," Ellen now said.

Swann here saw an opportunity to restore some goodwill. He said he would see if he could find one in Manhattan and Ellen immediately brightened. He retired that night certain that he need only come up with one of these dolls and the visit from the gas man would be all but forgotten.

One jogger and then another chugged past Swann. He continued on to work dressed as had become his style, wondering if he might shed a few more pounds if he put in a little exercise. He reflected that his new post would not offer even the occasional opportunity to run after criminals.

Again, all was quiet under the Plaza and the only change in the routine was that the meal period saw Swann cutting through the cosmetics section in Alexander's department store. All around him were women selecting paints and powders and perfumes, and his nostrils flared at a series of scents that each seemed too strong. A thin woman in a black unitard was spraying samples of a new fragrance. She chanted the name over and over.

"Obsession. Obsession."

In the toy department, Swann wandered past G.I. Joe and Masters of the Universe and Barbie. A matronly saleswoman reported that the last Cabbage Patch doll had long since been sold. He asked where else he might look, and the woman responded as she might to anyone in a suit and boutonniere.

FAO Schwarz was across from the Plaza. Swann entered to see a mink-covered rocking horse and a kid-sized Mercedes and any number of other items not for somebody who had to worry about the end of meal period. He hurried up to a saleswoman, unsure that this store would even carry what was the rage in Queens.

"Oh, yes," the saleswoman said. "But I believe they're all gone."

The saleswoman directed Swann to a bank of shelves, which proved to be empty save for a single box that lay on its side. He picked up the carton and peered through the cellophane window.

"You might try this," the saleswoman said.

Swann looked over and saw that the saleswoman was holding up a sort of upscale Barbie.

"The trends come and go, but they always come back to these," the saleswoman said.

Swann again peered through the cellophane window. He was due back at his post and he had just a moment to make a decision. He handed the woman the box.

"I'd like this wrapped, please," Swann said.

The saleswoman's brisk manner faltered. She glanced down at the box and back up at Swann.

"Is something wrong?" Swann asked.

"Uh, no, no no, nothing," the saleswoman said. "Cash or charge?"

Swann had never even applied for a credit card, and he took from his suit pocket $40 of what was to get him through to the next paycheck.

Jenny came rustling out of the living room in a pink taffeta dress, all the more beautiful because she so clearly felt herself to be so. Her excitement had brought rosy spots to her cheeks.

"Daddy!" Jenny said.

Swann hugged Jenny and looked past her into the living room. The birthday party had started, and the dozen or so children included Danica's son, William.

"Mommy!" Jenny said. "Daddy's here."

Ellen came up and Swann gave her the bag containing the wrapped present.

"Did you get it?" Ellen asked.

"The last one," Swann said.

Swann might have taken Ellen aside to elaborate, but she handed him a package of balloons and asked the children if they wanted one. Swann was instantly surrounded.

"I want red!" Jenny said.

Ellen went into the kitchen to join the other mothers. Swann raised a red balloon to his lips and exhaled with all his strength. The balloon rose in his fingers but refused to expand.

Swann sucked another breath in through his nose and huffed and snorted until the balloon began to swell. He was stretching the end in preparation for the knot when he heard Danica's voice come from the kitchen. The balloon slipped from his stubby fingers and sputtered wildly around the room.

"*Wooh,*" Jenny said. "Again!"

"No," Swann said.

"Yes."

"*No.*"

"*Yes.*"

Swann reinflated the red balloon and again stretched the end. The other children joined Jenny's chant.

"Yes! Yes!"

When Ellen reappeared, red, yellow, blue, green, white, and orange deflated balloons were scattered all about the living room.

"Great, Jack," Ellen said.

Swann began retrieving the balloons, one of which had sputtered as far as the kitchen doorway. He glanced inside to see a half dozen mothers seated at the table.

"I was thinking of sending William to Saint Augustine's," Danica was saying.

Swann was still stout enough that he was glad Danica was sitting with her back to him as he bowed to retrieve the balloon.

"Hi, Jack."

Swann had been greeted by one of the other mothers, but all six were looking at him by the time he was able to straighten.

"Hiya," Danica said.

Swann stood in his suit and now customary boutonniere. He again saw that faint but unmistakable spark of interest in those cat's green eyes. He felt his face flush.

"What are you, undercover?" Danica asked.

"I guess you might say that," Swann said.

When the time came for the cake, Swann mumbled along as everybody sang "Happy Birthday." Ellen reminded Jenny to make a wish.

"Don't tell anybody, or it doesn't count," Ellen said. "It has to be a secret."

Jenny seemed uncertain about this business of secret desire, but she closed her eyes long enough to speak a wish to herself. She blew out the candles that marked her fourth birthday. Everybody cheered.

Ellen began doling out cake and ice cream. Danica stepped in to help, and Swann noticed that the white band on her wedding ring finger was turning brown.

"Anybody doesn't got?" Danica asked.

Cake crumbs spilled from Jenny's mouth as she spoke.

"Daddy," Jenny said.

Danica walked over to Swann with a pink paper plate in her right hand.

"No thanks," Swann said. "I'm not really hungry."

Danica shifted the plate to her left hand. Swann watched her lick some icing off her right thumb.

"It's good," Danica said.

"I'm sure it is," Swann said.

Danica turned back to the table, and Swann stole what glances he dared as she ate the cake and ice cream she had offered him. He told himself that only a lowlife would eye a woman at his daughter's birthday party. He tried not to look again. He looked.

Ellen stacked the presents in front of Jenny, and the other children joined in ripping open the packages. Their voices grew more and more excited as they unwrapped two Barbie dolls, a talking pony, a wind-up tarantula and a play doctor's kit.

Finally, the small hands fell upon Swann's package from FAO Schwarz. The wrapping paper fell away in shreds and Jenny tore open the box. She gave a shout as she held up the gift.

"Look!" Jenny said. "A Cabbage Patch."

The mothers fell silent. The round, dimpled face of the doll Jenny held before them was the color of chocolate.

After a moment, Danica gave a short, throaty laugh. She and the other mothers all looked at Ellen, who was glaring at Swann.

"I guess it's time for the goody bags," Ellen said.

The presents had marked the end of the party, and Ellen began handing out sacks of sweets. Swann was standing by the front door as Danica went by with William.

"*Oooh*. I love roses," Danica said.

Danica went on down the stoop, and Swann considered whether high school might have been a different story if he had thought to wear a suit and a boutonniere. He then turned to face Ellen.

"It was the only one they had," Swann said.

"I wonder why," Ellen said.

The night ended with Jenny tucked in with her doll and Swann in bed beside Ellen.

"I did pay the gas bill," Swann said.

"You're supposed to," Ellen said. "Everybody's supposed to."

Ellen paused.

"Jackie, you're going to make people think there's something wrong with you," Ellen said.

Swann concluded that he was in bed with a woman who was coming to view him much as Fredricks did.

Swann awoke early, feeling tenser than when he had finally dozed off. Ellen and Jenny were still asleep and he had two hours before he had to leave for work. He stood at his front window, feeling as restless as if he were standing at the top of a subway stairwell.

Swann watched a neighbor go by with a dog, no doubt to walk along the park. His next thought was of the joggers, and a few more thoughts had him go into the kitchen for a knife.

Some quick work, and Swann's denims became cut-offs. He hit the sidewalk and took a breath of morning air. He then lowered his head and broke into a trot.

The only running Swann had done in the past decade had been in pursuit of criminals. He had no quarry fleeing before him. He was without the adrenaline of the hunt. His sole object was to boil off the very flesh that he was trundling along the park.

Other runners went by, some with the look of calm and ease Swann had seen in the man in the college T-shirt. Several faces were as red and contorted as he figured his own must be. A man nearly as stout as himself approached and they struggled past each other gazing straight ahead.

* * *

Swann leaned against the kitchen doorway in a sweat, face hot, chest heaving, knees ready to buckle. Ellen held up the two hacked-off legs of the denims, and he explained between gasps that he had made a pair of shorts so he could go jogging.

"For what?" Ellen asked.

Swann folded his arms over his chest and tensed his throat against the tumult of his jogged stomach.

"It's . . . good . . . for . . . you," Swann said.

Swann stepped from the shower as Ellen was cleaning the toilet bowl. He was inspired to make the announcement the gas man had interrupted several days before.

"I don't know if you noticed, but I dropped a few pounds," Swann said.

Ellen flushed and stood with the brush dripping in her hand.

"I'm not surprised," Ellen said. "You haven't been eating much."

Swann kissed Jenny as he left for work.

"Her, too," Jenny said.

Jenny held up the Cabbage Patch doll. Swann kissed the plastic cheek.

"What color am I?" Jenny asked.

Swann assumed that somebody must have passed a remark concerning the doll's complexion.

"White," Swann said.

Jenny pointed to the freckles on her arm.

"With brown spots," Jenny said.

The next morning, Swann was again by the park, running neither after nor away, but toward. He looped back home feeling that he had progressed exactly as far as he had pushed himself and he was in such good spirits that he expanded his regimen to include jumping jacks. He threw out his legs and clapped his hands over his head and he could have been back in the time the word had been *vigor.*

The new regimen imparted a sense of accomplishment even as Swann stood underneath the Plaza with Fredricks doing absolutely nothing. He might not have been battling evil and rescuing the innocent, but the end of the week did see his revolver slip from his waistband while he was getting ready for work. He cinched in his belt one more notch.

Swann celebrated this second notch at the Oak Bar, and the club soda was no less miraculous for being the last he could afford until his next check. He nonetheless found himself growing fretful in a realm that had seemed beyond all care.

Everywhere he looked, well-tailored outfits reminded Swann that his own suit was getting too big. The suit would become clownishly so if he lost additional weight, and yet he was hardly going to give up his regimen and return to gorging just so he could make his clothes fit. He still had no solution when he arrived home.

Swann stood in the kitchen, both his hands buried in his trousers. He might always have been inclined to fidget in his pockets, but he had not known this about himself because his pants had always been too tight. He had never before had room to jingle change.

"Money!" Jenny said.

Swann's weight loss left room in his pocket for Jenny's hand as well. Her smaller fingers wiggled about and then came out in a fist. She opened her hand to see the quarter and two dimes that remained of his last paycheck.

Jenny scampered down the hall, and Swann soon after heard a series of faint but distinct sounds come from her room. He recognized this as the clinking of coins dropping into the porcelain piggy bank that he and Ellen had received as a wedding present. Ellen had passed it on to Jenny so she would learn to save.

The routine of the days ahead ended each evening with Swann going past the Oak Bar, his fingers fidgeting in roomy pockets two coins short of a jingle. His suit became even baggier, and his belt was drawn in a third notch when he went to pick up his next paycheck. He saw that his overtime for the night of the shooting had made the six-week passage through the city bureaucracy.

"You're a fucking hero," Sullivan said. "You musta dropped twenty pounds."

Swann made the deposit at the cash machine no differently than always, but he withdrew only $20 of his usual $50. He then hit a button he had never had occasion to use before, thus causing the screen to inquire how much he wished to transfer into savings. The number he entered included the additional $30 he would ordinarily have withdrawn for himself. He placed that atop the $89.02 for the four hours of overtime that followed the killing of Daryl Coombs. *Beep*.

The morning run was the same twenty blocks, but felt less arduous as Swann took measure of his larger progress. His next check would include the overtime from the derelict, and he would probably be able to stash another $150 or so. That would put his savings around $275, which might get him within range of attire befitting someone who frequented the Oak Bar. The problem was, he had no idea what such a suit might cost.

After another tour under the Plaza, Swann walked briskly past the Oak Bar and turned down Madison Avenue to a pair of bronze and plate-glass doors. A salesman directed him to a wood-paneled elevator, and he rode up beside a middle-aged woman who wore a blue dress and pearl earrings. She seemed to feel he was crowding her, though by subway standards he was hardly in her vicinity.

Swann stepped out on the third floor to see rack after rack of suits. A salesman approached and eyed him in a way that made him all the more conscious of his ill-fitting attire.

"A forty-eight, am I right?" the salesman asked.

The salesman had been quite literally sizing him.

"I was a husky," Swann said.

Swann had only intended to browse, but he now found himself allowing a tape measure around his waist. The salesman hesitated on encountering the revolver.

"I'll be wearing that," Swann said.

The salesman had sized Swann correctly and led him over to the appropriate rack. Swann ran his eyes past an elegant solid gray and a nice summer-weight tan and other equally wonderful, definitely above-ground suits.

Swann then came to a navy pinstripe that looked very much like the suit worn by the man who had stood next to him the first time he visited the Oak Bar. He touched the sleeve and discovered that the material felt as remarkable as it looked, at once soft and strong, wonderfully smooth and substantial.

"Should we take a look?" the salesman asked.

Swann pretended to examine the suit, trying to locate the price tag. He sensed that asking what the suit cost might be something like throwing money onto the bar at the Plaza.

"Why not?" Swann said.

Swann was in the changing room when he noticed something else about the sleeve, this being the small white tag that showed the price to be $650. He could hardly step back out and announce that there had been a misunderstanding, so he went ahead and stuck a leg into the trousers. He felt the wonderful material run up his bare skin.

When he emerged, Swann stepped before a three-paneled mirror. He thereupon beheld proof in triplicate that the three notches felt like much more than they appeared, that fat covered by the finest of tropical wools looks primarily like fat.

"A beautiful suit," the salesman said.

"I think I'll have to think about it," Swann said.

Swann began his morning run feeling every ounce of his remaining bulk, and he sought to distract himself from the mounting pains in his chest and knees. He fell to pondering the matter of the suit, and he figured that he would still be $350 short after his next paycheck. He estimated that he could probably squeeze $50 from each subsequent check if he stayed out of the Oak Bar. That meant he would have the $650 right around New Year's Day.

Swann threw a little more kick to his step and went on to the matter of weight loss. He calculated that he had been cinching in his belt at the rate of roughly one notch every two weeks. This was the same frequency with which his paychecks came.

The next slap of his sneakers had Swann considering his wages and his weight as factors of a single formula. He reasoned that three months would give him more than enough time to trim himself to a figure befitting such a suit. He reached the end of his run deciding that on this New Year's he would show himself to be a Jack Swann as grand as he had ever imagined.

* * *

Swann kept his goal before him through all the next week, calculating on his morning runs that each day of exercise and diet trimmed him of another half pound, that every hour at his post beneath the Plaza put $5 more in savings, that each stroll past the brass-rimmed windows was one stroll closer to the night when slim Jack Swann would stride into the Oak Bar in his Brooks Brothers suit.

At home, Swann further economized by substituting damp cleaning for dry, steaming out the wrinkles by hanging his present suit in the bathroom with the water running hot. He managed to get several days out of his boutonniere by keeping it in a tumbler of water overnight.

Swann arrived at his next payday with his lapels slightly curled and his rosebud a little brown at the edges, but with the image of the true Jack Swann shimmering only brighter. His belt was drawn in another notch when he collected his check.

"You're a what-you-call-it," Sullivan said. "An inspiration."

Swann stepped up to the cash machine with the $136.10 in overtime from the derelict. A couple of pokes with the index finger sent that along with $50 into savings, bringing the total to $305.12. BEEP!

The suit hanging by the shower, the rosebud in the tumbler, Swann read Jenny another fairy tale. He was feeling that he was himself living happily as he kissed Jenny good night. His calm stayed with him as he retired down the hall with Ellen to sit before the television.

Then, right in the middle of some canned laughter, came a crackling sound from the box itself. A burning smell filled the air. The screen went dark.

"What happened?" Ellen asked.

Swann rose and flicked the power switch on and off.

"Try it again," Ellen said.

Swann flicked the switch twice more and flipped the channel dial and wriggled the power cord and banged the sides. He finally got a butter knife and unscrewed the back. He gazed for the first time at the mass of wires and circuit boards that could somehow translate unseen rays into television shows.

"It must have broke," Swann said.

Swann could do nothing more than replace the back.

"This time, I'll pick it out," Ellen said.

Two years before, Swann and Ellen had decided to dispense with the usual anxiety of what to get each other for Christmas and buy a new television as a joint present. Ellen had clipped a list of recommendations from a consumer magazine, and Swann had gone with Joseph to the store.

Joseph had become uncharacteristically vocal on seeing that all the televisions on the list were of Japanese manufacture. The result was the American set that now stood before them, showing only their own dim reflections.

"Maybe we can get it fixed," Swann said.

Swann flicked the power switch several more times before returning to his armchair. He had in childhood been fascinated by the notion that wherever he went the air was filled with invisible beams carrying whatever television shows were being broadcast at the moment. He now checked his watch and considered that "Falcon Crest" and "St. Elsewhere" were bouncing all around the room. He sat with Ellen in what at first seemed almost in answer to his new calm, but the quiet soon became silence.

Swann got all the morning exercise he needed wheeling the television up the street in a shopping cart with Ellen at his side and Jenny roller-skating ahead. They turned into the nearest fix-it shop, which proved to be one business that still dealt almost exclusively in American appliances. The shelves were crammed with toasters and electric clocks and vacuum cleaners that looked nearly new. The man behind the counter quickly diagnosed the trouble with Swann's television.

"It's no good," the man said.

Swann had the day off, and he could offer no reason why they should not go directly to Cousin Ozzie's Electronics. A salesman with slicked-back hair took Swann and family along a wall of televisions that rose on both sides from floor to ceiling. Almost all of them were Japanese, and Swann stopped before a sixteen-inch set whose cost would probably put his savings plan back not much more than a month, subway crime depending.

"That's list price," Ellen said.

Ellen crouched before a twenty-four-inch Hitachi that stood on the bottom shelf. The price tag reported the set had been reduced from $390 to $300.

"Here you got a ninety-dollar saving," Ellen said.

Ellen lowered her voice.

"You had some overtime coming, didn't you?" Ellen asked.

Swann could hardly squawk about the price and then show up a couple of weeks later in a new suit. His one hope was that the store would not take a check. That ended when he proffered the sole piece of identification he carried.

"No problem, Officer," the salesman said.

That night, Swann plugged in the Hitachi and pulled the power switch, causing whatever was inside to transform the invisible rays into the evening news. The lead story was of little concern to Swann. He was too busy looking at the anchorman's suit.

The salesman had not been lying. The Hitachi did indeed have terrific picture resolution, and Swann could make out every elegant pinstripe.

In the morning, Swann might have stayed in bed save for the thought that missing one day could too easily lead to missing another. He roused himself against the threat of seeing all that might not have been simply become what had been before.

On his run, Swann once more sought distraction in finance. He calculated he would have to save for seven months more to reach his goal. The image of a slim Jack Swann in a Brooks Brothers suit vanished into the morning haze.

Swann reached the end of his loop seeing nothing before him but distance. He returned home so distracted that he oversteamed his suit, removing the creases along with the wrinkles.

"I think you're next."

Swann was being addressed by a woman who stood directly behind him at the cash machines. He realized that the line had moved ahead one more place.

"Sorry," Swann said.

Swann stepped up to the vacant machine and made the necessary transfer to cover the check for the Hitachi. The screen flashed the new balance of his savings account.

"*$00.00.*"

Beep.

Swann arrived at District 1 with all the professional verve of Fredricks the day before a barbecue. Everything otherwise seemed the same until he encountered Mannering. No big, booming welcome. No big, flashing smile. No arm around the shoulder or slap on the back. Just a mumble and a scowl and a hand holding out a personnel order.

9/4/86
TRANSFER
The following transfer is ordered:
EFFECTIVE IMMEDIATELY

POLICE OFFICER	SHIELD	ID#	FROM	TO
Coleman, S.	3126	8473	D1	Anti-Crime

Swann looked up. Mannering would stay in "the bag," as the uniform was known. No Dirty Paddy. No Starsky and Mannering. No working *undercover.*

"A pygmy cunt," Mannering said. "I get beat out by a fucking nappy-haired pygmy cunt with size one and a half shoes."

Mannering crumpled the paper into a ball.

"What they ought to do is give the interviews on black history," Mannering said. "They'd fail them anyway, and they wouldn't be able to squawk about affirmative action."

Mannering then eyed Swann's oversteamed suit and day-old boutonniere.

"Maybe I ain't ready for plainclothes, anyway," Mannering said.

Coleman reported for her first day in anti-crime wearing a red leather pillbox hat, a black leather carcoat covered with big white stars, and high-top sneakers.

"Officer Coleman, where did you get that outfit?" Sergeant Quinn asked.

"My closet," Coleman said.

Quinn announced that he wanted to team the new arrival up with a more experienced officer. The hush that followed was long enough for Swann to look from Fredricks to Coleman to Fredricks to Coleman.

"I'll take her," Swann said.

Coleman's black eyes fixed on Swann. She seemed neither pleased nor disappointed.

"He'll do," Coleman said.

Quinn went on to the matter of the perpetual mess around the coffee machine. Swann remembered that the transfer order had said *Coleman, S.* Sharon? Sarah? Sandra? Sally? He was sure he had not guessed correctly when roll call ended and she came over.

"I'm Jack," Swann said.

"Simone," Coleman said. "You know, like Simone say let's get going."

Swann followed Coleman out the door. He saw that she had dyed her tail a familiar hue.

Swann's baggy shuffle was no match for Coleman's quick step, and she was half a dozen strides ahead when he reached the end of the passageway outside District 1.

"They really fucked you this time, Jackie boy!"

Mannering was at his post by the turnstiles, and he made his meaning clear by tilting his head toward Swann's new partner. Swann reckoned that the situation would only become worse if Mannering heard the truth from somebody else.

"I asked," Swann said.

"What?" Mannering asked.

Swann had made the break now.

"Yeah. I asked."

Mannering's last words reached Swann as he started after Coleman.

"Jackie boy, you know what happens to people who wear suits? They become suit people."

Swann hurried on to catch up with Coleman.

"Do you have to walk so fast?" Swann asked.

"No," Coleman said.

Coleman kept striding at the same pace until they boarded the downtown train that would take them to the uptown train that would take them to the station beneath the Plaza. He stood the post with Coleman, who was officially just another civil servant of the transit police variety.

"I see you dyed your tail," Swann said.

"Like it? It's po-lice blue," Coleman said.

At meal period, Swann as always turned toward the nearest stairway leading to the street. Coleman made for the steps that descended to the tracks.

"Where are you going?" Swann asked.

"To eat," Coleman said.

Swann followed less because of any unwritten rule than out of curiosity. He had never seen a transit cop begin a meal period by going deeper into the underground.

"Where?" Swann asked.

"Same place I always go," Coleman said.

Coleman got off the train at Times Square and Swann followed as she turned away from another set of steps that led up to the street. She took a stool at a subway soda fountain Swann had passed a thousand times without ever stopping. He gave his order only to learn from the counterman that this was one soda fountain that did not stock soda water.

Swann made do with black coffee, and Coleman asked for a hot dog. He watched her apply the mustard from a squeeze bottle in a single straight line.

"I'll give you the résumé," Coleman said.

Coleman said she had been a cop just two years, most of that time in Brooklyn. She added that was also where she had grown up. She mentioned a street whose name Swann had written on a number of arrest reports.

"I'm still living home," Coleman said.

Swann said that he was married and that he had a daughter and that he lived in Queens and that he had become a police trainee right after high school. He knew he was telling her only what she would have assumed.

* * *

Coleman hopped off her stool. Swann put down his coffee and started for the train that would take them back to their post. He had wrongly assumed her destination a second time.

"Now where you going?" Swann asked.

"For a stroll," Coleman said.

Swann had both traveled and patrolled the subway, but he had never heard of anybody who strolled the underground when they could just as easily be elsewhere. He also had never known anyone to stroll quite so fast.

"Are you in some kind of hurry?" Swann asked.

"No," Coleman said.

Swann stayed alongside Coleman, passing a Spanish record shop and a clothing store that sold imitation designer jeans that no self-respecting thief would wear. They continued past a sheet of plywood that covered what had once been a doorway.

"The Room," Swann said.

"I've heard talk," Coleman said.

The Room had been the place transit cops took prisoners to beat them, at least until one of those prisoners returned with a Legal Aid lawyer who caused a fuss. The case had gone the way of almost all civilian complaints, but questions had arisen about the blood spattered on the walls and slanted ceiling. Swann generally staved off memory as if it were hunger, and his particular memories of this chamber had him momentarily grateful for Coleman's pace.

When Coleman did slow, Swann understood that she had not suddenly become accommodating. He had also spotted the posse and he moved with her toward the turnstiles. The two of them were now in step with the young black men who ambled just ahead, carrying throwaways.

Swann felt his pulse quicken as he and Coleman followed the posse up the steps leading to the street. He reached the top and saw the teenagers turn the corner just as Daryl Coombs had. He stood at the edge of his domain, skin tingling, fingers flexing, heart pounding. He was acutely aware of the revolver cinched in his belt. He could not have said if he was scared or thrilled.

"Yo, we go after them, who's gonna watch the subway?" Coleman asked.

Swann had been threatened by innumerable bosses, and he had been subjected to endless grumbling from Fredricks. He had never until that moment been faced with an argument for staying in the hole that was more convincing than the threat of getting in trouble.

"Anyway, it's too easy," Coleman said. "It ain't hardly sportin'. You won't see those city cops coming down in the hole. You got to *work* to catch a crook in the hole."

After four more hours beneath the Plaza, Swann and Coleman signed out at District 1. She went off to black Brooklyn and he started across Central Park South. He was back at his own pace as he went past the Oak Bar.

Swann's arrival home prompted Ellen to turn away from the Hitachi and hold up a piece of paper he recognized as the new gas bill.

Swann got himself through his morning exercise and went down into the subway feeling fit mainly for a nap. He snapped alert when he saw that Danica was standing not more than twenty feet up the crowded platform.

At the screech of an approaching train, Danica's head swiveled in Swann's direction. He also turned, though not so much to peer into the tunnel as to prevent her from seeing him in his baggy, oversteamed suit and wilting rosebud.

Swann saw a pair of headlights appear and knew that Danica must also be watching them draw nearer and nearer. He did not steal a glance back at her until the first few cars had roared past and he was sure she would no longer be looking his way. He saw her standing with her face clenched against the gritty blast.

Danica boarded with no sign that she was aware of being watched. Swann squeezed in two cars down. He remained numb to those pressed against him as he felt himself carried into Manhattan with Danica.

At each station, Swann peered out to the platform, checking if Danica had gotten off. He did not see her again until he reached his own stop. She stayed two car lengths ahead all the way up to the street.

Danica turned away from District 1, and Swann checked his watch. He did not have to be at work for fifteen minutes and this was one instance where nothing in the Patrol Guide prevented him from following somebody beyond the top of the subway steps. He was stopped only by the sense that he would be too much like a posse trailing a vic. He did stare after her as she went down the block and disappeared around the corner.

On her second day of plainclothes, Coleman's closet had produced a bright red satin blouse, matching leggings, and green socks. Meal time again sent her to the subway soda fountain for a hot dog, and Swann sipped black coffee as before.

Afterward, Swann once more strolled the underground at Coleman's pace. They then returned to standing under the Plaza, as they did the next day and the next and the next. The sameness underscored the difference of his new partner, but that difference also heightened the sameness of everything else.

Swann still managed to get himself running each morning, and he had his belt drawn in another notch when he received his next paycheck. The day became all the more momentous when his after-meal stroll with Coleman brought them to an actual crime in the subway.

A sneak thief was dipping his hand into a woman's purse, and he did not seem to believe that two such uncoplike characters were indeed Five-O until he was lying handcuffed on the mezzanine. Coleman insisted that Swann take the collar, and the early morning landed him in ECAB, reading a newspaper. The items in the financial pages included a matter-of-fact account of a man who had sealed a billion-dollar deal, no dollar of which seemed to be his own.

"Officer Swann."

The public address system summoned Swann to an assistant district attorney who called him by his first name and who was not completely successful in concealing his amusement on seeing a cop in an outsized steamed suit. Swann, on his part, observed that the ADA's suit was not quite as nice as the pinstripe at Brooks Brothers.

"*Homeowners receive instant cash!*"

Swann stood in the early morning dark with Ellen dozing on the sofa just as she had been when he returned home from the shooting.

He had seen the Money Store commercial a number of times before, and he had never paid it any more heed than the ones that claimed that the right hygiene products can bring success in love and work. He now found he had an increased sensitivity to the word *cash*.

Still, Swann was not so interested that he waited until the end of the ad before hitting the power switch. He woke Ellen so she would not spend the whole night on the sofa, and she groggily trailed him into bed. All was as it was supposed to be.

At the start of his morning run, Swann told himself that he would be getting the overtime for the sneak thief collar in six weeks and that he could save enough for a suit by February. Probably. Hopefully. Maybe. Unless something happened. Like before.

Swann jogged back home with no new savings plan, though the next two weeks saw him still losing weight at the one-notch-a-paycheck rate. The only clothing he purchased was an eight-dollar pair of gym shorts to replace the now too large cut-offs. The closest he came to fiscal planning was the occasional daydream in which he stopped by the Money Store and got a bundle of Cash the way Ellen might stop into the supermarket for some Vim or Joy. That fantasy was partly obscured by the difficulty he had picturing a store that sold money. He had less trouble with his more frequent imaginings about Danica, these often coming after he stopped by the sidewalk florist.

Swann had a fresh rose affixed to his lapel as he once more sat with Coleman at the subway soda fountain. He sipped his coffee and absently registered a stir of tunnel breath, the rumbling of an arriving train coming to him with no more import than might the sound of the waves at the seashore.

Swann heard the train begin blowing the long-short signal of an emergency. He and Coleman were already off their stools when the wild-eyed faces of a posse appeared from the tracks below.

The teenagers were taking several steps at a time, materializing in a few great bounds. They hit the top with their arms pumping, their legs churning, their sneakers slapping the concrete, the emergency signal continuing to blare behind them.

On seeing Swann and Coleman, the posse scattered, ten, maybe fifteen of them exploding in all directions. The only thing to do was grab the nearest one, and Swann brought a gangly teenager down with the sort of tackle he might have executed in high school if he had made the team.

The teenager fought to escape, and Swann could have been back in Liberty Weekend as he felt young, desperate flesh struggling under him. Swann fought that much harder, seeking not to hurt, but to stop. He spoke quietly as the teenager howled.

"Don't make me kill you," Swann said.

Swann dug a knee in the teenager's lower back and managed to bring the arms together and snap on the handcuffs. He heard another cry of pain, and he looked over to see that Coleman had somehow managed to bring down a teenager at least fifty pounds heavier than herself. She had a thumb hooked around the teenager's ear and an index finger under his nose and when she yanked back the pain caused him to howl and snap his teeth. She yanked again.

"Do it," Coleman said.

Her teenager complied and Coleman slapped on the cuffs and looked over at Swann. He was not meeting the dull, resentful gaze of a civil servant making another collar for dollars. Her eyes were shining, and he was sure she was breathing hard from more than exertion. He was sure she was huffing with precisely the same excitement that charged his own chest.

"What I do?" Coleman's teenager asked.

Coleman yanked the teenager to his feet. He had not looked so big with Coleman sitting atop him, but when they stood side by side her head was even with his shoulder.

"Why don't we go find out?" Coleman said.

Coleman grabbed an upper arm about as thick as her neck and led the teenager down the steps. Swann followed with his prisoner, and now he could hear screams between the long-short blasts of the horn. He saw that the train was stopped three quarters of the way into the station and that a crowd was gathered by the second car.

A man reeled out of the crowd and vomited. Others were craning their necks and otherwise struggling to see what had caused the ones at the front to gather. Those who could see stood mesmerized and Swann had to repeatedly shout "*Police!*" as he shoved his prisoner through them.

Swann saw a single sling-back shoe on the concrete, and then he himself went mute. A young black woman in a pink dress lay pinned at the waist in the two-inch gap between the car and the platform. She was what transit cops call a "space case."

"It wasn't me," Swann's prisoner said. "I didn't push her."

"Shut up," the other teenager said.

"She wouldn't let go," Swann's prisoner said.

The woman was chest down, and her face was turned to the side. Her right hand was close by her head, clutching the strap of her oversized black leather handbag. The left arm was outstretched, clawing weakly.

Swann left his prisoner with Coleman and lay down by the woman. She was semiconscious, and her half-open eyes did not seem to see the face inches away. Her manicured nails were scratching on the concrete, and he took her hand for a moment. She moaned softly.

"I'm a police officer," Swann said. "An ambulance is on the way."

Coleman was trying to radio for an ambulance, but of course the portable did not work. Swann rose to guard the teenagers while she dashed to the pay phone. He looked over his shoulder at the ring of faces and asked if anybody had seen what happened. They all stood silent, their eyes on the woman.

Two uniformed cops appeared from the crowd. They were not happy to see Swann, but they agreed to lend him a flashlight and to watch the prisoners. He lowered himself through the larger gap where the first and second cars joined.

Swann squirmed in the dark space between the undercarriage and the tracks. The flashlight beam caught a pair of bare legs, and he saw that the woman was wearing the second sling-back shoe. Blood dripped off the toe.

Swann ran the light up the dangling legs and the rivulets of blood. He saw that the hem of the pink dress had been pulled up into a mangle of clothing and torn flesh. Intestines hung in red-and-blue loops. He caught a strong odor of excrement.

Swann scrambled back onto the platform and saw that the crowd had grown. Coleman had returned, and she, too, was asking if there were any witnesses to what had happened. Nobody spoke, and the only thing to do was to conduct a "show up."

Swann took the prisoners to within the woman's field of vision and ordered them to lie face down. They knelt handcuffed before her and then dropped their shoulders, gently lowering themselves onto their sides. They finally rolled onto their stomachs.

Swann again lay beside the woman and took her hand. Her upper half was unmarked, and not even her makeup was disturbed. He saw the precise black lines drawn under the lower lids of her unfocused eyes.

Swann asked the woman if she could speak, and her mouth opened slightly, the gloss on the lips fresh, unsmudged, a pink to match her dress. No words came, and he told her to squeeze his hand twice if she could hear what he was saying. He felt her fingers tighten once and again. He said he was going to ask her some questions and he wanted her to squeeze twice if the answer was yes, once if the answer was no.

"Do you understand?"

Two squeezes.

"Do you know what happened to you?"

Two squeezes.

"Did somebody push you?"

Two squeezes.

"Do you recognize anybody here?"

Pause. Swann watched the woman's eyes become more focused as they fixed on the face of one teenager. The eyes then moved to the other. Two squeezes.

"Are these two of the young men who pushed you?"

No pause. Two squeezes.

Swann now paused. To give the woman's statement the greatest weight he would have to take what was known as a "dying declaration."

"Do you know you are about to die?" Swann asked.

Pause. Two squeezes, slow.

"Do you know you have no hope of survival?"

No pause. Two squeezes, fast.

"Is everything you have told me the truth?"

No pause. Two squeezes, even.

Swann squeezed back once and then a second time. He held on to her hand as Coleman dragged the teenagers out of the woman's view and the paramedics did what little they could. A crew of emergency service cops inserted air bags between the car and the platform.

"I'm gonna stay right here," Swann said.

The woman's eyes had lost their focus.

"Take it easy," Swann said.

Swann heard the cough of a compressor and the hiss of the air bags inflating. The woman must have sensed that something was happening, for there was a sudden glint of awareness in her eyes. Swann tried to hold this last glimmer of what was *her* in his gaze.

"I'm here," Swann said.

The air bags rocked the car away from the platform, and the crushing pressure on the woman's waist was suddenly released. Her insides sloshed to the tracks, and her pretty face paled under her still perfect makeup. Her eyes lost their glimmer, going as wide and fixed and dull as those of Daryl Coombs at the end.

"I'm here," Swann said.

A final gasp escaped her glossed lips and reached Swann's face as a tiny puff of air. He caught a faint, familiar scent, and he felt her hand close with what might have been a spasm or a last hard squeeze, a final *No!* The grip then relaxed, and he felt the fingers open to the half curl of the dead.

Swann lay as still as the woman for a moment and then looked up to see another hand outstretched to help him to his feet. This hand was big and white and belonged to the balding city detective he had met on the night of the shooting.

"Good work," the detective said.

Swann got to his feet.

"Your partner says you got a dying declaration," the detective said.

Swann nodded and looked over to see Coleman standing with her back to him, watching the prisoners. The two stared straight ahead as if waiting for the next train.

"Some guys think you can't do better than getting the perp to write . . ." the detective said.

Swann understood the detective meant acquiring a written confession.

". . . but give me a dying declaration any day."

Swann gazed past the detective and saw that the crowd had gotten bigger. Somebody had strung up yellow crime scene tape.

"Not that I'd kick if I had both."

Swann glanced over to where two emergency service cops were unrolling a black body bag.

"I see you're still wearing that suit," the detective said.

Swann looked back at the detective, who was eyeing him as if there was something not quite proper about a cop wearing a suit without being required to do so by either position or occasion.

"Anyway, they're deciding now who's gonna take it," the detective said.

The detective nodded toward two men in suits who were huddled next to the stairway. Swann recognized one of them as the supervisor of the District 1 detectives. The other was no doubt the boss of the city squad. The city police also had jurisdiction in the subway, but they generally showed interest only in the event of a homicide. The result was that each violent death underground raised the question of who would officially take the case.

"This'll go to us," the detective said. "You guys took the last one."

The detective smiled.

"But hey, the important thing with a homicide is that everybody looks good," the detective said.

The detective again eyed Swann.

"Speaking of which, you dropped a few pounds, didn't you?"

The detective looked down at himself and shook his head.

"Wish the fuck I could."

The case did indeed go to the city police, and Coleman was detailed to join the balding detective in escorting the prisoners to the precinct. Swann remained to recover the woman's property once the crime scene was processed. He slapped the subway dirt from his suit and watched the routine begin.

One technician raised a camera and called for everybody to stand back so that only the dead woman would be in the picture. The flash fired several times, and a second technician began recording various distances with a tape measure, noting in inches precisely how much of the woman lay on the platform. He then checked the hands for defensive wounds and covered both with brown paper bags on the chance that there was skin or hair under the nails. He secured the bags at the wrists with yellow crime scene tape.

Swann stepped in to help lift the body, seeking a grip in her armpit, feeling that she was still warm there. He was so adrenaline charged that she seemed almost weightless, and he had no trouble turning her over.

A gloved hand prodded a drooping loop of intestine back into the mound of mangled flesh and dress. Swann and the others all seemed to turn gentle as they laid her on the white sheet that lined the body bag.

The second technician crouched to check the woman for other wounds. He ended by taking her chin in his fingertips. Her head lolled back and forth, the eyes fixed, the lip now curled slightly back, the makeup still unmarked.

"Just the obvious," the second technician said.

The first technician was standing with a clipboard that held a form known as a "body sheet," this bearing an outline of a figure not greatly more sophisticated than those Jenny crayoned. Swann watched him draw a rectangle above the waist to indicate the mangle.

The air bags hissed flat and the train creaked out of the station and a cop huffed as he bent over the body bag. The sound Swann knew he would remember was that of the six-foot zipper closing.

Swann entered the precinct squadroom, his left hand holding the woman's handbag and the sling-back shoe that had lain on the platform. He flexed his empty right hand, still feeling the dig of the body bag's canvas handle. The woman had seemed to grow heavier as they carried her up the steps to the mezzanine and on up to the morgue wagon.

Swann saw the teenager he had arrested now come out of the squadroom with the balding detective. The teenager's expression was unchanged. The detective was flushed and agitated.

"A real fucking tough guy," the detective said.

The detective might have vented some of his frustration with his fists if the prisoner had shoved a cop or insulted a desk officer's mother, but with a big crime like homicide comes a lot of attention. Slap around someone for disrespecting an officer, and he will take it as his punishment and plead out to time served. Slap around someone charged with murder and he might try to escape a twenty-five-year sentence by screaming police brutality. A bruise or a cut might then require an explanation.

"Not that it really matters," the detective said.

The detective opened the door to the holding cell and nudged the teenager inside. Swann saw the other teenager lying on the bench as still as if he had been left on a gurney. He was no doubt coming off a blast of adrenaline, and he had been arrested enough to know that justice was going to be a long, slow process. He had the peace of having done exactly what he was accused of doing, and he slumbered in what cops call the Sleep of the Guilty.

"Damn," the detective said.

The detective was patting himself.

"Anybody got a pen?"

"Yo."

Coleman had called out from the desk where she was filling out some paperwork. The detective took her ballpoint pen, and Swann assumed he wanted to be prepared in the event the second teenager agreed to make a written confession.

The detective stepped inside the holding cell and crouched to slip the pen between the first two fingers of the sleeping teenager's hand. He squeezed. Hard.

"Wakey, wakey," the detective said.

Swann had seen a variation of this trick performed in the subway in which a bullet was inserted rather than a pen. The public would see only a smiling cop lending a derelict a helping hand. The pain from the crushed knuckles was said to be enough to rouse anybody but the dead, and the teenager awoke with a roar, his eyes popping wide.

"Let's you and me talk," the detective said.

The teenager rose, his grimace smoothing to stone as the detective led him from the cell. The detective paused and held the pen out to Coleman.

"Thanks," the detective said.

Coleman said nothing and made no move to accept the pen. The detective dropped it onto the desk and looked at Swann.

"You look cute with a purse," the detective said.

Swann was still clutching the dead woman's handbag. He set it down on the desk as the detective disappeared with the second teenager into the interrogation room.

"Look what you did."

The first teenager was addressing Swann from the holding cell.

Swann went over and saw him fingering a tear in the knee of his leather-trimmed denims. The rip must have come when Swann tackled him.

"You know what these cost?"

Coleman called out from the desk.

"Tell the officer how much," Coleman said.

The teenager answered in the tone of a kid in class who knew the answer.

"Fifty-four, plus tax."

"And tell him how much you had in your pocket when you left your house."

The teenager gazed at Coleman, looking now like a fat kid who had been asked to state his weight. He would have been only more shamed if he had not answered. He succeeded in keeping his voice neutral.

"Thirty-five cent."

The teenager stared through the bars, his face a pool whose depth Swann could not gauge. Swann again flexed the hand that had felt the woman's final squeeze, that had carried the body bag. He checked his anger, knowing that a glower or a single word would turn the teenager sullen as a killer.

Swann wanted to know more. About this youngster. About all these youngsters who each night became the biggest power in the city. Maybe about how he had himself come to kill.

"I spent all mine on clothes, too," Swann said.

The teenager eyed Swann's baggy, oversteamed suit.

"You bugging," he said.

He grinned.

"What's your name?" Swann asked.

"Alvin."

"Alvin, do you know why you're here?"

"You arrested me."

Alvin's face lost expression. Swann perceived that he had to be more gradual, that he had to draw out that part of this teenager that grinned at the suit, the part that was like any other youngster. He had always found with Jenny that the best way to get the full story was to start before what she would consider to be the beginning.

"Alvin, what time did you get up this morning?" Swann asked.

Alvin assumed the same expression he had with the detective.

"I didn't do nothing," Alvin said.

"You didn't get up today?"

Alvin shook his head.

"I wish I didn't."

"What time?"

Alvin hesitated.

"Ten. Eleven."

"Then?"

"Then I get dressed. I say, 'Ma, you cook?'"

"What'd you eat?"

"Beef patties. I always eat before I leave. Got to."

Alvin was looser now.

"What'd you say when you left?"

"'I'll be back, Ma.' I go out my building and I run up on Kelly."

"Who's Kelly?"

Alvin looked down and again fingered the tear in his jeans. Swann feared he had nudged too hard. The hand that had held the body bag now reached through the bars. Swann gave Alvin a fatherly pat on the shoulder, speaking as he might to a son.

"Alvin, Alvin, we're just talking," Swann said.

Alvin did not shrink from the touch. Swann saw something flash under the surface of the pool. He ran his hand over the curve of the shoulder.

"You don't feel like talking about Kelly, no problem," Swann said.

Alvin's head dipped lower. He seemed embarrassed, defenseless before intimacy.

"Kelly a robber," Alvin said. "He say he taxed a man on Thirty-fourth Street for six hundred thirty-one dollars. He said, 'Yo, Alvin, this is MONEY.' All he doing is showing me bills."

"You must have been bugging."

Alvin grinned at Swann's choice of words.

"*Was I.* The rest of the posse, they there and they say, 'Yo, we going to get paid.' You got to have money, especially when it be nice outside."

Alvin was now speaking as if Swann or anyone else should understand.

"So we go to the city to get busy on dollars. I'm saying, 'You got to think positive.' You think you gonna get caught, you get caught. People say they ain't gonna get paid, nine out of ten times they get knocked."

Swann led Alvin to the arrival at Times Square.

"We see Platypus and he with a whole bigger posse. He say, 'Whas up? Let's get busy.' He want to bum rush a vic."

"How many in the posse?"

"Which?"

"Yours."

"Maybe fifteen."

"And his?"

"About fifty. They get whatever come along. See diamonds, get it. See jewelry, get it. See money, get it. They surround a vic and go in his pockets and everybody be gone. The vic, he don't know what hit. He just go, 'What? What?'"

"Did your posse go with them?"

"No, we wasn't with it. If you with a whole, whole lot, you might don't get paid. We stay with us and say, 'Let's take it up Broadway.'"

"Then what?"

"All you do is go hunting, go hunting for a vic."

Alvin said they had prowled uptown, with little luck.

"I felt like we was giving up when we see a poppy love."

"That's a vic?"

"In a suit."

"Like me?"

Alvin again eyed Swann's attire.

"Maybe."

Alvin's tone stayed offhand as he described trailing the man.

"Nobody going to just rush up on you and rob you," Alvin said. "They going to study you. See what moves you make."

Swann nodded as if this was only reasonable.

"The street was kind of active, so we hung back. The vic go in a store. I go behind to see what kind of money he got. He just take out the one dollar, but I see a print."

"This man didn't get suspicious when you came in behind him?"

"I had my own money. I buy a bag of pretzels."

"And then what?"

"Then there go my thirty-five cent. He go out the door and I say, 'Mister, you got the time?'"

Swann made a conscious effort to keep his own tone casual.

"That seems to be the thing to ask," Swann said.

"You got something that work, you stick with it. He raise his hand and I see the watch he got is gold. I see he got rings. I look in his eye, and I see he scared."

"And?"

"I go back to the posse. I say, 'Yo, that the vic.' We get on our throwaways."

Alvin's hand went to the blue jacket he was wearing.

"Let me ask you, how'd you learn about throwaways?" Swan asked.

Alvin shrugged.

"You just pick up basic things. Crime is crime."

"Then what?"

"The vic go down the block. Every time you go to rob, you do get that nervous feeling. You say, 'No,' but the money makes you say, 'Yeah.' This other kid, he get ready to fiend."

"How do you fiend?"

Alvin raised his arms to demonstrate on an imaginary victim.

"You put your one arm round the neck and push down with your other hand. They got it from wrestling on TV. It have something to do with the air to your brain. Heads try to scream. Once you scream, you let that breath out and it's over. You go right to sleep."

"How do you choose who does it?"

"Anybody can fiend a head. It not how fast you is. It how you sneak up. Once you got them, it's over."

"So this other kid does the fiend."

"He about to when the vic go in a building. And that was it. I'm feeling too soggy. I don't even want to eat my pretzels."

Alvin shook his head.

"That the way the night go. We was tired. Somebody say, 'Let's go, maybe catch something easy on the way home.' I wasn't really with it. I was just going home."

The story was nearing the killing. Swann sensed he should ease back.

"Now, how many times have you gone hunting for a vic?" Swann asked.

"On the real side? Not too many times."

"When was the first?"

"I got started when I needed money. I was real little, I was like a goody-goody. But you start to compare yourself. You be sayin', 'Yo, I'm going to get paid and get that, too.'"

"You been in jail?"

"First time, I was kind of scared. I was on the bus, I still couldn't really believe it. Soon as I got there, I said, 'I'm really locked up. This is it. It's over.' Third time I went, I knew what was up and everything."

"If you had gotten money this time, what were you going to do?"

"Get fresh. Adidas sneakers. Burgundy. Maybe sky blue. Jacket to match. A Guess vest. Would you believe a vest they be selling for eighty-five dollars. Money really doesn't last too long, you know."

"Yeah."

At that moment, the door to the interrogation room swung open. The detective was flushed again as he brought the second teenager back to the holding cell. The teenager's face remained stone.

"Am I interrupting something?" the detective asked.

"Me and Alvin here were just having a little conversation," Swann said.

"Well, the conversation's over," the detective said.

Swann watched Alvin's gaze go from him to the detective.

"What the fuck are you looking at?" the detective asked.

Alvin's face became the twin of the teenager who now stood in the cell with him.

"Nothin'," Alvin said.

The detective now spoke to Swann.

"Neither of 'em will say shit," the detective said.

"Maybe if we look at pictures we could come up with a couple others," Swann said.

The detective shrugged.

"We got the main players," the detective said.

"How do you know that?" Coleman asked.

The detective sniffed.

"What do you want for a misdemeanor homicide?" the detective asked.

A complete accounting was required for even a humble victim's property. Swann went over to Coleman and the dead woman's oversized handbag.

"We best start with the cash," Coleman said.

Swann reached into the woman's handbag, feeling past a package. He took out the wallet that the detectives at the scene had already checked for identification. He saw the card inside that had directed them to contact the woman's sister in case of an emergency.

"You go up and offer somebody a hundred million dollars if you can kill them, they gonna say no every time," Coleman said. "That same person'll go ahead and get killed trying to keep somebody from taking what?"

Swann took out a ten-dollar bill and nine singles.

"Nineteen dollars," Swann said.

Coleman recorded the amount on a voucher form. Swann glanced over at the holding cell. The teenagers were huddled, speaking low to each other.

"You really had him," Coleman said. "You would have had him writing."

Coleman was saying that Swann could have gotten a written confession. She pressed a stamp to a red ink pad for the next step of the procedure. She stamped EVIDENCE on the first bill and slid it across to him.

"Speaking of which," Coleman said.

Swann took up the pen and initialed the bill. The stamp again thumped EVIDENCE and he again scribbled JS and they kept going until the bills were done.

"What else is there?" Coleman asked.

Swann reached back into the handbag.

"One package," Swann said.

Coleman looked up at the package, which was wrapped in silver paper and tied with red ribbon done up in a big bow. Her voice turned uncharacteristically soft.

"A cop called to confirm they notified the family," Coleman said.

"He said the deceased was on the way there to drop off a birthday present for her niece."

Coleman paused. Swann was also staring at the package.

"The party's tomorrow, but our woman had to work," Coleman said.

Swann again reached into the purse.

"One key chain," Swann said. "One eyebrow pencil."

Swann's hand next chanced upon a half roll of mints. He sniffed the neatly folded end. He caught the scent that had been carried by the woman's final gasp.

"One pack of mints," Swann said. "She's eating a mint, eating a mint and waiting for the train, and one of them comes up and asks if she has the time."

"She tips to being *sized,*" Coleman said. "Maybe also that they're all jerked up. They had to be vexed that they did all that walking and couldn't find no real *vics* in the street."

"One address book. She tightens her hold on the bag."

"They figure she must have much dollars."

"One tin, aspirin. They wait for the right time."

Swann glanced over at the holding cell. The teenagers were settling onto the floor.

"She hears the train coming," Coleman said.

"One compact mirror. She looks in the tunnel. Sees the light. The train's coming to take her away."

"Baw! The posse sets it off."

"Somebody grabs the bag. One pay stub. Brown's Office Supply, $568 for two weeks."

"She holds on. She's *keeping* that present."

"One book of stamps. They pull harder."

"She still holds on. She ain't giving it up."

"They figure this must really be a score. One, no two, pencils."

"The train's coming."

"Somebody gets mad."

"Pull come to shove."

"She hits the tracks. The train's close. She tries to get back up. The train's trying to stop. She's halfway up."

"She still got the bag."

"She's still got the present."

"Is that it?"

"No."

Swann picked up the lip gloss of the same color he had seen on the woman's parted lips.

"One lip gloss."

Swann's eyes went back to the holding cell. The teenagers were both escaping into sleep.

"What's in the package?"

The balding detective had come over.

"It wasn't opened," Swann said.

"Well, you better fucking open it," the detective said. "You can't just voucher a gift. You have to know what's inside."

Swann tugged gingerly on the red ribbon and the bow came undone.

The woman had not used any tape and the carefully folded paper came away without a tear, revealing a carton with a cellophane window. He beheld a doll identical in every aspect to the one he had bought Jenny.

Five

THE LOOKOUT HEFTED an empty bottle as Swann and Coleman neared.

"That's right, we're police officers," Swann said.

The lookout tossed the bottle. Swann and Coleman crunched over past the broken glass of other alarms to see a group of gaunt figures scatter from a tenement stoop. A youngster of about fifteen ambled down from the top step like a school kid at a fire drill.

The youngster must have been the crack spot manager. Those who conducted the actual transactions were concealed under the stoop, no doubt with a handy back exit. The money and drugs were apparently exchanged through a six-inch chink that Swann saw between the third and fourth steps.

"They going to be out of business a good five, ten minutes," Coleman said.

Swann checked the tenement's address, but the building they were looking for proved to be farther down. They passed from the bright morning to a dark, creaking stairwell that had the same urine smell as the subway.

The smell grew stronger as they ascended into deeper gloom, and Swann had the sensation of going up into the depths. They finally reached the third floor, and he saw a thin stripe of light under a door that had been reinforced with plywood and sheet metal. He knocked.

"Who?" a voice asked.

Coleman said they were the police and several locks clicked. The door opened, and light poured into the gloom. A tidy, perfectly groomed woman stood in the doorway of an immaculate apartment. She had a boy about a year old on her hip. She might have borne an even stronger resemblance to her dead sister had her eyes not been red and swollen.

"You already been here to tell me," the woman said.

A little girl appeared wearing a neatly pressed dress that had a pink-and-blue floral pattern.

"Hi," Swann said.

The girl ducked behind the woman's leg.

"She don't understand what's going on," the woman said.

Swann held out a brown paper bag containing the present, the wrapping restored as best he could manage. The city detective had not wanted to release it but had relented when Swann suggested they could bend the rules a little for somebody who had given them a dying declaration.

"The personal effects were vouchered as evidence," Swann said. "We thought we should bring this to you today."

The woman peered into the bag, and she was flexing her jaw when she looked up. Swann understood that she was struggling hard to hold on to herself in front of the children. Her voice was tight as she invited Swann and Coleman to enter. He said they had to get going.

"No," the woman said. "Please."

Swann and Coleman stepped past the woman and into the apartment.

"I'm Estrella," the woman said. "But you already know that."

The woman named Estrella bent over and handed the present to the girl, who looked uncertainly at Swann and Coleman.

"They brought it, but it's from Auntie," Estrella said.

As the dead woman must have planned, the girl's excited fingers had no trouble with the ribbon and the untaped wrapping. She gave a shout no less happy than Jenny's on seeing the face in the cellophane window. She needed only a moment to open the box and hug the doll to her chest.

"She's three today," Estrella said.

A knock sent Estrella to the door. A woman who was rotund even by the standards of the old Swann came in with a girl about four. The girl noticed only the doll.

"Mommy, Cabbage Patch!"

The woman was looking at Swann and Coleman.

"These are cops," Estrella said.

The woman reached for her child.

"There's no trouble here," Estrella said. "I had a tragedy."

"Maybe we should go," the woman said.

"No," Estrella said. "I want Esme to have her little party."

Estrella raised her chin, blinking hard.

"It was my sister," Estrella said.

Estrella turned to the children.

"What game can we play?" she asked.

Esme and the other girl looked up from the doll. They stood silent as a single tear trickled from one of Estrella's brimming eyes.

"Does anybody have an idea?" Estrella asked.

The children remained mute.

"Excuse me," Swann said. "Do you have any balloons?"

The children were cheering when another knock came. Swann was nearest the door, and he opened to see three girls in their early teens whose eyes were glassy and vacant like those of the dead. They showed neither surprise nor interest on seeing a white man pinching the end of an inflated balloon.

Estrella stormed over.

"What you're looking for is down the hall," Estrella said.

Estrella slammed the door shut. Coleman picked up a deflated balloon from the floor.

"Let's make it a double," Coleman said.

Coleman blew up hers and Swann held his ready and at a cry of *Go!* from the children the two balloons sputtered around the room.

"Time for the cake," Estrella said.

The candles and singing and the secret wish all went just as at Jenny's party. Swann and Coleman were at the door when Estrella quietly asked exactly what had happened to her sister. They recounted what they knew.

"And you got two of them?" Estrella asked.

"Yes, Officer Coleman and I," Swann said.

"You going to get the rest?"

"No," Swann said. "Probably not."

"If it was us two, we would," Coleman said.

Swann was slightly surprised by the *we*. He took her assumption as a compliment.

"Who is it?" Estrella asked.

"The city detectives," Swann said.

"But it's you that work in the subway."

"Sometimes we take it, sometimes they take it," Swann said.

Swann here was speaking of the larger *we,* the transit police.

"How do you decide?"

Estrella was speaking of the even larger *you,* the cops of both agencies.

"We take turns," Swann said.

Swann heard footsteps and he peered through the open door to see a cadaverous man hurry by, the tails of his torn raincoat flapping.

"It's too bad you don't take turns with crack houses," Estrella said. "I musta been at the corner a hundred times calling the police about what's going on down the hall."

Estrella seemed ready to cry again as she closed the door. Swann and Coleman stood in the hallway momentarily blind, the locks clicking in the darkness.

"If only we weren't just transit," Coleman said.

Coleman was again using the *we* that was just the two of them.

"Yeah, we might go right down the hall there and do something," Swann said.

Swann's eyes had adjusted to the gloom, and he saw Coleman was looking at him just as she had when they were both holding the balloons.

A burly man tried to block their way, demanding a $2 fee per person. Swann held out his shield.

"Do you give a government discount?" Swann asked.

Swann and Coleman entered a front room the same size as Estrella's. Here was indeed a crack house, which was not to be confused with a crack spot, that being where the drugs were sold. This was where the stuff was consumed, and in the smoky haze hung a stench that surpassed anything in the underground. Emaciated crackheads leaned against the crumbling plaster walls and sprawled on torn mattresses. The only talk was in whispers, which made Swann's voice sound loud.

"Ahem," Swann said. "Five-O!"

Those crackheads who were "beamed up" reacted with much the same look of vague annoyance Swann saw in the subway when a conductor announced that a train was being held between stations. Those who were preparing to smoke rushed to fire up their lighters. The man in the raincoat had been opening a vial, and in his hurry to load his pipe he dropped a crumb of crack. He fell on all fours and began frantically searching the rubble-strewn floor.

Another man's voice boomed beyond a closed door across the room. Swann entered with Coleman to see that the windows of this inner chamber were covered by blankets. The sole light here came from a candle whose flame flickered on the face of a middle-aged man sitting in a worn chintz armchair.

The man was sweating, and his eyes were slow in rising from three bodies entwined on the floor. These were the girls in their early teens who had come to Estrella's door, and they looked even younger without their clothes. They were also sweating, and the paint chips and plaster that covered the floor stuck to their skin.

"Hole it, bitch," the man said.

The man said this to a girl who had paused to smoke a rock. To "hole" apparently meant to exhale crack smoke into another girl's vagina, for that was what she was preparing to do when she saw Swann's shield.

The girl sat up, letting the crack smoke leak from between her lips, making no effort to cover herself. The one who was about to be *holed* tugged at the man's pant cuff.

"I still get my bottle?" the girl asked.

The man kicked the girl's hand away.

"Shut up."

"I did everything I was supposed to," the girl said.

"What you supposed to do is shut the fuck up."

Swann and Coleman moved together, grabbing the man from the chair and patting him down.

"You won't find no drugs," the man said. "I don't touch that shit."

Swann checked the man's eyes, which did indeed shine clear in the candlelight. Coleman reported that the man's pockets contained only legal tender, a pair of $20 bills to be exact. That was enough to buy four jumbo bottles and seemed to be the source of his power over the girls.

"That money's his," the third girl said. "He didn't do nothing."

"Endangering the welfare of a child," Swann said.

The girl gave a hollow laugh.

"Who be the child?" the girl asked.

"The three of you," Swann said.

"You sayin' *he* the reason we in danger?" the girl asked.

Swann and Coleman dragged the man toward the door.

"Why don't we let these young ladies get decent," Coleman said.

In the larger room, Swann and Coleman gave the man a hard shove toward the hallway.

"It's too bad those other people give beatings such a bad name," Coleman said.

Coleman was speaking of those such as Fredricks. She and Swann were still rousting the various crackheads when the three girls emerged from the back. They were dressed, and one ran her fingers through her hair and combed out some flecks of paint. She stepped over to the man in the raincoat, who was still searching on his hands and knees.

"Yo, this it?" the girl asked.

"Yes! Yes! Yes!" the man said.

He was reaching out when the girl flicked away the fleck of paint with her fingernail. The man should have become angry, but he simply dropped his head and went back to searching. The girl followed the other two out the door.

The only others who remained in the room were a young man who slept on a mattresses and a woman who was repeatedly slapping him in the face. The young man's head rolled under her blows, but he did not stir.

"You don't sleep for five days, you do get tired," the woman said.

She gave a last slap.

"There only one sure way to wake a crack fiend and that to pick him up by the back of his pant." "That I just can't do."

Swann hoisted the young man by his belt, and sure enough, he began to move his arms and legs like some sort of insect. He babbled to himself as Swann and Coleman drove him and the others past the stripe of light at the base of Estrella's door. The older man in the raincoat was sobbing harder for his little piece of cocaine and baking soda than Estrella had allowed herself to cry for the loss of her sister.

Outside, the young man interrupted his monologue to shout out "*Five-O*," which caused the figures in line at the stoop to scatter. The fifteen-year-old manager was at that moment carrying a green plastic trash bag toward a pink Mercedes-Benz sedan. The car squealed away from the curb and rocketed past Swann and Coleman, the words STRICTLY BUSINESS painted on a strip of chrome below the door, the driver hidden by the tinted windows.

The manager broke into a run with his trash bag, and there seemed to be nothing else for Swann and Coleman to do but chase him. Swann leaped in pursuit with the new fleetness imparted by his jogging regimen, feeling strong and sleek and swift right up to the moment Coleman raced ahead of him.

Even the manager was no match for Coleman, though he was able to keep running a good quarter block after she had jumped on his back. Swann reached them then, and they all ended up in a pile on the sidewalk. Swann once again saw Evil become a youngster's face pressed to the pavement.

The manager was still clutching the trash bag, and the plastic tore when Coleman pulled it away. Coleman stuck in a hand and a rustling sound came as she felt around.

"Shit," Coleman said. "It's only money."

She laughed.

"Cash for trash."

Swann conducted the search, reaching the manager's $150 sneakers without discovering drugs or a weapon or anything else that could justify an arrest. Swann got the answer he expected when he asked where the manager had gotten the money.

"I found it," the manager said.

Swann informed the manager that he could put in a claim for the money at District 1 of the transit police. The manager's voice turned contemptuous.

"You mean like the subway? I don't ride no train."

"Your money do," Coleman said.

* * *

At District 1, Coleman emptied the bag on the front desk. The officer on duty opened and closed his mouth without speaking, and then he gave a little nervous laugh.

Other cops came over, and a good dozen of them were giggling and making lame jokes as Swann and Coleman sorted the crumpled cash into denominations. None of the bills was higher than a twenty and most were singles. Swann began with these and Coleman grabbed some fives. They counted softly aloud.

Cops who had ignored Swann for weeks huddled around, staring intently at the mounting pile of bills, listening to the muttered count grow higher and higher. Money was money, and here was more of it than any of these cops had ever seen, more than they would ever have at one time, more than they could make in a year of collars, a big, amazing pile of money, close enough to reach out and grab, but not one ratty bill of it ever to cross their palms.

Swann had counted out exactly the price of a Brooks Brothers suit. He glanced over to where Coleman was continuing to count out fives. He thumped down another single and another and another.

When the last bill was counted, Swann filled out a Form 161 property voucher. The usual criminal to encounter the transit police had less than $10 on him when he was arrested, and often the crime involved not much more. The assembled officers now heard Swann speak aloud an all-time transit police record.

"*Fifty-six thousand, three hundred and twelve,*" Swann said.

The desk officer's giddy nervousness took on an anxious edge, as if all he now saw before him was neat stacks of potential trouble. He handed Coleman the rubber stamp and the ink pad.

"I want it out of here," the desk officer said.

Coleman did the stamping and Swann took care of the initialing, just as they had with the space case. They were interrupted by Sergeant Quinn, and then a lieutenant, and finally a captain, each of whom demanded a detailed report on how the money had been recovered. The captain went so far as to ask how he could be sure they turned in everything that had been in the bag.

"Why wouldn't we have just took it all?" Swann asked.

"Well, you didn't," the captain said.

"No, we sure didn't."

"That doesn't answer my question."

Coleman reached for the next bill and again proved she could be expressive with a rubber stamp. Swann affixed his initials and they kept on until all $56,312 was sealed into plastic evidence bags, each bill marked EVIDENCE, each bill initialed JS.

Swann watched Coleman go down the steps leading to a train that would take her home to Brooklyn. He was becoming as accustomed to the blue-tipped tail as he was to the voice that rose from the stairwell.

"Yo! Yo!" Coleman said.

Swann stood there in his baggy suit, sore with fatigue, his hands grimy from counting thousands, his fingers cramped from initialing big stacks of bills, his pockets holding nary the price of a club soda.

"Five-O," Swann said.

"*Homeowners receive instant cash!*"

The commercial had come on again, not a half hour after Swann returned home from counting $56,312 that had been dropped by a youngster.

"*The Money Store. Where America goes for money!*"

"*Easy terms!*"

"*Instant cash!*"

"*Now!*"

Swann left Ellen in front of the Hitachi and went to Jenny's bedside. He could see in the dimness that she was sleeping on her back, her own Cabbage Patch doll at her side.

In the bathroom, Swann scrubbed the money grime from his hands. He drew a glass of water for his boutonniere and hesitated. He sniffed the bud.

Oooh. Roses.

Swann awoke so restless that he had no trouble getting himself jogging. He pushed his thoughts beyond saving into the realm of borrowing and remembered all those people in the financial pages he had read at ECAB. They were leveraging themselves to power and prominence, covering one loan with a bigger loan, buying things by borrowing against what they did not yet own. Even the government was out there, borrowing, borrowing, borrowing.

Swann ran on, returning to his house feeling not at all like a tycoon and very much like a husband and a father and a transit cop who had to be at the medical examiner's office to identify a body.

A half dozen stainless steel gurneys were parked by the double doors, the pallets battered like old roasting pans. Puddles of foul-smelling body juices sat in the dents.

Swann entered with Coleman, and watched as a female clerk yanked open the stainless steel door of a refrigerated compartment. The clerk sighed on seeing the tray inside rattle out empty.

Swann and Coleman followed the clerk into the autopsy room and along a row of unclothed corpses. The man on the first steel table had been stabbed. The young girl on the second had been shot in the head. The middle-aged man on the third looked as if he had been both shot and stabbed and maybe strangled as well.

At the fourth table, the clerk stopped and checked the toe tag. Swann could see that the body was that of a woman who had been torn and mangled at the waist. He could not see the face, for the forehead had been peeled down over the eyes.

A man in surgical garb was setting down an electric saw, and Swann surmised that the burning smell came from the heat of the circular blade cutting bone. The man removed the crown of the skull and cut back a membrane and reached inside with both gloved hands. His voice came from behind a mask.

"I'll be with you in a minute," the man said.

Swann glanced at Coleman and saw she was gazing at the table with her usual steady determination. He looked back at the woman. A long incision ran from the wound up the center of her chest, branching at the collar bones. The breast plate had been cut out and the layers of skin and fat and muscle had been peeled back. The various organs had been removed and placed on a side table in Ziploc plastic bags. The heart was light red in color and about the size of a fist.

Swann considered that this procedure must have been precisely the same for Daryl Coombs and would have been no different for Jack

Swann had things gone the other way. He fixed his attention on the slender hand he had held as he told this woman that help was on the way. The fingers were flexed just as they had been when he had slipped his own hand free.

"Twelve hundred and five grams," the man said.

Swann looked up and saw that the brain now sat on a hanging scale. He noted the convolutions and the line between the two hemispheres. The tissue was gray with a delicate pink tinge.

The man put the brain in a plastic bag and replaced the crown of the skull. He then pulled the skin back up over the forehead. A final tug changed the face's expression from worry to something closer to peace.

"That's her," Coleman said.

Swann felt a hush within himself as he spoke.

"Yes," he said. "That's her."

At mealtime, Swann and Coleman rode from their post under the Plaza to Times Square. He once more matched her pace, seeming to stay one step ahead of himself as they passed the spot where the space case woman had been pinned. They continued up the steps where the posse had fled and they stopped at the soda fountain. The counterman no doubt remembered the events of the day before, but he kept himself to what was of immediate consequence.

"The same?" the counterman asked.

Swann sipped black coffee and watched Coleman start on her hot dog, her jaw working under skin that seemed no more peelable for his knowing that it was. She looked past him and her eyes fixed on something.

"You think anybody really watches those things?" Coleman asked.

Swann turned and saw that Coleman was looking at one of the fifty closed-circuit cameras that had been mounted in the station with great fanfare two years before. He answered with the authority of his greater experience.

"Of course not," Swann said.

He reminded himself that they were dealing with a homicide.

"But maybe we better check."

* * *

On their after-meal stroll, Swann and Coleman stopped at the double steel doors leading to one room the transit police still maintained under Times Square. He knew this was CCTV, but he had never been inside. He now entered to see a large room bisected with clear Plexiglas.

Swann stepped with Coleman past the partition to a bank of fifty television screens that made him think of Cousin Ozzie's, only these were black and white and much smaller. They seemingly showed every possible view of the station's mezzanines, passageways, platforms, and stairwells. The lone cop assigned to monitor them was at this moment engrossed in a crossword puzzle.

"How you doing, Officer?" Swann said.

The cop glanced up.

"I'm Officer Swann and this is Officer Coleman. You working the day tour yesterday?"

The cop's eyes were already back on the puzzle.

"Yeah, so?"

"Did you happen to notice anything going on?"

"Nope."

Swann scanned the bank of video screens, stopping at the fourth one down on the second row from the right. It gave a perfect view of not only the soda fountain but the top of the stairs from which the posse had appeared.

"Does this record?"

"Nope. Five letters for 'whirlpool.'"

"Look!" Swann said. "She's got no clothes on."

Coleman was right with him.

"Holy God, you're right!" Coleman said.

The cop forgot the puzzle and his eyes searched the fifty monitors. "Where?"

"Ooop," Swann said. "She's gone."

Swann turned back with Coleman to the vacant area at the front, which seemed to have no official function. Swann only then noticed three wooden benches and a couple of battered lockers stacked against the far wall. These had been in the Room before it was sealed.

At the end of the tour, Swann once more parted with Coleman and crossed Central Park South at his own pace. He passed the Oak Bar, his suit feeling that much baggier, his pockets seeming all the more empty as he continued toward the train home.

The evening rush was beginning, and a glum multitude was converging on the subway entrance. Swann's watch told him that this was about the time Danica would be getting off work and he glanced about on his way down to the platform. He felt anew just how much he would rather encounter her while wearing an elegant, well-fitting suit.

On the ride to Queens, Swann's thoughts went from Danica to Brooks Brothers to the row of steel tables.

Money Samuel
Money Sergio
Money Steven
Money Store

Swann stood in the kitchen, his finger on the number, the sweat from his run dripping onto the open phone book. Ellen and Jenny had gone to a triple coupon sale, and the only voice Swann heard was that of his upbringing, *Neither a borrower nor a lender be.*

The voice did not stay Swann's finger from moving to the telephone keypad. He forgot the number halfway through, and he paused. He became aware that his brow was scrunched. He smoothed his face as if giving it a little tug.

Swann dialed again. He still might have hung up had the phone rung more than once. The woman who came on the line had an overly friendly tone as she explained that he could indeed secure a loan in twenty-four hours, just like on television.

"How much are you interested in?" the woman asked.

Swann had not thought this far, and he held the receiver away from his mouth, trying to formulate a number. The woman's voice was faint and far away.

"Sir?" the woman asked. "Are you there? Sir?"

Swann brought the receiver back to his lips.

"Yes, I'm here," Swann said.

"And?" the woman asked.

Swann was not entirely sure why the particular figure popped from his mouth. It might have been just a coincidence that the outer limit of his daring was also the very sum that the government of the United States had borrowed in the name of him and every other citizen.

"Ten thousand?" Swann asked.

"Fine," the woman said.

Swann said the assessor would have to appear within the hour. His watch showed that the knock at the door came in twenty-five minutes.

"Couple years ago, I would have bet this area was gonna go," the assessor said. "It didn't just stay, it's on the way up."

The assessor wore a checked sports coat that was kin to Swann's polyester suit. Swann presented him with the papers proving ownership of the house.

"Fifteen percent is the number," the appraiser said.

Swann thought for a moment that the appraiser was speaking of the interest rate.

"You get any more minorities than that, everybody starts moving out," the assessor said. "Only it seems like there aren't so many places to go."

The assessor departed ten minutes after he arrived, which gave Swann a half hour to ponder the matter. He was resolved to broach the subject of the loan with Ellen once she and Jenny returned. His nerve faltered when she held up a cash register tape that was nearly as long as she was tall.

"And that's with club soda," Ellen said.

Swann examined the numbers on the tape and saw that Ellen had paid $19.06 for $132.43 in groceries.

"You should thank God you're married to a redeemer," Ellen said.

Ellen was affixing this latest tape to the refrigerator door when the telephone rang. Swann had a fearful inkling who might be calling, but she would be sure he was up to no good if he broke with transit custom. He as always waited for Ellen to answer.

"He just stepped out," Ellen said.

Swann held his breath.

"I have no idea."

Swann watched Ellen's knuckles whiten on the receiver.

"Don't worry. I'll tell him the minute I see him."

Swann saw no need for Jenny to hear what followed.

"Who wants to play hide-and-seek?" Swann asked.

Jenny scampered off to hide. Swann turned to Ellen and kept to the old cave cop precept: use the truth as home base.

"I was just curious," Swann said. "It's not really different from saving. Only instead of putting away a little bit each month and having a bunch of money, you start with a bunch of money and then pay a little bit each month."

"Bullshit, Jack," Ellen said.

Swann and Ellen looked at each other across a distance they had already measured.

"I know, there's something wrong with me," Swann said.

Swann called down the hall.

"Ready or not, here I come."

Swann made a loud show of searching for Jenny and then started for her room and the curtain behind which she always hid. He had just reached her doorway when he heard her giggle.

Swann was off that day and the next, and he had every intention of calling the Money Store to say he did not want a loan after all. He still had not done so by the second morning, when he heard the phone ring. Ellen made no move to play the transit spouse.

"It's probably your friends," Ellen said.

The phone kept ringing and Ellen remained standing at the sink. Her eyes fixed on Swann as he picked up the receiver.

"Hello?" Swann said.

"Hi, it's Mary at the Money Store."

"Hello?"

"Mr. Swann?"

"Hello?"

"Can you hear me?"

"*Hello?*"

"I'll call back."

Swann hung up.

"There was nobody there," Swann said.

The phone rang again and Swann grabbed the receiver.

"Hello?"

"Mr. Swann?"
"Hello?"

Swann hung up, and in minutes he was dashing along the park on his morning run, a quarter in the pocket of his shorts. He set a personal best on his way to the nearest pay phone.

"Yes? Yes, hello, this is Jack Swann, I . . ."

"Hi! I just tried to call you. Your loan has been approved for the full amount, and you can pick up the check at your convenience."

"You know, I really . . ."

"Just ask for Ben."

Swann knew he should say that it had all been a mistake, that he did not want to take out the loan after all. He did the best he could.

"I might not be able to get there for a few days."

"That's fine. It's waiting for you."

The woman got off. Swann promised himself he would telephone her back to cancel the loan. He had yet to make the call ten days later, at which time Ellen placed the latest gas bill beside his coffee.

"You don't got to make a face," Ellen said. "You do get your check today, don't you?"

Swann gave a start before he realized that Ellen was not speaking of the check with which he had been preoccupied for most of two weeks.

"Yes, I get my check," Swann said.

Swann went into the bedroom to finish dressing. He stuck his revolver into his waistband and realized that an entire pay period had passed without his midriff shrinking anything close to a full notch. He started back down the hall wondering if he had been slacking somehow, but he reassured himself that he had kept to his regimen.

"You've hit your number!" Sullivan said.

Swann glanced down at his paycheck, figuring that Sullivan meant he had received some overtime. He saw only his base pay, the number for every cave cop of his rank.

"No, no," Sullivan said. "Your *number.* What you're supposed to weigh."

Sullivan's eye in this regard was keen. Even the outsized suit had not kept him from noting that Swann's weight loss had all but stopped.

"Now comes the hard part!" Sullivan said. "I mean, it's one thing to take it off. Keeping it off is something else."

Swann decided that Sullivan was right, that he had stopped shedding pounds because he had reached his true girth. He had slimmed himself down to the Jack Swann who had always lain beneath all that hunger turned to bulk.

"I don't think that'll be a problem," Swann said.

Swann came away from the cash machine with his usual $50 lost in his voluminous pocket, the check at the Money Store seeming much more in keeping with his *number.* He reached the next corner reasoning that he got paid twice a month, which meant he could easily squeeze out $100 for himself, which was not all that much less than the $158 monthly payment on a $10,000 loan from the Money Store. He figured that he was almost certain to make up the difference with overtime from the occasional legitimate collar.

Swann did not know anyone who would even think of doing this, but he also could not name any other civil servant who had ventured into the Oak Bar. He rounded out his reasoning by figuring that the loan would be for less than a hundredth of what he would have been worth had he been killed that night with Daryl Coombs.

Swann stepped off a bus in Queens to see a storefront nondescript in every way save for a sign that said MONEY STORE. He entered and stood sweating in his baggy polyester, his diminished stomach in a knot. He was suddenly not so sure he had discovered the transit cop's formula for leverage. He almost hoped he would be told that he had hesitated too long, that the check had been voided.

"I was supposed to ask for Ben," Swann said.

A man approached in a polyester suit that lacked even a fake buttonhole. He flashed a detective-sized smile.

"Mr. Swann?"

Ben produced a loan agreement and a ballpoint pen. Swann had only to sign his name and Ben presented him with a check for $10,000 drawn on some obscure bank in New Jersey.

"Thank you," Swann said.
"No," Ben said. "Thank *you.*"

The envelope containing the check disappeared into the slot, deposited in that one place Ellen would never think of looking, Swann's savings account. He then had the novel experience of stepping away from a cash machine with a grin. He smiled again as he passed the Oak Bar on the way home, and he found sitting in front of the Hitachi to be nearly tolerable.

Swann's morning jog saw him bounding along with such pep that he extended his usual route a mile to include a branch of his bank. He took a moment to call up the balance of his savings account.

"*$00.00.*"

Later, Swann stopped at the bank branch by District 1 and the next morning he again jogged to the one nearest his home. The days ahead saw him stop at a cash machine every few hours.

"*$00.00.*"
"*$00.00.*"
"*$00.00.*"
"*$10,000.00.*"

The awaited moment came at the branch near District 1 just after Swann had completed an evening tour. He thereupon faced a whole new concept of withdrawal.

All Swann's previous transactions had been determined by how much he could squeeze out and still keep the lights on, the phone connected, and the stove working. He now had simply to determine what sum might feel good in his pocket.

Swann decided that a thousand was a nice number, but discovered that the cash machine would dispense only half that amount in a single day. This was not even enough to buy the suit, and he decided he would return when the bank was open. He was sure that the cash machine limit was the only factor he had not taken into consideration. He arrived home convinced that he was in as much control as any of those financial page tycoons who bought companies with money they did not have.

Swann joined Ellen before the Hitachi and noted that the anchor of the late news was wearing a dark gray suit whose lapels were a touch wider than he himself would favor. A late-night cop show then came on, and a pair of actors enjoyed the sort of adventures he had imagined as a rookie but which were no match for what he was sure awaited him in the days ahead.

Ellen took Jenny on another shopping foray, so Swann had no questions to duck when he left early for work. He went first to the bank, arriving at a teller's window with a withdrawal slip and his police identification.

"How would you like it?" the teller asked.

"How about hundreds?" Swann asked.

The teller counted out ten bills and Swann decided that $1,000 was not such an outlandish sum after all.

"You know, maybe I could do with a little more," Swann said.

A squiggle on another withdrawal slip and the total became $5,000. The teller flashed him a look suggesting that a cop had no business taking out that much money, and this only served to convince him that he had asked for exactly the right amount.

Swann then left the bank with a pocket print that would have been impressive in any trousers less billowy than his own. He felt beyond flush, beyond any simple measure of wealth. John J. Swann had his hand on the lever.

The salesman's tape at Brooks Brothers showed that Swann had dropped two sizes since his previous visit. He went into the changing room with the same pinstripe suit in a forty-four, the small white price tag now just something he would later have to snip off.

Swann stepped before the three-panel mirror, slowly pivoting one way and the other, breathing in and setting back his shoulders. He had the sense he was seeing himself as he should be, as he had seen himself everywhere but in a mirror.

"I'll take it," Swann said.

The house tailor chalked a few adjustments at the sleeves and cuffs, the length of his arms and legs being dimensions of himself that Swann was powerless to alter.

"Two weeks from Tuesday," the tailor said.

Swann held out a $100 bill, thereby giving the normal course of things just a little nudge of the lever.

"What time tomorrow do you need it?" the tailor asked.

Swann found that even a suit such as his old one was greatly improved by having a bankroll in the pocket when the time comes to pay for something. He experienced not a flutter of anxiety when the sales tax alone proved to be more than he usually allotted himself in a pay period.

The salesman asked if Swann wanted the new suit delivered to his office.

"Transit Police District 1, Columbus Circle," Swann said.

"I see," the salesman said. "The number on Columbus Circle?"

"There isn't one."

"I'm sorry, sir, but I think every building has a street number."

"It isn't a building."

"Your office is not in a building?"

"It's in the subway."

"I see."

"Tell the guy to ask the clerk in one of the change booths. They'll know."

Coleman had not been impressed by a whole garbage bag of cash, and Swann was unsure that she would see the reasonableness of his plan. The money remained a secret lump that made no print in a pocket that could have hidden twice that sum.

After work, Swann went by the Oak Bar with enough in his pocket for maybe five hundred soda waters, plus tip. He decided he could wait one more day and went directly home solely because that was what he had decided to do. All went as usual until bedtime, when he stashed the bankroll in the toes of his shoes.

As he entered District 1 the next afternoon, Swann was most likely the only transit cop ever to report for duty with the expectation of something wonderful. Sure enough, there they were by the front desk, a stack of navy blue boxes, each bound with plastic ribbon of the same color as crime scene tape.

"You had a delivery, Mr. Swann," the desk officer said.

Swann took up the boxes.

"I guess Christmas came early this year," the desk officer said.

Swann understood what the desk officer was suggesting.

"With all due respect to your rank, sir, how dare you?" Swann asked.

The desk officer's impassive expression reminded Swann that this protestation was exactly what would have come from a transit cop who actually had dipped into the money from Estrella's block. Swann had an urge to say more, but he was unable to think of anything that would not be taken the same way. He called over his shoulder as he started for the locker room with his armload of boxes.

"Ho, ho, ho."

Swann opened the biggest box like a present to his true self, carefully slipping off the yellow tape, lifting the lid, and parting the white tissue paper. The pinstriped wool looked and felt no less wonderful in the locker room than in Brooks Brothers. He hardly noticed that Mannering and three other cops were making a point of not noticing him.

"So, this nurse goes, 'Do you love me?'" Mannering was saying. "What am I gonna tell her? 'Honey, love is a hard-on.'"

Swann left the suit in the box and turned his attention to those containing some items he had selected on the way out of the store. He opened the one containing the shirts and chose the white oxford cloth.

"She don't like that and says, 'Take your hard-on and get the fuck outta here,'" Mannering said. "Which I do after I take a shower. I got enough trouble without bringing home any more musk."

Swann began removing the pins from the shirt.

"I get home and I get in bed, and what do you think the wife says? 'You smell too clean. You musta taken a shower before you left your girlfriend.'"

Swann had already stripped off his clothes. They lay in a heap as he buttoned his new shirt just as if it were any other.

"So I get all pissed off and tell her, 'Fuck this, I had a long day and I'm going to sleep.' Then you know what she does? She hucks and says, 'I'm gonna spit straight up.' I say, 'What? What're you, crazy?'"

Swann was now ready for the suit.

"She just hucks again. I throw the sheet up over my head. You know what she does? She fucking farts and says, 'Now, get the fuck out of my bed.'"

Mannering roared, as he probably expected the others to do, as they probably would have if they had not been distracted by the sight of Swann standing in what had to be the very nicest suit ever worn in a transit police facility, lawyers included. He looped in his new black leather belt and cinched the silver buckle to the notch where he intended to remain no matter what.

Swann felt a final, private confirmation as he affixed a fresh rose to a real buttonhole. He then headed for roll call in his new suit, along with a pink foulard bow tie, tassel loafers, and a pearl gray homburg hat.

Sergeant Quinn could do nothing more than join the other cops in gawking. The only words came from Coleman.

"You *do* have more than one suit," Coleman said.

Coleman was herself wearing overalls with a leopard print of a much hotter pink than Swann's bow tie, and she said nothing more of his attire as they embarked. They boarded a downtown local and he remained as excited as when he had first been in uniform. The train lurched into the tunnel, and the glass of the doors presented him with a reflection that he would not have willed any different.

"*Oh, baby. Yes!*"

At Times Square, the doors parted for nobody in particular, but Swann stepped off as somebody very particular indeed. He still had this sense when meal period sent him with Coleman to the soda fountain.

Swann sipped coffee and felt no less distinctive for the hundreds of citizens who hurried by without giving him a glance. The first people to take as much note of him as he took of himself were in a passing posse, all of whose members seemed to find that the most striking element of his new tailored look was the pocket print.

For once, the underground offered a real vic, or at least so it appeared until the posse proceeded to check Swann's eyes. They then encountered a look that perhaps no poppy love had ever shown when suddenly surrounded by young black faces, the look of a man absolutely resolute not to muss his suit.

"I think you scared those poor children," Coleman said.

Swann set his coffee on the counter and joined Coleman in trailing the posse. He stood at the top of the subway steps again, toeing the border of his official domain, though his toes were in much nicer shoes than before.

"Now they going to vic somebody *really* weak," Coleman said.

Swann wondered if Coleman was suggesting that he should have allowed the posse to try robbing him. He went with her back down the steps for the mealtime stroll and his new outfit did nothing to help him keep up with her pace. His right foot began to chafe in his new shoe, and he for once gladly returned to standing under the Plaza.

Coleman did not further acknowledge any change in Swann until they were parting.

"You know, that tie is all right," Coleman said.

The right shoe chafed all along Central Park South, but otherwise Swann felt only perfect as he reached the Plaza. He strode into the Oak Bar with the feeling of keeping a rendezvous, and indeed the figure he sought came in with him, as elegant as anyone else there.

Swann ordered his usual miraculous club soda and could almost have believed that there had been some terrible mix-up at his birth, that he had been placed in a civil service bassinet by mistake, that somewhere a prominent family had found itself with a loutish cave cop. He was feeling every bit as grand as he looked when the bartender asked if he wanted another.

"Yes," Swann said. "Please."

Swann glanced at his watch and the thought came that it was about the time Danica would be getting off work. He finished his second club soda more quickly than the first.

Swann soon after descended into the subway, but he spotted no honey-colored hair among the throngs. He rode homeward making do with the company of his own image.

"What the eff is that?"

Ellen's first question was easy enough.

"A suit," Swann said.

"How much?" Ellen asked.

Swann considered a Mannering-style offense, but Ellen's look of absolute fury caused him to reconsider.

"Tell me you didn't blow your whole check," Ellen said.

Swann here felt but one giant step from home base.

"No, I didn't blow the whole check," Swann said.

"Just the part for the mortgage and the food," Ellen said.

Swann said nothing for fear of prompting her to ask for an actual accounting.

"And I'm sure you didn't pay the gas bill," Ellen said.

Swann still said nothing.

"You're just gonna have to take everything back to the store," Ellen said.

Swann looked at Ellen looking at him.

"Mommy."

Jenny was calling Ellen's attention back to the pumpkin they were preparing to carve. Swann watched them scoop out goopy handfuls of seeds and he stood amazed that Halloween was just a day away. He had hardly registered the passage of summer and here it was the end of October.

"Make the eyes first," Jenny said.

Ellen reached for a knife. Swann took his temporal bearings. A full year since last Halloween. Jenny had been a cat. A black leotard. A headband on which ears had been sewn. Whiskers drawn on the cheeks.

"Jenny, what are you going to be this year?" Swann asked.

"I can't tell you," Jenny said. "It's a surprise. Only me and Mommy know."

Ellen finished the eyes and the nose.

"Now the mouth," Jenny said.

Ellen began carving a smile. Swann's reckoning jumped ahead nine months to the shooting. That had been in July. Then had come August, September, and October.

"Daddy, you can be the same thing as last year," Jenny said. You don't even need a costume."

He thought back to the Jack Swann of last Halloween, the Jack Swan before all the changes of these past four months.

"What's that?" Swann asked.

"A policeman!" Jenny said.

The smile done, Ellen looked up.

"Yes," Ellen said. "That's exactly what Daddy is."

* * *

The woman who answered the door at the first house smiled on seeing Jenny in her white tutu, rhinestone tiara, floppy white rabbit ears, and magic wand. The woman then looked at Swann's bow tie and homburg.

"That's my daddy," Jenny said.

Swann continued as Jenny's daddy down a sidewalk crowded with knee-high bumblebees and devils and butterflies and robots and witches and pumpkins and clowns and bears and superheroes. A three-foot skeleton came out of the darkness holding hands with a slightly larger carrot. They were followed by a tiny fortune teller and a tiger pudgy enough to have been a young Swann.

"Trick or treat?" "Trick or treat?" "Trick or treat?"

Then Swann saw a miniature pirate approaching with the unmistakable figure of Danica Cowan Neary. She had on a black cotton sweater and tight jeans and she looked only like herself.

"Hiya," Danica said.

Swann stood before her with his cuffs breaking on his gleaming loafers, his belt drawn to that perfect girth, his bow tie a sporty dash of color, his hat set just so, his boutonniere a fresh bud. Her eyes again held an unmistakable gleam of interest.

"Are you supposed to be somebody?" Danica asked.

"A transit cop," Swann said.

Danica laughed just as she had on seeing the Cabbage Patch doll. William stepped forward, brandishing a wooden sword tipped with red paint. Jenny held up her wand, a stick tipped with a tinfoil star.

"Magic don't work on pirates," William said.

"*Doesn't* work," Danica said.

Jenny and William went together up the stoop. Swann stood on the sidewalk with Danica. One thing even his fantasies had not prepared him for was conversing.

"I see you're wearing a rose again," Danica said.

"Yes," Swann said.

Jenny and William came bounding down the steps and turned their separate ways.

"Bye," Danica said.

"See you later," Swann said.

Danica went off with her pirate, and Swann ambled along with his bunny fairy princess ballerina.

At home, Jenny put down her tiara and wand, and Ellen checked the sweets for razor blades and straight pins. Ellen then rationed out three pieces of candy, and Jenny was totally content until she finished them.

"One more?" Jenny asked.

"No," Ellen said.

"But Mommy, I *want* it."

"No."

Jenny looked at Swann.

"You heard Mommy," Swann said.

At District 1, Marie called out her standard greeting and howled when Swann clapped his homburg over his fly. A good number of his fellow officers continued to have trouble ignoring him, their looks passing from surprised to edgy. Cops who would not have hesitated to battle an armed robber seemed to feel seriously threatened by a bow tie and a hat. The exception was Coleman, who had on aqua sneakers and a white leather jacket.

"I still like that tie," Coleman said.

After the meal-time stroll, Swann descended with Coleman to the end of the uptown platform. A train was about to depart, and they boarded the last car just before the doors shut.

Coleman kept with transit cop convention and remained standing, her feet spread for balance and both hands free. Swann's own feet were still breaking in his new shoes, and he was unable to resist a vacant seat on the other side of the car.

As the train rolled out of the station, the door at the front of the last car was the sole portal through which anyone could enter. That included the police and thus the last car was the party car.

Or so Swann and his fellow cave cops believed. The party always seemed to end at the approach of anyone cop-like and Swann would enter with the feeling that the mirth had ceased an instant before he stepped inside. The teenage faces of those who rode back here would be not so much blank as fixed. Nobody would acknowledge him, yet everyone would seem acutely aware of his presence and the whole car would seem only to be waiting for him to leave. He would feel less a cop than an intruder, a spoiler of fun that would resume the instant he was gone.

The difference now was that the homburg and the bow tie appeared to leave these young riders uncertain Swann could be a plainclothes anything. He felt a dozen pairs of eyes studying him to see if he could possibly be what he in fact was. He had an irresistible desire to know exactly what his presence had always caused to vanish.

Swann bowed his head and closed his eyes and that seemed to be enough to convince them he was no threat. A young man cried out.

"Party over here!"

A whole chorus of young women replied.

"Pa-r-r-rty!"

Swann heard a pure, high voice begin singing wordless notes. Hands clapped and feet stomped in a single, driving beat. He smelled marijuana and cigarettes and he heard the hiss of a beer can opening.

Swann felt a jolt and heard the screech of brakes come through the fun. The beat stopped and the doors rattled open for the Fiftieth Street station, and he knew without glancing up that the teenagers had palmed their joints and cigarettes, ready to make them disappear at the first sign of a cop. He kept his head bowed and his eyes shut. He listened to the doors close.

The train entered the tunnel and the beat resumed and a group of young women chanted rhymes toward the other end of the car. From somewhere closer came a deep, breathy voice.

"Yo! There a vic."

Swann felt his heart thud hard and fast. His eyelids twitched and he knew that all he had to do was open them and raise his head. Things would almost surely end there.

Swann had no face before him to remind him of Daryl Coombs. He had only this voice gone excited at the sight of somebody asleep and defenseless, somebody *really* weak.

"I don't see no jakes," the deep voice said.

The voice was even closer now, in front and above Swann. His head stayed down and his eyes remained closed. He breathed as evenly as possible, and he did his best to keep his neck relaxed and his arms limp. He grew more and more intensely alert as he did all he could to look as though he were asleep.

"What if *he* a jake?" a second, squeaky voice asked.

"Look like that?" the deep voice asked. "If he a D, where his partner?"

Swann felt the jolt of the train braking for the Columbus Circle station. He experienced a jolt of his own as a hand landed on his shoulder. He fought to remain limp as a tingling spread down through his chest and out his limbs.

"Yo!" Coleman said. "Mister! Wake up!"

Swann raised his head and opened his eyes to see Coleman's face inches from his own. Her gaze met his in what he understood as a question. He dropped his head as if falling back into a drunken sleep.

"Well, the man can't say I didn't try," Coleman said.

"If he wake, we'll fuck him up," the deep voice said.

A jerk of the train caused the homburg to fall from Swann's head. The girls at the other end of the car exploded into laughter.

"You sure he ain't no D?" the squeaky voice asked.

Swann let saliva seep between his lips and dribble onto the floor. The whole car seemed to laugh.

"That ain't no D," the deep voice said.

The deep voice came from Swann's left, no longer above, but even with him and all business. The beat ceased and the girl's voices lowered and Swann knew what must be coming.

Swann was still surprised by the feel of a hand easing into his left pocket. The fingers were long and thick and they jumped on feeling the cash that had been making the irresistible print. They came away with the bankroll and the ensuing whoop was one of pure joy.

"A *stack,*" the deep voice said.

Swann opened his eyes. The roll of $100 bills was in the hand of a young man who wore a red hooded sweatshirt and was even bigger than his voice and fingers suggested. His expression went from ecstatic to shocked as Swann leaped from the bench.

"Five-O!" Swann said.

* * *

The young man would surely have been fast anyway, but the clutch of that much money made him Olympic. The chase ended only when he reached the front of the train. He whirled back to face a winded Swann.

"Look at this suit!" Swann said.

The young man looked.

"I am wearing a seven-hundred-dollar suit," Swann said. "If you fight and make me wrinkle it, I am going to kill you. Now, place your hands behind your back."

The young man did not resist until Swann tried to pry the bills from his manacled hand.

"Let go," Swann said.

Swann lifted the handcuffs, raising the young man's wrists six inches from his back.

"I said, 'Let go,'" Swann said.

Swann lifted the handcuffs another couple of inches and the fingers opened, though the first shriek did not come until Swann took the money. The bills were damp with sweat as they went back into his pocket.

At the next stop, Swan led the young man off the train. Coleman came out of the last car with a short, thin teenager, no doubt the owner of the squeaky voice. Swann's deep-voiced prisoner spoke.

"It look like an ordinary female."

Coleman came closer, holding up the homburg to let him know she had retrieved it.

"Very ordinary," Swann's prisoner said.

Coleman was only a few feet away now, and Swann could see the brightness in her eyes, the sparkle that again showed she shared his excitement in this work. She held out his homburg.

"As they say about a fool and his money . . . ," Coleman said.

Swann hoped that she was referring to his prisoner and not to him. She said nothing more, asking no questions as to how he had come to be carrying such a stack.

He carefully reblocked the crown of his hat and placed it atop his head.

"Am I going to jail?" Coleman's prisoner asked.

"No," Coleman said. "We're joking."

* * *

At District 1, the desk officer asked what happened to the complainant.

"He's right here," Swann said.

The desk officer looked on either side of Swann.

"Where here?"

"Here."

"You?"

"Lieu, what am I supposed to do, let them rob me and walk away?"

The desk officer asked what had been taken, and Swann held up his bankroll.

The desk officer did not speak until Swann moved to return the bills to his pocket.

"Voucher it."

The rules did indeed call for the money in question to be vouchered, but usually a person who recovered his own property was allowed to keep it.

"Lieu, it's mine," Swann said.

The desk officer clearly did not consider this a usual situation.

"I said voucher it," the desk officer said.

Coleman got out the stamp pad and began passing Swann $100 bills marked EVIDENCE.

"I ain't even gonna ask," Coleman said. "That way, when they ask *me,* I can say I don't know."

Swann felt he should tell her anyway, but for it to make any sense he would have to disclose so much more. He initialed one of his own bills and reached for another.

Coleman took the plastic evidence bag over to the desk officer, who gave the first official reaction to the sum Swann had been carrying in his pocket.

"You got to be kidding," the desk officer said.

The desk officer showed the paper to Sergeant Quinn, who was taking it into the captain when Swann and Coleman escorted the two prisoners from the district.

"That was thousands, right?" the one with the deep voice asked.

"Right," Swann said.

"And you a cop, right?"

"Right."

"It ain't right."

Up on the street, a uniformed city cop stood ready to lock the prisoners in the back of a paddy wagon. The one with the deep voice turned to Swann and shrugged.

"At least it was there for me," the prisoner said.

Coleman was taking the collar, and she started around to ride in the front.

"Good night, Officer Coleman," Swann said.

Coleman paused and looked at Swann.

"Good night, Officer Swann," Coleman said.

Coleman rode off to court and Swann crossed the street. The bank was closed, so he had to make do with the $500 maximum he could withdraw from a machine. He found the Oak Bar was just the place to go after being robbed.

The spell was momentarily broken when four young executive types about Swann's age arrived at the bar for a quick drink. They talked loudly of business, using such phrases as *cut his heart out* and *take no prisoners* and *send him home in a box* and *kick ass*. They seemed no more individual or interesting than the cave cops at Joey Farrell's Bar, and he further observed that they did not tip as well. They together left a single dollar for the bartender, or half what he himself put down after he had lingered over one club soda.

The television was off when Swann arrived home. He unknotted his bow tie as he listened to the sound of running water come from behind the closed bathroom door.

He went to check on the sleeping Jenny and then stopped into his own bedroom to take off a suit he was in no hurry to explain. He again stashed his bankroll in his shoes.

The water sounds had stopped, and Swann opened the door to see Ellen lying in the tub, completely submerged save for her knees and the oval of her face. Her eyes were closed, but he knew from the arch of her neck that she was awake.

Swann stood there in only his holey Jockey shorts, testing whether she would sense his presence, whether their bond held any magic. She finally did open her eyes, but only to gaze up at the ceiling. She gave no sign of seeing him.

Swann kept motionless, watching Ellen stare up from her watery silence. Her eyes flickered and caught a flash of something at the edge of her vision.

Ellen's eyes darted over toward him and her mouth popped open. Her expression relaxed, going from relief to nothing at all.

"You scared me," Ellen said. "I thought somebody was there."

Ellen again closed her eyes and eased her head back. Swann remained where he was, at the end of a day that had been vivid from the feel of the tropical wool going up his legs to the trembling of the thief's hand going into his pocket to the tang of the club soda flooding his mouth. He waited for some feeling to come with the sight of this naked woman who was his wife and the mother of his child.

Swann felt the warmth of the bath as he eased in one foot and then the other. The displacement caused the water to close over Ellen's face.

"Jackie!" Ellen said. "What are you doing?"

Water was sloshing onto the floor when the telephone rang. He closed his eyes and dipped his head below the surface, blocking out all but their coupling until he finally had to come up for air. The telephone was still ringing.

"Maybe it's something important," Ellen said.

Wet, nude, and half erect, Swann stood in the kitchen with a puddle forming at his feet and a familiar voice coming over the line.

"It's me."

Coleman then asked if she had awakened Swann.

"I was just in the bath," Swann said.

"The DA told me to call you. They want you down here eleven o'clock tomorrow morning, sharp."

The sound of the tub draining met Swann as he returned to the bathroom. He saw Ellen crouched naked on the floor, mopping up the spilled water with a towel.

"The DA wants me down in the morning," Swann said.

"Not still about that shooting," Ellen said. "I thought that was all done with."

Ellen rose.

"You sure you're telling me everything?" Ellen asked. "There's not something I don't know about?"

Swann took the towel and wrung it over the tub.

"It's just some guy tried to rob me on the train, and the DA wants to talk to me about it."

"What? Are you okay?"

"Fine. I'm fine."

Swann hung up the towel and followed Ellen's wet footprints down the hall. He was in bed when he felt some bathwater caught in his ear. He turned his head into the pillow and felt the bubble pop and trickle out.

Swann arrived at the eighth floor of the Manhattan district attorney's office at precisely the appointed hour, a fresh rose in his buttonhole.

"ADA Salinger, please," Swann said.

The secretary looked up and the sight of a man in a suit caused her to close her newspaper and straighten in her seat. Her voice and manner were solicitous.

"And you're mister . . . ?"

"Officer," Swann said. "Officer Swann."

The secretary relaxed and spoke in a superior tone.

"You'll have to wait."

"I have an eleven o'clock appointment," Swann said.

"Mr. Salinger is in court," the secretary said.

The secretary went back to her newspaper, and Swann walked over to a row of plastic chairs where a number of other cops were waiting to see prosecutors. A cop in a rumpled uniform stood up.

"You ADA MacPherson?" the cop asked.

"Sorry," Swann said.

"You know when he's coming out? This is the second day he's had me sittin' here."

"I'm here to see ADA Salinger."

"You're just a cop?"

* * *

Two hours later, Swann and his fellow cops were still sitting there. He went back to the secretary and she informed him he would now have to wait until at least 1 P.M.

"Mr. Salinger is at lunch," the secretary said.

At about 1:30 P.M., the secretary called out Swann's name and sent him down a narrow hallway to a small office. A man several years younger than Swann was sitting behind a desk wearing a dark blue suit and a red tie. The man held out his hand and asked for Swann's given name.

"Officer Swann," Swann said.

Salinger's eyes scrutinized Swann's suit, his homburg, his bow tie, his boutonniere.

"Mister Salinger, you had me sitting out there on my day off for two and a half hours," Swann said.

Salinger smiled.

"Since when do you guys object to a little overtime?"

"I don't earn my money sitting in a hallway until some junior DA decides to see me."

"How do you earn your money?"

"Excuse me?"

"I want to speak to you about how you came to have such a large sum of money at the time of the robbery."

Salinger opened a manila folder.

"Three thousand, three hundred and four dollars," Salinger said.

Salinger's tone suggested that the magnitude of the number was in itself evidence. Swann could not help feeling that to explain himself was to admit that a transit cop had no business carrying that kind of money.

"I withdrew it from my savings account," Swann said.

"Do you make a habit of carrying such sums?" Salinger asked.

Salinger was clearly used to intimidating cops, but Swann was one cave cop who could not be cowed by a suit. He had learned that all a suit meant was that the person wearing it had gone into a store and bought one. He felt a surge of anger that he was being called to account by somebody who surely had never gone home with muzzle flash burn on his cheek and a teenager's blood on his chest.

"Mr. Salinger, that's my money and I would appreciate it if you would give me a release form so I can get it back," Swann said.

Salinger was trapped by procedures aimed at minimizing the very thing he seemed to suspect Swann of doing. A district attorney had every right to hold on to stolen property until it was no longer needed as evidence, but money was different because the victim never received the actual bills. Those stayed in the property clerk's office, not just stamped, but punched with holes, that being an added precaution against their ending up anywhere other than the Treasury Department furnace, once the case was through the courts.

The victim, meanwhile, received a check for the recovered amount. Salinger had no legal recourse but to sign a form authorizing payment to John J. Swann for the exact amount about which he was being questioned.

For the first time in his career, Swann left the courthouse with a bounce in his step. He went directly to the basement of police headquarters and presented the release form at the property clerk's office. The cop took due note of the amount.

"Seems like things are going pretty good in the subway," the cop said.

"You wouldn't believe it," Swann said.

Swann got to a bank just before closing and presented a check signed by the comptroller of the City of New York. He had money orders drawn up for both the gas company and the Money Store, and he felt almost like a financier as he used borrowed money to meet the first payment on his loan.

Swann also submitted a withdrawal slip. His adventure seemed to be assuming a will of its own, perpetually urging him to take one step further, now telling him there was no sense having his money sit in a bank when it could be in his pocket.

The teller's expression only served to confirm that Swann was right to withdraw the full amount in his savings account, and the prospect that somebody might again try to rob him simply added to the excitement. He arrived at the Oak Bar with $8,000 making a tycoon-size print in his trousers. He had just one club soda only because he chose not to have another.

Swann then sauntered crosstown to the subway, checking his watch to confirm that he had plenty of time before Danica was likely to get off work. He went up the block to the corner where he had once seen her vanish from view.

When the honey-colored hair appeared in the rush-hour crowd, Swann dashed back down the block. He then returned at a leisurely pace, once again his cuffs breaking on his gleaming loafers, his belt drawn to that perfect girth, his bow tie a sporty dash of color, his hat set just so, his boutonniere a fresh bud.

Danica drew near, and Swann pretended to gaze in a store window. He watched in the glass as she stopped.

"Jack?"

Swann stopped.

"Danica," Swann said.

Swann produced an isn't-life-funny smile he had on occasion employed with a sergeant or a district attorney.

"I don't believe it," Swann said. "That's twice in a few days. How you doin'?"

"Don't ask. I just got off work."

"You work around here?"

"Up the street. I'm a receptionist. All day, it's 'Hopper and Levin, may I help you? Hopper and Levin, may I help you?'"

"I was just coming from the subway."

Danica took in his suit and bow tie and hat.

"You look like you're going somewhere," Danica said.

Her eyes had that gleam, and the effect on Swann was that of an emboldening ray.

"Actually, I was just going for a drink," Swann said. "You want to come along?"

"I don't know," Danica said.

Swann feared that he had just been more reckless than he had been at the Money Store. He was ready for her to go off and tell Ellen. He instead heard her laugh.

"Why not?" Danica said. "My son's with his father all week."

"There's a place a couple blocks away," Swann said.

Danica hesitated at the entrance and touched Swann's elbow.

"Here?" she asked.

Swann led Danica on up the green-carpeted steps, and the doorman nodded as they went through the polished-brass portal. She tossed back her hair and seemed to do her best to act nonchalant as she went with him through the carpeted lobby and on to the Oak Bar. He, on his part, made every effort to appear as if he were perfectly at ease escorting such a woman.

Swann asked for a table by a window. Danica took the chair held by the maître d', and Swann sat to her left. The waiter appeared.

"I'll have whatever you're having," Danica said.

Swann had been mesmerized by Danica for more than two decades, and yet he knew almost nothing about her, not even such a small thing as what she might like to drink. He could guess that she would not be enchanted by club soda, though he did decide she might like bubbles.

"Champagne?" Swann asked.

Danica smiled.

"Oh, I love it," she said.

Danica looked truly excited, which caused Swann to be pleased, at least until the waiter asked what particular champagne they wanted. Swann knew even less about champagne than he did about her, and he chose one he had read was served aboard the auto executive's yacht on Liberty Weekend.

"I go crazy for this dark wood paneling," Danica said. "Do you come here often?"

"I have been," Swann said.

Danica lowered her voice.

"Isn't it awful expensive?" she asked.

"What do you pay for a movie, five dollars?" Swann asked. "For a dollar more, you could get a drink here."

"Even champagne?"

Swann gave a shrug that indicated he was not worried about money, which at this moment he indeed was not.

"Champagne might be a little more," Swann said.

Danica sat back and Swann joined her in gazing out the window. People and traffic drifted by, as distant as the Oak Bar seemed all the times he passed on the street.

"Can I ask you something?" Danica asked.

Swann looked back at Danica. She now leaned toward him as if to say something intimate. He ceased to breathe.

"What was it like when you shot that guy?" Danica asked.

The waiter had returned, and this was surely not the usual chatter he overheard on arriving at a table to uncork a bottle of champagne. He nonetheless performed the task with aplomb, draping a white towel over the cork and twisting until there was a discreet *pop*. He poured a splash in Swann's glass.

"Would you care to taste the champagne?" the waiter asked.

"Oh, of course," Swann said.

Swann still did not like the taste of alcoholic beverages, and his palate experienced the champagne as an astringent bitterness.

"Perfect," Swann said.

The waiter filled both glasses and placed the bottle in a silver ice bucket. Danica took up her glass and Swann watched her mouth touch the rim. She pursed her lips and her throat rippled as she swallowed. His own throat contracted.

"I haven't had champagne since I got married," Danica said.

Swann made himself take another sip.

"You know, I never would have dreamed you were like this," Danica said.

"Like what?" Swann asked.

"Like all this," Danica said.

Danica finished her glass and Swann poured her some more. He was returning the bottle to the silver bucket when she leaned forward again.

"I'm sorry for asking you about that," Danica said. "It's only that it's something I can't imagine."

Swann suspected that he could go a long way with her by telling her precisely what it was like to kill somebody, but here he hit a wall. He could not trade on the dead Daryl Coombs, even to make time with the beautiful Danica.

"It was just something that happened," Swann said.

Danica seemed both disappointed and a little embarrassed. She smiled and raised her glass.

"Shouldn't we make a toast?" Danica asked. "With champagne, you're supposed to make a toast."

Swann raised his own glass, but he could not immediately come up with something they held in common that was appropriate to toast.

"What do you like best in the world?" Danica asked.

Swann looked across at Danica and her hair and lips and eyes.

"I don't know," Swann said. "A lot of things. What about you?"

Danica closed her eyes and went into whatever lay inside her magnificent exterior. Her eyes popped open.

"Tanned feet," Danica said.

Swann had no immediate response.

"Oooh, I love them!" Danica said. "You know, like when your feet get tan and then like you look down on them and you open your toes a little bit and the insides are like white. I like that. Yeah, even if it's like the slightest tan. I just like the look when my feet are tan. I don't know why, I just do."

Swann did not know why, either, but he was unreservedly willing to accept that there was indeed something wonderful about the space between her toes. He brought his glass forward to toast one part of her heretofore untouched by his adoration.

"To tanned feet," Swann said.

The glasses met with a *ching,* a pure, single note that came as clear to him as the solitary bell at his First Communion.

"*Oooh!*" Danica said. "You know what else?"

Swann just stared at her.

"Polished nails!" Danica said.

Ching. The glass rang as true and clear as before. Danica held out her left hand and spread the fingers. The nails were painted lavender, the finish of the enamel shining even in this dim light.

"I don't really work hard at my nails, you know," Danica said. "I don't really like to get manicures from people because I like the job I do better. Not that I do a great job, because I don't fuss. As long as they look neat and everything, it's okay with me."

Danica's tone became confidential.

"You know what they do when you get a manicure?" Danica asked. "They cut your cuticles."

Swann joined Danica in studying where the curved ridges of flesh met painted nail. Even here she seemed absolutely perfect.

"I don't really have a lot of cuticle," Danica said. "And I think what happens when they cut that, the more you cut it, the more it grows."

Danica looked up, her expression somber.

"I think people are ridiculous to pay for fake nails," she said. "All they're doing is making somebody else rich, because you can grow your nails. People say they can't, but they can if they just have patience, you know, and keep some polish on them. But you can't buy cheap polish. You have to use something a little more expensive, clear or whatever, so you don't attract too much attention to your short nails, and then eventually your nails will grow."

Danica laughed.

"When I was younger, I decided I didn't want to bite my nails anymore," she said. "I was about ten or eleven and I said to myself, 'Hey, you know, you're not biting your nails anymore,' and that was it."

Danica turned her nails in the dimness and she seemed to become wistful, as if she dearly missed a time in her life before the sight of her coming down a hallway set a boy thumping.

"Now I'm still at least not biting my nails," she said.

Danica drummed her fingers and the nails clicked on the tabletop, all her softness and shine ending in a sound of brittle hardness. Swann refilled her glass, and she later proposed toasts to *oooh,* bacon well done, gotta be almost black, and *oooh,* ice-cream cones, butter pecan, walnut, pistachio, anything with nuts, and *oooh,* crisp, clean sheets. Swann watched the *ahhh* toss of her hair before she took a sip and that *mmmm* ripple down her throat as she swallowed and the *Holy God!* tip of her tongue running across her upper lip afterward.

Finally, Swann upended the bottle to see only a few last foamy drops splash into her glass. Then came an incredible moment when she seemed to be reaching for his hand.

"I guess it's about time to go," Danica said.

She pushed back Swann's shirtsleeve and looked at his watch.

"Sometimes it runs a little fast," Swann said.

Danica held up her counterfeit Rolex.

"Mine doesn't run at all," Danica said. "It broke."

Danica looked about the twilit room.

"Anyway, it's getting late," Danica said.

"I'm in no hurry."

"Isn't Ellen expecting you?"

* * *

The bill came in a leather folder as if to dress up the vulgar necessity of payment. Swann casually dropped a couple of hundreds and rose with Danica to discover he was a little drunk as well as dazzled. He was not so inebriated that he failed to see her take a book of matches from the ashtray and slip it into her purse as a souvenir.

"You know what I need?" Danica said. "A bathroom."

The waiter directed Swann and Danica to a flight of stairs that descended to subway depth. Danica went through a white door that bore a brass plaque reading Ladies. Swann entered the one marked Gentlemen and passed an elderly black man in a white attendant's coat.

At the urinals, Swann took out his bit of flesh for which he had no appropriate name. He then washed his hands and the attendant held out a towel.

Swann accepted, feeling one sort of embarrassment he had not previously experienced. He met the tired eyes of the sole black person he had encountered since entering the Plaza.

"How's it goin'?" Swann asked.

"Fine, thank you," the attendant said.

Swann dried his hands and set a $20 bill in the white porcelain tip dish as if to make up for something and maybe as a sort of offering to his own good fortune. He sensed that the attendant's response would have been the same no matter what the amount.

"Thank you, sir, you have a good night now, sir," the attendant said.

Swann passed with Danica through the brass doors to a cool autumn evening.

"Cab, sir?" the doorman asked.

Swann looked at the yellow cab parked at the curb. The subway suddenly seemed for that other Jack Swann.

"Thank you," Swann said.

Danica got in first and scooted across the seat to make room for Swann. The door shut and there he was, for the first time in the back of a cab he had not commandeered to pursue a fleeing felon. His heart pounded not from a chase, but from sitting thigh to thigh with Danica in a close, dark space.

"Where to?" the driver asked.

"Richmond Hill," Swann said.

"Where?"

"In Queens."

The driver made no move to pull away.

"Did you hear me?" Swann asked.

"I heard you," the driver said. "And I don't go there."

"You do now."

"No. Get out."

"I'll get out when we get there."

Swann had heard that cabbies were loath to go to the outer boroughs, partly out of fear of being robbed, but more because they were unlikely to get a fare on the way back. The prospect of not making money now sent the driver into a rage.

"Out!" the driver said. "Or I drag you out!"

The driver leaped from the cab and circled toward the rear door on Swann's side. Swann reflexively hit the lock. The driver reached for the front door on that side and Swann locked that as well. The driver raced around to the other side only to have Swann lock the remaining two doors.

The windows were all shut and the keys were still in the ignition and the driver found himself locked out of his own cab. He cursed and waved his fists, but he was unable to do anything to Swann without first damaging the cab. The only response to his threats was a fit of giggles from Danica.

The driver finally surrendered and wheeled away from the curb in a furious silence. The cab hit a pothole with such force that Danica bounced against Swann, just as he had bounced into Coleman in the paddy wagon, only not like that at all.

"Sorry," Danica said.

Danica slid away, but not before Swann had caught a scent that was faint and overwhelming.

On the other side of the Midtown Tunnel, the cab ascended an elevated ramp that arched high over Calvary Cemetery. Swann's mother was buried there and he himself might have been interred beside her instead of speeding through the aboveground beside Danica. The cab descended to street level and the cemetery gave way to the sprawl of Queens.

As they rolled onto Danica's block, Swann met the cat's green eyes.

"Well, thanks," Danica said.

"Well, thank you," Swann said.

Danica glanced toward the driver and she was giggling again as she slid out of the cab. Swann listened to the click, click, click of her heels on the stoop. He smelled only the cab's evergreen air freshener.

"You ain't getting out?" the driver asked.

"No," Swann said. "I'm three blocks over."

Swann took the precaution of having the cab stop around the corner from his house, but he was so enraptured that he hit the stoop like someone who had been at the Oak Bar with Danica. He caught himself halfway up and passed through the front door doing his best to appear as he might on almost any night but this one.

Six

SWANN SET OUT for his post with a headache too slight to be penitential and no bother at all when he considered that the moderate throbbing at his temples came from having drunk champagne with a beautiful woman.

"Like I say, I won't even ask," Coleman said.

Coleman was referring to his pocket print, which again looked like a whole lot of money.

"But I can't speak for them," Coleman said.

Coleman flashed her eyes toward two men in raincoats who stood before an ad poster at the far end of the passageway outside the district, doing a reasonable job of not looking as if they were looking. Swann started with Coleman toward the trains and stole a glance back. The men were tailing them.

Down on the platform, Swann and Coleman sauntered a half dozen strides along the tracks. Swann stepped to the edge and peered back into the tunnel. The two men immediately turned as if they were also looking for an approaching train.

"You know what they think," Swann said.

"I also know I was there," Coleman said.

Coleman was not saying that Swann would never steal, only that she would have seen him if he had dipped into the bag of drug cash.

"It is my money."

"I wouldn't expect it to be anybody's else's."

After a while, one of the men glanced over his shoulder. Swann was still looking their way, and the man rejoined his partner in pretending to look for a train until one actually did arrive.

* * *

The station under the Plaza was not busy enough for the men to keep Swann under constant surveillance without being obvious, even by the standards of the Internal Affairs Division. They split up, one taking the street above, the other the platforms below.

That covered all the possible exits, and Swann felt himself sealed in the underground. He stood with the Oak Bar directly overhead, Coleman at his side and a big chunk of the suspect money nuzzled against his thigh.

She asked no questions, which made him feel more strongly that he should give her some answers. He was not any more sure that he could make as much sense to her as he had to himself. The result was that he had still said nothing when the time came for their mealtime trip downtown.

The man who was watching the platform spoke into his sleeve. IAD must have had radios that actually worked, for the partner hurried down from the street. The two men rode to Times Square in the next car from Swann and Coleman.

At the soda fountain, Swann peered over the rim of his coffee cup to see the IAD men keeping watch from a bank of pay phones. He might not have been able to convey his theory of leverage to Coleman, but he could relate what he had learned of the Dark Side over the years.

Swann said that the first thing you did when assigned to IAD was check your own file, known there as a *locator.* You saw that anonymous calls had been made to IAD whenever you were up for a transfer or promotion. You also noted the substance of those calls.

"Stuff only people close to you know," Swann said.

Swann was still looking at the two men and he was speaking to himself as much as to Coleman. He said that the second thing you did was check the locators of everybody you knew. You saw reports that one friend liked to peep in his neighbors' windows and another had been robbing the coffee money and you wondered if you really knew anybody. You learned that almost all allegations ended with the accuser's word standing against that of the cop. The question on the Dark Side was not so much guilty or innocent.

"It's 'substantiated' or 'unsubstantiated,'" Swann said.

"They used the 'un' word after the cops beat my brother," Coleman said. "He's not what you would call a big fan of the police."

"What'd he think of you going on the job?" Swann asked.

"He don't like it," Coleman said. "I told him, 'I'm not going to let a bunch of cops keep me from being a cop.' I asked him, 'Who do you want coming when you dial nine-one-one, them or me?'"

Coleman was speaking as if she did not consider Swann to be one of *them*. She rose for the after-meal stroll and began softly humming "Me and My Shadow" as the IAD men trailed them. He listened to her shift the tune around as she had with the classical music that rose from the park on Liberty Weekend.

She made this tune her own as well, and he was stepping with her to its cadence when they descended to the platform for the ride back to their post. He imagined going with her into the last car and maybe hearing the feet and hands take up her beat. The reality was he would also be boarding with their two shadows, the sight of whom would be sure to keep the last car the mirthless place he had until recently known it to be.

At the end of the tour, the two men trailed Swann and Coleman right up to District 1. She signed out and he did the same, and he emerged to see a new pair of men in raincoats waiting in the passageway, pretending to study the same ad poster. The first two men had spent the tour poised to record any straying from the subway system while Swann was on duty. This second team now stood ready to observe any ways he might stray beyond the bounds of the life he could be expected to lead on a transit cop's paycheck.

Swann knew that the smart thing would be to go home like a good civil servant, and he was considering doing precisely that when he heard a purring voice.

"Hiya!"

Danica was standing off to the other side of the doorway from the two men. She had apparently been chatting with Mannering, who stood slackjawed as she started toward Swann, who was himself altogether amazed.

"We keep bumping into each other," Danica said.

Danica's throaty laugh sounded no less fine here than at the Plaza.

"It must be fate or something."

Swann recovered enough from the surprise to introduce Coleman and Danica.

"Danica, this is Simone."

"Pretty," Danica said.

Danica was speaking of Coleman's given name. Swann realized he had never before said it aloud.

"Whas up?" Coleman said.

Danica seemed flustered by Coleman's flat gaze. She gave an all-purpose smile and turned back to Mannering.

"Nice talking to you," Danica said.

Coleman's gaze stayed flat as it went to Swann. She nodded farewell and headed for a Brooklyn train.

"She's a cop?" Danica asked.

Swann's attention returned to Danica, who would be called pretty before all else.

"Yes," Swann said. "My partner."

Swann was unable to figure a way to tell one's date that one is being followed by IAD, so he said nothing to Danica about the two men who trailed them along Central Park South. He remained conscious enough of his shadow's presence that he went up the carpeted steps to the Plaza feeling a touch like he might on duty when crossing the boundary between the subway and the street.

Danica seemed to have an easier time at least faking nonchalance than on the first visit. They again asked for a table by a window, and she appeared genuinely relaxed as she gazed out at the street. She had no cause to take any particular notice of the man in the raincoat who was watching the hotel entrance from the opposite sidewalk.

Swann turned his attention from the street to the room and lost the sense of having crossed a boundary. This did, after all, seem precisely the place to take a woman such as Danica, and she was just the woman to have in a place such as this.

The waiter brought the champagne and Swann again pronounced the astringent taste perfect. Danica said it was exactly what she needed after a day as a receptionist with Hopper and Levin, accountants.

"My boss had me call this restaurant, Angkor What?, and make a reservation."

Swann recognized the name as one of the new hot spots in the gossip columns he had read in ECAB.

"So when I call, it's like forget about it, they got nothing for like weeks. Can you imagine? So I tell this to the boss, and he tells me, 'Call back and say you were supposed to call a couple weeks ago, but you forgot and now you might get fired if you can't get your boss a seat.' I do that and it's still forget about it. I mean, it could have been true. And, it almost was, because my boss gets all mad like it really is my fault. So don't even ask me about today at work."

Swann stole a glance out the plate glass to see that the lone IAD man had spotted them in the window. The man immediately averted his gaze and the street did not seem so remote.

Danica drummed her fingers on the table, the nails making that sound of brittle hardness. Swann remarked that she had changed her polish from lavender to a bright red. She seemed surprised and truly pleased that Swann had noticed this small detail.

"Well, at least I'm still not biting them," Danica said.

She examined her nails.

"But I'll tell you, between work and home . . ."

Danica looked up.

"I guess you musta heard about it," she said.

"Somebody said something about some problems," Swann said.

"You know Timothy, my husband."

"We used to play as kids."

"I should say ex-husband."

Danica paused.

"He was so *cute,*" Danica said.

Swann just blinked.

"Among other things," Danica said.

Danica abruptly changed the subject, or so it seemed.

"The way I clean is, I start with the bedrooms and work my way out to the bathroom and the kitchen," Danica said. "Because that's the way you should. And the first thing I do is I do my vacuuming, which lets the dust settle in the meantime. Okay? Then I go into dusting, and I start with the bedrooms and I come into the living room, and at the same time I'm Windexing, too, the mirrors and things like that as I go along. Then I go into the bathroom and I do the usual with my foam cleaner, the bowl and all that kind of stuff."

Danica lowered her voice.

"William, you know, a young boy doesn't always, you know, hit where he's aiming at. And I got this *nose,* so then if I smell that smell, it makes me crazy. I get nuts. It's like every day I have to check the bottom of the bowl. You know how it is, you were a little boy once."

Swann nodded.

"Then it's the kitchen," Danica said. "I'm doin' that and I'm like dead and what's my husband do but come in with the mail. He belongs to this Vietnam book club, where you get all these books about Vietnam, though if you really want to know, all he did over there was be a cook. I don't think he even killed anybody, and about the only time he almost got killed was by his own guys when he forgot to heat the turkey loaf."

"Anyway, he gets these books and they come in these big sort of envelopes, padded, and when he tears it open out comes all this padding, this gray stuff, and it goes on my floor that I just did. I say something and he says, 'Okay, okay, I'll get the broom.' Now, I'm a vacuumer. I can't stand to mop. And I *hate* to sweep. I'll vacuum whatever you want, but don't give me a broom. I been with this guy like forever and he don't know even that. I don't even *own* a broom."

Danica ran an enameled fingernail around the rim of her glass once and then again.

"And now my son's with my husband every other week. This week is his."

Danica looked up.

"But if I hadn't married him, I would never have had William," Danica said. "Another kid, but not William."

Danica had said something profound. Swann was startled by her sudden transition from vacuumer to philosopher.

"And I wouldn't be drinking champagne in the Oak Bar," Danica said.

Danica dipped her fingertip into her glass and raised it to her mouth. The drop broke on her lips.

"Or maybe you would," Swann said.

Danica laughed and Swann raised his glass.

"Here's to vacuuming and drinking champagne in the Oak Bar," Swann said.

Ching. Swann sipped and glanced out the window. He thought for a moment that the IAD man had gone, but then he saw a gray unmarked car at the curb. The second IAD man must have fetched the car, and the two of them now sat inside, waiting.

"And sunsets," Danica said.

Ching.

"And taking walks wherever," she said.

The bottle was wet and icy in Swann's hand as he poured the last few drops into Danica's glass. She remarked that the hour must be getting late, and he raised his empty glass.

"Here's to getting late," Swann said.

Danica looked at him and giggled.

"For a minute I thought you said something else," Danica said.

Swann smiled, though he was not sure what she meant. He checked his watch and then made a show of leaning over to look at her Rolex.

"Mine's running fast again," Swann said.

Swann ordered a second bottle of champagne, and the hour was indeed late when they left the Oak Bar. They again went down to the rest rooms, and he placed a $20 offering in the tip dish. The attendant had the same response.

"Thank you, sir, you have a good night now, sir," the attendant said.

Outside the Plaza, Swann breathed in the night air to dissipate the effects of the champagne for which he had just paid a week's wages. He saw the unmarked car still waiting at the curb.

"That was nice," Danica said. "Thank you."

Danica's smile was smudged by inebriation. He felt his own buzz as something they shared.

"Anytime," Swann said.

No taxis were standing empty, and Swann was waiting for an unoccupied one to come along when he heard horse hooves striking asphalt. A horse pulled up a hansom cab and the driver called from his perch.

"Ride through the park?"

Swann had Danica at his side and yet he was still startled that somebody would take the two of them as a couple.

The carriage carried them into the park, and soon the only sound was that clip-clop of the horse's hooves. Swann gazed with Danica into a hushed stately wood. A big uptown moon was gleaming through the trees.

"Now I got another thing I like best," Danica said.

Swann stole a glance back and saw a pair of headlights trailing them as they started up the east side of the park. He joined Danica in watching the apartment buildings of Fifth Avenue rise beyond the trees, their lights golden and celestially remote.

Swann was peering up at the penthouse of the tallest building when one of the windows went dark. He kept his eyes on the small, black rectangle, understanding that whoever lived up there had flicked the light switch and was most likely slipping into bed, ready to slumber in lofty luxury. He checked behind them and saw the unmarked car's headlights, the IAD men still recording how Jack Swann, cave cop, spent his money.

Only the moon shone above the trees once the carriage reached the top of the park and began to clip-clop along the edge of Harlem. Danica was wearing just a light jacket over her dress, and she folded her arms against the late-autumn chill. Swann slipped off his suit coat and placed it over her shoulders.

"Now you'll freeze," Danica said.

"I'm okay," Swann said.

The lights of the Upper West Side appeared on the right. Swann saw Central Park South up ahead and knew the ride around the park was almost over. The IAD men would be following him back to Queens, where they would witness his return to his proper place when he was not underground.

Swann looked over at a moonlit glade that sloped down to the trees. He reached up and tapped the driver on the shoulder.

"Stop," Swann said.

"What?" the driver asked.

"Stop," Swann said. "You know, like 'whoa.'"

"What's the matter?" Danica asked.

Swann paid the driver and leaped from the carriage. He held out his hand.

"You said you love to take walks," Swann said.

The sound of the hooves faded as Swann started across the moonlit glade with Danica close at his side. The ground underfoot was soft and ethereally aglow.

"Isn't this dangerous?" Danica asked.

"No," Swann said.

Swann saw that her eyes had narrowed and were darting back and forth, peering hard at the shadows.

"Would you do this if you didn't have a gun?" Danica asked.

"No," Swann said.

Danica giggled, maybe still a little merry from the champagne, but also clearly titillated to be walking where the whole city was afraid to venture. Swann, in turn, felt an elation beyond that of drink and Danica's charms. He was a protector, if not quite the virtuous prince of Jenny's storybooks then close to the sort of hero he had imagined himself as a rookie. Let whoever lived in that penthouse take a stroll through Central Park at night.

The thump, thump of a pair of car doors was too distant to make Danica look back, but signaled Swann that the IAD men were trailing him on foot. He kept on, feeling Danica sidle closer as they reached the shadows beyond the glade. Her shoulder was brushing his as they started up a path that curved into a dark grove.

"Where are we going?" Danica asked.

"I have no idea," Swann said.

Fallen leaves carpeted the path as it wound through the trees and around a rock outcrop, dipping down into a black hollow and rising up into a thicket. The path there forked into two blind curves.

"You decide," Swann said.

Danica peered from one to the other as if looking for a clue. She began to wag a painted fingernail back and forth.

"Eeenie meenie miney moe, catch a . . ."

Swann touched her elbow.

"Let's go this way."

Swann and Danica wound through more trees and eventually came to an esplanade vaulted with tall, spreading elms. Cast-iron lamps shone softly on two long lines of deserted wood benches.

Swann and Danica walked slow and silent up the center as if striding up the aisle of a cathedral. He glanced back but saw nobody. He decided IAD must have taken the other path.

* * *

The esplanade opened into a large square, and Swann continued with Danica past a half dozen rows of empty seats that were arranged before a deserted bandstand. The two then came to an ornately carved limestone balustrade whose steps descended underground like an oversized subway stairwell.

At the bottom of the steps, Swann and Danica passed through a dimly lit tunnel. They stepped from there into a second square that had a fountain topped by a bronze angel with outspread wings. There was a small lake beyond, the glassy black water ringed by thick trees and bare rock.

Swann and Danica stepped to the water's edge. A fish nipped some morsel off the surface, and Swann watched the circular ripple slowly widen and vanish. Then all was still and serene in this hidden place at the center of the City of New York.

Swann peered down by the polished toes of his loafers and saw the mooncast reflections of himself and Danica. He looked up. Her eyes were shining and staring back at him.

Ching.

Swann eased toward Danica and the perfect face of his greatest desire filled his entire vision. She closed her eyes as she had when she was pondering what she liked best.

Swann shut his own eyes. He had much the same desperate feeling as on that night of Liberty Weekend almost four months before when the trigger of his revolver had begun to slide from under his sweating finger. He leaned forward until his lips touched Danica's ever so lightly. The warm softness was as unreal as the heat of a muzzle flash.

Swann slid his arms around Danica, feeling the tropical wool of the suit jacket still draped over her shoulders, burying his face in her honey-colored hair. Her lips brushed his neck and he kissed her a second time. She began to stroke his back and his sides and he felt splendid under her touch.

Swann's own fingers trailed down the furrow of her back, but his boldness ended at her waist. He ran his hands up her sides until he neared her breasts, and he became aware of a growing discomfort in the vicinity of his revolver. The trouble became more acute when she began nibbling his ear lobe. He reached down between their bellies and heard her breath catch, as if she were not sure she wanted things to go further.

"My gun," Swann said.

Swann's ear filled with giggling, but then Danica suddenly pulled away. His first thought was that she must have realized whom she was kissing. He then saw that she was looking away from him and toward the tunnel through which they had come.

"I saw somebody," Danica said.

Swann looked over, but the IAD men must have ducked back into the shadows. He considered simply saying that he did not see anyone, but she was sure to see them again.

"I'm being followed," Swann said.

Her eyes went from the tunnel to Swann. He saw that same gleam of interest as on the morning after the shooting.

"For real?" Danica said.

"For real," Swann said.

Her eyes returned to the tunnel.

"By who?" Danica asked.

"Other cops," Swann said.

Those soft lips pursed. Her next question was there without her asking.

"My partner and I recovered a bag of money and they think I took some," Swann said.

The eyes were back on Swann, that gleam of interest undiminished. Her voice was a low purr.

"You might have told me," Danica said.

Danica's smile shone in the moonlight and she was all the more beautiful for seeming a little excited.

"I mean, what if we got really carried away with them watching?"

Danica kissed Swann lightly on the lips. His words came spilling out as she pulled away.

"I didn't take money," Swann said. "I would never do that."

Swann would have said more had Danica not kissed him again. Her tongue plunged into his mouth as if seeking the taste of what had set her eyes shining. He pulled her to him and his tongue moved with hers.

* * *

The renewed stirring down by Swann's revolver seemed an unequivocal and increasingly insistent indicator of what was important. He had, after all, not gazed after her for years hoping he might someday know her views on police corruption. He had not dreamed that she might stand with him in some moonlit spot and know he would not take money. His fantasy had always been to be doing exactly what he was doing at this moment, although he had never conjured up a scenario in which IAD was watching.

"Come on," Swann said. "Let's lose these fucks."

Swann took Danica's hand and led her from the square to a trail that curved along the water's edge. Their steps sounded in hollow unison on the wood planks of a small footbridge, and they soon after came to a maze of paths that rose and fell and twisted and forked in a thick and brambly undergrowth. She stifled a laugh as he led her into the deeper darkness of a thicket.

The wood bridge was far enough away that the thud of other feet was barely audible. Swann then heard a muttering, and he peered through the branches to see the two IAD men come up the path. He froze and held his breath as they passed not six feet from the small clearing where he hid with Danica.

"Fuck," one of the men said.

The men took another few steps and stopped. Swann had just enough light to see Danica clap a hand over her mouth.

"I told you we should have went the other way," the second man said.

Swann did not so much as blink as the men went back past them. He then turned to Danica and they stood facing each other until they heard footsteps going back over the bridge. They then kissed and kissed again and her low purr broke the silence.

"What else would you never do?" Danica asked.

Swann's mouth went to her throat. His fingers fumbled with a button of her blouse and he kissed the bared skin and he undid another button and another. The blouse parted to prove the inadequacy of his imagination and his hands then established how deficient a sense sight can be. He cupped a breast in each palm and seemed to be at the extreme end of experience from the shooting of Daryl Coombs.

The revolver became an object to be cast aside, and the tropical wool suit trousers felt in this instance much more wonderful coming off than they had going on. Swann stood with his pocket print lost in the heap at his ankles, his bow tie still neatly knotted, his full if not remarkable erection now poking up from between his shirttails.

Swann ran his hand down over Danica's belly and his tactile sense was as acute as if he were riding shut-eyed in the last car. His fingertips reached the soft curls he expected and yet was still amazed to find.

Swann ended up bare-bottomed on the ground, Danica atop him. He felt her hand slide between them.

"Do you have anything?" Danica asked.

"Excuse me?"

"Birth control."

"I didn't really expect this."

Danica laughed.

"Me, either," Danica said. "Just be careful."

Danica's hand tightened on Swann and guided him into her and for the first time he entered a woman other than Ellen.

The fit was no less perfect, and Swann's emotions became as clear as the messages sparking from his nerve endings. Feeling and feelings seemed to travel along the same pathways, and he experienced the paired thrills of not just realizing a fantasy but also of deciding he had been absolutely right to have had it. He kissed her as if ending a long separation, and he commenced to move in the hot slick of this rightness.

Danica soon began to moan in time with his strokes, slowing when he slowed, speeding up when he sped up, welcoming him each time he returned. She seemed ready to go on and on as he quickly neared the point where he would have to withdraw in the name of contraception. A fantasy of twenty years was about to end in under five minutes.

Swann took a deep breath and opened his eyes wide and gazed up into the night sky just as he had while firing the shot that could just as easily have killed him. He began to count soundlessly to himself with the cadence of a doctor pressing on a bloody chest.

One.

Two.

Three.

Four.

The urgency subsided and Swann closed his eyes and went back up to full speed. Danica's moans lengthened into wails and he felt her go rigid. He experienced a sudden and imperative need to resume his silent counting.

One.

Two.

Three.

Four.

Swann continued, pumping on and on as if he were championing all the fatsos who did not Get the Girl. She began to toss her head and make deep sounds in the back of her throat. She shuddered and went limp.

Swann suspended his count and stroked on, feeling all his desire and vitality compress to a single, straining force. He brought himself right to the threshold, a single thrust of the hips from what everything in him was mounting toward.

Then, in that last instant, the rightness became a precipice. Swann withdrew and skidded between their pressed bellies, holding his breath as if a momentous event were imminent. The clasping and the thrills and the cries and the sweat and the gasps all ended with him throbbing exactly as he would have with Ellen, which was to say about as momentously as a finger drumming on a tabletop.

Swann rose with Danica and took a shirttail to wipe a smear of semen from his belly. He looked to see her rub a corresponding smudge into her skin like a dollop of lotion.

"That's what I call getting late," Danica said.

Swann hiked up his trousers and tucked in his damp shirttails and cinched his belt to the notch he had deemed his true girth. He peered down at the dark floor of the clearing for his revolver and saw a black shape. He stooped to feel a rotted stick.

"Let me know if you run across some panties," Danica said.

Danica crouched beside him, and they were both patting the churned leaves when a rustling came from the surrounding undergrowth. They froze, though the sound was too faint to be anything but a small animal. He looked at her, hunched low, head up, peering into the dark.

*　*　*

Swann rose and slipped his revolver back into his waistband as he watched Danica pull up her panties. He had imagined them to be white when he had reached down to peel them off, but he now saw that they were black. The elastic gave a little snap, and she stuffed her panty hose in her jacket pocket. She took his hand.

Swann emerged from the thicket feeling confirmed in a way not contemplated by the Church. The path took them through a small gap in the underbrush and up to a park building that looked like a small castle. They passed onto a rock overhang that jutted high over the lake. They gazed together across the glassy black water to the lights of midtown Manhattan.

"Very nice," Danica said.

Swann and Danica continued along the path, circling the far side of the lake and coming to where they had first kissed. His legs had a spring they had not possessed before, and, had the question been put to him, he would have said that he had discovered the true secret of *vigor.*

III

Seven

THE SWANN OF A WEEK BEFORE would have been content to take the subway home. The Swann of even a few hours before might have been willing to bicker with a cabbie over going to Queens. The Swann who now came out of the park took Danica up to a black stretch Lincoln with livery plates.

A $100 bill also proved lever enough to send a limousine driver scrambling to open the rear door. Swann slid inside with Danica and reclined as if he never traveled any other way. He listened to her sigh as she stretched out her legs and rubbed her palms on the gray velour upholstery.

Danica's hand was on Swann's as the ramp beyond the Midtown Tunnel took the limousine up over Calvary Cemetery. He asked the driver to honk, and Danica gave him a look.

"Just saying hello to my mother," Swann said. "You got anybody?"

"There's my grandfather Ernie," Danica said.

The limo's horn again sounded out over the graves of Swann's mother and Danica's grandfather Ernie and a quarter million other uncelebrated dead. Swann rode resplendently on, and he could have been the very King of Queens as he rolled into Richmond Hill with Danica's head resting on his thumping chest.

The limo stopped for a red light and Danica raised her head to gaze out the window. She suddenly slipped down toward the floor.

"Isn't that your father?" Danica asked.

Swann saw that Danica was right. Joseph was standing at a bus stop, his old Marine duffel bag at his side. The streetlight overhead showed that he had a black eye. He was tilting his head one way and then the other as he attempted to make out who was on the other side of the tinted glass.

Swann slunk down beside Danica and instructed the driver to run the light. The driver refused and Swann held up his badge.

"I am a police officer and this is an emergency," Swann said.

The limo lurched through the intersection. Danica asked what Joseph was doing standing in the dark with a shiner and a duffel bag and if he had seen them and what he might do if he had and whether he might tell Ellen. Swann gave the same answer to each question.

"I don't know."

Danica sat up and stared at Swann. The plush cushions beneath him became as uncomfortable as a subway bench.

"This is really crazy, isn't it?" Danica asked. "I mean, like, you're married."

The driver hopped out as Swann and Danica sat looking at each other. Her eyes were bloodshot and his own had the same gritty feel as after a night at ECAB.

"Yes," Swann said. "I'm married."

The door opened.

"But, I gotta say, tonight was great," Swann said.

Danica kissed him and he would have been sure this was the end had she not ever so lightly bitten his lower lip.

"See ya," she said.

Danica slipped out and Swann saw that dawn was breaking outside the tinted glass.

"Where to from here, Officer?" the driver asked.

The limousine pulled over at Swann's corner, becoming something even harder to explain than a cab. He told the driver not to bother with the door and ducked out, quickly putting a dozen steps between him and the ride that had seemed so splendrously fitting high above the cemetery. He looked up and down the street, more worried about an early-rising neighbor than he had ever been about IAD. He then checked again, finding himself suddenly less sure of his senses now that he was back in the place most familiar to him.

Clarity returned with the click of the front-door lock, and Swann passed into a hush disturbed only by his own small noises. These ceased when he reached Jenny's bed. He checked on his sleeping child as he would no matter where he had been.

Swann heard his own light steps as he went into the bathroom, there to sponge any traces of seed from his belly. He scrubbed lower upon seeing that the slick of his joining with Danica had dried to a dander of crusty flakes.

Swann then sniffed his fingers. He washed his hands once, and again, feeling as solitary as a lone thief. He did not consider that Mannering most likely did the same after seeing the nurse, or that the Prince of Vigor himself might well have ducked into a presidential washroom on the way from Marilyn Monroe to the First Lady.

"What time did you get in last night?"

Ellen was dropping a slice of bread in the toaster. Swann was wearing his gym shorts, having just completed his morning run, which had done nothing for a headache quite severe enough to be penitential.

"I don't know," Swann said. "Late."

Ellen thumbed down the toaster's lever and turned to Swann. He had not consciously chosen to use that word *late,* and he felt it hang there as a measure of his duplicity.

"I grabbed somebody on the way home," Swann said.

Swann had again not intended any double meaning. He concentrated on taking a sip of coffee.

"That's twice in two days you didn't call," Ellen said. "I had cooked."

"Chicken again," Jenny said.

"I'm sorry," Swann said.

Swann looked at Jenny, he feeling a full second meaning of his words, she chewing Cap'n Crunch so that milk brimmed from her lips as she spoke.

"Did you shoot him?" Jenny asked.

"No," Swann said.

Swann unthinkingly handed Jenny a napkin. She wiped her mouth.

"Before I forget, your father called," Ellen said.

Ellen was going into the refrigerator for something, and Swann could not see her face to judge if the whole conversation had been a trap. He spoke as casually as is possible when you are praying that the limo glass was as opaque as it seemed.

"Oh yeah?" Swann said. "What did he say?"

The refrigerator door shut and Ellen turned to him holding a jar of grape jelly.

"Just that he was going away and that he would send you a postcard," Ellen said.

"From where?"

"That's what I asked him. He wouldn't say."

Ellen turned to the toaster, whose timer had long since ceased to function. Her own sense of time prompted her to lift the lever and the toast popped up, golden brown.

Swann arrived at District 1 with an acid stomach and his temples throbbing hard enough that for once he welcomed the dimness of the subway. He saw the first pair of IAD men waiting at the same place down the passageway, and what regret he had felt at home was offset by imagining the report that must have been on Lieutenant Gentile's desk at that very moment.

Subject and unid. female white went to Oak Bar and were observed drinking what appeared to be champagne. Subject and female then traveled by carriage into Central Park, there continuing by foot, at which time the undersigned continued surveillance on foot, whereupon subject and female were lost from view.

The other officers knew by now that the Dark Side was trailing Swann, and his good cheer seemed to anger some who would have otherwise been able to smirk at his misfortune. More appeared to have the typical reaction to an officer's being under investigation, which was to avoid him as though he had some deadly strain of cooties.

As he crossed the muster room, Swann caught Mannering looking at him. Mannering quickly turned away, just as the men from IAD might. Swann experienced another little lift of vigor on considering that the great swordsman Paddy Mannering must be desperate to know how Jack Swann could possibly attract so beautiful a woman as Danica.

No such interest was evident in Coleman, who greeted Swann with the same flat look she had given him the night before.

* * *

At meal, Coleman was still maintaining a certain reserve, and she seemed to pay even more attention than usual in applying the mustard to her hot dog. Swann looked over at the IAD men, who were once more watching from the bank of pay phones. He thought of those last moments with Danica in the limousine and he bit his lip, deciding that if nothing else courtesy dictated he give her a call.

Not that he was going to make a goom call with Coleman there. He fumbled to make conversation as he had been doing since the start of the tour. He now again found IAD a handy topic.

Swann resumed his recitation on the Dark Side, saying that the newcomer to IAD found that the only cops who still spoke to him were the ones who had the most contemptible locators and were hedging against future trouble. You were shunned as a *rat* by the good cops and you had to shun the bad ones and you were left with just your work.

Only, cave cops just did not have much opportunity to be corrupt. Bigtime corruption in the subway was shaking down gays in the bathrooms and a transit IAD investigator went from one petty allegation to another.

"And how're you going to show you're not just some petty scumbag when you spend all day trying to prove some cop is working in a bar or going home early?" Swann said.

Coleman tipped her head toward the IAD men.

"Don't take this the wrong way, but I don't think they're worried about whether you're going home early," Coleman said.

Swann gazed back at the two men, thinking how excited they must be to have what seemed a case of real corruption, just like with the city police, just like in the movies. True evil and therefore a chance to prove themselves good.

"I'm going to hate to disappoint them," Swann said.

He felt he had talked himself to where he had to tell Coleman, and tell her he did.

"What you mean, 'Money Store'?" she asked.

"You might have seen the commercials," he said.

"I don't really watch too much television. It's boring."

Coleman had finished her hot dog. She wiped her mouth and looked at the streak of mustard on the napkin.

"I was wondering . . . ," Coleman said. "I thought maybe you hit the lotto or something."

She shook her head, but she was smiling as she did so. He sensed that if she did not completely approve, she at least appreciated his spirit.

"I have to admit, you're not boring," she said.

Near the end of the after-meal stroll, a passing posse took an interest in Swann's pocket print. He played the fearful vic, secretly grinning at the thought of his shadows being forced to take appropriate police action and come to his rescue. That fantasy ended when one of the older members spotted the men from IAD and let out a shout.

"Five-O!"

The posse moved on toward the turnstiles, with Swann and Coleman trailing them as far as the top of the subway steps. The two then returned to the underground and the IAD men found themselves ahead of the people they were supposed to be following.

The IAD men stepped over to a token booth, pretending to be in need of directions as Swann and Coleman went by. One spoke in a raised voice so as to be heard by the clerk behind the bulletproof glass.

"How do we get to the uptown trains?"

Swann's words came by reflex.

"Just follow us," Swann said.

Swann turned to see Coleman purse her lips to keep from laughing.

At the end of the tour, Coleman went her way and Swann went his, the evening pair of shadows trailing behind. IAD got a turn to watch him stand at a pay phone.

"Hopper and Levin, may I help you?"

Swann had been inside this woman and yet he had no idea of the nature of their bond. He might as well have been trying to guess what she would toast.

"Hi, it's Jack . . . Swann."

"Hiya!" Danica said. "I was just . . ."

Swann heard the trill of another call coming in.

". . . hold on."

The switchboard was one of those that pipe in music when a caller is on hold, and Swann had some easy-listening tune in his ear as he glanced over at the IAD men. He felt a twinge of sympathy for these cops who were even more ostracized than himself, who were no doubt as excited as he would be by a big case.

Danica came back on.

"Now, what was I saying?" Danica asked.

"You said you were just something," Swann said.

"Oh yeah. I was just thinking of you."

Danica waited for Swann to speak, he being the one who had called. His fantasies had never taken into account that he might realize them and he had no idea what to say. "It was good to see you" or "I had a nice time" would cover the drinks at the Oak Bar and maybe even the carriage ride and the stroll through the park, but they did not seem adequate for the events in the thicket.

He welcomed the trill of another call.

"I'm sorry," Danica said.

"That's your job," Swann said.

"Don't remind me. Every freaking day."

Swann found himself with something to say.

"But you never know what fate might bring," Swann said.

"*Oh,*" Danica said. "You mean like maybe when I come out of work tomorrow?"

Swann was fatigued from the previous night's escapade and he might have forgone the Oak Bar had he not considered the report that would be landing on Lieutenant Gentile's desk. The club soda was no less wonderful for being almost obligatory and maybe a little more so for not tasting anything like champagne. He stood with his back against the bar and saw that a couple was at the table where he had sat with Danica. He looked beyond them to see that one of the IAD men was standing across the street.

As Swann left the Oak Bar he heard a shout.

"Officer! Officer!"

Swann whirled as if he were in one of his hero fantasies. He saw that he was being addressed by the limousine driver from the night before.

Here was a truly chance encounter, and Swann was willing to take it as genuine fate. He ended a brief conversation by holding out a $100 bill and the driver recited aloud their arrangement.

"Quarter to five tomorrow outside your office."

* * *

Swann's shadows left him at the end of his block, for whatever transpired once he had gone up his stoop was apparently of no official interest. He was sitting down for a few bites of flounder when the thought came that his next meeting with Danica would be an actual date and that he probably should buy her dinner. He felt as low as a man who would think of his goom while eating with his wife and daughter.

Swann banished any further thoughts of Danica just as he would have banished any thoughts of his family had he been with her. Jenny went in to take her bath, and Swann crouched by the tub, playing whale to her mermaid.

Swann and Ellen kissed Jenny good night. The rest of the night took the two of them them from the television to bed, where they kissed each other good night. Part of him remained as absent as on the night of the shooting. The rest of him seemed more intensely present than ever.

For the second time in a month, rapid transit was rapid. Swann arrived in midtown twenty minutes before he had to report for duty and he crossed to a pharmacy. He had proved himself a champion with Danica, and he was in this place only because he stood a good chance to have sex with her again and he should by all rights have swaggered up like the envy of men everywhere. He instead found himself mumbling and averting his eyes as he asked for condoms.

The man at the register did not make things easier by asking such questions as "What kind?" and "How many?" Swann requested a brand he remembered hearing spoken of in junior high school.

"Plain or lubricated?" the man then asked.

Swann had not anticipated such a choice. Plain might be too plain, but maybe lubricated was not plain enough, though perhaps lubricated would be more considerate, though plain seemed somehow nicer, less mechanical if not exactly romantic.

"Both," Swann said.

His purchase in one pocket, his money in the other, Swann reported for duty still unsure where he might take Danica for dinner. He had seen a suitably elegant dining room at the Plaza, but to go there would make it seem he knew of no other place, which indeed he did not. He was so preoccupied that only on encountering Sullivan did he remember that this was one of those days by which he had until very recently measured his existence.

"You got to be the first cop in the history of the world who forgot it was payday," Sullivan said.

Sullivan presented Swann with his check.

"I don't care about you and money," Sullivan said. "I don't really care about what happened with Fredricks. You're still my hero. You don't just take it off. You keep it off. That's the real test. Just look at that woman with the talk show, what's her name."

Coleman appeared in the yellow satin jacket she had been wearing back when she had first addressed Swann in a tone of kinship.

"Coleman, what's the name of that talk show woman that lost all that weight and put it right back on?" Sullivan asked. "You know . . ."

Swann knew that Sullivan was speaking of one of Ellen's favorites and that the woman in question was black.

"She doesn't watch television," Swann said.

"But I do get paid," Coleman said.

Sullivan handed Coleman her check.

"See, even she don't forget payday," Sullivan said.

Swann still had his own paycheck in his hand. He pocketed it without bothering to check the exact amount.

At the end of the tour, Swann parted with Coleman and headed off as quickly as if he were still matching her stride. His invigorated step was impeded when he encountered Mannering and several other cops on the steps. He trudged behind them to the street.

"Officer!"

Mannering and the others turned just as Swann had outside the Plaza. Swann slipped past them, and the driver held the door as he climbed into the back. The door shut and he peered through the tinted glass. A grinning Mannering was standing among fellow officers who did not seem to know how to react.

* * *

Swann watched through the limousine's rear window as the IAD men made for their unmarked car. He rode off to Madison Avenue and saw Danica gazing about a bustling street for nobody but him. She was wearing a clinging red dress hemmed high up her thighs. Her hair was drawn tightly back with a black ribbon, which had the effect of making her eyes seem even bigger.

"That's her over there," Swann said.

"I remember," the driver said.

Danica recognized the driver as he hopped out to open the door. However her day at work had gone, she seemed only delighted as she stepped inside.

"Hiya."

Danica's scent seemed unusually strong, and even the polish on her fingernails appeared to have an extra sparkle. He watched her steal a glance through the rear window.

"The gray car," Swann said.

Danica laid a hand on Swann's thigh.

"Are you sure it's a good idea for them to see you spending all this money?" Danica asked.

Her eyes were shining.

The limousine felt more deliciously extravagant for pulling over after only seven blocks. Swann alighted with Danica just beyond the entrance to the punishment post and they went into the Plaza for a bottle of champagne. They returned to their waiting ride slightly tipsy.

"Where to?" the driver asked.

Swann had been considering this question as Danica sipped and talked. She had been speaking of more troubles with her boss when Swann had been seized by a notion that struck even him as crazy. The idea had become more reasonable after he had another glass and considered how such a move would raise him in her esteem. If he was successful.

He understood that he might fall just as far if he failed, and yet that very risk gave the idea more appeal. He certainly had no thought that any part of him might want to lose her. He felt only the spirit of his adventure overtaking him once more.

"Where to?" the driver asked.

"I thought we might try that restaurant Angkor What?," Swann said.

"Jackie, I think to go there you really have to *be* somebody," Danica said.

Danica spoke as if they were both only playacting. He answered with the boldness of somebody who was pretending to be who he really was.

"Ms. Neary, are you ready to learn a little something about police work?" Swann asked.

The gray car was a half block back when the limousine pulled up to a curb in downtown Manhattan. The driver opened the door and Swann slid out behind Danica. They faced a row of four squat buildings fronted by a single colonnade. He saw no sign or awning indicating which of the four identical portals was the entrance to Angkor What?.

"I know it's one of these, but I couldn't tell you," the driver said. "I never had anybody who didn't know."

Swann assumed that the theory here was apparently the same as with the Room in Times Square: Anybody who belonged there was supposed to know where it was.

A couple approached in loose-fitting clothes of the sort worn by the younger movie stars on talk shows. They strode through the third of the four doorways as surely as if there had been a neon sign. Swann and Danica followed them into a waiting area that had palm-frond wallpaper.

A number of people stood at a small bar, while others lounged on rattan furniture that might have come from a 1930s movie. Some of the men gave Danica the usual gawks, but most who glanced over at her were apparently looking for something more particular. They did not seem to see this in her, and certainly not in Swann. They looked away as if a gust of wind had rattled the door.

Swann and Danica stayed behind the couple as they stepped up to a low podium that was very much like the maître d' stations in those same 1930s movies. The illusion ended with the maître d' himself, who wore not a dinner jacket but a billowy white dress shirt with the collar buttoned. His trousers were black and loose-fitting, though not quite baggy by the standard of Swann's old suit. He also wore white socks, and, of all things, black police shoes.

He took the couple's name and checked the log.

"Yes, for two," the maître d' said. "I'm afraid there will be at least an hour wait before something opens up."

"But it's nine now," the man said.

The maître d' seemed already to have forgotten the couple. He looked over toward the front door and he suddenly straightened. His cool gave way to a welcoming smile.

A short Hispanic woman had arrived in a gray rubber dress that fit her well-exercised torso like a wet suit. She was in no way as pretty or arousing as Danica, but she did have an aristocratic air of self-assurance. She was escorted by a man who was razor-commercial handsome and who dropped behind her as she brushed past Swann and Danica.

"I meant to call ahead," the woman said.

"Never a problem, Gabriella," the maître d' said.

Swann felt Danica's elbow prod his side.

"*You know who that is?*" Danica said. "*That's Gabriella Millar.*"

Swann nodded, having seen this woman's face in who-knew-how-many photographs. Gabriella Millar had once been married to a British rock star, thereby becoming someone whose life was documented in gossip columns and magazines and on television. She received the maître d's attention with a faint smile that suggested it was only her due.

The maître d's own smile vanished as he turned away from the booth where he had eagerly seated Gabriella Millar. He strode back and gave the couple a reproachful look for still standing there. The couple retreated to the bar.

The phone rang, and the maître d' brusquely informed the caller that the place was booked for the next two weeks. He then became abruptly solicitous.

"You should have said so. Come right in, Mr. Parker. Your table's waiting."

The maître d' hung up and turned to Swann.

"Nice to see you," Swann said. "How you been? Two for Swann, nine o'clock."

The maître d' glanced at the log.

"I don't show anything here," the maître d' said.

"It has to be there," Swann said.

The maître d' did not recheck the log, which suggested that Swann was telling a relatively common lie.

"Perhaps if you would like to wait at the bar, I'll see if something opens up," the maître d' said.

The maître d' spoke by rote, but his look was intent and he was apparently administering a standard test for this situation; if the person in question acquiesces too easily, said person is almost certainly lying and can be left at the bar until he tires and leaves. This only proved to Swann what was already obvious, that Angkor What? did not get many transit cops.

Swann had used the short trip to the restaurant to prepare himself as any experienced officer might. He had remembered in detail what had never happened, and he needed no further thought to know how a man who had actually made a reservation would act. He took half a step forward and gradually tightened his voice.

"I made a reservation for a table at nine and that is what I expect," Swann said.

The maître d' looked back at the log.

"It's going to be at least an hour," he said.

Swann discreetly pressed a $100 bill from his bankroll into the maître d's hand.

"Listen, I know it's very busy, but whatever you could do, I would appreciate," Swann said.

The maître d' seemed to have a blind newsdealer's faculty for sensing denominations through the palm. He was suddenly agreeable.

"There is a wait," he said.

The police shoes seemed not entirely inappropriate, for the maître d' said this in the same tone in which Fredricks might say, *You did see that nigger raise his hands to me.*

"I understand," Swann said.

A $100 bill was proving as much a lever here as at Brooks Brothers, and Swann felt nearly at ease as he led Danica over to the bar. They stood next to the well-groomed couple and drank glasses of champagne that tasted to him every bit as horrible as the stuff at the Oak Bar.

"*Did you really call?*"

Danica was whispering.

"Yes," he said.

Danica lowered her voice still further and asked if Swann had really been able to make a reservation.

"Yes," Swann said.

Swann said this looking directly into her eyes, and she seemed thrilled that he showed no sign he was telling anything but the truth.

"What does this all have to do with police work?" Danica asked.

Swann felt himself brim with all she did not know. He had often felt this way with Ellen, but he had never told her even as much as he now told Danica.

"Nothing," Swann said.

Danica giggled.

"You're terrible," Danica said.

"Is that a compliment?" Swann asked.

Danica set her gaze as even as his own.

"No," she said.

"Swann," the maître d' said.

Swann went over with Danica, and the maître d' began to lead them toward the jam of small tables off to the left. Swann stopped beside the booth just beyond the one occupied by Gabriella Millar.

"This would be fine," Swann said.

The maître d' was being roughly half as agreeable as he had been with Gabriella Millar, which suggested that full benefits of celebrity were here worth about $200. Swann tested this calculation with a second bill.

"That shouldn't be a problem," the maître d' said.

He set two menus on the table. Swann settled opposite Danica and casually surveyed the room. The people at the more remote tables were looking at his booth as if they were trying to figure out who this couple *was*.

Swann then saw a woman with lavender highlights in her short blond hair cross the room. She was wearing a black miniskirt and sheer black stockings, and more than looks she had a *look*. She did not seem to be really a waitress even as she stopped before Gabriella Millar's table and took a drink order.

"San Pellegrino," Gabriella Millar said. "Large bottle."

The waitress went over to the bar and then approached Swann's table.

"A large San Pellegrino," Swann said.

"I might as well try some of that, too," Danica said.

* * *

The waitress left without doing anything so waitressy as write down the order.

"I didn't know this was a wink's," Danica said.

Danica had unrolled her napkin and found a pair of chopsticks. One thing the maître d' and the lavender blond definitely were not was Chinese, and Swann sought some explanation in the menu. He found himself quite beyond his experience with restaurants, which was limited to diners and Chinese take-out.

Swann sought guidance by eavesdropping on what Gabriella Millar ordered, but she only asked for "the usual." He would have been unable to determine even the national origin of the offerings had Danica not queried the Oriental busboy who came up with a large green bottle.

"Excuse me, is this Chinese food or something?" Danica asked.

Danica could not quite make out the busboy's reply.

"*Come here?*" Danica said.

"*Khmer,*" the busboy said. "Cambodia."

"Oh, I think my husband might have went there when he was in Vietnam," Danica said.

The busboy gave Swann an empty look. She corrected the misapprehension.

"But, I mean we're separated," Danica said.

The busboy poured not just a splash for Swann to taste, but two whole glasses. Danica ventured a sip and exclaimed aloud. Swann reached for his own glass, prepared for a taste no less unpleasant than champagne.

What happened was a little like the reverse of the miracle of the club soda. The stuff whose elegant label identified it as San Pellegrino was a few weak bubbles from what might sputter from his kitchen tap in Queens.

"Yes," Swann said. "That's exactly what it is. Water."

The waitress reappeared to take their order, and Danica told Swann to choose for her. He, in turn, avoided trying to pronounce the names by pointing. He discovered that the very occidental waitress had her own way around the Cambodian words.

"A number three, and a number twenty-five," the waitress said.

"And a fork, please," Swann said.

* * *

The Oriental busboy carried up a tray. Danica's expression dimmed when his small, scarred hand placed before her a mound of what looked like raw red meat. This, he said, was *Nhom Lor Hong,* salad of sliced beef.

Swann got his fork, as well as a plate on which a large green leaf was folded into an envelope. He pried it open, and a puff of steam curled up. He saw a pool of pale liquid and a whitish square of *Amok Cabo Gien,* filet of fish in coconut milk.

Swann had not tried a new dish since the Belgian waffles at the 1964 World's Fair, and he had not encountered a completely novel taste of any kind since the night he and Ellen first attempted oral sex. He now cautiously took a fleck of the fish between his lips.

An odd, slightly sweet, faintly tangy, and completely marvelous flavor seeped through Swann's mouth. He looked across at Danica as she ventured to try a tendril of the raw beef.

"*Mmmmmm,*" Danica said. "How's yours?"

"Terrible," Swann said.

Danica laughed and Swann took another bite of fish, truly enjoying food for the first time since the shooting. He was about to suggest that Danica try some when he saw her freeze, a tendril of meat pinched between her chopsticks.

"Oh God, oh God, oh God," she said.

Swann turned to see what had caused Danica to name the power to which he had appealed while wrestling with a gun. He saw a man he had seen somewhere before and whose voice was oddly familiar.

"Hello, Gabriella, nice to see you again," the man was saying.

Gabriella Millar's tone was suddenly less detached.

"Oh, *Ron,* how are you?" Gabriella Millar said.

Swann realized that the man was Ron Parker, the television actor who played Dewy London, man-with-a-badge extraordinaire. London drove a supercharged Ferrari and killed three or four bad guys a week with a silver .45 automatic he kept under the jacket of his ultrachic suit. He never had to sign out or sit in ECAB. He was, in fact, the least cave of cops.

Ron Parker followed the maître d' past Swann's table to the next booth. He proved to be duck-footed and much shorter than he appeared on television. He did have a redhead at his side who was almost surely a model, of the same breed as the one in the Calvin Klein underwear billboard.

Indeed, the woman rivaled Danica, who was whispering again, sounding more excited than she could ever be by IAD. Or Jack Swann.

"*Oh God, forget about it, get out of here,*" Danica said. "*Wait'll I tell William.*"

She raised her chopsticks, but then lowered them.

"I was just thinking that I can't tell William. My mother asked me where I was going tonight and I told her to the movies with my girlfriend."

Danica popped the tendril into her mouth but seemed not even aware she was chewing.

"What's he doing?" she asked.

Swann looked past Danica to Parker, who was sitting with the detached air of someone on post. Swann could not escape a certain fascination in seeing this image of the air become blood and bone and skin.

"He's picking his nose," Swann said.

Danica tucked her hair behind her ear, at the same time turning her head and snatching a glimpse in a way IAD might have done well to study. Her eyes flashed back to Swann and she giggled at his fib.

He dipped his fork into the open leaf and held out a piece of the moist and tender fish. She offered him a sliver of meat that proved to have a flavor that was not quite citric and not quite peppery and not quite anything else he knew.

"Nice to see you, Ron."

Gabriella had risen behind Swann and she was calling over his table.

"Maybe we'll see you later at Eleanor's," Ron Parker said.

Swann remembered from his ECAB reading that this was *the* spot where people of the financial pages mixed with actors and such.

"I don't know, I think I have something to do tomorrow," Gabriella Millar said.

When the busboy came up to clear the table, Danica was nibbling on a shred of lettuce garnish.

"*Oooh,*" Danica said. "Crisp."

The busboy took up the plates.

"Your food is really quite terrific, you know," Danica said.

"Thank you," he said.

"Oh, you're welcome," Danica said.

The busboy went off.

"If you ever have dead lettuce, okay, like the lettuce is dead . . ."

Swann only wished that Ron Parker was eavesdropping.

". . . what you do is put it in a bowl with some cold water and some ice cubes in it and you put it in the refrigerator an hour or whatever and it'll be crisp as anything. And I'm not lying."

The check showed that dinner at Angkor What? came to only about five times as much as at a diner, water included, bribes aside. Swann was rising with Danica when the busboy stopped before Parker's booth with a tray. The busboy called out Parker's order, drawing out the word, which did not come easily to his tongue.

"Hamburger."

Danica was once more whispering as they started toward the door.

"*Why would he ask for that here?*" she asked.

The answer came to Swann instantly.

"Because he can," Swann said.

Swann was accustomed to encountering all sorts of weather shifts on returning from the underground to the street, so he was not surprised to see a heavy rain had begun to fall since they had passed through the unmarked portal. He and Danica dashed to the limousine, and they landed in the back more breathless than might be expected from their sprint.

"Where to?" the driver asked.

Danica turned to Swann. She was all the more beautiful for the rainwater beading on her face.

"Eleanor's," Swann said.

On a dark block of Fourteenth Street, Swann peered from the limousine to see a crowd of maybe seventy people standing in the downpour. Most such assemblies of his experience were drawn by the sight of somebody in trouble, but he saw no bleeding figures or young men in handcuffs, no yellow crime scene tape. He saw instead a rectangle of black velvet ropes of the sort he had seen in banks and at movie theaters. These particular ropes blocked off a doorway that was painted black and was, of course, unmarked by any sign or awning.

The driver said that the place had something called a door policy and that not everybody could gain admittance. A suggestion of how he measured Swann and Danica's chances came when he handed them an umbrella.

The gray unmarked car was parked across the street, and the IAD men no doubt enjoyed the sight of Swann huddling with Danica at the edge of the crowd, the rain drumming on the umbrella. Several people were calling to a tall young man who stood in the shelter of the doorway beyond the ropes. He was wearing a long white scarf, a black overcoat, a black beret and, of course, black police shoes.

"Jonathan."

"Can I talk to you a minute?"

"Jonathan. Jonathan."

"My sister's in there. She has my keys."

The young man did not appear even to hear the supplications. He scanned the crowd, not making eye contact, not overtly spurning anybody. He simply ignored them, which kept them standing there, their very rejection making it seem as if deliverance lay in getting through the black velvet ropes.

"Over here, Jonathan."

"Jonathan, please."

"Can I just go in and peek? I came all the way from Florida."

"Jonathan."

Danica gazed at Swann expectantly, as if a man who could get a table at a hot restaurant must surely be able to get into a hot nightclub. He looked over to see two men and a woman stride ropeward with the same sureness with which cops cause crowds to part.

"How are you tonight?" Jonathan asked.

"Good," one of the men said.

Jonathan unhooked the rope to allow the trio through. The unchosen continued to cry out as he returned to the doorway.

"Jonathan! I'm Michael Jackson's lawyer!"

"I'm Michael Jackson's mother!"

"Quiet!" Jonathan said.

The supplications immediately ceased.

"Take one step back," Jonathan said.

The whole dripping mass obeyed, so that Swann and Danica were no longer standing at the edge. Swann had a choice of either complying with Jonathan's command or standing amid the crowd, both of which would have been unacceptable even if IAD had not been watching. He strode ropeward, as unequivocally as he would at a crime scene.

As with the two men and the woman, Jonathan gave no sign of seeing Swann and Danica until the last instant. As with the others, he stepped over and reached for the rope. Unlike with the others, he left the rope hooked. He smiled as he spoke to Swann.

"It's just you, right?" Jonathan said.

"No, it's two," Swann said.

Jonathan paused as if he were waiting for Swann to understand what he had really said.

"It's very crowded right now," Jonathan said. "I'll see what I can do."

The price of celebrity treatment at Angkor What? had been $200. Swann dug into his pocket only to see Jonathan turn away and unhook the rope on the other side. Four young black men sauntered through in street attire that was complete with gold chains and oversized nameplates.

"I thought he said it was too crowded," Danica said.

Swann could only conclude that Danica's outfit spoke too much of Queens. He saw no chance of getting Jonathan's attention again, and his hand went from his pocket to her elbow. He moved to lead her away.

"No," Danica said. "Let's just watch for a while."

Danica glanced across the street at the gray car. Swann understood that having somebody looking on made the situation all the more unnerving for her. He took no joy in seeing how stunned she was to be disregarded like some fatso.

Swan guessed there was a quota for black males; Jonathan ignored several who were attired much like the four he had let in. Black remained the predominant color of the clothes worn by a succession of Caucasians who were admitted.

"What is it with this place?" Danica asked. "This is ridiculous."

"You're right," Swann said. "It is ridiculous. Let's go."

Swann took Danica's hand, but she yanked it away and stood with her red dress garish for all the fashionable black.

"Where?" Danica asked.

Danica's pointed tone suggested that Swann might have won the gamble at Angkor What? only to lose it here. He was reprieved at least for the moment by a commotion at the curb. A murmur rose from the crowd and photographers began firing off flashes.

None other than Ron Parker passed through the ropes shouting obscenities at the photographers. That appeared to be the behavior they wanted and they seemed thrilled when he threw a punch. No matter that such a right hand would have drawn laughs in the last car of the subway. He went through the unmarked doorway very much the tough guy.

"If you think about it, you can see how Elvis isn't dead," Danica said.

Swann could offer no reply. He looked over at the gray car and saw that not all the cameras were pointed at Ron Parker. The IAD man on the driver's side was wielding a telephoto lens to record what Lieutenant Gentile would no doubt take as a victory.

"I mean, I'm not saying I really believe Elvis is alive or anything," Danica said. "I'm just saying I can comprehend him wanting to be dead for a couple of years. You know, to like have a little bit of life without going everywhere and having people go crazy over him."

Swann decided to test just how well he had represented the fatsos of the world that night in the park.

"It's getting late," Swann said.

Danica looked at Swann and then made a show of checking her broken counterfeit Rolex.

"My goodness," Danica said.

Eight

THE RAIN ruled out the thicket, but the entrance to the Plaza was marked in big gold letters for all to see.

"You know, I have work tomorrow and I don't have any clothes," Danica said.

"We don't have to stay," Swann said.

"You mean just check in and like do whatever and leave?"

"We could head for Queens now if you'd rather."

She breathed in deeply and sighed.

"I'm starting to feel achy. Like I might have to call in sick tomorrow."

"Really?" he asked.

"Yes."

Swann needed neither lie nor bribe to secure a room. The desk clerk did ask for identification and seemed to do his best not to appear surprised when Swann produced his badge. Swann looked like anything but a cop, but was a cop, but had more money than any cop should have and therefore was probably not just any cop, but was still just a cop.

"I was hoping for a room high up and overlooking the park," Swann said.

Swann parted the yellow drapes and peered down a dozen stories from one of the windows that had shone so bright and remote the night they had ridden through the park. The street and the trees and meadows and pathways now all lay in wet darkness at his feet.

"Are they there?" Danica asked.

Swann saw the gray car at the curb below.

"Yes," Swann said.

Swann turned from the window. Danica stood incandescent in this place removed from the street by $450, plus tax.

"What's going to happen with them?" Danica asked.

She came close.

"They'll follow me until they decide they're not getting anything . . ."

He brought her closer.

". . . then they'll call me in."

He nuzzled her neck.

"Then what?"

"They'll ask me where I got the money."

She raised her chin and he kissed her arched throat.

"And?"

"And I'll tell them the truth."

He brushed her hair back from her forehead and ran his fingertips down the plane of her cheek. He felt the stirring that had told him down in the park what was truly important.

"I'll tell them I borrowed it."

He closed his eyes as he kissed her, but the image of her seemed to stay before him. He was slow to pull away. Their mouths were just parting when she spoke.

"What if they check?"

The tip of her tongue flicked his lips.

"They'll see I borrowed it."

She laughed as she had at the bar at Angkor What? when he said he had made a reservation.

"I really did," he said.

"You *are* terrible," she said.

"No, really, really."

"I'm sure you did."

She giggled and her hand fumbled at his waist. He felt a tug as she unhitched his belt from any notch at all. She was reaching into his Jockey shorts when his revolver slid down his pant leg.

"Ooops," she said.

Her fingers closed around him and the weapon clunked against his ankle and this was the very moment a knock came at the door.

* * *

The bellhop was opening the champagne when he spied the revolver Swann had placed on the bedside table. He glanced up at Swann and then acted as if he had seen nothing at all.

"I'm a police officer," Swann said.

Swann put his handcuffs beside the revolver. The bellhop did a reasonable job of pretending he went to $450 rooms to open bottles of Dom Perignon for cops all the time. He left with a $20 tip.

"Champagne?" Swann asked.

Danica had been staring at the instrument with which he had killed Daryl Coombs and thereby first drawn her attention. She took a glass and sat on the end of the bigger-than-king-size bed. He sat in the armchair to the side.

"I can understand," Danica said. "About the money."

Danica's gaze shifted to the huge gilded mirror on the opposite wall. The glass showed her sitting on the oversized bed in this room with creamy white walls and thick rose carpet.

"You know, the other night I was thinking and I thought, 'I don't know, I feel like I want a lot of things,'" Danica said. "Not that I'm a greedy person. I guess I just feel like I'm getting older and I want nicer things. I guess you get like that. I can make ends meet, but I can't always have extras, you know? I go to Duane Reade or whatever and get my shampoos and Q-tips and tissues, things like that, necessities. I have to have those things and they add up and I don't like going to the store and saying, 'Gee, should I get this now?' I don't like that feeling of not being able to get something, you know what I mean?"

Danica's eyes went to the mirror. She absently patted her hair.

"I'm talking too much, right?" Danica asked.

Swann responded as he might to a district attorney or a sergeant or, for that matter, Ellen.

"No, not at all," Swann said.

"Anyway, what was I saying?" Danica asked.

Swann went blank for a moment. Then it came to him.

"Wanting things," Swann said.

"Right."

Danica's eyes returned to the mirror. She again patted her hair.

"You know, the other night I'm putting William in bed and I start thinking that Christmas is not that far away and that I don't want to have happen this year what happened last year, which was that I was going nuts with that damn Ghostbusters car and I couldn't find it anywhere and I felt sick Christmas morning when he didn't have it to open."

Swann nodded, deliberately listening lest Danica think he was not.

"Anyway, I tell William, 'I know it's not even Thanksgiving, but what do you want from Santa this year?' And he says, 'There isn't a Santa.' It turns out he got that from some kid at school, so I told him, 'Well, so and so doesn't know what he's talking about.' I just hope he believes me, because that is the best part of their life. See, when you believe in Santa Claus, you think so long as you're good, he's gonna come to your house, and if you don't get exactly what you wanted, it's just because he decided to give you something else. After you don't believe in Santa Claus, it means that your father couldn't afford it or your mother didn't want to spend the money or something like that. Everything starts being who your parents are or where you come from and how one kid can get it and you can't. And then all you do is *want, want, want.*"

Swann now had to make no effort to listen. He raised his glass.

"Here's to Santa Claus," Swann said.

Ching. The champagne left a wet crescent on Danica's upper lip. Swann kissed her and fell onto the bed with this woman whom every man alive was supposed to be want, want, wanting.

"Shouldn't we take our clothes off?" she asked.

He could only agree, and here he was able to undress without having to stash his bankroll in his shoes. He did come to the matter of his holey Jockey shorts, a problem he solved by whipping them off at the same time as his trousers.

He stood before her and he could not help but note that she was less mesmerized by his whatever-you-call-it than she had been by the revolver that was supposed to be but a symbol. He did not figure on becoming any more spellbinding as he prepared to put on a condom.

"I already have something," she said.

He should not have been amazed that she had planned on being intimate with him. He was.

One.

Two.

Three.

Four.

The secret count once more enabled Swann to champion all past and present fatsos. They had lain silent for a long while when she spoke.

"You know, I can't believe you did that," she said.

He had a panicked moment, but he could think of nothing he had just done that was more exotic than what had transpired before in the thicket. He decided she must be speaking of the cash, and he prepared to tell her the whole story of the Money Store, just as he had told Coleman.

"We're sitting there with Ron Parker and you say, 'He's picking his nose,'" she said.

He continued to lie silent. She sat up and reached for her champagne.

"You know who I used to really like?" she asked. "Bruce Springsteen. Did I have a crush on him! I used to say, 'Oh, if I ever saw him on the street, I'd lay a lip lock on him. Oh, forget about it.'"

Danica rose and took her glass to the window. She peered down at the street as he gazed upon the backside he had so often admired after she had passed him by.

"One of them's getting out of the car," Danica said.

Swann picked up his own glass as he came over. An IAD man was crossing the street toward the Plaza's entrance.

"He's gonna see if we're in the Oak Bar," Swann said.

"Then what?" Danica asked.

"He might check the front desk. And they'll tell him we're up here. And he'll go back to sitting down there."

The man had disappeared from view, but Swann and Danica remained at the window, their eyes on the street.

"So what about you, you ever have a crush on anybody when you were younger?" Danica asked. "Cher, something like that? Bo Derek, maybe?"

Danica dipped her head to take a sip of champagne. Her hair fell forward and shrouded her face.

"You," Swann said.

Danica shook back her hair.

"I mean like a celebrity," she said.

"Three times the Blessed Virgin," Swann said.

"You *remember* that?"

"Three times beast of the manger."

Danica looked at Swann as if she were trying to picture him with a papier-mâché head and hemp tail. He dropped his gaze to the street and chanced to see the IAD man returning to the gray car.

"He's coming back," Swann said.

Danica was watching with Swann as the IAD man stopped at the opposite curb. The front desk man must have given him the room number, for he turned to gaze upward, no doubt counting the stories, one, two, three, four.

"Can he see us?" Danica asked.

The IAD man was not likely to know which window on the twelfth floor was theirs, though he still might be able to spot them. Reason dictated that he would be able to distinguish their small figures just as they could see his.

"Maybe," Swann said.

"Here," Danica said.

She held out her champagne for him to take. He stood with a glass in each hand, feeling her tongue swirl in his navel, steeling his knees as she descended further. He peered with half-closed eyes over her head to see the IAD man climb back into the gray car. The man must not have spotted them, for this was one time he most definitely would have been looking like he was looking.

Swann himself contemplated the sight of Danica Cowan Neary licking him like a lollipop. All the tenets of being male said he was living what should be his greatest fantasy. He brought the two glasses together.

Ching.

Swann and Danica soon had better reason than most guests to appreciate the cushiony thickness of the carpet. He progressed kiss by kiss up her inner thighs with the aim of doing for her as she had for him. He caught the scent he had been so careful to scrub away after their first joining.

"You might taste something," Danica said.

Swann extended his tongue and he did indeed taste something, in particular what seemed to be the very spermicide that Ellen sometimes used. Danica's thighs closed around his ears, and he heard only the coursing of his own blood as he tongued the bud-numbing stuff. He was lost in the familiar when she unclamped her legs and reached for the bedside table.

She held out the handcuffs that had been on the wrists of big, bad men and had not so very long before restrained the final thrashing of the dying Daryl Coombs. He was, it seemed, looking at the flushed face of somebody who actually wanted to be handcuffed and that same *crrrrick* came as he closed a bracelet around one of her slender wrists. He reached for the other, but she grunted and held up her hand for him to stop.

Swann immediately complied and wondered if he had misjudged everything, if this was not what she wanted at all, if now she really was saying he had gone too far. He watched her mouth open and he waited for her to begin by calling him some sort of weird sicko. He would apologize, but what would he say then, that he thought *she* was some sort of weird sicko?

Instead, Danica extended her tongue and the polished nails of her free hand picked something off the downturned tip. She held up a black pubic hair pinched between thumb and forefinger and then cast it away. She held out a second slender wrist for shackling.

Swann ended by reaching to the night table for his key ring. He flipped aside his house key and used the tiny silver one to free her wrists. Danica sat up, and this seemed to be a moment when he should say something.

"You're so beautiful," Swann said.

Danica gave Swann a polite smile that she was no doubt conditioned to give when she received this compliment. She was clearly not in the slightest need of such a phrase, but he could come up with only one other thing to say that was at all appropriate.

"I'll get the lights," Swann said.

Danica slipped into bed as Swann went over to the wall switch. He paused in darkness at the window and saw that the gray car was still there, the two men probably making at least a mortgage payment in overtime.

Swann made for the faint outline of Danica's form on the mattress. He lay beside her feeling as if he had been on some crazy amusement park ride that had climbed and plummeted and twisted and turned and bobbed and weaved and spun around and now glided back to exactly where it had started. Sperm had met spermicide and Jack Swann was in bed with Danica.

"Hadn't you better make a call or something?" Danica asked.

Swann here found that going beyond all sexual bounds made it no easier for him to discuss his family with Danica. He was grateful he had already telephoned home; whatever the two of them had just done together, he could never have made the call with her in the same room.

"I already did," Swann said.

Swann felt himself blink.

"I said I made an arrest," Swann said.

Swann was again in the realm of unintended double meaning. Danica cut her laugh short.

"I shouldn't," Danica said.

The two of them lay in silence. Swann next heard the rustle of her toes in the bedclothes.

"*Oooh,*" Danica said. "I love them. Crisp sheets."

Nine

DANICA WAS almost immediately asleep, and Swann lulled himself by listening to the faint rise and fall of her breathing. The next thing he knew, the telephone was ringing and he could not imagine who could possibly even suspect Jack Swann was staying at the Plaza. A groggy caution kept him silent after he picked up the receiver.

"Hello?" a voice said. "Hello?"

Swann did not speak.

"Mr. Swann?" the voice said. "This is your wake-up call."

Swann thanked the owner of the voice and went into the bathroom. He stepped into a gleaming porcelain tub, tore the blue-and-gold wrapping from a bar of soap, and turned big brass-and-enamel taps so elegant he might have been showering in hot San Pellegrino. He emerged from the roiling steam as he might at home, only the towel about his rosy middle bore the royal blue Plaza logo.

Swann's footsteps were dream silent on the thick carpet as he crossed to the closet. He got his first reminder that he was soon returning to the life of Jack Swann when he pulled on his holey Jockey shorts. A second reminder came when he took up his revolver.

The condoms would certainly qualify as EVIDENCE should Ellen find them, and Swann discarded both packets into the polished-brass wastepaper basket. He then pocketed his bankroll, donned his homburg and knotted his bow tie before the gilded mirror. He turned toward the bed.

Danica lay on her back, her hair spread upon a white pillow edged with the same royal blue as the logo on the towel. He heard himself quietly speak her name. She did not respond, and he leaned closer.

"Danica."

Swann set a hand on her bare shoulder, her skin soft, warm, unreal. He gave a gentle shake, but she did not stir. She remained beyond the reach of his touch or voice. He was left alone with the face and body that had set him wanting for so long without knowing anything more about her than what she looked like.

"Danica."

Swann shook her a little harder, as he might with a dozing derelict, getting much the same feeling of jostling a shell, of summoning somebody who had slipped away.

"Hey."

Danica stirred and opened her eyes. Swann watched her form suffuse with the conscious self that had not figured in his fantasies, that he was only now coming to know.

"I have to go to work," Swann said.

Danica sat up holding the top sheet to her chest, her other hand brushing crusts of sleep from the corners of her eyes.

"You're just going to leave me here?" Danica asked.

Swann apologized and bent down to kiss her.

"Don't you feel a little achy?"

"If we call in sick, a lot of times they check to see if we're home," Swann said. "In my case, they're gonna know I'm not home."

Danica asked if he could wait until she was dressed and he said he could not and that she should order room service when she wanted breakfast. His hand went into his pocket for his bankroll just as her hand reached for his fly. He heard the zipper go down and he found himself saying something that sent him farther beyond his imaginings than anything that had transpired the night before.

"No," Swann said.

Danica seemed only to be encouraged, and Swann was compelled to make a second, more emphatic refusal. She peered into his now open fly as she spoke.

"You don't look like you're so sure," Danica said.

Swann gazed down at the growing bulge of this one appendage over which he had no control. His hand closed around the other print in his trousers, the bankroll. He made what seemed to be the logical suggestion.

"Not go home?" Danica asked. "Just stay here? Tonight, too?"

She fell back onto the bed.

"Tomorrow is Saturday," she said. "But I don't even have a toothbrush."

Swann peeled $500 off the bankroll.

"What about you?" Danica asked.

"Get me a toothbrush, too."

"Don't you have to go home?"

Swann found the prospect of speaking of his wife and child even more difficult than the night before. He pushed away any thought of his family just as he had banished any thought of Danica at his dinner table.

"I can always say I made a collar."

"Again?"

"It's happened before."

"With who?"

"No. I mean really."

Danica remained dubious and Swann remained in a hurry to get to work. He offered the only quick solution.

"You mean I just stay if I want and go if I want?" Danica asked. "Do they give you the money back?"

Swann told Danica not to be concerned about such incidentals and turned to hurry out.

"Hey," Danica said. "Don't forget your thingamajigs."

Swann looked down and saw the open handcuffs that were lying where he had left them the night before. He quickly retrieved them and mumbled a farewell, this being the first time he had been rendered sheepish by an item of standard police equipment.

In the lobby, Swann counted out another $450, plus tax, for the coming night. The nervousness of the day clerk suggested that he must have heard about the guest who was not only a cop but had cops asking about him.

The sky had cleared and the air was fresh and Swann dashed along rain-washed Central Park South, dodging puddles, the daytime IAD men trailing behind. The two remained in the passageway as he entered to see Marie at her usual spot just inside the door.

"You fly open," Marie said.

Swann had no time for jokes, and he strode on into the anti-crime room just as roll call was about to begin. Coleman was there in matching pink leather pants and jacket. She raised an eyebrow and he had the irrational thought that she somehow knew he was coming not from home but from the Plaza.

"What are you, *ready?*" Coleman asked.

Swann followed Coleman's gaze and saw that his fly was indeed open, exactly where Danica had left it.

Swann stood twelve stories and one dim and dingy mezzanine beneath the room where he had lain with Danica. He decided she had likely bathed and he pictured her now standing at the window directly above him, the morning sun on her face, a plush towel wrapped around her middle, her toes bare and untanned on the carpet. He was not sure what she would decide, but he did know her well enough to give silent thanks that he had not told her exactly where he was posted. She would have come to see him, and he did not want to face Coleman after having his goom breeze by to say whether or not she intended to spend another night at the Plaza.

As it was, Coleman seemed almost to have accepted that he was bound to be like his fellow officers in at least one regard. Mealtime again as always sent them to the subway soda fountain, the IAD men on this occasion pretending to browse at a newsstand. She ate only half her hot dog, and he inquired if she was feeling all right.

"It's probably just the surveillance," Coleman said.

Swann and Coleman were beginning their after-meal stroll when they fell in behind a passing posse. Mannering happened to be patrolling the mezzanine, and any hard feelings he may still have harbored did not keep the amusement from his eyes on seeing a posse trailed by two cops who were, in turn, trailed by IAD.

At the top step, Swann watched the posse slip off into an afternoon that proved even finer than the morning. He then returned with Coleman to the never-changing underground, flashing his shield to the token clerk as they went back through the turnstiles. They were starting across the mezzanine when he saw Mannering striding right toward them, as definite as a whole way of life, his words booming with the Voice of Command.

"HOLD IT RIGHT THERE."

Mannering brushed past, and Swann looked back to see that the IAD men had just gone through the turnstiles. They would not have wanted to show the clerk their shields with Swann around and that gave Mannering a pretext to stop them as fare-beats.

"THAT'S RIGHT. YOU TWO."

The IAD men realized that Mannering was addressing them, and one reached for a pocket, no doubt intending to show his shield.

"LET'S KEEP YOUR HANDS WHERE I CAN SEE THEM, FELLAS."

Swann became aware of what Mannering must have already heard, the rumble of an arriving train. He turned to Coleman. They had only an instant to decide whether to accept the opportunity Mannering was offering.

"So?" Swann asked.

The rumbling grew louder, as insistent and enticing as a subway noise could ever be. Mannering was Mannering, but IAD was IAD. And mischief was mischief.

"So, yo!" Coleman said.

Swann and Coleman reached the downtown platform as the train's doors were opening. They stepped aboard and waited to see if Mannering would prove able to create a sufficient delay.

The doors had just rattled shut when the IAD men came bounding down the steps. The two could only stand and try not to look as though they were looking as Swann and Coleman rode away.

"They gonna be mad now," Coleman said.

Swann could have been a youngster again, with Coleman as his best buddy, the buddy he would have liked to have when he lumbered through the woods with the plastic gunbelt cinched to his outsized waist.

"Yes, they are," Swann said.

The train braked and the spell broke. Swann and Coleman might have made a getaway, but they were still due back at their post in just a few minutes. He stepped off with her at the next station feeling once more a cave cop.

On the uptown side, Swann waited with Coleman for the train that would take him to where his shadows were almost surely waiting for him. The IAD men would know that wherever he had gone, he would have to come back to his post. They were no doubt hoping they would at least be able to report him for returning late from meal.

He felt the breath of an approaching train and with that came the thought that he should take advantage of what unshadowed minutes remained.

"So?" he asked.

He tipped his head toward the end of the platform. She eyed him, as if weighing whether she should help him push something that might already have gone too far.

"So?" she asked.

"Yo," he said.

The first cars rocketed past as Swann and Coleman neared the end of the platform. Her voice came to him through the roar.

"Are you a vic?" Coleman asked.

Swann had been spurred by a desire to hear that "Pa-a-rty" again. He became a kid once more at the thought of how IAD would react to him becoming a crime victim a second time.

His next thought was that Danica might be expecting him at the Plaza.

"You mind taking the collar?" Swann asked.

Swann now felt like just another cop with a goom.

"I would be the one being vic-ed," Swann said.

The train stopped. There it was, the last car.

"True enough," Coleman said.

The doors parted.

Swann slumped onto a bench and bowed his head as the doors shut. He sat closed-eyed in the momentary stillness, telling himself that he had a right to ride where he wanted. The money he had felt he had a right to borrow was again making an inviting print in his pocket.

A jolt signaled that the train was starting, and a principle as basic as leverage caused Swann to rock in the opposite direction as he left the station. A voice called out the all-clear and he heard shouts and laughter. Somebody to Swann's left started clapping.

Others took up the beat with their hands, feet and sputtering mouths. Swann found himself wriggling along with his toes, and he would have been almost content not to get robbed. The last car seemed the merriest, most wonderful of places right up to the instant a hand came out of the beat and slammed the plastic seat beside him.

Swann played the dozing drunk, his head down, his body limp, swaying ever so slightly with the motion of the car. He heard a laugh and then an excited voice.

"He out for the count."

The beat stopped and Swann tingled as he waited to get hit. His heart raced. His ears strained to pick up the smallest sounds. He almost jumped when another, deeper voice boomed out.

"Yo, leave that man alone."

For a few thudding heartbeats, the only sounds were those of the train. Swann heard the first voice again, the excitement giving way to bluster.

"Fuck you then, faggot."

The beat resumed and Swann concluded that the would-be robber had backed down.

When the train braked for the next stop, Swann lolled his head as if he had been roused by the jolt. He gazed blearily about like a man trying to orient himself. He took care not to make eye contact with Coleman, who was seated directly across from him, clapping her hands and tapping a foot.

The beat ceased when the darkness outside the windows gave way to the light of the Times Square station. Swann saw teenagers palm joints and stash beers and pinch off cigarettes, but he was unable to guess who was the would-be robber and who was the protector.

As the doors opened, a big, fearsome-looking young man rose from the opposite bench. He passed Swann on his way out and addressed him in the deep, booming voice.

"You should be more careful on the train."

Swann felt obliged to mumble some gratitude. He waited until his protector was on the platform before dropping his head and pretending to sink back into a stupor. His last image as he closed his eyes was of Coleman still sitting across from him, silently nodding a beat that was taken up by the whole car as the train returned to the tunnel.

Swann knew that all the serious thieves would normally have gotten off at Times Square, but the underground did not often offer a vic such as he appeared to be. He was sure he would not have to wait long before the would-be robber moved to regain some pride along with what was making that nice pocket print.

The hand that came out of the darkness this time felt no bigger than Jenny's as it shook Swann's shoulder. He heard the soft voice of a child.

"Mister."

The beat lost some of its drive and Swann heard several riders giggle. He parted his eyelids ever so slightly and saw a pair of red sneakers about the size of Coleman's.

"Mister."

Swann was ready to raise his head and chase this child away. He then heard the voice he had expected.

"That's mine."

The would-be robber now sounded indignant, as if he were citing a legitimate claim. Swann was preparing for the follow-through on this claim when he heard a third voice. The tone was low and determined and menacing.

"Step off, nigger."

The beat disintegrated into a panicked scramble. The stomping gave way to a scuffling toward the next car. The laughter and excited shouts turned to yelps of fear. Swann understood that the child was with an older friend and that the friend must have drawn a gun.

The car went into a curve, and Swann swayed with the motion, keeping his head down. He was uncertain if he should leap up and tackle whoever had the gun or wait for a cue from Coleman. He did not know which was more likely to save somebody from getting shot, which was more likely to get somebody shot. His Brooks Brothers suit sure was not bulletproof and seemed at this instant to possess all the power of a scrap of cloth.

He then felt the child's hand dig into his pocket, sure and steady in the tumult. It was slipping away when there came a gunshot of stunning loudness.

The shock must have caused the tiny hand to lose its grip on the bankroll, for bills were fluttering to the floor as Swann raised his head. The child stood before him, even smaller than the size of the red sneakers had suggested. A teenager was sprawled to the left, the arms reaching up.

Swann was looking only for the gun and he saw it in the hand of a smaller teenager to the right. Coleman was already diving for it and he leaped for it as well, his ears still ringing from the shot, hearing his own shout join the screams as his hands closed around the steel.

Swann was again wrestling with a teenager for a gun, but this time Coleman was with him. He felt her strength join his own and they wrested the gun free. She tucked the weapon in her waistband as he snapped on the cuffs, and they looked at each other across their prone prisoner, both breathing hard. He saw that her shirt and face were speckled with a fine spray of blood.

Swann's bankroll was scattered on the linoleum, now part of a crime scene and therefore not to be touched until the photographs had been taken and the detectives were done. He stepped over the strewn bills, and the ringing in his ears seemed to vibrate down into his nerve fibers as he crouched over the shot teenager. He understood that this must be the would-be robber.

The arms that had been in that last, stretching reach now lay limp. Swann saw that the bullet had punched a small, neat hole just below the left eye. A trickle of blood ran over the cheek into a large pool that leaked from the back of the head. These were not the gushing injuries of a living person. Only gravity fed this widening puddle and its floating clumps of brain tissue and shards of bone. The puddle's edges were traced by the jolting of the train no differently than if somebody had spilled a can of soda.

"That's it, you take a hard look," Coleman said.

Swann thought Coleman was talking to him, saying he was responsible. The quivering of his nerves did indeed seem to carry that very message. He looked up to say something, and he saw she had not been speaking to him. She had been addressing the child whom he had seen when he first opened his eyes.

The child now stood six feet away, looking like a fugitive from the third grade. His right cheek bulged as he chewed slowly on a huge wad of gum and gazed down at the dead teenager who must not have been willing to back down a second time. He only seemed to consider that he might have reason to flee the police when he glanced up and saw Swann looking at him.

The child's oversized sneakers slapped on the linoleum as he dashed toward the next car. Swann knew the train was nearing a stop and that might mean chasing this tiny figure into the station. He yanked a red wood handle at the end of a rope that is just inside the end doors of every car. The train stopped as if it had suddenly realized something.

Swann continued into the next car to see that the surprise jolt had caused the child to lose his footing. The child was just scrambling back up when Swann grabbed him. He stood in creased designer jeans and a white T-shirt with a huge Gucci logo across the chest and a black leather bubble coat with a brown fur collar. His cheek was back to bulging as he calmly chewed his wad of gum.

"I ain't ascared of no jakes," he said.

The child grinned, showing a gold cap on each eyetooth. Swann brought out the handcuffs that had last been on Danica. He closed them to the last ratchet only to discover that the manufacturer had not anticipated that criminals could come in such a small size. The bracelets hung loose on the child's wrists as Swann led him back.

The teenagers who had been making the beat were crowded at the door to the last car, shouldering each other to catch a glimpse of the body. Swann called for them to stand back and entered to see that Coleman had the shooter on a bench.

Swann set his prisoner next to the shooter. The child sat with his feet not quite touching the floor, his legs swinging out and back as he stared down at the dead teenager. The puddle was bigger, maybe eighteen inches across, and the jolt of the emergency brake had sent the blood fingering into the scattered money.

The conductor who entered was black, as were most of those who sold the tokens and maintained the tracks and repaired the cars and ran the trains. He had come to see who had pulled the emergency brake and to get this particular train running again. He halted when he saw the body.

His eyes then went to Swann, showing both sorrow and anger, seeming to mark at once what bound and what separated him from this teenager who lay shot to death at the end of his train.

"Can we continue into the station?" the conductor asked.

"Yes," Swann said.

The conductor ducked into the cab to reset a switch. He left the car without looking back and in a few moments the train jerked into motion. The pool of blood ran toward the rear, leaving the bills behind, stained and glistening.

Swann looked at Coleman. She had no doubt assumed the would-be robber would get the money. She must have positioned herself behind him, ready to make the collar, only to see the smaller teenager pull the gun and fire. The bullet had exited the back of the head, misting her with blood and, Swann now saw, leaving a small piece of skull in her hair.

Swann raised his hand without thinking, brushing the bit of bone from the crinkly hair of a sort he had felt only when pushing somebody's head down into the back of a radio car. He surprised himself by doing this, though not so much as he surprised her. She swatted his hand away with such sudden force that he was left wondering just how steady her steadiness was.

"You had something in your hair," Swann said.

Coleman brushed her own hair, though the bit of bone was gone.

"And you got sprayed a little bit on your face and also on your shirt."

Coleman glanced down at her shirt.

"It comes out if you soak it with something," Swann said.

Coleman looked up.

"I know," she said.

The train eased into the next station and a young woman started to board, but stopped on seeing a body sprawled before her. Her expression changed from weary to startled.

"This train isn't going anywhere for a while," Coleman said.

"I guess not," the young woman said.

The young woman paused.

"How much is that?" the young woman asked.

She was speaking of the money.

"A lot," Coleman said.

"I guess so," the young woman said.

The young woman left. Coleman next spoke to Swann.

"The shooter is definitely going as an adult. You best hope shorty here is on the up with his moms."

Coleman was alluding to one possible complication that Swan had failed to anticipate. Standard practice dictated that the arresting officer took the adults down to central booking while the partner handled any juveniles. The time involved in taking a juvenile collar was largely determined by whether a parent or guardian agreed to come to the district and assume custody. The officer otherwise had to escort his underage prisoner to the juvenile jail in the Bronx, and that usually meant waiting hours for transportation.

Swann would have liked to be able to tell Coleman that he was not someone who would worry about so incidental a thing while standing over a dead kid. The problem was, he might well have Danica waiting for him at the Plaza.

"Shit," Swann said.

"Are you supposed to be talking like that in front of me?" the child asked.

Uniformed cops, paramedics, and detectives. The routine commenced. Swann and Coleman prepared to escort their two prisoners from the scene, but nobody seemed to be sure whether they should go to the precinct or District 1. Detectives of both the cave and city persuasion conferred to decide whose turn it was to take the case, and the child started to get fidgety much the way Jenny might.

"Why we just standing here?" he asked.

"Have you been arrested before?" Swann asked.

"Never."

"*Never?*"

"I was in Family Court."

"For what?"

"Running wild."

"What else did they call it?"

"Armed robbery."

"You had a gun?"

The child tipped his head toward his friend.

"No, he had it."

A tall transit detective finally came over.

"Swann, maybe you can help us," the detective said. "That space case, with the woman. Was that the last one or the one before?"

"The last one."

"Then this one's ours. Take them to the district."

Swann lifted the crime scene tape, and he saw no significance in it being of the same color and feel as the stuff on the Brooks Brothers boxes. He crouched under with the child and Coleman followed with her prisoner and they squeezed through the citizens who were straining to see what had happened. They continued into a shoulder-to-shoulder crowd of those who had no hope of seeing anything and were simply waiting for the trains to start running again.

Swann was starting up the steps when he heard cheers, and he knew that the train must be rolling out of the station to make room for the ones waiting behind. The train would clatter on through station after station until it reached the yard, each car empty save for the last, the detectives in their suits standing over the teenager who lay dead amidst the bloodstained bills.

Swann then saw the IAD men scurrying toward the scene. Their office would have been routinely notified of any shooting where a cop was present. They seemed panicked and furious even as they continued to try not to look as though they were looking.

A silent Swann continued toward the street with a silent Coleman behind him.

At District 1, Swann searched his prisoner, his hand feeling huge in these pockets just as the child's had felt tiny in his own. The child also kept his money in the front pocket, and Swann came out with a quarter, two pennies, and a fluff of lint that he picked out before setting the coins on the front desk.

"How about something to eat?" the child asked.

Coleman's voice was hard.

"Next time, eat before you do your crime," Coleman said.

"With twenty-seven cent?" the child asked.

Coleman took the older prisoner over to the holding pen. Swann seated the child on a bench, handcuffing his right wrist to a steel ring set in the wood plank.

"How about at least some water?" the child asked.

He was grinning again and swinging his legs back and forth as he had on the subway.

"How about first we speak to your mother?" Swann asked.

The child's grin vanished and his legs stopped swinging. He said that his mother was at her job and that he knew neither her work number nor the name of the company.

"What if something happened to you?" Swann asked. "How would somebody get hold of her?"

"Something did happen to me," the child said.

Swann said he would try calling the child's home anyway and asked for the number. The child said he did not have a telephone, and Swann said he would send a radio car to the address.

"You don't believe me," the child said. "What, my mother can't work?"

The child gave no sign he was lying and in fact seemed truly offended. Swann would have been pushing the matter only because he had Danica waiting at the Plaza.

"Okay," Swann said. "We'll wait 'til she gets off work. What are the chances your mother will come get you?"

"Is there some reason why she wouldn't?" the child asked.

Swann had no reply.

"How about that water now?" the child said.

Swann filled two Styrofoam cups, giving one to the child and taking the other over to the holding cell. The shooter was lying on the bench at the back of the cell, already in the slumber of the guilty.

Swann took a sip himself, the water icy on his lips, pure on his tongue. He looked around for Coleman, but she was nowhere in sight. He watched a uniformed cop pull on latex gloves and empty a clear plastic bag containing the money onto a desk a few feet from where the child sat. The blood had turned a brownish red.

"You get the mother?"

Swann turned to see Coleman. She must have been in the women's room. Her face was shiny from scrubbing.

"Not yet," Swann said.

Swann's saw the reddish brown flecks still on her blouse.

"I better voucher this," Coleman said.

Coleman took the teenager's gun from her waistband and sat down. Swann watched her remove her shield from its leather holster and use the pin to initial the weapon.

He had only been after a little more mischief, and she had gone along, nonetheless. She had seemed as stunned as he himself was by the enormity of what had actually transpired.

She now seemed determined just to keep with the routine. She finished scratching a tiny SC just above the trigger guard, then recorded the weapon's make and serial number on a voucher form.

Swann looked over at the pile of bloody bills. The uniformed cop had begun his count. One. Two. Three. Four.

"You know, that's a lot of fucking shlamolies."

The balding city detective was at Swann's side.

"How'd you do with that case, where the woman was pushed in front of the train?" Swann asked.

The detective kept his eyes on the mounting pile of counted bills.

"I should be so lucky they all go like that," the detective said. "The DA was very happy."

"And you only got the two?" Swann asked.

"What's it matter, two or ten?" the detective said.

"Please," the uniformed cop said. "You'll fuck up my count."

The older prisoner had been taken from the holding cell to the squadroom to assist with the investigation. The uniformed cop finished the count, wrote down the total, and began a second count to make sure. Swann watched the bills pile up again, knowing that even so safe a realm as the subway had the occasional terrible crime such as the space case, but also knowing this most recent horror was of his making. He felt as if he had levered the world, but not to any place he had intended.

The uniformed cop then took out the ink pad and the rubber stamp. Swann listened to the thump and saw that the letters did not show where the bills were stained.

— VI — CE

— DE —

EV — — — E

The child gave a shout.

"I know! EVIDENCE!"

The child looked from the bills to Swann.

"When you get that back it still got that word on it?" he asked.

"I get a check," Swann said.

"Who get the money?"

"It gets destroyed when your case is done."

"They throw it away? I go to jail for it and they throw it away?"

The child spoke as if truly aggrieved. He asked for some more water and Swann held out his own cup.

"You can have this," Swann said.

"I saw you drink from it," the child said.

He scored *P* on his empty cup with his thumbnail.

"That's so you know this one's mine," the youngster said. "*P* for Pharaoh."

Pharaoh sipped from the refilled cup marked *P* and pumped his legs. His bright eyes moved about the district, stopping at the front desk.

"That man look like he sizing you," Pharaoh said.

Swann looked over to see that he was standing between a child who was on his way to jail for robbing him and the man who was leading the effort to prove he had himself stolen that same money. Lieutenant Gentile did in fact seem to be sizing him, appraising how much fear he had, waiting for him to show that fear by turning away and making himself busy.

"Excuse me," Swann said.

Swann brushed past this man who was not just some unfortunate from the Dark Side. Three more strides took him to the pay phone, from which he called directory assistance. He spoke loudly enough that Gentile could not help but overhear.

"THE PLAZA HOTEL, PLEASE."

Swan dialed the number.

"MR. SWANN'S ROOM, PLEASE."

He listened to the phone ring in the room where he had slept the night before. He now prepared to ensure that Gentile would overhear him tell the beautiful Danica that he really had no way of being sure when he would be free and that the best thing would be for her to check out and come back another night.

The phone kept ringing. Swann pictured the bed made, the big towels folded, as if he and Danica had never been there. The operator came back on to say there was no reply and to ask if he wanted to leave a message.

"Could you just say that Jack called and I'll call later."

Gentile was making for the squadroom with such obvious fury that Swann felt justified in all his adventures save this most recent one. He returned to Coleman as she slid the older prisoner's gun into a manila envelope.

A transit detective escorted the older prisoner from the squadroom back to the holding cell.

The prisoner scuffled inside and stood behind the bars seeming simply bored.

"You're fifteen and you say you got two kids, what was it, twenty months and sixteen months?" the detective said.

"And?" the prisoner said.

The detective flashed a listen-to-this look at the front desk.

"And that's not possible," the detective said. "You can't have two chiles who *bees* four months from each other."

The prisoner stared out at the detective, not looking at all bored now.

"You tell that to they mothers."

Pharaoh roared and slapped the bench with his free hand but quieted when he caught a stern look from Coleman. She gave the same look to the detective.

"Detective, if you're done now, I got some police work to do," Coleman said.

Coleman took out an on-line booking sheet and called for the older prisoner to pay attention. Swann got started on his own paperwork, and ceased to think of anything else as he recorded that he was taking into custody Pharaoh France, Jr., male, black, age ten, four feet three, sixty-five pounds. Another section inquired whom the prisoner resided with and "Relationship (Guardian/Agency, etc.)."

"Most time, my mother," Pharaoh said.

Swann noted the mother's particulars and came to the entry for the father's name, address, and business number.

"I told you, I live with my mother," Pharaoh said.

"It's just something I need for the sheet," Swann said. "Pharaoh France, Sr.?"

The youngster nodded.

"Address?" Swann asked.

"Look!" Pharaoh said.

Pharaoh extended his fingers and slipped his hand from the handcuffs.

"Very good," Swann said. "Now, please."

Pharaoh worked his hand back into the manacle. Swann completed the rest of the paperwork and all the answers fit no less than always. His watch showed that it was past five o'clock, and Swann arranged for a district in Brooklyn to send a radio car to notify Pharaoh's mother.

Swann was summoned to the squadroom. He was there directed to what he assumed was the same chair where the older prisoner had sat. An assistant district attorney introduced herself as Ms. Curry, but did not ask for Swann's name. Lieutenant Gentile sat off to the side, fiddling with his pipe.

Nobody seemed much concerned with the shooting itself and that made the details starker in the telling. Swann described hearing the shot and raising his head. He had a vivid memory of the teenager taking a last, straining reach at nothing.

"And that's it," Swann said.

Curry had been taking notes on a yellow pad. She set down her pen.

"I understand that you make it a practice to encourage such robberies," she said.

The remark came as if this was what she had been waiting to say all along.

"I make it a practice to lock up bad guys," Swann said. "That's what I do. That's what I am. I'm one of the good guys."

"What is one of the good guys doing with that much money?" Curry asked.

Swann was almost ready to give in, if only to show her that she was wrong about him. He then became aware of the wet popping of Gentile's mouth on the pipe stem.

"I do not see that it's anybody's business but my own," Swann said.

"Now that somebody is dead, don't you think that changes things somewhat?" Curry asked.

"For the dead kid it sure does."

"And, I'm afraid, for you."

Curry paused.

"Don't you think this has gone far enough?" she asked.

Curry was speaking as if Swann was toying with them. She was entirely right, but neither she nor IAD nor anyone else seemed able to fathom how he could possibly have the gall to get himself robbed a second time, for twice as much. None of them could see that he could do so only because he felt armored by the truth, because he was not a crook at all.

"If I was a Rockefeller, you wouldn't be asking me where I got my money," Swann said.

Gentile spoke for the first time.

"I have to tell you, Officer, you are not a Rockefeller."

Swann went from the squadroom to the coffee machine. Mannering had just poured himself a steaming cup.

"I guess you heard about the shooting," Swann said.

Mannering took a big slug of hot coffee that must have scalded his mouth and throat. His eyes watered.

"Jackie boy, these things happen," Mannering said.

Mannering blinked rapidly and blew across the rim of the cup. Swann poured his own, knowing he should thank Mannering for the moment of freedom, but unable to express gratitude for something that had ended in death.

"They're gonna give you a hard time," Swann said.

"Who?" Mannering asked.

"IAD."

"For what? The Patrol Guide clearly states that a member of the service should properly identify himself upon entering the system. As, I might add, did you and your partner."

Mannering hit this last word hard. His look said that IAD might be IAD, but things were still things.

"By the way . . . ," Mannering said.

Mannering's voice became unexpectedly intimate.

"... you still seeing that one I saw?"

Mannering was speaking of Danica.

"Yes," Swann said.

Mannering smiled as to a fellow swordsman.

"It's that bulge to the right," Mannering said.

Mannering was referring to the bankroll. His smile broadened.

"Jackie boy, it's too bad you got to be such an asshole at the same time," Mannering said.

A clerk summoned Swann to a departmental phone. He picked up and he had no sooner identified himself than Pharaoh's mother was shouting at him.

Swann spent a full minute calming the mother down. He proceeded to describe the circumstances of the arrest and she demanded to know why he had waited so long to notify her. He said he did not have her work number. That set her screaming again.

"What, you think everybody can get a job?" the mother asked.

Swann said he had only been going on what Pharaoh had said. The mother hushed, seemingly given pause that her son would lie about her being employed. Swann heard a car horn and understood she was calling from a pay phone.

"Put my boy on," the mother said.

Pharaoh freed himself from the handcuffs and slid off the bench. He tucked the gum in his cheek as he raised the receiver to his mouth, looking intimidated for the first time since his arrest.

"Hi..."

Swann could only guess what the mother was saying. Pharaoh's mouth twitched. His jaw clenched. His head drew back, but he kept the receiver to his ear. He spoke in a small, polite voice.

"If they hadn't arrested me, I wouldn't be here," Pharaoh said.

Pharaoh relaxed for a moment, his eyes going to Swann.

"The voice on the phone is asking her for five cent," Pharaoh said.

The mother then came back on. Whatever she said caused Pharaoh's eyes to well.

"Yes, Mama, I'll tell the officer," Pharaoh said. "But you know I ... Hello?"

Pharaoh set the receiver into the cradle.

"They disconnected her," Pharaoh said.

"What did she want you to tell me?" Swann asked.

"She say you want me so bad to arrest me, you can keep me."

Swann went to the front desk and said he would be needing transportation to Spofford, the jail for juveniles. The desk officer said that the one operational car was on a job and might not be done for several hours. Swann headed for the pay phone to make some calls of his own.

Danica picked up on the second ring.

"Hiya!"

The voice came to him as the vibration of all her magnificent parts. He was suddenly less resolved to tell her to go home.

"It's Jack."

"I kinda figured."

"I tried you earlier."

"I just got in. I was out shopping. I hope you don't mind, but I spent almost everything you gave me. It just went, you know what I mean? What time is it, anyway?"

Swann felt no urge to make jokes about it being late. He glanced at his watch and said that it was a little after 7 P.M. He told himself that this was past the time he should also call Ellen.

"You know my watch is broken," Danica said.

"Listen. I made a collar and I'm gonna be tied up for a while," Swann said.

Danica said nothing for a moment. Swann heard the television playing in the background.

"You sure you dialed the right number?" Danica asked. "Isn't that what you were supposed to tell somebody else?"

"There was a shooting," Swann said.

"Oh, no! You had another one? Are you all right?"

"I'm fine. I wasn't in it."

Swann was telling the truth, but it did not feel at all like home base.

"What happened?"

That trill of *interest* joined the hum. Swann gave a quick account, but she asked more questions and seemed to have no sense that he was less and less interested in answering them.

"Well, you got who did it," Danica said. "That's good."

Swann quickly said that his entire bankroll had been vouchered as evidence and that he was going to be busy for hours.

"Maybe we should make it another time," Swann said.

Swann could not quite believe he was telling Danica Cowan Neary that she need not wait around for him in a room at the Plaza. Neither apparently could she.

"You mean just go home?" Danica asked.

Swann inquired if Danica had enough cash left for a cab, and she said that even if she did, she was not anxious to battle with some cabbie about going to Queens. He kept himself from saying that a cabbie would likely be willing to take an unescorted Danica anywhere.

"I really don't mind waiting right here," Danica said.

Swann was searching for something to say when he heard a knocking in the background. He could not at first tell if it was actual or simply on the television.

"I gotta go," Danica said. "That's them."

"Who?"

"The room service. This morning, I did what you said and called and asked for some coffee, and when the guy came I gave him one of those hundreds. But he didn't have change, so he said I could just sign. So when I got back, I was a little hungry and they had this menu here, so I called them."

The knocking came again. Danica lowered her voice.

"I've been writing 'Danica Swann,' because I didn't know if we were supposed to be married, or what," Danica said.

Danica dropped her voice still lower as she asked how he was going to be able to pay the bill. Swann said he would be reimbursed the next morning.

"Then everything's fine," Danica said.

* * *

Danica got off and Swann stood there.

"You done?"

Swann saw that another cop was waiting to use the phone, likely for a goom call of his own.

"One minute," Swann said.

Swann reached into his pocket only to discover he had used his last quarter. He had only three nickels, and he had an idea how the cop would respond to Jack Swann of the famous bankroll asking to borrow a dime.

"You better go ahead," Swann said.

A paddy wagon had just arrived for the adults and Coleman was taking the older prisoner from the holding cell. He called to Pharaoh, voicing his first concern since his arrest for homicide.

"I hope my cousin don't sleep in my bed while I'm gone."

Swann asked Coleman if she had a dime so he could call home. Her prisoner again called to Pharaoh.

"You hear that? All that money and he need ten cent."

Pharaoh replied as if defending Swann.

"That's all right. He get a check for thousands."

Pharaoh called to Swann.

"Right?"

"Right," Swann said.

Coleman held out a quarter.

"I figure you're good for it," Coleman said.

Swann took the coin, his gaze going from the reddish brown flecks on her blouse to her scrubbed face and eyes that still seemed determined just to keep going.

"Catch you later," Coleman said.

A manacled arm in one hand, the paperwork in the other, Coleman set off for court. Swann went with his quarter to the pay phone and called Ellen to say he had made a collar. He did not tell her about this second shooting and he told himself it was because he did not want her to worry.

"You better say good night to Jenny," Ellen said.

Jenny came on the line sounding as happy as if all was right with the world.

"Hi, Daddy."

"Hi, sweetie."

Swann coursed with feelings that he pushed away when he was with Danica, that he now fought to keep from his voice.

"Shouldn't you be in bed now?" Swann asked.

"Mommy was just reading to me. Are you coming home?"

"Not tonight."

"Good night, Daddy."

"Night, night."

Pharaoh was yawning by the time the radio car was free, and he rode in the back beside Swann, drooping toward a sleep as innocent as might overcome Jenny at the end of an exciting day. They soon came to the corner of the streets named Tiffany and Casanova and the white brick Spofford Detention Center.

Pharaoh woke at the rattle of the chain-link gate. He climbed out with Swann, and the only sound as they crossed the main yard was the hum of the high-intensity lights that glinted off the razor ribbon. The hot glare made the youngster's face hard.

In the reception area, Pharaoh observed decorum and allowed Swann to employ a key in removing the handcuffs. A guard wearing latex gloves seemed to forget all else on seeing Swann in his homburg and bow tie.

"I'm with transit," Swann said.

A city cop had just brought in two older youngsters, and they did not have to be told to strip off their gold jewelry and leather coats and designer jeans and name-brand sneakers and tube socks and nylon underwear. The youngsters then stood with only their postures, and Swann watched them exaggerate the square of their shoulders and the tilt of their heads, clearly doing all they could to maintain their sullen hardness, to will themselves into more stony stuff than pubescent flesh.

"Welcome home," the guard said.

Pharaoh had only removed his sneakers, and the guard grumbled for him to hurry. Pharaoh grinned.

"And get rid of that gum," the guard said.

Pharaoh's grin vanished and he dropped the gum in the trash bin. He pulled a sock off his right foot only to reveal another. He removed this second sock and there proved to be a third and he kept going until five pairs lay in a mound before him. He hung his head and his bare toes curled on the concrete floor. His words were barely audible.

"I ain't really ten," Pharaoh said. "I'm eight."

The guard stopped laughing. Children under ten could not legally be lodged at Spofford.

"So, you decided that maybe being locked up ain't so great?" the guard asked.

Pharaoh did not answer, and the guard turned to Swann.

"I can always tell when these little motherfuckers are lying," the second guard said.

Pharaoh raised his head.

"I'll let you call me that," Pharaoh said.

The guard ignored Pharaoh.

"I just can't always tell what they're lying *about,*" the guard said. "Maybe he's eight and he said he was ten and now he's scared and he's sayin' he's eight. Or maybe he's really ten and he said he was ten and now he's scared and he's sayin' he's eight."

Pharaoh spoke in the same tone as when he had been arrested.

"I ain't ascared of nothin'," Pharaoh said.

Pharaoh rattled off the phone number of a neighbor who was sometimes willing to fetch his mother and put her on the line. The guard went into a side office. Pharaoh turned to Swann.

"I had orange Ballys, but they got too small," Pharaoh said. "These Adidas, they my brother's."

He smiled.

"I get paid, I'm gettin' new Ballys," Pharaoh said. "Sky blue. Seventy-eight fifty. Plus tax."

Swann had yet to find the proper tone to employ as arresting officer of somebody four feet three. He tried speaking something like a guidance counselor.

"Well, it's nice to have goals."

"Yeah, I got that."

Pharaoh ran an index finger from one gold-capped eyetooth to the other.

"And I'm going to get it straight across," Pharaoh said. "Eighteen carat. Little niggers got gold in they mouth, you know they be getting *money.*"

"Not *gold,*" Swann said. "I said '*goals.*'"

"I just want to be rich like you," Pharaoh said.

Swann could think of nothing he could say.

"If I be out for Easter, I be looking *fly*," Pharaoh said.

Pharaoh himself now spoke not unlike a guidance counselor.

"Girls see you with fresh clothes, with jewelry, they be on you," Pharaoh said. "They give up they body."

"What do you know about that?" Swann asked.

Pharaoh turned solemn.

"I know you got to take a shower with them first and make sure they clean," Pharaoh said.

The guard came out of the side office.

"The mother says, 'What's it matter how old he is?'" the guard said. "And I tell her if he's not at least ten, we can't keep him. She says, 'Then he's ten,' and she hangs up."

Pharaoh took off the leather bubble coat and the T-shirt with the Gucci logo and the Calvin Klein jeans and red nylon underwear.

"Don't you lose my Gucci shirt," Pharaoh said.

That and the rest of Pharaoh's outer garments went into a paper bag marked with his name.

"P-h-a-r-*a*-*o*," Pharaoh said. "Not *o*-*a*."

"Don't sweat it, little man," the guard said. "We know who you are."

The guard handed each of the prisoners a worn blue bathrobe and discount-store sneakers without laces and Jockey shorts of the type Swann wore. Pharaoh went off to the cells with his arms filling only half the sleeves and the bottom breaking in folds at his feet.

The two nighttime IAD men were waiting in the passageway on Swann's return to District 1. He left them outside the Plaza and ascended in the elevator to the hushed corridor twelve plus one stories above his post. He rapped lightly with a single knuckle on the door to room 1211. No answer came, and the possibility that Danica had gone home brought nearly equal measures of regret and relief. He then heard the murmur of the television and he knocked again, with four knuckles now, but still restrained. He received no reply and he surmised that Danica must be asleep.

Swann returned with a key he obtained at the front desk, saying he did not want to awaken his "wife." He entered to find the lights on and the television playing. Danica was sleeping atop a remade bed, wearing only a towel like the one he had wrapped about his middle that morning.

Swann went to place his revolver on the bedside table and saw the tray that room service must have brought. She had ordered a hamburger and had left it half eaten, scalloped by her last bites.

Danica slept on. Swann hit the power knob on the television and crossed to the window. He could see the IAD men standing across the street, their hands dug into their raincoat pockets. He set his fingertips against the pane. The glass was cold.

"It's you."

Danica had awakened. She sat up, squinting.

"Hi," Swann said.

"Are they down there?" Danica asked.

"Yes."

Danica raised her hand to cover a yawn.

"I was going to surprise you," Danica said. "But I fell asleep."

Swann surmised that she had planned to greet him naked at the door.

"There wasn't much I could do," Swann said.

"What time is it?" Danica asked.

Swann knew Danica was not being suggestive. He checked his watch and said it was 5:05 A.M. She swung her legs off the bed, reflexively holding the towel to her breast with one hand while the other tugged it down lower on her thigh.

"I'll be right back," Danica said.

The sound of Danica brushing her teeth came from the bathroom as Swann emptied his pockets. He had no bankroll but he did have his handcuffs and shield. He put these beside his revolver along with the paperwork he was to take to Family Court after the weekend.

Danica was done with her toothbrush and Swann was puzzled to hear the light clicking on and off several times. She emerged without the towel but he did not mistake this as a belated surprise. She was simply going to bed.

"I guess you probably don't feel like talking about it," Danica said.

Swann knew that she wanted him to talk about the shooting.

"No, I don't," Swann said.

"I can understand," Danica said.

Her eyes stayed on him. He stood silent.

"If you want to brush your teeth, yours is the blue one," Danica said.

Swann removed the blue toothbrush from its package and reached for a toothpaste tube that had a single neat fold at the bottom that Ellen would respect. Swann made a fold of his own, brushed as always, and set the blue toothbrush next to the pink one Danica had bought. He could have been home until he flicked off the bathroom light. The toothbrushes glowed in the dark.

Swann returned to the room to see that Danica had taken the same side of the bed as the night before. He turned off the lights before he undressed, even in darkness removing his Jockey shorts along with his trousers.

"Notice something about the toothbrush?" Danica asked.

"Yes," Swann said.

"I thought you might get a laugh out of it."

He slid into the newly crisp sheets opposite her, on the side of the bed that would have been Ellen's side at home.

"It really is late," Danica said. "I'm sorry, but I think I just have to go to sleep."

He was himself exhausted, in no condition to represent even a lone cave cop.

"Do," Swann said.

She rolled toward him and gave him what felt exactly like a goodnight kiss. He lay with the taste of the toothpaste in his mouth, and he had a familiar sense of being intensely present and yet not completely there.

The wake-up call seemed to come much too early, and Swann did not so much regret rising from that particular bed as from any bed at all. He headed for the bathroom feeling only fatigue, and made another neat fold at the bottom of the toothpaste tube. He dressed and took up his things from the bedside table.

Danica had also been awakened by the telephone, and she gazed at him with drooping eyes as he told her to call room service when she got hungry. He would pay for it after he was reimbursed.

"It's funny, really," Danica said. "Them having to give it back to you."

Danica's words carried the implicit assumption *when you stole it in the first place.* Swann said only that he would be back as soon as possible.

"I'm not saying it was your fault yesterday or anything, but I would appreciate it if you didn't have to arrest anybody before you get back," Danica said.

"Don't worry about that," Swann said.

The procedure for obtaining a release form was the same. The cop at the Property Clerk's office had pecked out F-I-V-E T-H-O-U when he burst into laughter.

"You must be making them crazy," the cop said.

Swann left the building feeling no mirth of his own. The daytime IAD men trailed him through the sunshine and he felt almost ready to give up if only that did not also mean giving in.

Swann had never been to a check-cashing store before, but he also had never needed to meet a room service bill on a day the banks were closed. He now entered a dingy storefront a few blocks from the courthouse. The room was bare, the ceiling waterstained.

He joined a line of people who most likely had neither checking nor savings accounts and who were waiting to pay two percent of what little they had to cash a check or obtain a money order. Here were people with less than no leverage.

When his turn came, Swann stepped up to a scratched sheet of plastic whose most prominent scar showed that its bulletproof qualities had been tested and proved. He presented the checks along with his shield and police I.D. card to the young Hispanic woman on the other side. She gazed from the four-year-old photo to him.

"I lost a little weight," Swann said.

Swann removed his homburg so as to look more like the picture. She signaled her acceptance that he was still himself by reaching into the cash drawer.

Swann worked the hat brim around in his hands as he watched the bills fall soundlessly one atop another. The woman was no less careful than the detective wearing the latex gloves, the last single marking 98 percent of what had been officially recorded as the amount peeled wet and sticky from beside a young corpse not yet gone cold.

Ten

The subway dropped Swann several blocks from the Plaza. The IAD men stayed right behind him as he made his way up Fifth Avenue. He broke stride when he saw a huge polished-brass logo identical to that on the front of Pharaoh's T-shirt.

Curiosity sent Swan into the Gucci shop. Well-dressed people were inspecting handbags, scarves, shoes, blouses, jackets, and just about everything else you could stamp with the double G logo. There were, however, no T-shirts, and he surmised that these must be strictly street-corner, black-market items.

Swann glanced out the plate-glass window to see that two shadows had taken up position across the street. They seemed more fidgety than usual, and that could be partly explained by their seeing their big-time crook in such a store. They also were surely still furious about the events of the day before.

At this reminder of his mischief's result, Swann was transported back to the shooting. The money in his pocket could have been those same bloodstained bills.

He returned himself to Gucci by scrutinizing the merchandise and he came upon an Italian wallet. He ran his fingers over the creamy leather, having no conscious thought of Ellen before deciding it would be perfect for her coupons.

Swann bought the wallet with two $100 bills and resumed his stroll up Fifth Avenue. He peered over his shoulder to see one of the IAD men ducking into Gucci, no doubt to check on the purchase. He had gone only another few paces when he spied something in a window that he thought might be nice for Jenny.

Swann returned to the street with a French red velvet dress so beautiful it was arguably worth the cost. The two IAD men were standing together again, but one of them was sure to stop into the dress shop as soon as he moved on.

Move on he did, from store to store, inspecting beautiful things that seemed to be from everywhere in the world but America. He bought Joseph an English white dress shirt that had mother-of-pearl buttons.

He also purchased an oversized Swiss fountain pen whose nib was eighteen-carat gold. He smiled as he pictured Coleman handing it over the next time a detective asked to borrow a pen.

In FAO Schwarz, Swann passed a new shipment of Caucasian Cabbage Patch dolls and a display case of pricey dolls nearly as pretty as Danica. He left the store with a four-foot purple giraffe.

Swann still had a sizable bankroll unspent when he came to a jewelry store. The window displayed a number of expensive watches, and he remembered Lieutenant Gentile's suggestion on Liberty Weekend that he buy a more accurate timepiece.

The IAD men were still behind him, and Swann entered with the thought of them later presenting Gentile with a copy of a receipt for one of these watches. He happened to first see a case of women's watches bearing price tags a fraction the size of what had been on his suit. He left the store with his bankroll all but gone, one of the tiny white pieces of paper having borne the biggest price he had ever seen, $2,495 for a gold-and-silver lady's Rolex.

Danica was seated on the edge of the bed, and she was back to wearing nothing more than a bath towel. Swan felt a little dizzy, though this was likely less from the sight of her lustrous thighs than from the nail polish fumes.

"I thought maybe you had made an arrest or something, so I decided I might as well do my nails," Danica said.

"I'm sorry, I just needed to be by myself for a little while," Swann said.

Swann set down the packages.

"I guess so," Danica said.

The purple giraffe fell over. He set it upright.

"It's for Jenny," Swann said.

"I'm sure she'll love it," Danica said.

Swann watched Danica extend a forefinger and carefully set a tiny brush at the base of the nail. She drew the brush to the tip in a single slow stroke.

"You probably still don't feel like talking about it," she said.

She meant the shooting. He said nothing, and she returned her attention to her nails, dipping the tiny brush into the bottle of scarlet and painting the thumb.

"Now comes the hard part," she said.

He saw that she had finished the left hand and was ready to begin the right. This meant she had to work the brush with fingers whose nails were wet.

"If you get a little smudge, you can always smooth it out with a little remover, but it's really better not to have one," she said.

He continued watching until the last finger was done. She began the process again.

"I hope you don't mind, but I was looking at those legal papers," she said.

She was talking of the Family Court paperwork he had left on the bedside table.

"He's not much bigger than William," Danica said. "He's in jail now?"

"Yes. Until Monday."

"Then what?"

"Probably nothing. Probation."

"You mean like in school if you got caught smoking?"

He briefly described the juvenile justice system while she finished the second coat.

"And it's like their own little court?" she asked. "*Family* Court."

She began to shake both hands vigorously.

"Now maybe you could turn the tap for me," she said.

He followed her into the bathroom. She stood before the sink, still shaking both hands.

"It's terrible to say, but this was the point I first *really* missed my husband," Danica said.

He reached first for the handle marked with a golden H.

"No, no, no!" she said. "Haven't you ever seen anybody do this? Just the cold."

He complied and stepped aside. She stuck the fingertips of her left hand under the running tap.

"This wouldn't be so bad if it could be warm water," she said.

She removed her left hand and stuck in her right. He remained in attendance, turning off the tap once she was done, and following her back into the room. The air was still thick with fumes.

"Now we just have to wait a little while," she said.

She resumed her perch on the bed, hands up, fingers splayed. He sat in the armchair feeling no insistence in the thud of his heart. He could not gauge the wait by looking at the nails. The polish did not change shades as it dried.

"It's called Fire Ruby," she said. "I had a couple of dollars left over, and when you didn't come, I went down to this little drug store they have here. There was this Fire Ruby for like four eighty-five, and I figured the sales tax and I had just enough and I thought, 'Here I am at a place like the Plaza, counting pennies like I was at Duane Reade.' It's a good thing I happened to already have the remover."

She scrunched her brow as she slowly brought her thumbnails together.

"You got to be real gentle, because if it isn't dry, it'll stick, and you don't want any more than a tiny little pull mark," she said.

The nails came away without sticking.

"Now, I better get dressed if we're going out," she said.

Danica rose and let the towel drop. She certainly was as magnificent as ever but her magnificence seemed less consequential. He knew that the differences was not in her.

Danica bit the sales tag off a new pair of white silk panties with her equally white teeth. She pulled them up her thighs and as in the thicket the elastic snapped against her belly.

"Where do you want to go?" she asked.

Danica seemed only reasonable for expecting that he might take her somewhere after keeping her waiting in the hotel for a night and a morning.

"I spent pretty much everything I had," Swann said.

Danica had started to roll up one leg of her panty hose.

"What about room service?" she asked.

"I kept enough to pay room service," he said.

Danica unrolled the panty hose up over her leg. Her skin shone through the material as she drew it taut.

"That was a lot of money," she said.

Swann found himself relieved to be speaking of the money as something that was gone.

"Yes, it was," he said.

"Can you imagine if that kid had got away with all that?"

Danica rolled up the second leg of the panty hose.

"What's that name?"

"Pharaoh."

Swann held at once the sight of Danica pulling up her panty hose and the memory of Pharaoh taking off his fourth or fifth pair of socks.

"I saw his father's got the same name, and he doesn't even know where his father is," Danica said. "'U-n-k,' that means 'unknown,' right?"

Danica opened a box and parted the white tissue inside and took out a new dress in the style worn by most of the women who had gained entrance to Eleanor's.

"I had got this for last night," she said.

Danica drew the simple black sheath over her head. He watched her give a series of sharp little wriggles as she pulled it down over her breasts, stomach, and thighs.

"We could go to a matinee movie or something," she said.

Danica laughed and turned around for Swann to zip her. Her perfect flesh disappeared under the material as his hand went slowly up the furrow of her back. He drew her hair aside and fumbled with the tiny black hook at the top.

"I mean, I could go get enough for that at the bank," she said. "It could be my treat."

Swann could have kissed the bared nape of her neck and drawn down the zipper and they would have gone on another fabulous ride. He fitted the tiny black hook into the tiny black eye.

"I'm going home," he said.

Danica turned around, and more than anything her face showed shock. He shared at least a good part of her surprise, for he had heard the words as if they had been spoken by somebody else.

"This just isn't right," Swann said.

The words were no less spontaneous, but this time Swann felt them in his mouth and his throat and his chest. Danica did not seem any less stunned.

"What kind of bullshit is that?" she asked.

Swann said nothing.

"I mean, when did you figure this out?" she asked. "I could have told you it wasn't freaking *right* before we started."

Danica's shock was becoming fury, but she seemed to decide that the one humiliation worse than being dumped by Swann would be to let on that it bothered her. She calmly opened her purse and took out various tubes and containers of makeup.

"If you think you can wait a minute, I'll go down with you," she said.

Danica went into the bathroom, and Swann looked about the grand surroundings he was quitting. His eye chanced upon the watch that she had left on the dresser. He discovered that her broken counterfeit was one of the better kind. It felt as hefty as the genuine Rolex he now set down in its place.

Danica emerged with her hair brushed back, her makeup applied.

"You might as well keep this," she said.

Danica held out the blue glow-in-the-dark toothbrush with a solemnity that seemed not at all ridiculous.

Danica absently slipped the Rolex over her wrist. She then noticed something that caused her to give a sudden start. She studied the face and held the watch up to her ear.

"I can't believe it," she said.

She held out her slender wrist much as she had two nights before.

"Look," she said. "It works again."

Swann watched the sharp golden needle tick, precisely marking the passage of one second and another and another.

"I bet maybe it's a sign of some kind," Danica said.

Swann did not dare tell her the truth and light up her already gorgeous face and maybe cause her to hug him. He might then have been unable to leave.

"So I guess your watch must be running right," she said.

Swann gave her the time. She turned the tiny knob on the side of the watch with the very thumb and forefinger that had so perfunctorily picked his pubic hair off her tongue.

"Twelve . . ."

Swann saw the hour and then minute hands move into place.

". . . forty-six."

Her watch was ticking in sync with his.

"Time to go," she said.

The summoned cab rolled up. Swann decided that he should part with Danica here, before the entrance to the Plaza and not outside her house in Richmond Hill. He handed her all that remained of his bankroll after a room service tab that included a $22 hamburger. He told her she would be riding alone.

"That's all you have?" Danica asked.

Swann shrugged.

"How are you going?" Danica asked. "You don't have any money."

"What do I need money for?" Swann said. "I ride the subway free."

Swann set down the giraffe and his packages on entering his house. He experienced a new sense of quiet, maybe even serenity, as he went through the mail on the small table by the door. He saw several bills, but thankfully none from the gas company. He also came upon a postcard of a squat modern building, and he flipped to the back to see a cramped, tiny script he only vaguely recognized. The hallway was too dim for him to make out the message, and he stepped into the brighter light of the living room.

At that moment, Swann realized that the reason for at least part of his new serenity was that the television was off. He then noticed a smell, faint but distinct and no more pleasant than that of nail polish. The smell was of cheap pipe tobacco, and his worst fears were confirmed when he saw Ellen jump up from the sofa.

Ellen's face contorted and she issued a series of accusations that were all the more terrible for being entirely true. Lieutenant Gentile had been there, and he had no doubt told her everything he knew.

"They showed me a picture, and they wanted to know who was the *pretty girl,*" Ellen said. "I don't know why I didn't tell them."

That she had even then remained a transit cop's wife now seemed to send Ellen past a limit. She seized the television.

Swann stood amazed as Ellen lifted the Hitachi in her spindly arms. He was fully astounded when she pitched it at him. It fell short, hitting the floor with a crash.

Ellen screamed for Swann to leave, and shards of the broken screen splintered underfoot as he backed into the hallway. He heard a second, tiny voice and turned to see Jenny standing in the doorway to her room.

"Daddy," Jenny said.

Ellen stepped between them. Swann suddenly felt as if he had never quite known her. She looked at him as if she had known what he was all along.

Jenny began to cry and Swann decided he would only be making the situation harder on her if he stayed. This was hardly a time to give presents, so he took the giraffe and his other packages with him as he went down the stoop. The door slammed shut.

The house suddenly no longer his home, Swann wondered where he might take himself. Joseph had gone away somewhere with a duffel bag and Swann had no key to his father's house and all he had in his pocket was a broken counterfeit Rolex.

He started up the block, hoping to see the IAD men who had trailed him from the Plaza. He figured they might have been detailed to linger at the corner and report on the results of Lieutenant Gentile's visit. He was ready to go up and tell them that their boss was the one who had gone too far, that if he had lost, they had not yet won.

Swann saw only his neighbors out with their families on a fine Saturday afternoon. He trudged toward the one place he could go, the subway.

Eleven

AT DISTRICT 1, the desk officer looked up and remarked that Swann was not due to work for two days.

"I came in a little early," Swann said.

He stashed his purchases in his locker and then lay back on a wood bench and tipped his homburg against the fluorescent light overhead. The cops working a four-to-twelve had just left, and the room would be quiet until the midnight shift came in.

Swann felt the vibrations of the trains rumbling through the station and on under the city. He was possessed by a weariness as deep as the understanding that he could have seen this coming, that he had only himself to blame, and that there was nothing he could do about it now.

Swann tried to excuse himself with thoughts that he had only gone after what every man who stared at Danica on the street wanted, that he had only borrowed the way half the world seemed to be borrowing, that he had only sought a little leverage and vigor. The weariness kept closing in, and he dropped off like some new prisoner falling into that profound first sleep of the guilty.

Swann awoke to voices and slamming locker doors. He kept still, his hat over his eyes, listening to the midnight guys getting ready to head out and the evening guys coming in, each and every sound familiar, but sharpened in his private darkness.

Somebody muttered and somebody else laughed and he knew it was about him. He kept feigning sleep as he would in the last car, not moving even after the final lock had clicked shut and the last footsteps had faded out the door. He felt his heart pumping and the hardness of the bench under his back and an itch where his hat rested on his nose. He scratched and laid his hand back on his chest. Sleep was long in coming now that he was waiting for it.

When Swann awoke again, the locker room was deserted, and he sat up knowing only by his watch that morning had come. He lay back down and went over all that had happened the day before. He remembered the postcard.

Swann took the card from his suit jacket pocket and he had no trouble making out the tiny script in the harsh fluorescent light. He realized he was looking at his father's handwriting for the first time since high school, when parents were required to sign report cards. He now read the only written words Joseph had ever addressed to him:

"The people are nice (mostly). The food is not as bad as you would think. The big problem is that there are a lot of nuts here. But what can you expect?"

Swann glanced up at the caption in the corner of the postcard, which said that the building pictured on the front was the Veteran's Administration Hospital, Brooklyn, N.Y.

Joseph sat in a dayroom on the seventh floor, wearing the same blue pajamas as the other patients. He turned slowly at the sound of Swann's voice and shuffled over in paper slippers. His face was flushed and his eyes were glassy. The right eye was blackened.

"Why the suit?" Joseph asked. "Something else happen?"

Joseph sounded dull, distant. Drugged.

"I've just been dressing this way," Swann said.

Joseph grew no more animated as he took in the bow tie and boutonniere and homburg.

"Looks that way."

Swann sat down on a plastic chair facing his father.

"So, I guess you got my postcard," Joseph said.

Swann asked how he was and Joseph said he was okay and Swann asked what somebody who was okay was doing with a black eye in a psychiatric ward. Joseph spoke in a monotone of getting off work and being even more tired than usual and going down into the subway with the single hope that he would not have to wait long for a train.

"What do you think happens? I'm not there thirty seconds and in comes this train, one of them new ones, the ones the Japs built. But I'm not really thinking about that. All I'm thinking is, 'Now if I can just get a seat.' I don't know how it happens. I sit all day and the only thing I got in my mind is I don't want to stand all the way home.

"I get on, I see this one seat open. There's this woman going for it, and like part of me wants to give it to her. But I go for it."

Joseph paused where he would most likely have shown embarrassment had he not been medicated. The effect on Swann was to make him feel closer to his father, for he had to imagine the emotion the blank face and glassy eyes and toneless voice did not convey. He felt that part of himself that intuitively understood his father, the part that seemed to be the same stuff.

"I get there a step ahead of her. I feel bad about taking it, but I take it."

Swann could picture Joseph making for the seat as if it were something more than a place to sit. Another shit day at the ZMT machine, but the train comes right away and there's a seat. A bit of luck.

"But I didn't really fit because this is a Jap train and the seats are made for Jap asses, not American asses. I had to really squeeze in, and I'm all pressed up against this big Puerto Rican woman on one side and this tall fucking jamuke on the other."

Swann knew "jamuke" as one of the remarkable number of terms for black people, none of which he had ever before heard employed in so flat a tone, without the slightest inflection of fear or contempt or unease.

"The woman, I don't mind her so much because I can tell she's doing her best to fit in the space for a Jap ass. The jamuke is a different story. He's skinny, but he's sitting there with these fucking long legs spread out like he had a regular American seat, which means he's halfway into my Jap-size seat.

"That's when it all hits me. I fight in a fucking war and kill these Japs. The Japs kill all these guys I know. Now, here I am, beating out a woman for a seat on a Jap train and I don't even fit because it's for a Jap ass. I got to squeeze in between a fat PR and a moo who's sitting there like it's some kind of throne. That's the world I fought for: a moo sitting on a Jap seat like he's a king."

Swann understood that Joseph had been afraid to ask the black man to move over. Swann also knew how keenly Joseph the soldier and father and man of the house must have felt the shame of that fear.

"At the same time, I got the woman I beat out looking at me like I was some kind of lowlife, which is exactly how I felt. I decide to get up and I step away and I watch the woman go and say to the moo, 'Would you mind moving over a little?' You know what this fuck says? He says, 'Oh, I'm sorry,' and moves over, or at least as far as the Jap seats will let him."

Swann now pictured Joseph riding on into Queens, all the more shamed, all the more tired.

"Two stops later, the moo gets off, but it's not like I'm going to sit next to this woman. I stay where I am until I get to my stop. I go for the door and what happens but I bump into this other fucking moo who's trying to come in."

Joseph was out of breath, as if he had not been droning, as if he had been speaking no less excitedly than would have fitted what he was saying.

"And that's when I hit him," Joseph said.

"Excuse me?" Swann asked.

"I think that's *exactly* what this other moo was saying," Joseph said. "But before I heard what he said, I'd already hit him. Well, maybe more like shoved him."

"Let me guess," Swann said. "And that's when he hit you."

Joseph pointed to his blackened eye.

"Hard," Joseph said. "Though I think your guy hit him harder."

"Excuse me?" Swann said.

"I wish you wouldn't keep saying that," Joseph said. "Your guy, the cop. All the white people had run out of the car, and one of them must have got a cop. The cop comes in, takes one look at the situation, and that's when the cop starts hitting the moo. I tell him to stop, because I had started it. He gives me a look like you're giving me now. He says, 'What are you, nuts?' And I say to myself, 'Maybe I am. Maybe I am fucking nuts.'"

Joseph then lowered his voice.

"I had already been here to the VA to visit Jethro. You remember. The Vietnam guy from the post office."

Swann did indeed remember the long-haired young man who worked at the ZMT machine beside his father, the two of them punching out ZIP code after ZIP code as the envelopes flashed before them, keeping to the maxim Thinking Is Counterproductive.

"The stool next to you," Swann said.

"Not anymore," Joseph said.

Joseph spoke in a monowhisper.

"He checked himself in here and convinces them he's got this delayed stress syndrome. That's where you get fucked up about something and don't know about it until later."

"That's too bad," Swan said.

Joseph kept to the monowhisper.

"What're you, nuts?" Joseph said. "He swung himself a hundred percent disability. He stands to get one thousand, three hundred and thirty-five dollars a month, tax free. And he never has to sit at one of them fucking machines again."

Swann had never heard his father come any closer to complaining about work than an unthinking sigh or the joke about keeping productive.

"Well, Vietnam was a fucked-up war. But the one I was in was pretty fucked up, too. Who's to say I can't have stress that's a little more delayed?"

Joseph's eyelids drooped as he waited for Swann to appreciate the wisdom of his proposition.

"Besides, it's not like these Vietnam guys got to ride around in trains made by Viet Cong. It's not like every other thing they see in the world is marked 'Made by the V.C. and go fuck yourself.'"

Joseph leaned closer.

"So I ride this other Jap train out to here, but this time I'm not visiting. This time, I tell them I want to sign myself in. They don't really listen to me until I tell them about hittin' the moo."

Joseph stopped and nodded hello to a patient who went by wearing a football helmet. Joseph explained to Swann that this patient had served in Vietnam and had appeared on a magazine cover with a field bandage wrapped about his face. The bullet wound underneath had healed twenty years before, but his nose was gone and one of his eyes had shifted up toward his forehead. The other had dropped down by his cheek.

"He has the helmet so he won't hurt himself when he bangs his head on the walls," Joseph said.

Joseph then pointed out a former tank driver who each morning set a book face down on a table and spent the rest of the day carefully edging it a sixteenth of an inch back and forth. Another patient was scurrying frantically about, begging for a cigarette.

"Come on, come on, give me one, come on, come on, give me, give me," the patient said.

Joseph told Swann that one thing you should never do in a nuthouse was give anybody a cigarette. This advice was borne out a moment later, when a visitor acceded to the patient's pleas. Two other former warriors immediately hurried over, demanding they get a cigarette, too.

"I think one of them doesn't even smoke," Joseph said. "He just wants to have what everybody else has. Nuts think that's the way things should be. They think that it's supposed to be even."

Swann reached over to touch Joseph's forearm.

"Well, at least the cop didn't lock you up," Swann said.

"I think he was going to, but I told him you were my son," Joseph said. "He said you're nuts, too. He said you were going around all dressed up in a bow tie and a hat. He said you're going to jail."

Swann spoke the first thing that popped into his mind, which happened to be the truth.

"They're jealous and they can't stand anybody being different," Swann said. "They see a bow tie, they go wild."

Joseph's glassy eyes stayed on Swann.

"Believe me, I didn't do anything wrong," Swann said.

Swann was now speaking strictly in terms of the penal code.

"I don't even know how to tie one of them," Joseph said.

Swann decided that this was not the time to tell Joseph of the money and Danica and what had happened with Ellen.

"It's easy," Swann said. "It's just like tying your shoes."

The two IAD men were by the flagpole out front, the sea breeze snapping the stars and stripes overheard. They had been waiting for him when he came out of District 1 and he had figured that some cop looking to curry favor with the Dark Side must have tipped them that he was sleeping there on his day off. He had been too anxious to pay them much heed on the subway ride out to see Joseph.

Swann now left the hospital grounds with them right behind him. He had an urge to confront them, but he checked himself, perhaps because he knew that the larger blame was his own. He led them through a bright, unseasonably warm Sunday afternoon.

He soon neared a subway entrance. He had nothing to do and no place to go and he was unable to think of any reason he should leave the sunshine for a dim hole.

He ambled past the entrance and along the broad avenue beneath which this subway line ran. He was truly achy from a night on the bench and he reached the next station tired enough to have come from a shift in the mail room. He kept going, deciding that one place he could go was for a walk, knowing that the IAD men were tiring along with him, certain that after the shooting in the last car they would have to stay with him no matter how far he trekked.

The trains trundling underfoot, Swann went through Bay Ridge and Sunset Park and into South Brooklyn. He passed Irish and Italians and Swedes and Puerto Ricans and Chinese and blacks and they all looked at this weary man in the homburg and bow tie as if he were an outsider.

Night was nearing when Swann reached the wooden walkway over the Brooklyn Bridge. The Manhattan skyline appeared before him, and each heavy step brought him nearer to the skyscrapers built by the ironworkers. Joseph never had spoken about his work at the post office, but he had often told the younger Swann about the men who walked hundreds of feet in the air on steel beams ten inches wide.

Joseph said that the people on the street believed that no Caucasian would do such a thing, and that a myth had arisen that those men up on high steel were Mohawk Indians who possessed some natural sense of balance the same way blacks had rhythm. There were, in fact, never more than a few Indians up there, and most ironworkers were, like Joseph's own father, Irish who had come by way of Newfoundland.

Swann walked on, gazing at the Empire State Building. He remembered holding Joseph's hand on the night in his tenth year when he peered from the observation deck to the street far, far below. He recalled that he had at one point tried to determine where in the twinkling sprawl of Queens were the few blocks that comprised his home and school and known world.

Swann then remembered descending in the elevator, again taking Joseph's hand, feeling connected to something big, distinct in the squeeze of tourists. That feeling came back to him as a kind of clue as he now crossed the darkening waters toward the tower his grandfather had died building.

At the span's midpoint, Swann looked to his left, out across the harbor to the Statue of Liberty. He saw for the first time the new torch that had been lit by the President himself, the upraised beacon that was no longer a beacon at all, but the glint of spotlights off what he could not help but think of as *goal leaf*.

Swann reached the far side as weary and footsore as some storybook messenger from beyond the realm. He took a last look at his grandfather's tower and descended into the underground. He was exhausted, but a glance back told him that he was in no worse shape than the two men who had shared one of the city's longest strolls since the opening of the subway.

At District 1, Swann lay down upon a locker-room bench. His great relief deepened to a feeling that he had come to the end of something. He then began to feel the wood plank beneath him hitting the very places that were sore from the night before.

Swann would have tossed and turned had that been possible on an eighteen-inch plank. He lay awake, figuring that the narrow bench was still a good eight inches wider than the beams the ironworkers walked. That got him thinking of what Joseph had said one day on appraising a teenage son who was by any measure rotund.

"Well, you're no Indian."

Swann was still not asleep when the midnight shift headed out. He finally dozed off for a couple of hours, and he rose as bleary as those cops who commuted from the most distant suburbs. They at least were freshly washed and shaved, and if they were not in suits, they had on something other than what they had been wearing all weekend.

The Family Court building was not open to the public until 9 A.M. and the usual line stood at the plate-glass doors. The majority were, as always, minorities and almost all the adults were female. He surmised from one woman's bruised face that she was seeking an order of protection. A second woman had a toy fire engine under her arm and might have come hoping to regain custody of a child.

Others were no doubt seeking child support and a good number were there because either a son or daughter had been arrested. Swann tried to guess which might be Pharaoh's mother, but none bore an obvious resemblance.

Swann stepped off the elevator on the fourth floor a few paces from the holding pen where Pharaoh would be sitting, back in his Gucci T-shirt and the rest. A guard was just pulling the door closed to this place the youngsters called the TV Room, and Swann heard the thme song of a show he had liked as a child and that Jenny often watched. He went down the hall thinking that after Ellen's feat of surprising strength, Jenny was one kid who would not be seeing Looney Tunes this morning.

Swann turned into an office and presented the paperwork that had last been read by Danica. The procedure was much the same as at ECAB, only without the roomful of nodding officers. Juvenile arrests entailed filling out an extra form, and the prospect of any effort that could otherwise be avoided was enough to keep many officers away. That made for less waiting time, which, in turn, reduced the dollars to be found in such collars. And that made officers with mortgages prefer the more lucrative adults.

Swann expected questions regarding his bankroll, but the prosecutor apparently felt this was outside Family Court's purview. The process was only protracted by a wondering look or two, and he was back down in the lobby in less than half an hour.

The doors had been opened and those who had been lined up were inside and more women had arrived. A toddler lurched through the metal detector and the mother moved instinctively to catch her, but the buzzer went off and a court officer ordered her back.

Swann intercepted the girl and led her to the mother. The woman watched him as closely as any mother would a man of his present appearance, and yet what he felt most keenly as he returned the child was not that he was rumpled or unshaven. What came to him most strongly was that he was as absent a father as Pharaoh France, Sr., and so many others.

Swann found a stray $10 in his suit coat and he stopped by the salad bar at a Korean grocery before returning to District 1. He arrived shortly before roll call, and he would have noticed Coleman first even if he had not been looking for her. She had reported for duty in a black body stocking and outsized overalls like a farmer might wear, except these were made of quilted purple satin and were hemmed at the knee. She seemed as alert as ever, though his condition would have been apparent to anybody.

"I got to say, you're looking a little de-pressed," Coleman said.

Swann groped for a response that fell between saying nothing and telling everything.

"I've been having a few problems," Swann said.

Swann realized he was not telling her anything new.

"I'm out of the house," Swann said.

Coleman looked about as surprised as if a crook had told her he had been arrested.

"I'm sorry to hear that," Coleman said.

Coleman's voice did carry an undertone of sympathy.

"What can you do?" Swann said.

Coleman asked no more questions than she had about the money.

"You know that woman you met?" Swann asked.

"Danica," Coleman said.

Swann was surprised that Coleman remembered her name.

"We had kind of a thing," Swann said.

Coleman nodded.

"I ended it and I went home, but IAD had been there. They had told her."

"Bad break," Coleman said.

"Hey, what more can they do?" Swann asked.

The answer to that question came at roll call, when Sergeant Quinn announced that Officers Swann and Coleman were being taken off patrol *forthwith,* as in immediately. Swann would henceforth assume Sullivan's clerical duties in the anti-crime office. Coleman was being transferred to work at the radio console at the operations unit, which was crassly known as the transit police "crack unit" due to the large number of women assigned there.

"See how many times you can get robbed at a desk," Quinn said.

Swann looked at Coleman and felt a swelling in his chest such as might come just before a chase, but what he had come to was a finish. He apologized for landing her in duty even more dreary than standing the punishment post.

"It was two of us," Coleman said.

Swann could think of nothing to say other than what he would have said on parting with just some other cave cop. The difference was he meant what he said.

"It's been good working with you," Swann said.

"Likewise," Coleman said.

"I guess I'll see ya around."

"Chances are."

Coleman then puffed out her cheeks and crossed her eyes.

Swann went into the office where Sullivan was whiling away the last days before his retirement.

"My hero," Sullivan said.

Sullivan proceeded to instruct Swann in his new duties as what cave cops called a "house mouse." These included the occasional operation of the computer, and to this end Sullivan tossed Swann a slender manual.

"What you do is do what it says in here," Sullivan said. "You need what they call an access code to get in, but I won't be needing mine."

Sullivan wrote down four digits which were also his shield number.

"So, you be me."

The computer instruction complete, Sullivan left for a meal. Swann started on the manual, pausing every few minutes to perform his primary function, which was to answer the office telephone. Most of the callers were women asking for male officers, with the wives sounding either bored or burdened and the gooms sounding a little uneasy and maybe a little thrilled to be calling a police station.

A number of the cops were not even working that day, but Swann uttered the usual *He's out in the field*. He only diverged from standard transit police response when a female asked for Fredricks with the tentative voice of somebody recently met in a bar.

"Is that guy still telling people he's a cop?" Swann asked.

Two gooms and a number of spouses later, Fredricks's wife called. That was proof in itself that she was unaware he had taken the day off.

"Don't tell me about any field, because he just called to say he made a collar," the wife said. "I could lie and tell you one of the kids was sick, and then you would have to put him on."

Swann could not have told the truth without feeling like Lieutenant Gentile.

"He must have called you from the field," Swann said. "He's probably on his way in with the collar."

Swann hung up and wiped his palm on a pant leg that retained only a phantom crease. He then seized the receiver and dialed what had been his home. He heard Ellen pick up, and he got out a first word.

"Hi . . ."

Swann heard a click and he sat with the dial tone in his ear. He finally set down the receiver and sought whatever escape was possible in a computer manual. He did, in fact, find a certain comfort in something so concrete and relatively simple.

The computer proved to be not much more difficult to operate than a cash machine, and he was soon ready to give it a try. He punched in Sullivan's code and a list known as a "menu" flashed onto the screen.

Swann wandered the keyboard with a single finger. He entered an *x* next to an item marked "Complaint Report File" and pecked a few more keys. The screen went blank for the instant that was all the computer needed to search through more than a million homicides, rapes, robberies, and assaults. Flash, from out of a decade's mayhem appeared the official details regarding the shooting of Daryl Coombs.

"See, there's nothing to it."

Sullivan had returned.

"But you're gonna get to hate it. One time I decided I would get it crazy, and I told it to give me all the arrest reports involving twos."

Sullivan seemed to assume that Swann knew what he meant by *twos*.

"I figure it would blow up or something, but all it did was come back and say, 'More than a hundred.' You ask for anything that's a lot and that's what it says. Big high-tech machine, and it says 'More than a hundred.'"

Sullivan's finger stabbed the screen where Daryl Coombs's race was reported. The numbered boxes showed he was *(2) black*.

"No shit," Sullivan said.

Swann understood that "twos" was the most recent expression for blacks, which he had not heard owing to Coleman's constant presence as his partner.

He sent the report of the shooting back to where it had come from and he hunted out another few keys. Flash, here was the beating of the derelict duly recorded as a violation of Section 120.05 of the Penal Code, assault on a police officer. The format was identical, and Swann could see the smudge on the screen from Sullivan's finger where the derelict's race was also given as 2.

"Hey, that's that thing where you had a problem with Fredricks."

Sullivan leaned close. His breath smelled of alcohol.

"Remember that when you tell these fucks to do something, they do it because they know you're willing to do what you gotta do. If you don't do the right thing, then they're gonna fight every cop they run into."

Sullivan leaned even closer, his voice tight.

"I know things."

Sullivan then straightened and smiled. His voice boomed again.

"Maybe I don't."

Sullivan patted his belly and laughed.

"I can't even keep off ten pounds."

Swann dispatched the report on the derelict and called up the report on the space case, which he saw was classified as closed.

"One thing that computer can tell you is that it don't matter what you do or what you don't do." Sullivan said. "Everything just goes in there and so what?"

Joseph's sad, drug-dulled face was still that of a father who had come home straight from work every night, who had kept himself and his family solely on what he earned, who had always seemed to lead exactly his life; a rock with no need of a lever. Swann had come to the psychiatric ward with the intention of keeping to idle chatter, but he was still the son who in earlier years would have reached for Joseph's hand. Son now told father all about the Money Store and Brooks Brothers and the Plaza.

Joseph listened with an expression as blank as the computer screen until the tale came to the affair with Danica. He straightened under his hospital garb and whatever drugs he was on did not keep the glint from his eyes.

"No shit," Joseph said.

Swann was feeling at once better and worse as he then told of breaking off the affair. The light in Joseph's eyes faded.

"Hunh," Joseph said.

Swann went on to recount how he had been thrown out by Ellen.

"That's rough for Jenny," Joseph said.

The tone was slurred but fatherly. Swann remained sure he had not mistaken the nature of the glint.

"Yes," Swann said.

"And Ellen, of course."

"Yes."

A nurse announced that visiting hours were over. Joseph kept the fatherly tone as he said that Swann's childhood room was there if he wanted it. Swann said he needed a key.

"There should be one on my dresser," Joseph said.

Swann gave Joseph a look that was perhaps a little like the one he had received from Joseph when he said that he had left Danica.

"I mean I need a key to get in," Swann said.

"A couple weeks ago, I started thinking that everybody figures your door's locked, anyway, so fuck it, why bother?" Joseph said. "Just go on in. It's all yours."

Joseph's dulled eyes gazed straight into Swann's.

"Though, if you wanna know, you're the one who belongs in a nuthouse."

Swann's return to his childhood home was witnessed by the IAD men, who must have been thankful that he had not decided to walk. They watched from the corner as he turned the knob and found that the door was indeed unlocked. He entered feeling as if he had been awaited.

One thing Joseph shared with Danica was an aversion to sweeping.

He also did not like vacuuming, dusting, scrubbing, picking up, or any other kind of housework. The result was a decade of dirt where Swann's dead mother had for so long labored to keep what she called *shipshape.*

In his room, Swann stripped off his rumpled suit and stood in his holey Jockey shorts before the narrow bed in which he had spent all the nights of his younger years. He had lain here wanting Danica, but he had left here to be with Ellen and now he was back.

Swann pulled down the spread and saw that the bed was made with a precision that Joseph could never have managed. This had to be his mother's work, a few moments of her years of domestic drudgery preserved here before him, the blanket tucked taut, the top sheet folded over and smoothed by her hand.

Swann slowly pulled back the covers and slipped into the bed. He lay with the fold of the top sheet across his chest, his heart thumping with no desire for anything but sleep.

IV

Twelve

SWANN ROSE in the morning leaving the bedclothes a twisted, wrinkled heap. He was less achy than if he had slept on the bench, but he felt no more rested as he reached for the suit which lay in a heap by the bed. The thing seemed a discarded throwaway, but he was sure to have at least one more funeral to attend.

As he put the suit on a hanger, Swann patted the jacket for the glow-in-the-dark toothbrush. He also came upon the paycheck that had seemed incidental. He was back to a life where he had to count his money as carefully as if it were evidence, where he could not spend beyond what he earned. His bankroll was gone but the loan remained, and he went into the bathroom calculating how he would meet the next Money Store payment.

Celeste was not around to keep Joseph from squeezing the tube from the middle, and Swann had to work some of the stuff up from the bottom. He brushed while figuring that all but five-o of his regular wage would go to Ellen just as before. The difference was that what had always been his pocket money would have to meet all his expenses for the next two weeks.

Swann rinsed and set the toothbrush in the same slot of the ceramic holder that he had used as a boy. He computed that he would now be living on $3.58 a day, give or take a penny.

In his parents' room, the sheets and blankets lay as Joseph had left them the morning he had stood at the bus stop with his duffel bag. Swann searched for something to wear and extracted a pair of Joseph's chinos from a mound of clothes that sat atop the dresser.

He stepped into one leg and then the other and pulled up the pants of the father who had sometimes seemed so big and other times seemed so small. The cuffs were a half inch or so shorter than would have found favor at Brooks Brothers, but the waist fitted perfectly.

He reached back into the laundry pile and pulled a gray sweatshirt over his head. He looked back at the bed that his mother, Celeste, had never left unmade. He thought of her, and he remembered the glint that had come into Joseph's eye when he had spoken of Danica.

Marie offered no jokes when Swann entered District 1. He expected his fellow officers to be smugly pleased to see him again looking like one of them, but several seemed closer to being disappointed. He could not have said if they harbored secret rebellious urges of their own or if they simply missed having so obvious a target for scorn.

In the anti-crime office, Swann set a cup of coffee on the desk and started filing papers and answering the telephone. He again called what had been his home, and Ellen once more hung up before he had completed his first word. He was back at his duties when a uniformed cop paused outside the office with a portable radio on his gunbelt.

Coleman had begun her own new assignment, and her voice came remote but unmistakable through the static as she attempted to communicate over transit radio with some other cop in the underground.

Coleman: "[Unintelligible] repeat."

Caller: "[Unintelligible] to Central."

Coleman: "Unit calling. You're [unintelligible]."

Caller: "[Unintelligible]."

The cop with the radio on his gunbelt strolled out of Swann's earshot, but others happened by. The tedium of his day was broken periodically by Coleman's voice.

At the end of the tour, Swann rose from the desk with rival pains in the head and back. The cops who had been out on patrol returned, and Swann got a measure of how unhappy he must look when he saw Fredricks smile.

"Look," Fredricks said. "A *real* cop."

Joseph was again in the dayroom. He worked his mouth and licked his lips as if he was preparing to say something momentous.

"Hi," he said.

Joseph resumed his mute stammering, which Swann surmised must be a new side effect of the medication. Swann inquired if Joseph was sure he wanted to continue his quest for a disability. The answer came in the military terminology that was prevalent on the ward.

"That's an affirmative."

Swann and Joseph sat across from each other like two passengers in a subway car so empty there was no luck to getting a seat. Swann asked a question he was not aware he had until he posed it.

"Not for nothing," Swann said. "But, when you were in high school, was there one girl you would have died for but never even looked at you?"

Joseph stopped licking his lips.

"Antoinette," Joseph said.

"And?" Swann asked.

"And? And nothing."

Swann arrived home with a mailroom slump to match his father's clothes. He felt all the more Joseph-like as he took from the freezer one of the four packages of fish sticks Ellen had given him to take over the morning he had gone to get his tie knotted. He rubbed away some of the frost with his index finger so he could read the directions.

Once he had the fish sticks in the oven and the timer set, Swann searched for a plate only to discover that they were all in the great pile of dirty dishes that rose from the sink. He ran the water hot and squirted in some soap and proceeded to wash the first dish of his adulthood.

Swann pulled the plate from the suds, clean and shining, and he was inspired to keep on scrubbing through dishes and silverware that had grown multicolored molds. He had a big stack of clean dishes when the timer on the stove went off. The sound was remarkably like that made by the buzzer outside the grand jury, the signal that he had been held blameless in the shooting of Daryl Coombs, that officially he had nothing to worry about.

Swann knew where the potholders were from all the occasions the sound of the oven timer had summoned his mother to take out a roast or a turkey or maybe a pie. He now opened the door, to see the three crusted rectangles.

When he had finished eating, Swann went to the sink to rinse the plate he had just washed. His earlier dishwashing had left a puddle in front of the sink, and he mopped it up.

That done, Swann decided he might as well clean the whole floor. He could only guess which of the cleansers under the sink was appropriate. He decided on ammonia, which smelled most like whatever was used in the subway, and he poured a half bottle into a bucket of water. He sent the squeegee back and forth, back and forth, until he had an expanse of gleaming linoleum.

Swann emptied the bucket in the bathtub, sponged up the grime left around the drain and continued scouring until the whole bathroom sparkled. He went into the living room with the vacuum cleaner, and he came to understand how Danica could get a kick out of causing dirt and dustballs to vanish wherever the chrome pipe pointed.

After he had vroomed through the other rooms, Swann dusted, and one quality of such work was that he thought of nothing until he came to his parents' bed. He tugged at the wrinkles left by his father and tucked the corners as he had so often seen his mother do. He smoothed the coverlet and the thought came that this was the place of his beginning just as the sidewalk in front of the theater had nearly been the place of his end.

Swann then headed for the gleaming bathroom to attend to the last thing in the place in need of scrubbing, himself. He trod squeaky clean into his room and came to what seemed a sort of test. He went ahead and made the bed even though he would be slipping inside the moment he was done.

In the morning, Swann remade the bed and drank coffee from a cup he had washed the night before. He sipped with his back against the kitchen counter, watching the sun pour through the window onto the floor. The restored gleam brought a memory no brighter than the day he had found his mother clutching a mop handle and struggling to catch her breath. He washed the cup again and left for work in his father's clothes.

Swann passed the street where he had lived. He remembered that first morning that might not have been, and he pictured Jenny on roller skates, streaking fearlessly toward him and Ellen. He continued toward the subway hoping to catch a glimpse of his wife and daughter much as he had once kept an eye out for Danica.

Evening returned Swann to the hospital, and he saw that Joseph's side effects had extended to twitches of the head and tremors in the limbs. Swann urged Joseph to forget the disability before he was truly disabled, and the involuntary twitches were joined by a very deliberate shake of the head.

"That's a negative," Joseph said.

Swann tried to make small talk. He again asked another question he did not know he had until he posed it, this about his mother.

"You know that," Joseph said. "We met in Coney Island."

"And?" Swann asked.

"And, I guess you'd have to say it was the lipstick."

The IAD men might have been looking or not looking for all Swann noticed on the ride back to Queens. He was too preoccupied with what he had heard in the hospital, with ordering it into a story, adding what he already knew and what he sensed must have been, running it all through his head as he might after questioning some crook.

Swann could see Joseph at eighteen, an apprentice ironworker learning to walk the narrow beams up amidst the winds that had killed his father. His one day off a week had been Sunday, and he had been lazing through this lone afternoon free of peril when the news of Pearl Harbor came over the radio. He had enlisted the very next morning, and the months ahead had seen him go from working the high steel to clawing for cover on the coral of a Pacific Island called Peleliu.

Swann pictured Joseph in a firefight, tearing open a wooden ammo box and discovering a three-inch square of white paper that a female munitions worker must have slipped inside. Bullets were whizzing and shells were exploding and men were screaming and dying and Joseph himself might have been but an instant from death as he stared at the imprint of a red lipstick kiss.

Joseph had still been carrying the paper kiss stuck inside his helmet a month later, when a bullet struck his shoulder. The helmet had been left behind as he was carried semiconscious to an aid station. A corpsman had there declared him the recipient of what was termed a "million-dollar wound," that being the value placed on being hurt badly enough to be evacuated but not so seriously as to be crippled.

Swann already knew that Joseph had been shipped home with enough permanent stiffness in his shoulder to be classified as 20 percent disabled. No evaluation had been made of his mental state, though he might have been said to have returned home more sane; he had refused to go back up on the steel, and he had not been dissuaded by news that those who died on the job were now paid for the entire day, even if they fell in the morning.

Swann knew also that Joseph had applied to the post office because it had preferential hiring for veterans. Joseph's own mail had brought his regular disability checks, which reset the value of his wound at exactly $23 a month.

What Swann had not known until this evening was that Joseph had spent his first check on a spree similar in spirit if not in scale to his son's adventures in leverage. He had ended up at the Atlantis Bar in Coney Island and there he had chanced to spy a young woman. She had been wearing lipstick of the same shade as the paper kiss he had lost the day he was shot.

Swann went into the house and the shipshape rooms and lingering scents of ammonia and scouring powder. He ate his three fish sticks and he washed the dish and he made his bed in the morning. He arrived at work on time and Marie was back to calling out her usual greeting.

As he arrived at the hospital that evening, Swann considered that he was seeing his father much more now than when they had been living two blocks apart. He asked Joseph no more questions about the past. He did try to lighten things by asking if the hospital served fish sticks.

"Not yet," Joseph said.

Joseph resumed silently working his mouth and licking his lips, the side effects seeming more pronounced since the last visit. Swann once more pressed Joseph to leave, saying he could not stand to see him this way.

"Why do you come?" Joseph asked.

"Because you're in the hospital," Swann said.

"But I'm not sick," Joseph said.

Swann turned angry.

"All the shit going on everywhere and you're bringing this on yourself," Swann said.

Joseph might have become no less angry had psychopharmacology allowed.

"You're fucking right," Joseph said. "That is exactly what I'm doing."

Swann bought a newspaper on the way back to Queens and spent the night as if his childhood home had become a tidy, private ECAB. He read cover to cover, and when he came to the financial pages he saw that the whole country seemed to be borrowing, borrowing, borrowing with ever more abandon. He felt a vague anxiety, although there was apparently no reason to believe that the fortunes of the world's greatest and richest nation were in any way subject to the same forces as those of Jack Swann, cave cop.

Swann continued his reading, the anxiety fading as he went through the comics and gone altogether when he came to the food section. He saw there a coupon good for twenty-five cents off a liter of club soda and his own adventures in leverage now led to his taking up a pair of scissors and snipping along the black dotted lines.

Swann had the next day off, which allowed him to arrive at the hospital during office hours. Joseph's doctor was clear-eyed and gave at least the impression of being attentive while Swann explained that Joseph was faking. The doctor answered with clinical talk about nightmares, irritability, difficulty in concentrating, and other classic symptoms of post traumatic stress disorder, known in the business as PTSD.

The doctor then produced a roll of paper that he said any policeman was sure to recognize as a polygraph tape. Swann saw no reason to say that the only lie detector ever employed by the transit police was a baseball bat that prisoners in the Room were told would strike them if they prevaricated.

The doctor proceeded to explain that Joseph had been wired to one of these machines the day before. The even lines at the beginning of the tape showed Joseph's blood pressure, pulse rate, and muscle tension while he listened to music. The lines turned jagged at the point the doctor had played a thirty-second recording of what was termed "moderate-intensity combat sounds stimulus." This established to an almost 90 percent certainty that Joseph was indeed suffering from PTSD. He was, in other words, a fake fake.

The doctor added that one hundred days of periodic combat was the limit the average infantryman could withstand psychologically and that Joseph had fought steadily for almost twice that. The doctor also said that case studies of World War II veterans had shown that those who fought the Japanese suffered a greater incidence of lasting psychiatric disorder than those who battled the Germans.

"Fighting is apparently more savage when the enemy is of a different race," the doctor said. "Apparently, the enemy does not seem quite *human.*"

The doctor related this with the continuing detachment of somebody for whom such things as savagery and race were abstract matters. Swann left without saying that Joseph had no doubt been coached by Jethro on the symptoms and must have figured a way to beat the polygraph. He also did not bother to say that people of other races can seem considerably more human once you shoot them.

Swann went down the hall thinking of the times he had heard transit police bosses speak of a war against what they often called *the criminal element.* The chiefs who talked this way were invariably white and by *element* they meant black teenagers.

Swann entered the ward to see a therapist who was black soothing a patient who was white, the one whose football helmet kept him from hurting himself. Swann sat down with Joseph and told him that the doctor had decided he was in fact sick.

"See," Joseph said. "It's working."

The black therapist walked by.

"How are you today, Joseph?" the therapist asked.

The therapist almost surely knew the details of Joseph's trouble on the train, yet his voice carried only kindness.

"Okay," Joseph said. "How're you?"

Swann almost asked Joseph his feelings about this *jamuke.* He did inquire how Joesph had beaten the polygraph. Joseph looked about and spoke in that monowhisper, adding a grin to the side effects.

"I thought about combat."

Swann arrived back in Queens with the whole afternoon ahead of him and IAD still right behind. He had the coupon in his pocket and he stopped into a supermarket. The club soda was marked Special Today, but Swann had learned enough from Ellen not to be surprised that it was selling for the usual price.

As he waited in the express line, Swann stole a look through the store's plate-glass windows just as he had at Gucci. He saw that the IAD men were at a pay phone across the street. One yawned and they both seemed only bored now that he had returned to a life no more interesting than that of the average transit cop.

"Eighty-nine cents, please."

Swann felt vaguely embarrassed as he presented the coupon, but he also felt a slight lift on leaving the store with twenty-five more cents than he would have otherwise. This tiny boost became inspiration as his eye reflexively went to where his two shadows stood.

The IAD men moved away from the pay phone as Swann approached. He proceeded with what was surely the very thing to do with his redeemed quarter.

"Hello?" Ellen said.

"Don't ha —"

Click.

"— ng up," Swann said.

The call lasted just long enough for Swann to lose the quarter. He then saw that the IAD men were still walking. He had thought that they had only been by the pay phone so as not to look like they were looking. He realized that they must really have been making a call to their office and that Lieutenant Gentile must have finally decided that there was nothing more to be gained from the surveillance. The time was fast approaching when Jack Swann would be summoned to officially explain his bankroll.

Swann started walking in no particular direction other than away from both Joseph's place and the house he still thought of as his home.

He let the traffic signal on the next corner determine whether he would turn.

The light flashed from red to green and Swann continued straight. He looked back, almost wishing IAD was still trailing him. He trudged ahead with just himself, feeling for a moment that he had lost his audience, that the show was over.

After several blocks, Swann decided on a destination that happened to be in that general way. He began to tire, but he kept going as he had along the subway line in Brooklyn. This trek took him beneath the elevated highway where he had ridden with Danica in the limousine.

Cars and trucks passed overhead as a weary Swann stood upon the scruffy cemetery plot where he would someday be buried however things went. He had no thought of that, only of the woman who lay in the adjoining plot.

Swann stared at his mother's name on the squat marble tombstone and read again the years of her life. He calculated that she had been nineteen on that night in Coney Island.

Swann remembered Joseph telling him in the psychiatric ward that Celeste had first gone to a neighborhood saloon, only to be told that women were to keep to the tables at the back. The Atlantis Bar, it seemed, had let even women belly-up, and Swann now pictured her standing at the bar, her lips painted that particular shade, a glass in the calloused hand that had helped build the very ship on whose deck Japan had surrendered. The peace had brought the soldiers home to reclaim their jobs, and she was having a drink after her last shift at the Brooklyn Navy Yard. She had thrown her final pay up on the bar, and at nineteen the most exciting work she could have looked forward to was being a waitress or a cashier or a salesgirl or something else no man wanted to be.

Joseph had seen the lipstick and he had stepped over, drably Irish, a man who had been able to impress people only when he had been up on the steel high enough for them to imagine him a Mohawk. Celeste might not have been in a favorable mood toward men in general, and indeed Joseph would tell Swann that she had answered his offer of a beer by saying she bought her own.

Everything might have ended right there had Joseph not dropped the only money he had ever received without working atop the last wages she would ever earn for her labors. She had laughed, and Joseph would later recount to Swann exactly what he had thought.

"I'm in."

Swann opened the bottle of club soda and raised it in a toast to Celeste. He took a long drink that would have tasted grand to anybody thirsty from a long walk.

The way back seemed longer, and the moment Swann arrived at the house, he sought the armchair. He recalled as one all the afternoons in his childhood when Celeste had sat here. The young face he had pictured at the Atlantis Bar took on the sad lines of the face he had known.

Celeste had gone from building the U.S.S. *Missouri* to keeping house for Joseph Swann. A moment had often come near the end of the day when her domestic labors were done and Joseph's tired step had not yet sounded on the stoop. She would fall into this very armchair and stare off while her son attempted various strategies to get her attention. He could now see her lined face and hear her voice, more hollow than tired, telling him to go, go and get himself something sweet.

After a while, Swann went into the kitchen. He ate three fish sticks and washed the lone dish afterward and returned to the living room. Memory passed with him into evening, that time after dinner when Joseph would assume the armchair and Celeste would shift to the sofa and young Swann would sprawl on the floor.

Swann remembered that the television had gone on as automatically as the lights, but he could not recall any particular moment of all the nights they had spent gazing at the flickering screen. Two, three, sometimes four hours a night, almost every night, for year after year, and he could reclaim no more than the names of a few shows and their characters. Even these melded into those he had later watched with Ellen.

The thought of television did recall a night when Joseph had stayed in the kitchen after dinner and helped him with a grammar school assignment to bring in something about their family. They had constructed a model of the Empire State Building out of cardboard, with a toothpick for the transmission tower which his father had told him broadcast invisible beams of television.

Swann now considered that he need not have gone back a whole generation to his grandfather's tower, that the same cardboard could have made a fine model of a battleship. He pictured Celeste washing dishes and tidying up, silent while he and Joseph cut and pasted. He wondered if she had felt as forgotten as indeed she was.

Swann was sure Celeste had chosen to remain silent in many circumstances, and that silence seemed to still hang in the house as he went down the hall to what was again his room. He was lying down when he remembered that Celeste had helped him make the papier-mâché head he had worn as a beast at the manger in the class Christmas pageant. He had shared the stage with Danica, but his one clear recollection was of peering through the eyeholes to see his mother and father smiling back at him.

Swann's last thoughts before sleep were of Jenny, who would never again see her mother and father as a single approving presence. His regret over his recent deceptions gave way to a wish that he had been able to maintain a larger fiction.

In the morning, Swann had no sooner risen than he was making the bed. He was tucking in the blanket when the telephone rang. He picked up to hear Sergeant Quinn, and he understood that Ellen had abdicated her position as transit spouse to such a degree that she had given the number where he might be reached.

"I just stepped out," Swann said.

Sergeant Quinn thereupon informed Swann that he was to report to IAD that very morning.

Swann figured Coleman would also be summoned and he knew he owed her a telephone call. Their relationship had always ended with work, so he had to first ring District 1. He got her home number from a clerk and dialed.

"Speak."

The voice was male. Swann decided not to be too personal.

"Officer Coleman, please."

"Not here."

Swann thought this might be a variation on the standard transit response.

"It's very important," Swann said. "Are you sure she's not there?"

"Did you hear what I said?"

Click. Swann lowered the receiver, all but sure Coleman was gone, guessing that she was either at IAD or on her way there. He had failed to foresee that they might not be able to talk before she was called down. He realized that in telling her about the Money Store he should have told her not to resist if IAD ever pressed her about the source of his cash.

He now hoped she would not get herself in trouble by evading the question he had resisted answering.

The appointed hour saw Swann enter a Brooklyn office building and ascend in an elevator too slow to bring a dip to his stomach. He had known all along that this moment would come, and he could no longer tell himself that he would worry about it later; now was later.

At the thirteenth floor, Swann stepped off into the dim hallway that had the look and feel of the underground. He pushed a buzzer beside an unmarked wooden door. A voice asked him to identify himself, then instructed him to wait.

He looked at the closed door and thought that Coleman might well be inside at this very moment. He still bristled at the thought of being forced to tell IAD where he got his money. That did not keep him from hoping that she would tell them whatever she was asked.

He saw that the floor was littered with cigarette butts ground out by other cops who had been called here, and he decided the wait was intentional, designed to unnerve. He was himself pacing and rattling the change in his chinos when the door opened. He pulled his hands from his pockets and prepared to stride manfully in only to see Coleman appear.

The door shut, and they stood alone at the portal to the Dark Side. She looked unfazed, and he momentarily relaxed. He was filled with the simple feeling that he was glad to see her.

"So?" Swann asked.

Coleman eyed Swann's decidedly civil service attire.

"So, I hope you're only dressing like that for them," Coleman said.

Coleman had herself chosen to face the IAD wearing black bicycle pants and a cow-print top.

"Listen . . . ," Swann said.

Coleman held up a hand, accepting unsaid the apology he was about to offer for causing her to be summoned.

"I tried to call you this morning, but you were already gone," Swann said. "I hope if they asked where I got the money, you just told them."

"They seem to have their mind made up about that," Coleman said. "All they asked was did I see you take it and did I take some, too."

Coleman winked.

"I told them a person doesn't have to steal to dress nice."

Swann was not sure whether she was referring to him or herself.

"I also told them that the way they should know you didn't take money was that I would have locked your ass up."

He thanked her.

"Don't think I wouldn't have," she said.

She hit the button to summon the elevator.

"I was going to call you this morning, too," she said. "But they didn't have your new number at work and I didn't want to bother your wife."

That word *wife* seemed to hover there.

"If you ever need me, my father's Joseph," Swann said. "It's in the book."

Coleman boarded.

"I would wish you luck, but I don't think luck's got anything to do with it," she said.

She waved as the elevator doors closed. He went back to jingling his change.

A plainclothes sergeant finally opened the door. He turned to call out a warning to those inside.

"I got somebody coming!"

Swann heard scurrying sounds as he followed the sergeant into a deserted squadroom. IAD investigators were not supposed to be seen by other cops, and they had secreted themselves in the side offices. The doors were cracked and from each a single eye peered out at the case of real, big-time corruption.

The only door from which nobody was peeping was the one Swann was ushered through. He was left to sit alone in a windowless room that had a frayed green carpet. He was growing increasingly tempted to crack the door and peep out himself when the sergeant returned with Lieutenant Gentile.

Gentile sat down at a steel desk and tapped his pipe onto the edge of a cut-glass ashtray. He had brought a thick folder that could only have been Swann's locator.

"I would have guessed you would be wearing a suit," Gentile said.

Gentile was himself wearing a blue suit of a lusterless material. He opened the file and began to flip through a stack of field reports that no doubt progressed from the shooting of Daryl Coombs to the finding of the drug money to what transpired afterward.

"We have a saying here," Gentile said. "'If it looks like a duck and walks like a duck and talks like a duck, it's probably a duck.'"

His eyes were on Swann.

"I guess I should thank you for having the nerve to report you were carrying such a large sum when you were robbed," Gentile said.

Gentile maintained his stare long enough to establish that he considered this reporting of the truth to be the ultimate arrogance, a dare. The tobacco-stained fingers resumed turning the reports, these including the very ones that Swann had smiled at imagining on Gentile's desk.

Swann's jaw clenched as Gentile came to the last sheets. One of these would be a summary of the interview with Ellen.

"You had no cause to go to my house," Swann said.

Gentile slowly turned over the last report, this probably documenting the phone call the IAD men had made while Swann was in the supermarket redeeming his first coupon.

"You had no cause to involve my family," Swann said.

Gentile took a stack of photographs from a manila envelope at the back of the file. He held up an eight-by-ten-inch black-and-white print of Swann and Danica standing with the rain-drenched crowd outside Eleanor's.

"Pretty girl," Gentile said.

Gentile returned the photos to the envelope and closed the file.

"I think we can begin," he said. "What time do you have, Officer Swann?"

Swann told him.

"Did you buy yourself a new watch as well?" Gentile asked.

"No," Swann said.

"If I remember correctly, it had a tendency to run a little fast. Did you have it repaired?"

"No."

Gentile glanced at his own wrist.

"Well, it certainly seems to be running fine now," he said.

The sergeant turned on a tape recorder and noted aloud the time, date, and place of the interview, as well as those present. Gentile began filling his pipe from an economy-sized tin and asked Swann to think back to the two occasions he had been robbed in the subway.

"I really have only one question," Gentile said.

Gentile paused here to light his pipe, and Swann thought back not to the last car, but a squadroom and the night when he had sat spattered with Daryl Coombs's blood, his hands shaking. He had listened to this same voice say that one matter concerning the shooting had not been addressed, that there remained the question of Swann's being outside the system.

Now became then as the match sizzled, and Gentile leisurely popped his lips on the stem, waiting for fear and doubt to take hold. Whatever way others might cope with working on the Dark Side, Gentile had embraced IAD's power to intimidate, and Swann had challenged it even before he became a suspected thief.

"How did you come to have so much cash in your possession?"

Swann felt his cheeks burn hot, as if they remembered the sear of a muzzle flash.

"With all due respect to your rank, sir, I can't see how it is any of your business," Swann said.

Gentile had not even bothered to pose this general question to Coleman. Swann had no doubt that IAD had indeed already made up its mind and he did not imagine that Gentile expected him to confess. The query's purpose was made clear as Gentile calmly reminded him that under Chapter 4, Section 2.5 of the Department Manual, any officer who refused to answer questions put by IAD could be suspended on the spot.

"Do I need to repeat the question?" Gentile asked.

Swann knew that with suspension his wages would stop as abruptly as his paternal grandfather's had when he fell off the Empire State Building. The bills he would be unable to pay would include the installments to the Money Store and that meant he would lose not just the gas meter, but the whole house. He would be putting his wife and daughter in the street.

"Well?" Gentile asked.

Swann also knew that within the very minute he refused, he would have to reach into his waistband and surrender his shield and the revolver with which he had killed and which had almost killed him. Swann had no love for this weapon, but he rebelled at the prospect of turning it over to this particular man. The feeling was intensified by his sense that Gentile would be happier receiving his revolver than his answer.

"Should I take your silence as a refusal?" Gentile asked.

The moment was no easier to bear for being what Swann could have foreseen from the start. His father's clothes now felt more fitting than the Brooks Brothers suit. He appreciated as seldom before how much harder it can be to tell the truth.

"I borrowed it," Swann said.

Gentile gave the same lidded stare he had given the night of the shooting, when Swann said his watch was running fast.

"Suppose you tell us exactly where it was you *borrowed* from?" Gentile asked.

The second answer came as easily as a lie.

"The Money Store," Swann said.

Gentile again gave the lidded stare.

"Why not the tooth fairy?" he asked.

The sergeant spoke for the first time.

"No, Lieu, there really is a place called that. It has the commercial with Phil Rizzuto. You know, the Scooter."

Gentile silenced the sergeant with a stern look and took several slow pulls on the pipe. Swann's clearest feeling was the headache the smoke was starting to give him.

"And can you tell us how much you borrowed?" Gentile asked.

"Ten thousand dollars," Swann said. "You can check with the Money Store if you want."

"Oh, we will," Gentile said.

"Just ask for Ben," Swann said.

Swann had nothing else to tell. He sat empty save for the hope that Gentile was more than a little annoyed that all those reports had been for naught.

"Tell me, was this before or after you recovered the bag of money in Brooklyn?" Gentile asked.

Here Gentile posed a question Swann had not expected. Swann now thought back to the room at the Plaza, when he had told Danica that he had borrowed the money and she had still seen some scheme at work, when she had been so titillated she had reached for his belt before he could say anything more.

"After," Swann said.

"How much was in that bag, sixty-six thousand?" Gentile asked.

"A little less."

"Maybe about ten thousand less."

Gentile seemed to have decided that the loan was a ploy to account for the skimmed drug money. The notion struck Swann as only ridiculous, but apparently it was easier for Gentile to accept than the idea that a cave cop would put up his house to borrow ten grand and head for the Oak Bar.

"Lieu, I have answered all your questions, and when you check with the Money Store, you will see I have told you only the truth," Swann said. "I am prepared to answer any other questions you might have."

The lidded gaze narrowed.

"I have nothing for the moment," Gentile said. "Though I am sure that I will have some in the future."

The sergeant turned off the tape recorder and called out a warning that again brought the scurrying noises. Swann walked back out by the cracked doors and the peeping eyes that believed him guilty of one sin he had not committed. He was sure that he had nothing to worry about from IAD, that he had done nothing to warrant a departmental trial, much less an indictment. He passed on to the street where the eyes did not look at him at all and he was left with only himself in judgment.

*   *   *

Swann was just walking into Joseph's house when the phone rang.

"It's me."

Coleman asked how he had fared with IAD. Swann said he had simply told the truth.

"Anyway, what can they do?" he said.

"That's probably what they're thinking right now," she said.

Swann heard himself laugh, but the remark stayed with him after he hung up. He shook off a chill that came when he recalled Lieutenant Gentile's last words. The man from the Dark Side had really been saying that he might not be able to get Swann now, but somehow, some way, the time would surely come.

Swann had a day off still before him, and he had an urge to run, or at least go jogging, but he had neither cut-offs nor sneakers. He settled for taking another walk, his initial course determined only by a desire to go in another direction than the day before. He let the traffic lights again guide his meandering until he felt the tug of a destination that seemed the right distance, as measured by both blocks and memory.

The Unisphere looked to Swann as if a quick rub with one of the cleaners under Celeste's sink would restore it to what it had been when it had stood as the centerpiece of the 1964 World's Fair. The pavilions had long since been demolished, but the stainless-steel globe remained, hardly tarnished since the day young Swann had circled it. He had been looking for Pelelieu. His mouth had been stuffed with what would be one of his two clearest memories of the fair, a Belgian waffle.

An older Swann walked around the now dry fountain at the globe's base, still unable to pinpoint the Pacific island where Joseph had been shot. He stopped and gazed out across the grounds where he had once passed with his parents through a vision of a glorious time to come.

Joseph, Celeste, and Jack had gone with the crowds from Progressland to the World of Tomorrow to the Avenue of Science. The only promise he had yet to see realized was the clattering ZMT machine in the Mailroom of the Future. The fairgrounds had become a flat expanse of browned grass that fit seamlessly into the landscape of what had come to be.

Swann started back across the scrabble of what was, the fair's notions of the future seeming to be of the very stuff as his own fantasies of Danica and of being a hero. He felt harder pressed than ever before to forsake the belief from which his imaginings sprang. He had called upon the facts to prove himself not a thief, and the facts now seemed to be calling upon him to accept that he had been wrong ever to believe that something remarkable had been sparked in the joining of a bleary postal worker and a disconsolate housewife.

Swann passed along a spindly row of trees that were still not much more than saplings and which would need years more before this place lost the feel of a huge vacant lot. He guessed that this particular patch was about where the Vatican pavilion had been. There, a moving sidewalk had carried him into a darkened chamber where a halo of spotlights had shone upon a marble sculpture of the Blessed Virgin cradling the crucified Jesus.

These years later, Swann remembered the hush he had felt within himself in that one moment before the conveyor belt carried him away from the Pieta. He was sure that the feeling had not been religious in the sense the Church might have hoped, any more than he had been accepting the teachings of the nuns when he had lain on the sidewalk appealing to the Almighty to save him from his own revolver.

Indeed, Swann still could not have described the power to which he had made his most desperate plea. Had he been called upon to declare the mystery of his own particular faith, he would have had trouble articulating it much beyond saying that the hands of its making had come to include those of Michelangelo and Daryl Coombs.

Thirteen

SWANN CARRIED ON with his duties as a house mouse, and the workdays ahead passed as though he were serving an indeterminate sentence for having harbored too grand a conception of himself. He might have retained the right to his revolver, but it was now just a discomfort at his groin when he reached for a TP-30 form.

Swann remained at his desk during those meal periods when he and Coleman would have been strolling the underground. He did continue to hear her every so often over a passing cop's radio, and he deduced she was off Thanksgiving Day when the voice of another dispatcher crackled through the static.

Swann knew little about her life outside work other than that she did not watch television. He tried to picture her at home, on that street in Brooklyn, sitting down to a turkey dinner with her brother and the mother she had mentioned on occasion. She had never spoken of her father or, for that matter, of a boyfriend.

Swann had his own Thanksgiving dinner at the hospital with Joseph. They sat near the patient who spent each day pushing a book back and forth a fraction of an inch. He was doing the same with his plate.

"Better not ask him to pass the gravy," Joseph said.

Back in Queens, the route from the subway again took Swann past his block. Ellen's parents had moved to Florida, so he figured she and Jenny must have eaten their turkey at home, his chair standing empty at the table. Swann arrived at Joseph's street too restless just to sit inside. He embarked on another of the long walks that had lately taken the place of jogging. He caught himself peering back over his shoulder. He again almost wished he still had his shadows.

The traffic light went red, so Swann turned. He felt another tug of memory and he went by his former grammar school. He could have been shadowing himself as he ambled by his old high school.

In retrospect, the sight of the teenage Danica coming down the hall had affected him a little like the Pieta, but also a little like the Belgian waffle. He passed the school remembering a day he had seen his Blessed Waffle stroll hand in hand up this same sidewalk with Timothy Neary, who had looked all the more sleek and handsome in his Marine Corps uniform.

Farther on, Swann came to Pip's ice cream parlor, where a teenage Swann had gone in the company of only his appetite. He could not have Danica, but he could order the mountain of ice cream, syrups, fruit, nuts, sprinkles, and whipped cream that was listed on the menu as the Kitchen Sink. His waitress often was a thin girl his own age he would not have called pretty. Her nameplate read ELLEN.

Young Swann had taken to sitting with Ellen at the end of her shift, watching her count her tips, the stacks of sticky coins marking the day *good* or *bad* or *about the same*. He had then walked her home, and he had finally dared to brush her hand with his fingertips. She had pressed her palm against his, and they had continued hand in hand, just like Timothy and Danica.

A lone Swann now trailed this memory up to the house where Ellen had lived. His thoughts went to a night when her parents had been at a Knights of Columbus dance. She had led him down to the finished basement, and he remembered that the only light had been a small bulb over her father's aquarium. They had wriggled and gasped as they fumbled in each other's clothing, and she had seemed the only girl in the world.

Two decades later, Swann retained the image of her pale form bouncing off to the bathroom afterward. He had peered down at himself and noticed a smear of something dark. He had wiped it with his fingers and held his hand in the aquarium's light to see that it was her blood.

The next recollection Swann had was of her return from the bathroom. He remembered how she had shimmered in the lone bulb. He remembered their exact words to each other.

"I love you," Swann had said.
"I love you," Ellen had said.

Two more paydays took Swann almost to mid-December. He was undertaking Sullivan's former task of handing out the paychecks when he once more heard Coleman's voice carried by a burst of static. He looked up to see that the radio was held by Fredricks.

Swann thumbed through the checks. These were the last before the holidays, the ones for that pay period in which everybody had been out "working for Christmas," summoning all their wits and guile to make as many arrests as were possible in the underground. The alphabetized stack on his desk represented the very most each of these cops could achieve as measured by money.

"Fee . . . , fie . . ., fo . . . , Fredricks," Swann said.

Swann held up the check and watched Fredricks go intent for the instant needed to make sure that the collars had indeed become the extra dollars. His face then slackened into its usual expression, and he looked like a child who had not gotten all he wanted for Christmas. He might have long since ceased to believe in such silly things as Santa, but desire still seemed to rise in him as expectation.

Disappointment on his face and the biggest check he could muster in his pocket, Fredricks departed to play Santa for kids who were still in that time of which Danica had spoken, who still believed they had only to be good to get what they wanted.

The last check was Swann's. He would not have minded a little overtime to help him meet the next Money Store payment, but he did not feel the sort of disappointment that Fredricks and indeed most of the other officers had shown.

Swann had, after all, received and spent a much larger check with unhappy results. The most comfort he could draw from the experience was that he was one cave cop who had done his Christmas shopping early.

The afternoon before Christmas, Swann arrived at the hospital to escort Joseph home. Joseph was back in his own clothes, having been discharged as an outpatient and awarded a full disability. He had his duffel bag over his shoulder, and in his hand he clutched an audio cassette of actual World War II combat sounds much the same as those which had been used to prove him a fake fake. The difference was that this recording was subliminal, below the level he could consciously register. He was to listen at home to what he could not hear and thereby give vent to the fears he did not know he had.

"The idea is to become de-repressed," the doctor said.

Father and son walked to the subway, and Swann hoped the train would be American built. The train was Japanese, but Joseph did not register any objections, perhaps because nobody was going to crowd a man who was twitching and jerking and licking his lips.

Joseph did stop twitching for a moment when he arrived home and discovered everything shiny clean. He looked about as if the place had been visited by Celeste's ghost.

"What, you got a girl in?" Joseph asked.

Joseph assumed the armchair. Swann went to the supermarket and returned having made his biggest redemption yet, a $2 coupon for a turkey. He set the oven according to the instructions on the plastic wrapper and basted at the prescribed intervals. The bird had begun to turn a golden brown when he retired to the living room.

"What, you cook, too?" Joseph asked.

"I don't know yet," Swann said.

He sat on the sofa and proved not much better at making small talk at home than he had at the hospital. Joseph answered with a few monosyllables.

Only when a click came from the cassette recorder did Swann realize that the silence between him and his father had been filled with inaudible screams and gunshots and explosions. Joseph turned the tape over and Swann strained to hear the combat sounds, but he was no more successful than he had been in his childhood attempts to see the invisible beams.

Swann might have himself been succumbing to the subliminal as his thoughts went back to his eighteenth birthday and the cavernous main sorting room at the General Post Office. The ZMT machines had been still years away and he had gone down a long row of clerks who sat sorting mail into banks of cubbyholes. His father had been down toward the end, sitting on a gray metal stool.

Swann must have called to Joseph then just as he did now.

"Dad."

Joseph looked over from the armchair where he had always sat as the one who had been to war, who made the money and set the rules, who was the Man of the House.

"At least you won't be sorting any more mail," Swann said.

Joseph nodded.

"At least I won't be sorting any more mail," Joseph said.

Joseph went silent again. The tape kept playing those inaudible sounds of war.

"Remember when you had me come to your job?" Swann asked. "When I turned eighteen?"

"I remember," Joseph said.

"And you took me down to that train?"

"After that supervisor wouldn't let me step off. Four freaking minutes."

Swann had forgotten that part, but at Joseph's reminder it came to him as clearly as if it had popped out of hiding. He remembered how Joseph had held one hand aloft and continued to sort with the other until a man wearing a tie had come over.

Joseph had asked to *step off*, saying that his son was turning eighteen that day and had come to visit. The supervisor had said that it was still four minutes to meal and Joseph had been forced to keep sorting until the meal break was announced over the public address system. He had only then been allowed to rise from his gray stool and he had crowded with the other clerks around the time clock, his half-hour break ticking away.

The teenage Swann had not been too young to understand how his father must have felt. The full-grown Swann could see that those feelings lingered.

"You still got me to the train," Swann said.

"That, I did," Joseph said.

Father had then led son out of the main sorting room and through hallways and stairwells and onto a train platform at Penn Station. Swann remembered going through billowing steam to see what Joseph said was the midnight train from Dover. He had watched the workmen's clothes darken with sweat as they unloaded one long aluminum box and then another and then another. Each had contained the body of a young man killed in Vietnam and presently en route home for burial.

"Sounds like it's time," Joseph now said.

The oven timer was buzzing.

As if in a variation of the IAD axiom cited by Lieutenant Gentile, what Swann took from the oven looked like a cooked turkey, smelled like a cooked turkey, and tasted like a cooked turkey.

"A little dry," Joseph said. "But not too bad."

"Maybe I could baste a little more," Swann said.

Swann forked in another mouthful of turkey and gazed across the table to see Joseph doing the same. There had been thirty-seven aluminum boxes on the train platform that night. The sight of them had been enough to convince Swann that Joseph was right, that he should seek something that made him draft exempt, something like becoming a police trainee. He had taken the tests for both the city and the transit police, and he had gone with the one that called him first.

"The salad's nice," Joseph said.

Swann took a bite of salad, which he had prepared using a little tip he remembered from Danica.

"You can't say the lettuce isn't crisp," Swann said.

After he had cleared the table and washed the dishes, Swann went to the bedroom closet where he had transferred his purchases from Fifth Avenue. Joseph accepted his present with a polite but absent thanks and tore half-heartedly at the wrapping paper.

"I'll be," Joseph said.

He fingered the mother-of-pearl buttons of the white dress shirt and asked where Swann thought he might wear such a thing.

"Out," Swann said.

"Where would I want to go?"

"I don't know. Out."

"The only place I'm going is to sleep."

Joseph put the shirt back in the box and went to bed. Swann himself had no place to go other than his own room, but he was not ready for sleep and he lay still dressed atop the shipshape bed. Memory came upon him again, as unbidden hunger once had. He saw himself a rookie in his new transit police uniform, going day after day without being called on to do anything more heroic than give directions. The moment had finally come when he heard a scream for help and he had dashed across the mezzanine a savior. He had stopped dead on seeing that the shrieks were coming from a black man who was being beaten by Sullivan.

"*God, stop!*"

"*Nigger motherfucker!*"

Swann shifted on the bed, breathing deeply in and slowly out. He listened to a car speeding too fast up the block outside and then all was still again. He got flashes of Sullivan dragging the black man over to a scarred door, of the Room with its slanted ceiling and blood-spattered walls, of the two cops who put down their lunches to join in the beating, of the thumps and screams, of the black man kneeling, his head bowed, blood dripping into the concrete as he apologized for daring to ask *Why?* when an officer asked him to stop.

Sullivan had turned to Swann and said that he could not take the collar because he had pipe band rehearsal that evening. Swann had protested that he could hardly be the arresting officer when he had not witnessed the offense.

Sullivan's reply now came back to Swann word for word.

"*Don't worry, kid. I'll tell you what you saw. All you got to do is use the truth as home base.*"

That became the night when Swann first fetched napkins and ice, first touched black skin, first felt warm blood run with melting ice between his fingertips, first conducted a strip search and peered into a man's bare backside, first fingerprinted somebody, first put somebody in a cage, first rehearsed a lie before the bathroom mirror in District 1. The words had been suggested by Sullivan.

"*Only necessary force was used to effect the arrest.*"

And first called Ellen to say he could not meet her as planned. She had been at work and her boss had been calling to her in the background as she congratulated him on his first arrest. He had been in District 1 with Sullivan at his side, and he had seen no way to say anything except that he would see her when he was done.

The routine had been even slower then, and forty-eight hours had passed before Swann had told his lie and the black man had pleaded guilty to resisting arrest in exchange for being released on time served. The two of them ended up descending into the subway together, and Swann had found himself holding the gate open so the man could save himself the fare. Swann had heard three more words that would stay with him.

"*No, thank you.*"

Swann had not slept for three days when he arrived at Pip's to walk Ellen home. The manager had congratulated Swann on his first arrest, insisting he have a Kitchen Sink on the house. Ellen had sat with him in her polyester uniform with its nameplate.

These thirteen years later, after they had married and had a child and broken apart, he wondered if the outcome would have been different if he had told her everything about that first arrest.

He gazed about his bedroom and saw that he had left the closet door open. The four-foot purple giraffe stood with its suede ears perked, its glass eyes staring right back at him.

Christmas music was coming from Holy Child Church. Swann figured that the midnight mass must be nearly over. What sounded like the whole congregation was singing "Silent Night" as he hurried past with the giraffe tucked under an arm, the other packages in hand.

Jenny had been drawing on the pavement again, only what Swann made out in the streetlight was not a wobbly attempt at a hopscotch cross. The wild scribbling went in big, frenzied loops, then tightened into knots so furious that the chalk stick had crumbled.

Swann eased the key into the lock and slipped inside the house. He saw the tree standing not in the usual place by the sofa, but in the corner where the television had been. Ellen had managed without him to place the star on top. She seemed to have taken even more care than usual in hanging the ornaments.

A freer spirit was evidenced on the lower branches, where Jenny had tossed handful upon handful of tinsel. Swann laid the presents at the base, failing to see the milk and cookies that she had left out for Santa. His foot knocked over the glass. The clink caused him to flinch.

Swann could not just leave the milk spilled on the floor, and he avoided the added noise of fetching a sponge from the kitchen by pulling off the sweatshirt he was wearing. The spill gone, he decided that it did not seem right to leave the cookies sitting next to an empty glass.

The cookie stuck in Swann's throat like some gooey Host when he heard the creak of a floorboard. He could do nothing but stay absolutely still and listen to another creak and then another. He saw a silhouette appear from the hallway.

Ellen was in a crouched position with both arms extended, as she had no doubt learned from some cop show. Her hands held the elegant little Walther PPK he had bought back when he was first a cop and had seen in a gun shop an opportunity to have one thing in common with James Bond.

"I thought you were a burglar," Ellen said.

Swann noted that Ellen kept the weapon raised. He quickly explained that he had only been delivering some presents.

"You wouldn't shoot Santa, would you?" Swann asked.

Ellen lowered the weapon with a little grunt of defeat, as if a bullet would be useless against the cause of her hurt.

"Fucking Danica," Ellen said.

Ellen spoke this name in a tone that continued to resonate in Swann after she had ordered him out and he had returned to the street. He knew that she had not been speaking of the Danica who shopped at Duane Reade and hated sweeping and had truly profound notions about Santa. She had meant the same Danica who had so long inhabited Swann's fantasies.

The cold had Swann shivering, and he pulled on the milk-damp sweatshirt. He left the block thinking that long before Ellen became a redeemer she must have measured herself by the standard of what everybody was supposed to want, that she must have sometimes wished that she was a girl who drew stares when she passed down the hallway, a girl who left the boys yearning without their knowing anything about her but what she looked like, who would have needed only a smile to get whomever she wanted.

The conclusion was as obvious as the instructions on a frozen turkey. He turned onto the next block considering that he was not necessarily the man Ellen would have picked if she could have chosen anybody, that she had very likely settled for him just as he had settled for her.

Midnight mass was over, and Holy Child Church stood dark. Swann had earlier been too intent on his mission to notice that the Christ

Child had been laid in the crêche's cradle of straw. His eyes went from the small plaster figure to the very steps which he and Ellen had once descended as newly pronounced *man* and *wife*.

Swann remembered that their family and friends had applauded and flashbulbs had popped on all sides as if they were some kind of celebrities. A silver limousine had whisked them off to the reception, and they had drawn rousing cheers when they danced and when they kissed and when they fed each other cake. They had then headed for a honeymoon in the Poconos, and he now wondered if Ellen had understood any more than he that the people who cheered and threw rice were sending the new Mr. and Mrs. Jack Swann off to a life exactly like their own.

Swann turned down Joseph's block, thinking of the wedding night and how even the bed had been different, round and satin-sheeted. He had entered her so hurriedly he had felt the faint cool of the contraceptive goo not yet completely warmed by her heat. They had been in their new home when he first saw a tube of spermicide sitting out in the bathroom, and it had shrunk from the bottom, fold by fold like toothpaste, as familiarity joined them even in bed. Those first hot couplings in her family's basement seemed to have been not so much a miracle as an enticement, or perhaps simply a passage.

One step had remained, and perhaps he and Ellen had both unconsciously hoped that this was what was missing. The night had arrived when he had encountered none of the usual goo and he had indeed felt a new intensity. They had soon neared the moment against which they had always taken precautions and she had wrapped both her arms around him as if she were pitching herself overboard and taking him with her.

Swann had been sure they had conceived the very first time, or at least the second. He had learned otherwise when he saw her panties soaking in the bathroom sink just as he would years later see his T-shirt.

The next month they had tried again, the attempts becoming progressively less memorable. The familiar had taken hold again, but he had seen no more panties in the sink and she had gone to see the doctor.

Now, as he arrived back at Joseph's house and his own bed, he remembered Ellen's return from the doctor. He saw her burst through the door as if she could not wait to tell him, only to hesitate and say nothing, momentarily unable to speak.

Swann overslept and he woke on Christmas morning with just minutes to wash and dress. He shouted a "Merry Christmas" through the closed door of his father's bedroom.

"You, too," Joseph said.

Swann's hurry fell away as he went by his block. He had no thoughts of the past or how he had come to be where he was. He thought only of this present moment and where he was not. He knew that Jenny would be by the tree, seeing Santa had been there, but most likely not feeling Daddy's presence even in spirit. He felt more absent than if he had died, not even a ghost.

At District 1, a two-foot plastic tree stood by the front desk. The holding cell had been decorated with a banner whose legend, HAPPY NOEL, had been rearranged to read HAPPY LEON. The cell was empty, for the cops had developed their usual holiday blindness to anything that might entail spending the night at ECAB. This was one of those instances when time was more important than overtime.

Roll call showed that the only cops working were rookies without families and those who, like Swann, were out of the house. Fredricks, and no doubt Mannering, were at home being as good fathers as they were cops on the witness stand. Hardly a wife or a goom called all morning, which left Swann without even the usual distractions of the telephone.

Swann rocked back in the chair and grabbed the two plastic arms and realized he had seen Sullivan do exactly this. He rose and wandered the district, passing the radio room. He ducked inside.

Swann returned to his desk with a portable radio, but several minutes passed without so much as a burst of static, and he checked twice to make sure the thing was on. He finally heard a crackling.

"[Unintelligible] central," a cop said.

"[Unintelligible] go," Coleman said.

After a moment, the Christmas morning quiet returned. Swann reached for a pen to perform some clerical duties and was reminded that he had one present remaining in his locker. He looked at the portable radio and its silence became an invitation. He picked it up and pressed the transmit bar.

"*So?*"

Swann got no response, and he wondered if transit police communications had been unable to convey even this brief a message. He was back to sitting and doing nothing when the telephone rang.

"*Yo!*" Coleman said.

Swann arrived first at the subway soda fountain, and he was halfway through a cup of coffee when he spotted Coleman approach wearing a bright green leather overcoat and gold earrings the size and shape of door knockers. She smiled on seeing him and his mouth moved to answer with the same. He discovered he was already smiling.

Swann had told Coleman on the phone that he had something for her, but she nonetheless seemed more flustered on receiving a gift than he had ever seen her at a shooting or a morgue. Her hands looked not just small, but delicate, as she carefully tore away the wrapping and held up the oversized pen. She unscrewed the cap and saw the eighteen-carat nib.

"I was thinking I needed something to sign in and out with," she said.

She had told Swann that she also had a present for him, and she produced a small package from her overcoat pocket. He ripped at the paper with absolutely no idea what might be inside. He certainly did not expect what he saw.

"Get it?" she asked. "Yo! Yo!"

He slipped the loop at the end of the string around his ring finger and gave an experimental toss of his new police-blue yo-yo. He could not remember the last time he had even seen a yo-yo. He had last touched one when he was not much older than Jenny was now, when he had himself believed all was as well as in the storybooks, when he had thought his father a hero whom his mother was happy only to serve, when he had not yet started want, want, wanting.

The yo-yo spun down to its limit, and he found a familiar comfort as it thwacked back snugly into his palm. He tossed it again and heard laughter.

He had been so diverted that he had failed to notice a passing posse. The members of the posse had certainly noticed him, and their hilarity showed that they saw him as neither a vic nor Five-O. They themselves seemed for a moment less like crooks than simply kids, though they regained the bearing of a wolfpack as they neared the turnstiles and the steps leading to the street.

"There's some vic up there who's about to find he ain't alone on Christmas, after all," Coleman said.

Swann and Coleman were due back at their respective duties, and they were saved from even considering whether to trail the posse. Her cheer dimmed at the prospect of returning to the communications unit. He blurted another apology for having landed her there.

"Swann, you know what your problem is?" she said. "Your problem is that you . . ."

She cupped her hands over her mouth and nose and made a sound remarkably like that of radio static.

". . . [unintelligible]."

As Swann entered District 1, the desk officer gave him a smug look that showed continued pleasure in seeing him reduced to a house mouse in civil service attire. Swann gave a flick of his wrist and got his first indication that a yo-yo might incite as much ire among his fellow officers as a suit. He kept tossing through the rest of the tour and attempted an old childhood trick in the muster room.

"You call that an Around the World?" a cop asked.

Swann continued to practice at home, the yo-yo also proving to be a good way to pass the time while Joseph put on his subliminal tape.

"Jackie, what made you buy a yo-yo?" Joesph asked.

"Somebody gave it to me."

"For what? Who gives grown people yo-yos?"

"My partner."

"I thought you were working inside."

"My old partner."

"Fredricks gave you a yo-yo?"

Swann had made no conscious decision not to tell Joseph that he had been working with a black female.

"The partner I had after him," Swann said.

"I don't know what kind of cop gives people yo-yos."

The only sounds were subliminal.

The turkey lasted another couple of days. Swann would have tried cooking something new had he not been restrained by what the financial pages would have termed his "deficit." The country's deficit was well over a trillion dollars but seemed to be having no effect at all. Swann's few thousand of debt promised to keep them to a fish-stick diet at least until Joseph's first disability check came.

On New Year's Eve, Swann did splurge on two modest steaks, these proving even easier to cook than the turkey. He and Joseph afterward turned on the television for the traditional broadcast from Times Square. The show's host was chatting cheerfully at a booth in the center of the square, as relaxed as might be expected in an area closed off by more than a thousand helmeted city cops.

Swann watched as a camera swept along the police barricades to show the people on the other side waving and cheering and blowing noisemakers. He had in other years been posted directly beneath this scene, and he knew that this was the big night for posses. They were surely in the shadows beyond the reach of the television lights, snaking silently in single file, scouting out vics, waiting for the big moment when everyone would be distracted.

The famous ball commenced its slow slide down the pole atop the building at the center of the square. Swann listened to a quarter million people begin shouting out the last seconds of 1986.

"Ten!"

"Nine!"

"Eight!"

"Seven!"

Swann knew the posses would have their throwaways on.

"Four!"

"Three!"

"Two!"

"One!"

"Happy New Year!"

Swann saw the people at the barricades hugging and kissing and raising bottles of champagne. He knew that just beyond camera range other citizens were beginning 1987 with a forearm across their throats, a flurry of hands punching and tearing. He looked over to wish his father the best in the coming year, but he saw that Joseph had fallen asleep as if he had been watching just another TV show.

Swann was off New Year's Day, and the following morning he was back at District 1. He found his fellow officers beginning the new year with the dedication of those hoping to make up for holiday expenses by hunting up some overtime. The wives and gooms were back to calling, and everything generally went along as usual through the end of that tour and on into the next. The only relief in the routine came from the portable radio he had taken to keeping on his desk.

"Unit [unintelligible]," Coleman said.

The phone rang and Swann picked up expecting another wife or goom.

"Officer Swann, please," a woman said.

The tone was serious, bordering on official. He had a moment's anxiety regarding the Money Store but reassured himself that he was up on his payments.

"He's out in the field," Swann said. "Can I take a message?"

"I'm calling from Roosevelt Hospital for Danica Neary," the woman said.

Fourteen

DANICA SAT ON A GURNEY, holding surgical gloves filled with ice to both sides of her face. Her head seemed twice its normal size and had a purplish cast. Her lips were ballooned and her nose looked broken. Her smooth skin was torn over her left cheek and in front of her right ear. Her honey-colored hair was dark and matted with dried blood. More blood covered her forearms and still more was splattered over the front of her blue suit. Her eyes were swollen nearly shut, and she looked for all the world like a prisoner who had been to the Room.

"Hi," Swann said.

Danica looked at Swann and opened her mouth, but no sound escaped. Tears seeped from her slitted eyes and his instinct was to embrace her, but he was not sure she wanted to be touched at all. He laid a hand lightly on her shoulder so that she could easily shrug him off. She instead leaned into his touch and lowered the two ice-filled gloves.

"Oh, God," Danica said.

She dropped her head and sobbed as he stroked her matted hair with a tenderness that had not entered their lovemaking. She finally looked up, her nose running, the tears streaming over her battered face.

He took the ice-filled gloves and pressed them against her cheeks as if holding fistfuls of diner ice. She was no longer his lover and she was not a friend in any usual sense and yet she was also not just an acquaintance. He could only think of speaking to her as he would any other victim of a crime.

"Do you know who did this to you?" Swann asked.

Danica shook her head.

"What happened?"

Danica raised an index finger to her lips, a smear of dried blood on the knuckle, the nail painted a brighter red, shining and perfect.

"I lost this filling the other day," she said. "At the dentist . . . there were all these magazines . . . all they talked about was fitness . . . fitness this . . . fitness that . . . getting in shape . . . staying in shape . . . That got me thinking."

Swann understood that she was doing what he had known many crime victims to do, that she was trying to understand in her own mind how she had come to be attacked, how she had put herself in that spot at that time. The voice escaping those ballooned lips went calm, almost matter-of-fact, still halting, but eerily like her discourse on vacuuming.

"I made it my resolution . . . you know, for New Year's . . . to exercise, maybe eat better . . . which is why instead of lunch today . . . I decided I'd do what one of those articles said . . . get an apple, go for a walk."

Little of what she was saying would mean anything to a detective working the case, but each detail was significant to her, and he paid her all the attention she needed. Her words came more evenly as she described going with her apple into the park and finding the small, still lake with the fountain and turning onto what she called *that path you might remember.* She said she had been playing her Walkman and that the only sound she had heard was what had come from the earphones.

"Barry Manilow," she said.

The memory seemed as vivid to her as the chill of the ice was to Swann's fingers, but now her voice became so detached that she sounded like a witness rather than a victim. She might have been talking of somebody else who had been on that winding trail, listening to the song "Copacabana," hearing no mutters or scuffling to warn her before she was swarmed from behind and pummeled by what seemed like a hundred black fists. One of the hands ripped away the Walkman, and then she had been able to hear them. A young voice had shouted "*Get the watch! Get the watch!*"

"They musta thought it was real or something," she now said.

Swann had thought that the shooting in the last car would be the final horror that he would precipitate. He had thought that by spending the last of his bankroll he could unlever the world from the place he had not intended.

He now held the ice to Danica's face and met her slitted gaze and told himself that this was not the time to tell her about the switch. He listened to her describe in that same distant tone how the hands had kept hitting and how she had fallen and how she had tried to cover her face with her arms as they started kicking.

"You almost want to give up, let it happen, like let 'em kill you so long as it's over," she said.

He did not say that he had himself been to that moment, just before the first shooting, in which she had taken such interest.

"Then, you get this thing like you can't let it happen," she said. "You go *wild*."

She paused.

"Or at least I did," she said.

Danica described how she had flailed her arms and how that was when she had first seen the blood and how that was when she had started to scream. She remembered that she had kept on screaming as her attackers went away.

"Laughing," she said. "Those niggers were laughing."

Neither anger nor terror nor hysteria edged into her voice as she described staggering down the path she had come. She had not encountered anybody until she had reached the fountain by the lake, and there she had seen a man who was walking a small dog. Then, after all the years of being whistled at and ogled, the one time she needed a man's help, he scooped the dog up in his arms and fled.

Danica had fallen to her knees, sobbing and shouting for help until she had remembered her mother saying that people are most likely to come running if you shout *Fire!* She had tried this, and people had come to see a fire and found only her and one of them had called the police. Two uniformed cops had driven her to the hospital, and they had asked her if she could describe her attackers and she had said, *You know, black*. The next question had been whether she might be able to identify them if she saw them and she had said no. The cops had said, *Okay, thank you,* and they had left and she had been wheeled off for x-rays and now she was waiting to be examined by a plastic surgeon.

"I'm not sure why I had the nurse call you," she said. "I guess I was upset when it seemed like the cops weren't gonna do anything."

He caught a glimmer of expectation behind the slitted lids. She who had been his Blessed Waffle wanted him to be a Hero Cop.

"Did you notice anything about them?" he asked. "Do you remember what any of them were wearing?"

He felt her shake her head between the two gloves of ice.

"Did any of them have scars? Did any of them call each other by name?"

She shook her head twice more.

"It was like before you know it, that was it, and after it happened, I couldn't believe it happened, you know?" she said.

Her features were too swollen for her to have any clear expression. The continued calm of her tone told him that she *still* did not quite believe what had happened and that she would have a very bad time after she got home. He did not mistake her present composure to mean she was ready to hear him say how the case would go; that once the cops reported that she *[x] Cannot identify* the matter would end without even being referred to the detectives.

"Maybe they assaulted some other people tonight," he said. "Maybe the squad has a line on these guys."

She said nothing, and he understood that she was waiting for him to say that he would get the people who had done this to her. He took another small step from home base.

"Then, there's a good chance an informant will give them up," he said.

She looked past him and called to a pair of male orderlies.

"Excuse me, is there some way I could get some water?" she asked.

The orderlies walked by as if they had not heard her, as if she were not there at all, as if she was some fatso in a high school hallway.

"I'll get it," Swann said.

Danica took back the ice-filled gloves while Swann went to a water fountain. He returned with a paper cup to see a man in surgical garb holding up a sheet of x-ray film. The film showed the milk-white outline of a skull.

"Okay," the surgeon said. "Let's take a look at you."

The surgeon asked if Danica had double vision or ringing in her ears, and she replied that she had both. He brushed a fingertip over her right cheek and she reported that she did not feel anything. He wiggled her front teeth.

The surgeon then said he needed to determine if there was any serious nerve damage. He asked her to *Raise your eyebrows like you're surprised or frightened* and then to *Flare your nostrils like you're angry* and then to *Grimace like you're in pain.* She had little trouble until the last command.

"*Smile,*" the surgeon said.

Danica raised only the right, uninjured corner of her mouth. The surgeon asked her to smile again and Swann handed her the paper cup of water. Swann raised his empty hand as if he also held a cup.

"Here's to tanned feet and crisp sheets and Santa Claus," he said.

Both corners of Danica's mouth rose at least in the direction of a smile. The surgeon nodded and hurried off saying he wanted to start stitching her up immediately. Danica took a sip of water and returned the cup to Swann. He helped her lie back upon the gurney.

"Maybe it doesn't matter if they get caught," Danica said.

Danica raised her painted fingers to her cheek and began gingerly feeling around the edge of the gash. Swann's attention fixed on a much smaller, inconsequential wound on the back of her hand.

"But every time I see one of them I'm gonna go, '*Maybe that's one of the ones,*'" Danica said. "Every time I see a black face, I'm gonna be like —"

Danica stopped talking, for the male orderly who had ambled up was black. He must have overheard, but he said nothing as he began rolling the gurney down the hallway.

Swann walked alongside, and they passed the trauma room where Daryl Coombs had died. He saw that the table was covered with a fresh sheet and that the floor was gleaming and that everything was ready for whoever was next.

His eyes returned to Danica and her wounds. He laid his hand on hers, covering the scratch she must have received when the posse snatched the watch he had given her, the watch it would have known to be real, the watch that had marked her as a vic.

"Don't worry," Swann said. "We'll get these guys. I promise you."

* * *

Swann rounded a blind curve and saw a dark splatter on the dirt path. He had lied to Danica at the hospital only to spare her the truth, and yet he had still come here as if there was a chance he could make good his pledge to catch her attackers. He stared down at the splash of blood from the woman who wanted him to be like Ron Parker and the other cops she saw on television. She wanted him to be the Hero he had ceased even to imagine himself.

He stepped around the stain and continued in the direction she had said the posse had fled. He peered into the clearing where the two of them had hidden from the IAD men and where they had coupled like two happy forest creatures. He now moved deeper into the Ramble, his senses sharpening as though he were another sort of animal, one beginning a hunt.

He soon came to the castle, and he was crossing the terrace when his eye caught something white. He stepped over to see a jacket that had apparently been yanked off in a panic and now lay inside-out by a line of shrubs. The rest of the throwaways were strewn nearby, and he began to pick them up only because he felt he could not just leave them there.

As Swann descended into the subway, a woman called that he had dropped one of the throwaways. She placed it atop the pile he had carried from the park. He continued on into District 1.

"Oh, now you bring your laundry to work," the desk officer said.

Swann crammed the throwaways into his locker after counting an even dozen items of the previous year's styles.

In Times Square, Swann stood a few feet from where the host of the New Year's Eve broadcast had been on the air live. The cameras were gone along with the lights and the barricades and the thousands of helmeted cops. The usual evening crowd filled the sidewalks and the few uniformed officers on duty were gathered in front of a frankfurter stand known to give "discounts" to the city police.

Swann took out his yo-yo, keeping himself to the basic toss as he studied the posses that went by. There had been a dozen throwaways and he could only think to look for a posse that size. The numbers varied from nine to seventeen to six.

* * *

Swann was still counting heads when he heard music rise over the noise of the street. He looked up Broadway to see an open white Suzuki Samurai jeep with chrome everything and a row of six spotlights blazing atop the windscreen. The music grew louder as the jeep drew nearer, and the very air seemed to vibrate with the same sort of beat he had listened to closed-eyed in the last car.

As the jeep rolled slowly past, Swann saw that the backseats had been replaced by huge speakers that faced skyward. Two kids sat in front, and the one at the wheel was maybe sixteen and wore a knit cap and ski goggles. The second was a much smaller youngster who had on a white leather overcoat. Swann recognized him as the eight- or maybe ten-year-old Pharaoh.

The jeep pulled over by a wall where street photographers had taped up cloth backdrops. A half-dozen teenaged girls were striking movie-star poses before a banner bearing a six-foot reproduction of the Louis Vuitton trademark. The words stitched overhead read GO FOR WHAT YOU KNOW.

The instant after the camera flashed, the girls broke their tableau and began moving to the music that was blasting from the jeep. The driver raised his ski goggles and sat with Pharaoh, the two of them expressionless as Swann approached.

"Yo! Yo!" Swann said.

Swann gave the yo-yo a toss. Pharaoh knitted his brow, not immediately recognizing this yo-yo-flinging Caucasian in civil service attire.

"Five-O," Swann said.

Pharaoh then smiled and showed a change of his own, this being a third gold tooth. He offered a variation of the traditional greeting *What's happening?* to a man he had last seen in a suit, homburg and bow tie.

"What happened?" Pharaoh asked.

Pharaoh leaped from the jeep in a pair of new Air Jordan sneakers that appeared to be his size. He also had on a three-finger gold ring and a gold chain whose links were one-inch replicas of the Gucci "G."

"You don't even look like you," Pharaoh said.

Swann took a quick count of a passing posse: sixteen.

"You do look like you looking for somebody," Pharaoh said.

Swann explained he was pursuing a posse that had beaten and robbed a woman of her Rolex.

"It's not good to rob females," Pharaoh said.

"I'd have to agree with you there," Swann said.

"They scream," Pharaoh said.

Pharaoh asked where the attack had occurred and Swann told him.

"I thought you was transit," Pharaoh said.

"She's a friend," Swann said.

Pharaoh's gold teeth flashed again as he grinned.

"She nice?"

"Yes, she's a very nice woman," Swann said.

"No. Is she *nice?*"

"Yes, but that has nothing to do with it."

Pharaoh gave another gold smile.

"Un-hunh."

He shrugged his small shoulders.

"Well, I'll keep an ear out," Pharaoh said. "I hear anything, I'll let you know."

Pharaoh spoke nonchalantly, but he had a light in his eyes. He had been locked up at least twice. He surely had seen the police beat people and call them "nigger" and lie about it afterward. He was still unmistakably excited by the prospect of being one of the good guys.

That did not mean Swann was about to recruit a child as an informant.

"What about him?" Swann said.

Swann was referring to the young drug dealer who was at the wheel of the jeep.

"I'll tell him you only transit police," Pharaoh said. "He don't even ride the trains."

Swann was forced to be more direct and simply say that he did not want to put somebody of Pharaoh's age at risk. Pharaoh's face clouded.

"I was old enough for you to put in jail," he said.

Pharaoh stood as somebody who believed he had just been told he could only be one of the bad guys. Swann was groping for the right thing to say when he saw another posse go by. Only eight.

"You have fun robbin' people when you're young," Pharaoh said.

Pharaoh spoke as of some distant time.

"You feel like you're doing something. It's a *real* thing. But that's childhood days. That's when you're supposed to have fun."

"I seem to remember somebody had their hand in my pocket not so long ago," Swann said.

"Yo, I learned my lesson. If you're gonna do something, you really should go for some *serious* money. What's the most you gonna get vic-ing somebody? Two hundred?"

"You did a little better with me."

"And you know nobody would believe me. They all thought I was lying about the money because I was ashamed for having vic-ed a cop. They all said, 'He a cop, how could he have G money?'"

The biggest posse yet was filing by on the other side of the street. Pharaoh again waxed nostalgic.

"Somebody see like a hundred niggers coming at them, they ain't got nothing to say," Pharaoh said. "You with a posse, you *big*."

"What are you now?" Swann asked.

"*Large*," Pharaoh said.

Pharaoh said this slapping his hands flat against his chest.

"The younger you are and the more you got, the larger you are," he said. "It ain't about big no more. It about *large*. That's it; big to large."

Through the music came the universal electronic signal emitted by cash registers and cash machines and EKG monitors, only this was faster and more insistent than could have been triggered by the wildest heartbeat. The driver of the jeep looked down at the beeper clipped to his belt and gestured for Pharaoh to hop in.

Pharaoh dropped his hands and muttered to Swann as if they were in league.

"I hear anything, I'll find you," Pharaoh said.

Pharaoh rode off and Swann pondered why this eight- or ten-year-old criminal was so determined to be his ally. *Large* was about money. But the *big* for which this youngster pined was about the tingle of power and the thrill of the hunt.

Maybe, Swann thought, Pharaoh here saw a chance to join a hunt without risking jail, to run with three thousand cave cops. Pharaoh surely did not imagine that on this case Swann was a posse of one.

Joseph was sitting in the armchair amidst what Swann at first took to be silence. He then saw that the cassette player's little red light was lit.

"Ellen called," Joseph said. "She said to call her."

The mention of Ellen's name caused Swann's pulse to race as if they were courting again. He was more nervous dialing his own home than he had been on even the first call to the Money Store.

"Hello?" Ellen said.

"Hi," Swann said.

"Oh."

"I heard you called."

"Yes, I did. I wanted to tell you that I opened my own account at the bank. I think you should have your own."

"I'll start giving you a check when I get my check."

"I don't like taking money from you. I always worked before the baby, and I'll go back as soon as things settle down."

"You don't have to."

"I wouldn't do it because of you. I'd do it because of me. Okay?"

"Okay."

"Now that's more or less worked out, I think we should work out something with Jenny. You're still her father and that's one thing that's not going to change."

Ellen ended by saying Swann could see Jenny the following morning.

Swann went up the stoop as he had so many times before, but he stopped at the door and knocked as though he had become somebody else. Ellen answered, her expression suggesting she wished it was anybody but him.

"Hi," Swann said.

"Jenny, it's Daddy," Ellen said.

Swann listened to Jenny clump slowly down the hall. She appeared with her gaze cast at the downward angle of somebody off to Central Booking.

"Hi," Swann said.

Jenny fixed him with a look that suggested it was a good thing she was not a bunny fairy princess ballerina. She would most likely have used her wand to transform him into something as slimy as she now gave him reason to view himself.

Swann and Jenny walked silently up the block and into the park. He took out his yo-yo.

"Wanna try it?" Swann asked.

Jenny said nothing and Swann returned the yo-yo to his pocket.

They went on past the patch of grass where Danica had first gazed upon him with interest. He now looked at his daughter's downcast eyes, and he was mute with all that he could not explain to her.

The McDonald's beyond the park seemed altogether elegant compared to the subway soda fountain that had replaced the Oak Bar as Swann's main hangout. He went to the counter as Jenny wandered over to a small indoor carousel. She was astraddle a pink horse when he brought her an Egg McMuffin.

Swann gave the carousel a spin and he was trying to formulate something to say to Jenny when her face came around no less disconsolate than before. He pushed again and the face reappeared, unchanged. She spoke her first words to him.

"Go away."

Jenny's eyes were welling as she continued around, and she had tears on her cheeks when she reappeared. He stopped the carousel and her expression firmed to a mask as he brushed away her tears.

Swann began to say how sorry he was. Jenny interrupted with the question she had posed so often about such simple matters as the darkening of the sky at night and the rudeness of belching.

"Why?"

Swann could not tell the truth and he did not want to tell a lie.

"There are a lot of reasons," Swann said.

Jenny's unaltered expression told him that she had taken his response for exactly what it was worth.

"Jenny, I want you to know that I love you more than the whole world," Swann said.

Swann was convinced this was absolutely true, but he also understood she had every reason to doubt him. He could see that he was not going to make up for actions with words.

"Don't you want your food?" Swann asked. "It's getting cold."

"No," Jenny said.

Swann checked a parental impulse to tell her she had to eat.

"Well, let me know if you get hungry," he said.

He pushed the carousel and she came around and all that had changed was that she had been around one more time.

* * *

Jenny dashed ahead up the stoop and stood waiting by the door. Swann could hear that Ellen was blasting the radio as she had when she was single. He knocked.

"You don't have your key?" Jenny asked.

Swann did in fact have his key in his pocket, but he could well imagine Ellen's reaction if he opened the door as if nothing had changed.

"I think it's better if we let Mommy open the door," Swann said.

Swann listened for footsteps and heard only an old Temptations song. He knocked again, louder, though not so hard as he might have.

"Why can't you just open the door?" Jenny asked.

Swann crouched down so that his eyes were even with hers.

"Sweetie, I don't live here anymore," he said.

"You still have a key," Jenny said.

The door opened. Swann looked up at Ellen, who stood with the radio behind her blasting music from even before they met, back when he had first decided that he wanted Danica more than anyone else. He would not have been surprised if the teenage Ellen had listened to this song picturing herself with someone like Timothy Neary.

Swann now rose from beside their child and watched Ellen turn away. She swung back with a bulging plastic garbage bag.

"This is yours," Ellen said.

Swann saw that Ellen's hand was bare of both engagement ring and wedding band.

"Daddy was knocking and you didn't hear and he wouldn't use his key," Jenny said.

Ellen's look told Swann he had made at least one right decision regarding her. He rose and reached in his pocket, figuring that things might be easier if he gave her the key. He was working it off the ring when he was inspired to hand it to Jenny.

"Next time, you can open the door," Swann said.

Jenny accepted and stared down at the key in her hand as if it would tell her how she should react. She stepped over to Ellen's side.

"And I don't need to knock even if I'm with Daddy?" Jenny said.

"Even if you're with Daddy," Ellen said.

In his childhood room, Swann opened the garbage bag and saw that even in these circumstances Ellen had folded his clothes. He put the shirts and socks in the top drawers of the dresser. He consigned the pants and underwear to the bottom, these of no use unless he inflated to his former girth.

Ellen had not forgotten Swann's sneakers and gym shorts. He was now able to go for a jog, but he could summon little vigor to lighten his step. He chugged on with only the heavy-limbed determination to have achieved something from his recent adventures, even if that was nothing more than a waist size. He kept running until he was so tired that he was happy to be heading back to his solitary bed.

In the morning, Swann's legs still ached enough that he almost welcomed his clerk's chair at District 1. He entered NEARY, DANICA into the computer and the screen flashed a report confirming that her attackers were officially described only as numerous black males. The stolen property was marked as *one (1) Walkman cassette player and one (1) yellow metal watch*. The case had already been marked closed because the complainant *[x] Cannot identify.*

Swann checked for other robberies that day in the Central Park area and saw that a man had been attacked only twenty minutes before Danica. A spark of hope died when Swann read that this victim also *[x] Cannot identify.* He hit the Exit button and the only question that seemed to remain was when he would tell Danica that he had failed.

That, and when he would tell her about the watch. He was still unsure in both regards when he telephoned to see how she was faring.

"Hi, Jack."

Danica's voice was empty. He knew she now believed what had happened to her.

"You feeling better?"

"I'm all right."

Swann could have been listening to himself in the days after he shot Daryl Coombs.

"Can I tell you something?" Danica asked. "I don't think you should call me just because of what happened to me."

He was no longer listening to anybody but a beautiful woman whose beauty had been kicked and punched from her face. He understood that someone who had so long been an object of desire could not bear being an object of pity, particularly if the pity came from a man who had rejected her when she was in her glory.

"I just wanted you to know I'm still after these guys," he said.

He figured he could at least let her imagine he was out rousting crooks and grilling suspects, that she was still a beauty to be avenged.

"Thank you," Danica said.

He hoped he was not really thinking of himself when he also decided that he would do her no good by telling her about the watch. He considered that she need never know, unless the posse was arrested and the Rolex was recovered. That was hardly likely.

"Take care," Swann said.

"You, too."

The Hero Cop hung up and spent the next week filing reports and answering phones. The closest he came to action was listening to the scrambled transmissions on the portable radio he continued to keep on his desk.

"[Unintelligible] forthwith," Coleman would say.

On payday, Swann distributed the latest checks to those who wanted more so badly that they expected it. He again watched their faces slacken with the disappointment of people who clearly felt themselves to be living neither big nor large.

Swann examined his own check with the sole concern that he have enough to pay the Money Store and cover whatever Ellen and Jenny might need. A house mouse has next to no opportunity to make any kind of collar, and the second shooting had left him with no desire to get robbed in the last car again.

Swann would not be getting overtime, which meant he would very likely have to take a second job. He was pondering this prospect when the phone rang. Ellen was calling to ask if he would take Jenny that night.

"I have a date," Ellen said.

Swann could not at this moment have ascribed a particular size to how he was living.

"Good for you," Swann said.

"You mean for *you,*" Ellen said. "If I meet somebody, then you don't got to feel like such a scumbag. That's how fucked up it is. I do something to feel better, you feel better. But I'm not gonna sit around feeling bad just so you do."

"I'm glad to hear that."

"See what I mean?"

The small pink suitcase had until this day been used only for Jenny's make-believe trips to such places as Way Over the Rainbow.

"Here's what she'll need," Ellen said.

Ellen handed Swann the suitcase and what he noticed this time about her hand was that the nails were painted an opalescent pink. He felt a stab of shame and what he himself could not believe was jealousy. His knowing he was more than wrong did not stop him from still feeling she was *his* wife.

"Jenny!" Ellen said. "Your father's here."

Jenny clumped up to the front door and dodged both a hug from Swann and a good-bye kiss from her mother. She went down the steps by herself and he hurried to catch up only to have her ignore him all the way to Joseph's house.

Joseph was off at his weekly group therapy session, so Swann and Jenny would be eating alone. He enlisted her in an attempt at lasagna and she remained too remote for him to discern whether she was surprised to see her father cooking. She did bring full concentration to bear on her assigned task of adding the cheese and sauce.

"You're doing great!" Swann said.

Jenny said nothing, though she did seem to take even more care in spreading the sauce with the back of a spoon.

The timer went off and the sauce and cheese were bubbling as Swann took the tray out to cool. Jenny set the table and they began eating, she seeming to possess no greater appetite than himself.

"How is it?" Swann asked.

Jenny kept her head down.

"Good," Jenny said.

The phone rang and Swann picked up to get a second unexpected call of the day. A fellow officer informed him that somebody named Pharaoh had just called District 1. Swann was to meet him on Forty-second Street in one hour.

Swann hung up certain that Pharaoh would not have reached out for him unless he had some information. Swann then faced one difficulty of a sort never faced by the Hero Cop of the myth, this being the absence of a baby-sitter.

"Jenny, how'd you like to take a little trip with Daddy?" Swann asked.

"No," Jenny said.

"Jenny, Daddy has to meet a criminal," Swann said.

Jenny raised her head and Swann saw that the general fascination with cops and crime reached even to his four-year-old daughter.

Thieves were sizing up marks and hustlers were hissing offers of beat drugs and crackheads were firing up glass pipes. Jenny did not duck the protective hand that Swann laid on her shoulder as they walked down Forty-second Street.

Pharaoh had yet to arrive, and Swann watched with Jenny as the street photographers prepared for the evening. She attempted to read aloud the legend on a backdrop covered with dollar signs.

"Muh, muh, muh-o . . ."

"'More,'" Swann said. "'More is more.'"

Swann proposed they get their picture taken. Jenny tucked her hair behind her ears and stood formally at his side, tilting her head against him as the flash went off.

Swann paid the photographer $7, or what was supposed to get him through two days under his present budget. He and Jenny then watched their image appear on the Polaroid, father and daughter materializing together, their silhouettes first and then the most prominent features, the brow and mouth and eyes. The nose that she got from him.

Swann saw that Jenny had smiled for the camera and he looked up to see that she was smiling now. He handed her the photograph and the smile vanished.

"You don't want it?" Jenny asked.

Swann was reminded how delicate things were between them. He suggested they get another photograph so they could both have one. They were stepping over to the backdrop again when rap music came blasting up the block.

Pharaoh leaped from the white jeep, his eyes again saying he was no less excited to be helping a cop than he had been to rob a vic. He did falter on seeing Jenny. A four-year-old girl clearly did not fit into his fantasies about working undercover.

Swann introduced Jenny and Pharaoh, and they eyed each other, she in a bargain-store parka and knit cap, he with his gold teeth and three-finger gold ring and new leather baseball cap cocked sideways.

"Why is your ring so big?" Jenny asked.

Pharaoh struck much the same pose as the last time, when he had spoken of living large.

"Little niggers got gold, they be making *dollars,*" Pharaoh said.

"My daddy says that's a bad word," Jenny said.

"'Dollars'?"

"No, silly. The other."

Pharaoh glanced at Swann as if he were trying to figure how father and daughter had come to discuss the word *nigger.* He then looked back at Jenny.

"Niggers just be calling each other that," Pharaoh said.

"Can I try your ring?" Jenny asked.

Pharaoh did not appear entirely pleased with this prospect, but he complied nonetheless. The ring looked even bigger on Jenny's hand.

"Cool!" Jenny said.

Pharaoh laughed the way he might if he and Jenny were in a schoolyard.

"Your daddy buy this for you?" Jenny asked.

Pharaoh's face went blank.

"No," Pharaoh said.

Pharaoh slapped the front pocket of his leather pants. Swann noted that there was a print to match what he himself had gotten through the Money Store.

"I get paid," Pharaoh said.

The photographer interrupted to ask if Swann still wanted another picture. Swann said that he did, and a surge of camaraderie prompted him to invite Pharaoh to join them.

Pharaoh declined but responded with an offer of his own. Jenny stood before the camera wearing not just the ring, but the hat as well. She cocked the brim sideways, to the angle worn by its owner.

"Officer, you got a wife, too?" Pharaoh asked.

The flash came in the next instant. Now it was Jenny's turn to become serious.

"They're separated," Jenny said. "She caught him being *bad.*"

Jenny took off the hat and removed the ring as if they no longer suited her mood. Pharaoh gave Swann an appraising look, as if weighing whether he was dealing with a good guy after all.

"About the lady," Pharaoh said.

"What lady?" Jenny asked.

Pharaoh paused to slip on the ring and place the hat just so. Swann did his best not to appear at the mercy of an eight- or ten-year-old criminal.

"A lady that had got hurt in the park," Pharaoh said.

"What happened to her?" Jenny asked.

"She got robbed and beat down," Pharaoh said.

Pharaoh leaned closer to Swann, his voice again assuming a tone that said they were in league. Pharaoh had apparently decided to keep him as one of the good guys, if only so he could now be one himself.

"One of them is name Knowledge," Pharaoh said.

"Knowledge?" Jenny said. "Is that a boy's name or a girl's name?"

"Boy," Pharaoh said. "He from Brooklyn."

"I'm from Queens," Jenny said.

Pharaoh kept his eyes on Swann, waiting for some acknowledgment.

"You shouldn't be doing this," Swann said.

"What, I should be robbing people?" Pharaoh asked. "You came here, didn't you?"

"Yes," Swann said. "I did."

"Me, too," Jenny said.

Pharaoh was still waiting.

"Good work," Swann said.

Pharaoh shrugged as if he had only been doing what a fellow good guy should. His pleasure was more apparent for his effort to conceal it.

"I'll give you my beeper number so's you can let me know when you get them," Pharaoh said.

"Get who?" Jenny asked.

"The people that hurt the lady," Pharaoh said. "I'm helping your daddy."

Jenny looked up at Swann as she might have before all the trouble.

"Are you going to get them, Daddy?"

Swann would have had a hard enough time lying just to Pharaoh.

"I'm going to do my very best," Swann said.

Jenny dropped her eyes, as if she had seen enough of Swann's very best. He uttered the same pledge he had made to Danica, only this time he felt that he might be telling the truth.

"Yes," Swann said. "I'm going to get them."

Pharaoh roared off in the jeep with the music blasting. Swann reached into his nearly printless pocket and paid another two days' allotment for the second photograph. He saw that the camera had caught them in the instant between Pharaoh's question and when it registered. Jenny was at his side, the big gold ring shining huge on her hand, the hat turned saucily to the side, her smile, like his own, a millisecond from falling.

"I want that one," Jenny said.

Swann gave her the photograph. The meeting with Pharaoh had left her enough at ease in Times Square that she dipped from under Swann's hand when he began to guide her crosstown.

"What are you going to tell your mother about tonight?" Swann asked.

"What?" Jenny asked.

Swann took a step without speaking.

"You're going to tell her exactly what we did," Swann said.

Swann glanced at the Polaroid in her hand.

"Though you don't have to go out of your way to show that picture."

Swann tucked Jenny in, saying that she would be sleeping in the bed where he had slept when he was her age.

"Where do you sleep now?" Jenny asked.

"Tonight I'll take the sofa."

"When I'm not here, where? Here?"

"Yes. Here."

Swann bent and kissed her good night.

"I don't get a story?"

Swann looked over at the bookshelf. He remembered that his mother had brought over all his old storybooks when Jenny had been born.

"I guess I could remember one," Swann said.

The Frog Prince. Beauty and the Beast. Cinderella. None was right for a child who was just learning that her father was no prince and her parents were not going to live happily ever after.

"Ummmm . . ." Swann said.

Maybe the princess could like the frog better than the prince. Maybe Beauty could turn into the Beast. No. Those were not right, either.

"Come on, Daddy," Jenny said.

Swann looked at the sidewalk Polaroid she had propped on the night table.

"Once upon a time, there was a boy named Pharaoh . . ."

Swann recounted the story of his first encounter with Pharaoh, leaving out the shooting but going into great detail about the five pairs of socks.

"But why did he wear his big brother's shoes?" Jenny asked.

"He had no money to buy his own," Swann said.

"Is that why he was stealing?"

Swann felt that a simple yes would have been allowing an excuse, while a simple no would have been unfair.

"Sweetie, sometimes people have a number of reasons why they do things," Swann said.

Jenny waited for him to say more. He realized that he had no simple explanation for how a youngster not much older than she had been out vic-ing. He bent to kiss her good night again.

In the morning, Swann dropped Jenny at what was still her home. Ellen immediately spotted the picture Jenny did her best to palm. Swann explained what had happened.

"Mommy, Daddy's going to get some bad guys who hurt a lady," Jenny said.

"Good for Daddy," Ellen said.

Fifteen

AT DISTRICT 1, Swann sat down at the computer and called up the nickname file. He pecked out K-N-O-W-L-E-D-G-E and the machine needed only an instant to report a total of eighty-seven black teenaged males who had criminal records and who lived in Brooklyn and who were known on the streets as Knowledge. He requested a printout of each one's particulars, and the result proved to be longer than he was tall.

Swann began by crossing off those who were presently incarcerated, and Knowledge was apparently not a lucky name. The total dropped to sixty-one and the next to go were those whose records indicated they were primarily drug peddlers. *Knowledge* was popular in this line, and the list dwindled to forty-two.

Of the remaining Knowledges, Swann made a small *x* next to the nineteen who had been grabbed in Manhattan for robbery in concert with multiple others. His eyes went from name to name, searching in vain for some telling detail, some clue.

"I have a [unintelligible]."

Swann looked up at the portable radio on his desk.

"[Unintelligible]," Coleman was saying. "Forthwith."

Swann's eyes returned to the list. He was all but certain that the youngster he sought was among them. He also knew that he would need more than a posse of one to identify this youngster and the rest of Danica's attackers.

"[Unintelligible]."

Swann took up the radio, but hesitated. Danica had been his goom and Coleman seemed to have definite feelings in that regard. Still, what Danica had become was a vic and Coleman was most definitely Five-O, the only Five-O to whom he could turn.

He pressed the transmit bar.

"So?"

Swann was again the first at the soda fountain and Coleman once more arrived smiling. His own smile may have looked a little nervous, for she had been on post at the radio console when she telephoned to say *Yo!* and there had not been enough time to explain why he wanted to meet. He now told her that he was trying to track down a posse that had attacked Danica.

"That's the woman . . . ," Swann said.

Coleman tilted her head as if there was something she did not understand.

"I, you know . . . ," Swann said.

"I know that," Coleman said. "What I don't get is why they vic-ed her."

Swann checked his reflexive answer, which, in keeping with the transit police catechism, was that Danica was white.

"One thing they know is what's *real,*" Coleman said. "And that watch was slum."

Swann decided he had no choice but to tell Coleman the story of the two Rolexes.

"I don't know about love, but I'm getting to know a lot about stupid," Coleman said. "And it was stupid to let that girl walk around not knowing she had on a watch worth a thousand."

"Three," Swann said.

"What you pay for something and what it's worth are two different things," Coleman said. "What something's worth is what you can get for it."

"Is it worth it to you to help me get who did it?" Swann asked.

Coleman studied him, as if speculating what else he might not have told her.

"Don't you have to be at a desk somewhere?" she asked.

"No. Off duty. On our own time."

Coleman did not immediately respond, and Swann figured he knew why; cops were expected to take action if they happened to encounter a crime off duty, but neither he nor she nor anybody else had ever heard of cops hunting crooks on their own time. Even cops who actually were crooked stole only on duty.

"It's not like we'd be leaving the subway," Swann said. "We don't have to be there in the first place. We can be anywhere we want. Who's to say?"

"IAD maybe."

Coleman had given Swann a similar warning after the interview. He reminded himself that he was armored by the truth.

"We have nothing to worry about," Swann said.

"I wasn't really worried about me," Coleman said.

"Well, don't worry about me," Swann said. "Worry about this."

Swann produced the list of nineteen Knowledges. Coleman grew more intent as she looked from entry to entry.

"Does she know about the watch now?" Coleman asked.

"I thought it would only make it worse," Swann said.

Swann sensed Coleman disagreed, though she said nothing and her eyes remained on the list. She apparently had no more luck finding a clue than he had and perhaps that made the challenge irresistible.

"Least he don't call himself Supreme," Coleman said. "There's three Supremes just on my block."

In keeping with their plan, Swann boarded the subway in Queens before dawn. The posses had by this hour returned home and the last car rattled into Brooklyn empty save for himself. He tossed the yo-yo and decided he was getting nearly as good as he had been in the third grade. He remembered Joseph asking, *What kind of cop gives grown people yo-yos?*

Swann kept tossing as he pondered this question. He tried to picture Coleman in the third grade and he wondered whether that male voice on the phone had been her father. He decided it had sounded too young. He remembered the anger in the tone, which could have been that of a lover hearing another male. Or maybe it was the brother who had taken the unsubstantiated beating, assuming Swann must be one of her fellow cops.

Swann attempted an Around the World and he was not so sure he was on par with the third grade after all. He remained alone as the train went from station to station, soon only one stop from where he and Coleman were to meet. He thought of her unspoken position on gooms and debated whether it rose from general principle or was more specific to him.

He tried another Around the World, this at least putting him in the range of grammar school. He decided that more than anything his gooming had seemed to disappoint Coleman. That suggested she had held him in some esteem, and that meant she must have seen more in him than he beheld in the solitary reflection he now caught in the door window.

His reflection vanished as the train pulled into the light of the next station. The doors opened and he saw that Coleman was waiting on the platform as they had arranged. She boarded wearing her purple overalls and it struck him that he had known her long enough to see her in the same thing twice. He knew her well enough to detect that she was slightly apprehensive, which was only reasonable, given that their last escapade had ended with a kid's death.

He welcomed her with an Around the World even worse than the first one.

"You better work at that," Coleman said.

"I am," Swann said.

The train pulled out and his reflection reappeared with hers.

"You sure you want to be doing this?" he asked.

She met his gaze in the glass.

"It's what we do, isn't it?" she said.

Two more stops and they climbed out of the subway. He of course asked her none of what he had been wondering about her. If she had been wondering anything about him, she did not say so. They walked silent through the early morning darkness to the housing project that the computer had given as the residence of the first Knowledge.

Swann returned the yo-yo to his pocket, this being one time when they wanted to look as much as possible like Five-O. The windows were dark and the whole building seemed to be slumbering. He tingled at the chance that they might get lucky, that the one they were after might be here, sleeping, unsuspecting that they were nearing.

As the piss-scented elevator rose, Swann thought of Danica and how she had smelled as they ascended to their room at the Plaza. He saw her face as it had been then, and what he remembered was not her beauty, but her delight.

A subway-sized jolt signaled that Swann and Coleman had reached the floor they wanted. The apartment they sought was three doors down the hall. His knock brought no reply. She hit the door with an open hand, and the sound boomed in the stillness. A scuffling came from inside the apartment.

"Who?" a voice asked.

Swann held his badge up to the peephole, and the door opened. He and Coleman bade good morning to a woman of at least 250 pounds who wore a sheer, baby blue nightgown over a full suit of thermal underwear. He kept his voice casual as he asked if they could speak to her son.

"Knowledge?" the woman said. "You mean Clarence."

Swann and Coleman were now in a delicate position, for the woman had only to refuse them admittance and they would be left with no legal recourse other than to stand in the hallway and hope Knowledge emerged. The woman would not be at all confident about confronting people who had badges and guns, but if they challenged her too directly, her pride might send her right into defiance.

"Listen, it's no big deal, but your neighbors don't need to know your business," Coleman said. "Do you mind if we step inside?"

The woman surely did not believe that some cop was going to be concerned about embarrassing her, but the lie offered her an excuse to yield.

"I don't know why you got to be bothering people at this hour," the woman said.

Swann and Coleman entered, their true intentions running between them like a current. He thought she had played it perfectly, but he took care to show nothing as they followed the woman through an unheated apartment to a bedroom the size and temperature of a meat locker. The woman shook the middle of three youngsters who lay on a single bed under a pile of blankets and jackets. The boy rose in a red Gucci sweatshirt, a little puff of vapor escaping as he spoke.

"Whas up?" Knowledge asked.

The questioning began in the kitchen, beside an oven that had all four burners going.

"How come they call you *Knowledge?*" Swann asked.

"I don't know," Knowledge said.

"But you *do* know why we're here?" Swann asked.

Knowledge said nothing.

"Three clues: 'Manhattan, 'Vic,' 'Watch,'" Coleman said.

Knowledge still said nothing. Swann had to consciously keep himself from looking at Coleman. They just might have gotten the right one on the first try.

"Clarence, what did you do?" the mother asked.

Knowledge lowered his eyes. Swann understood they were dealing with a youngster who was still capable of being ashamed in front of his mother. Coleman must have sensed this as well.

"You know, you don't really seem like a criminal," Coleman said. "Your mother didn't raise you to be like that, did she?"

"Well, did I?" the mother asked.

Knowledge might not have had to answer the police, but his mother was another matter.

"No," Knowledge said.

Knowledge's eyes were still fixed on the floor. Coleman continued to play it perfectly.

"And it's not like you're out robbing every night, is it?" Coleman asked.

Coleman was offering Knowledge the opportunity to present himself as not such a crook, to use the truth as home base. He looked up and his voice had a hopeful lift.

"No," Knowledge said.

Swann here saw a place to join in.

"I bet it was only two or three times," Swann said.

Swann had nudged too hard. Knowledge reacted as if he were being tricked, which indeed he was. He cocked his head to the side and a stoniness came into his eyes.

"I ain't do nothing," Knowledge said.

Swann remembered that Alvin, the teenager from the space case, had started out this way. Only, this youngster seemed almost anxious for a little brutality. He could then make these cops in the wrong and bring his mother to his defense.

Swann raised a hand and Knowledge seemed ready for anything but the fatherly pat he received on the shoulder. Swann felt muscle and sinew under his palm and he thought of Danica in the hospital. He smiled.

"Knowledge, Knowledge, we know you're not like those other people," Swann said.

"I got nothing to say," Knowledge said.

Knowledge had gone edgy. He seemed not at all sure how to react.

"Knowledge, everybody wants to buy clothes, impress girls, show you ain't soft," Coleman said.

Swann at this moment had no trouble avoiding eye contact with Coleman.

"And, you know, today's your lucky day," Coleman said.

"What you mean?" Knowledge asked.

Swann might have posed the same question.

"We're going to give you a chance to explain," Coleman said.

Swann now understood where Coleman was going. He still had his hand on Knowledge's shoulder and he pulled the youngster to him.

"We're going to let you tell your side of the story," Swann said.

Swann kept Knowledge in the embrace, shaking off any thought of Danica, beckoning his long experience in fakery. The more energy he put into the sham, the more intensely he felt a bond of true intent with Coleman.

"You sure this is gonna help me?" Knowledge asked.

"The truth shall set you free," Coleman said.

"That mean probation?"

Coleman gave a brief, sharp laugh that did not end with a smile. Knowledge looked from Swann to her to his mother, who had stood silent as whatever virtue her son retained was used to draw out his guilt. The mother could not intervene without making him feel that his innocence was only foolishness.

"Tell them," the mother said.

Knowledge's eyes went to the stove, staring at the blue circles of flame as he spoke.

"I only hit him once," Knowledge said.

"*Him?*" Coleman asked.

"Who him?" Swann asked.

"What about *her?*" Coleman asked. "The *lady?*"

"Lady?" Knowledge said. "It ain't a lady. It a man."

Swann and Coleman were compelled to go ahead and get the details of the attack on the man. Knowledge turned out to have been in one of the posses Swann had pictured in Times Square on New Year's Eve.

"You know, when everybody *watch* the ball go down," Knowledge said.

Swann told the mother that city detectives might be coming to visit. Knowledge seemed to have decided that this was indeed his lucky day and he gave what seemed a completely genuine smile to these two cops who were leaving without arresting him.

"Bye," Knowledge said.

The apartment door shut, Swann looked at this woman with whom he had almost seemed to be of one mind. He wondered all the more who she was.

Coleman had the day off and her home station was only three stops down. Swann stayed aboard a train that soon became crowded with early workers. The yo-yo stayed in his pocket as he rode toward District 1 and his upended existence.

On his arrival, he sat down at the computer and found a New Year's Eve robbery complaint that matched the details Knowledge had provided. He telephoned the assigned city detectives and said that he had been working something else when he encountered a youngster who had confessed to the crime.

"Listen, the complainant can't I.D. and I'm sure he's not going to be thrilled about going to court," the detective said. "So there's no reason to be pursuing this thing."

Swann had seen on the computer screen that this case, like Danica's, had been closed because the victim *[x] Cannot identify.* The detective was not interested in going to a lot of trouble over a case for which neither he nor anybody else was any longer responsible.

"Of course not," Swann said.

Swann was allowed an hour with Jenny after work, and he had no sooner picked her up than she asked the question.

"Did you catch them?"

Jenny's expectant look made clear just how much she needed Swann to prove himself a good guy in at least this sense. He told her about running the name in the computer and visiting the first Knowledge.

"And nineteen take away one is eighteen," Swann said.

"That's a lot," Jenny said. "But not too much."

* * *

Morning after morning, Swann rode a predawn train, tossing his yo-yo. Coleman would be waiting, sometimes sleepy, always perking up as they began another adventure in the hours before either of them might have to report for duty.

"You sure you want to keep doing this?" Swann asked.

"Until we're done," Coleman said.

The computer printout would send them to the next address and he would again wonder if the youngster they were rousing was among those who attacked Danica. He would again have to push away any thoughts of her as he embraced this latest suspect.

And he would again feel that intimacy of intent with Coleman as they proved the latest Knowledge vulnerable in exactly the same way as the first. They would then discover that this was not the one they were after.

Afterward, Swann and Coleman would return to their no less separate lives. He would go through the day and into the night with the anticipation of the next dawn's mission. The very object of the hunt was a reminder of his responsibility for Danica's suffering, but he forgot IAD and he began to feel as if his duties at District 1 were merely a sideline.

The real work began the moment he resumed the off-duty hunt with Coleman. They were in the subway on their way for a sunrise interview with the tenth Knowledge when she expressed his own feelings exactly.

"It's like we're our own, off-duty police department," Coleman said.

The two of them passed from the underground to the street as if they were not transit cops at all. They interviewed another suspect in a case with which the city police could not be bothered. Swann only wished this had been the one they were seeking.

That afternoon, Swann picked Jenny up for a few off-off-duty hours. He had not failed to notice that few of the Knowledges had a father in evidence, and perhaps that helped make him more overbearingly a father to Jenny.

"You sure nothing's wrong?" Swann asked.

"Why do you keep asking me?" Jenny asked.

"I'm sorry."

Jenny did not have to tell Swann that he also kept saying that. He at least had the hunt for the lady's attackers to fall back on. He told her that he and Coleman had questioned another Knowledge that morning.

"Nineteen take away nine was ten," Swann said. "So, nineteen take away ten is what?"

"Nine!" Jenny said.

On a day they were both off, the printout sent Swann and Coleman to the residence of the eleventh Knowledge. Coleman was raising an open hand to knock when the door swung open.

A woman of about thirty stood in a cheap down coat and white nurse's shoes. She looked even more tired than the typical early morning worker, and she slumped against the door frame when she saw the two police badges.

"Now what more do you want?" she asked. "You already arrested him."

Swann and Coleman quickly ascertained that her son had been picked up for robbery in Manhattan the previous night.

"Me, I got a job to get to," the woman said.

Swann and Coleman trailed the woman down the hallway only because that was the way out. She ignored them and said nothing until they were descending in the elevator.

"*Knowledge,*" the woman said. "The other day, this boy come to my door and say, 'I come to get Knowledge.' I said, 'Who are you, truth?' He say, 'No, I'm Menace. Truth is downstairs.'"

Swann and Coleman were still right behind the woman when she reached the entrance to the subway, and she demanded to know why they were following her. Swann explained that they were simply catching the same train.

"You came here by *train?*" the woman asked. "What kind of police are you?"

The woman went down into the station along with other solitary early workers who were bundled in clothes that had been bought with an eye more toward price than style. No cop-like characters were in evidence to keep anyone from strolling through the exit gate. One early worker after another dropped in a token, starting the day a dollar behind on the way to carry and clean and cook before the rest of the city got going.

Knowledge's mother had already deposited her token before Swann and Coleman could motion her through the exit gate with them. That might have been the end of it had Coleman not sneezed just as they all reached the platform.

"Bless you," the woman said.

Coleman thanked the woman and said that the troubles with Knowledge must be very hard on her.

"Rondell," the woman said. "His name is Rondell."

The woman gazed into the tunnel, but the train was long in coming and she ended up turning back to Swann and Coleman. She said that Rondell's nickname was not entirely off, for he had won awards for both spelling and math at his grammar school graduation. She remembered that the other children had been more interested in what was on his feet.

"All they be saying was, 'What kind of shoes you got?'" the woman said.

The woman glanced down at Coleman's black Nikes.

"He got them," the woman said. "He got them in four colors. He have on the orange ones when he go out last night."

A screech sent the woman's attention back to the tunnel. Headlights appeared in the darkness.

"Look at his shoes and see what you see," the woman said.

At the back of Police Headquarters, Swann showed his face in the small window and the steel door to Central Booking buzzed open. He entered with Coleman beside him, and a uniformed cop directed her to the pair of footprints painted on the floor to mark where prisoners should stand before the mug-shot camera.

"Step up, take off your hat," the cop said.

Coleman held out the shield that she already had on a chain around her neck and continued with Swann to the desk at the back. Swann followed the procedure he had seen detectives use when removing prisoners for lineups. He wrote in a log book that they were taking out sixteen-year-old Rondell Harris *re: investigation.*

* * *

For the sake of appearances, Swann cuffed this latest Knowledge until they were outside and around the corner. Knowledge stood in orange Nikes, looking around for their police car. Swann steered him up the street, placing an arm around his shoulder.

At a coffee shop on the next block, Swann and Coleman sat Knowledge down in a rear booth. The youngster ordered a hamburger, and began as had most of the others.

"I got nothing to say," Knowledge said.

Swann remembered the mother's last words to them, and he peeked under the table. He remarked that Knowledge's left sneaker was a lighter shade than the right.

"They come that way," Knowledge said.

Swann was sitting beside Knowledge to facilitate the embrace he now applied. Coleman went to work with soft tones and Knowledge soon confessed that he had stolen the right sneaker from Sneaker World in Brooklyn.

"You see, they don't watch what they got on display because they don't think niggers are gonna take only one sneaker," Knowledge said.

Knowledge described going from store to store to store in search of a left sneaker of the same brand and size and color. A less dedicated thief might have given up after a week of such effort, but he had pressed on and he had finally found one in the window of Sneaker Palace in Manhattan. He had not realized until he was home that this one had been faded by the sun.

"I put the dark shoe in my window when it nice out, but it still got a way to go," Knowledge said.

The waitress brought the hamburger and a grape soda, along with coffee for Swann and Coleman. Knowledge was silent until he was done with the ketchup.

"You didn't take me out to talk about sneakers," Knowledge said.

He sucked some ketchup from his right pinky.

"Knowledge, you've already been arrested for last night," Swann said.

Coleman followed with the line they had taken to using as a precaution against any more unsolicited confessions.

"We already know about the lady in Central Park," Coleman said.

Knowledge pulled the pinky from his mouth, making a little pop. He was the first who did not ask what lady they were talking about.

"We don't care about that robbery . . . ," Coleman said.

Coleman was keeping her voice indifferent but Swann was sure her pulse was racing at the speed of his own.

". . . we want you to tell us about all the other robberies you did."

"I don't know nothing about no robberies," Knowledge said.

Swann applied another fatherly pat on the shoulder.

"That would sure come as a surprise to those cops who locked you up last night," Swann said.

Coleman now used the names the mother had mentioned in the elevator.

"Not to speak of Truth and Menace," Coleman said.

Swann felt Knowledge stiffen under his hand.

"Come on," Swann said. "They even told us you're the one who got the Rolex."

"They said that?" Knowledge said.

Knowledge's tone could only be described as hurt.

"I didn't get nothing," Knowledge said.

Swann heard at once the voices of the other diners and the clatter of dishes and the rattle of the cash machine drawer. It all came to him as the silence before Knowledge's next words.

"I was just there," Knowledge said.

Swann fought off an almost overpowering urge to look across the table at Coleman, to exchange just a glance saying that yes, they finally had their youngster. He kept his eyes on Knowledge and shrugged.

"That's not what *they* say," Swann said.

Knowledge met Swann's gaze.

"They lying," Knowledge said.

Swann held the eyes of this youngster who had helped beat Danica bloody. He smiled.

"You know, I almost believe you," Swann said.

"I don't know," Coleman said. "You better tell us the whole story."

Coleman spoke as if she found the matter only tedious.

"It was just something that happened," Knowledge said.

"I mean from the beginning," Coleman said.

Knowledge sighed and said that he and his posse had met up at the usual place, in front of his housing project. Nobody had felt much like going to school, so they had hopped a subway into Manhattan.

"Somebody started saying, 'Let's get paid,'" Knowledge said. "That's all it needs is one person to say, 'Let's go on a spree. Let's go *wiling*.'"

"Wiling?" Swann asked.

"Where you be wild."

"Oh, *wilding*."

"Actually, it's *wiling*," Coleman said.

Coleman spoke as if Swann had said *cold* instead of *cool*. He was given an excuse to look at her, but he had to keep his expression as uninterested as hers. He was sure that her thrill was matching his.

"Thank you," Swann said.

"Like I told you, *wiling*," Knowledge said. "They were saying, 'We're going to get somebody. We're going to get money.'"

Swann could have been listening to Alvin of the space case. Knowledge continued, his account bringing the posse to Central Park and the fountain by the lake. A youngster known as Justice had spotted a woman.

"She was like blond, but I didn't really look at her," Knowledge said. "She had on music. Justice say, 'Look at that watch!'"

Swann swallowed. He pictured Danica with the watch glinting on her wrist, the music from the Walkman blocking out the sounds of the posse coming up behind her as she went up *that path* into the Ramble.

"Anybody see something, they say, 'I want it,' and there ain't nothing more to say," Knowledge said.

"Who hit her?" Swann asked.

Swann was still managing a casual tone.

"I don't know," Knowledge said. "Everybody is ready to hit first so everybody else will say, 'See how he hit her?' The first hit will always be the best because after the first the person will either buckle or cover up."

The cadence of the other interrogations made Swann expect that Coleman would step in about now. She said nothing and he guessed that she was letting him run the questioning out of deference to his relationship with the victim.

"What did the lady do?"

"She buckled and she was like, 'Stop! Stop! Why you hit me? What did I do?' Now, everybody was like, 'Shut up.' She was crying and they was laughing. They was just hitting her and kicking her for fun."

"*They*? You mean *we*."

"I just saw all the rest of them hitting her, so I hit her."

"You were just a follower?"

"I wasn't following nothing."

"You were a leader?"

"I wasn't a leader neither. There is no leader. Everybody is just together."

Swann had long observed this about posses. He noted now that Knowledge put particular emphasis on the word *together.*

"Anyway, that was it," Knowledge said. "That was like the end."

Knowledge took a bite of hamburger and chewed as calmly as Swann was trying to keep himself.

"Who got the watch?" Coleman asked. "Justice?"

Coleman must have sensed that Swann was nearing a limit.

"No, first one to pop it, keep it. This other kid. They call him Pinnacle."

"Does he still have it?" Coleman asked.

"He won't say. Everybody ask him what he do with it. He act like he don't hear them."

"And who got the Walkman?"

"Justice. I know because he said, 'Listen to what kind of music she got,' and I listened. It was *terrible.*"

"What'd you get?"

"Nothing."

"You sure now?"

"After all I told you, would I be lying to you?"

"Maybe a little fun?"

"You might as well say that. But only a little bit. We go down to the Deuce and everybody talk about how they get their licks off and they laugh."

Swann returned, casual as before.

"What were they laughing at?" Swann asked.

"They find it funny to see people's expression," Knowledge said. "Most people, it's like, 'Why me?' Everybody laugh about that and talk about what they did. How much heart they got."

Knowledge sat back and held his hands palms up. His next words held for Swann some of the logic of the financial pages.

"You really got nothing to lose," Knowledge said. "Say we took something and the cops catch us. They take it back, but we ain't paid nothing for it."

"The posse gonna keep showing its *heart?*" Swann asked.

"Not today," Knowledge said. "This is Friday. Date night. But they be out the next night."

Coleman turned over her paper place mat and unscrewed the cap of the oversized Fifth Avenue pen Swann had given her. Knowledge stared at the big eighteen-carat nib. He looked up, wary, when Coleman asked him for the names and addresses of everybody in the posse.

"Menace and Truth didn't tell you?"

"They also told us you took the watch," Coleman said.

Knowledge's notions of everybody in a posse being together did not keep him from giving Coleman what she wanted.

"Pinnacle, that's with two *n*'s," Knowledge said.

"Thank you," Coleman said.

Knowledge was back to staring at the nib.

"That's not slum," Knowledge said.

Swann shifted on the bench. The posse's ability to recognize real gold had gotten Danica hurt.

"I got it for Christmas," Coleman said.

She held up the pen and Knowledge's eyes stayed on the nib. Swann had an idea how to make the case harder for the city police to discard.

"Knowledge, you seem to spell pretty well, so I tell you what," Swann said. "We're going to give you a chance to tell the DA exactly what happened and explain to him that you're really a nice guy and you really didn't do anything. And we're going to let you put it in writing so nobody can change your words."

Knowledge shook his head and let out a sigh.

"You mean every single last thing?" Knowledge asked.

"All you got to do is write the truth," Swann said.

"The truth is a lot of writing," Knowledge said.

"I don't know," Coleman said. "We have to be sure that the robbery in the park was the only other one. Look me in the eye and tell me you're not lying."

"I'm not lying," Knowledge said.

Knowledge definitely could have used some time before a mirror.

"Okay," Coleman said.

Coleman held out the pen and Knowledge could not resist. He rolled the thick black barrel in his fingers, turning the nib in the light. He then smoothed the back of the place mat with his palm and began, speaking each word aloud as he progressed from the ride into Manhattan to the attack.

"*Truth kick her mostly in the face. It wasn't bleeding a lot. Just dripping.*"

Knowledge paused like a schoolkid grown weary of his homework. Coleman threatened to tear up the paper if he did not tell the whole truth. He hunched protectively over the statement that would almost guarantee him a felony conviction. He completed the account and added a postscript.

"*I'm not that type of guy you may be thinking. I'm not a criminal. I'm just a regular person that go get some money sometimes. I am a very con . . .*"

Knowledge looked up and closed his eyes, going inside himself, as Danica had in choosing a toast.

"S-i-d-a, no, e," Knowledge said.

He bent back over the place mat.

"*. . . considerate.*"

Knowledge handed back the gold-nibbed pen.

"I had won an award for spelling, you know," Knowledge said.

Swann and Coleman did not want to arrest Knowledge for the case involving Danica until they had captured the rest of the posse. They took him back to Central Booking and returned to the street cheering themselves.

Swann whooped, feeling at once elated and horrified and exhausted and wild. He would have hugged Coleman had he not remembered how she had slapped his hand away when he brushed the bit of bone from her hair. He stood daunted as he had not been when he was only faking affection with the eleven Knowledges. It seemed that even with embraces the lie was easier than the truth.

"I know what we are," Coleman said.

The two of them might have at other moments been of one mind, but he could see that she now had no notion of what he had been contemplating.

"The off-duty police department," she said.

Swann was happy enough just to laugh with her.

"That's it!" he said. "The ODPD!"

He and she seemed more together than any posse until they came to the mezzanine where those bound for Brooklyn part with those headed for Queens. He did not imagine that they would do anything but once more go their separate ways.

"Tomorrow?" Coleman asked.

"Tomorrow," Swann said.

Sixteen

FROM THE SPLINTERED WINDOW of an abandoned building, Swann and Coleman watched the first member of the posse appear across the street at the meeting place. They had obtained mug shots in the basement of police headquarters and studied them on the subway ride to Brooklyn. Swann now decided that this was Gee Wiz, age fifteen.

Gee Wiz stopped in front of the housing project, his hands buried in the pockets of his black leather down coat. He lowered his head when more threatening-looking males passed, this being almost all of them. He did gaze at the females and received more attention in return than the teenage Swann ever had.

Suddenly, Gee Wiz cocked back his head and folded his arms across his chest in a hard-guy pose. He raised an arm and slapped hands with a second posse member who appeared out of the night. This was thirteen-year-old Justice, the one who had told the posse he wanted the Rolex on Danica's wrist. He had ended up with the Walkman, almost certainly the one whose earphones he was now wearing.

Moments later, these two greeted sixteen-year-old Truth. He was bigger even than Justice, with a thick neck and barrel chest. He was the first of the posse who looked individually tough.

More members appeared, and they all seemed to grow a bit more relaxed and confident with each new arrival. Swann recognized Menace and Destiny and Tickle and Reality and Gridlock and Sideswipe and Rampage and Pinnacle, with two *n*'s, who had gotten the Rolex.

The posse's shouts and hoots reached Swann like cries from a playground. He and Coleman eased further back from the window to ensure that the youngsters did not spot them. He watched them stroll away from the project, their limbs moving loose and in leisurely time with those of the others. Each of them had a throwaway tucked under an arm or flung over a shoulder.

"I'll follow them and you follow me," Coleman said.

Swann listened to her feet crunch evenly away on the broken glass that littered the floor. He kept watching from the window until he saw her crossing the street. He picked up the gym bag he had brought from District 1.

Coleman ambled in pace with the posse, and Swann trailed her, a block behind. He was back to trying not to look like Five-O, and to that end he was wearing his homburg and bow tie as well as his suit. The tropical wool had felt like so much finely spun pretense, but he himself felt entirely genuine as he now followed the small figure in red leather. The reflective strip on her black backpack shone as she strode with perfect poise through a crowd of crackheads and on past a dice game and a row of drunks who were pulling on quart bottles of beer.

He saw her hand shoot out and catch a yellow rubber ball that bounced off a stoop. She tossed the ball back to a little boy in a down coat, pausing to say something Swann was too far away to hear.

She continued through another knot of crackheads, and Swann reached the stoop where the little boy stood. Swann did not at first realize that the boy was speaking to him.

"The lady up ahead said to tell you don't be staring at her behind," the boy said.

Swann had not, in fact, taken note of any female hindquarters in several weeks, and he had paid no attention at all to this particular *behind* since his initial appraisal some months before. He now could not help but look at these two small knots of muscle that clenched in the tight leather pants up ahead.

Coleman and her behind suddenly broke into a sprint. Swann peered ahead and saw that the posse had reached a subway entrance and that the last of them was disappearing down the steps. He threw himself into a dead run.

Swann stood with Coleman on the mezzanine, winded from the sprint, hearing the voices of the posse down on the platform. She asked if he had received her message and he said only that he had.

"Don't try to tell me you didn't look," Coleman said.

A waft of tunnel breath and a rumbling saved Swann from having to respond. He and Coleman waited at the top of the steps, listening to the screech of the brakes and the rattle of the doors. They gave the posse a moment to board the last car.

Swann hit the platform with Coleman and they slipped into a middle car as the doors were about to close. They walked in tandem toward the back until they were two cars from the end.

Coleman continued on. Swann stayed where he was until the next stop. He there stepped onto the platform and strode quickly down to the last car.

Swann boarded as if he had been waiting at the station. He got the same reception his attire had previously earned him in the last car, with some youngsters uneasy, almost certain he was no threat, but not quite. Truth and Pinnacle in particular seemed to be sizing him as a possible vic. He was sure that even the most experienced youngster could not guess what was making the round pocket print where the bankroll had once been.

The answer became apparent to everyone after Swann reached into his trousers. He began tossing the yo-yo and scattered laughter erupted into general hilarity as Coleman repeated her Christmas Day joke so the whole car could hear.

"Yo! Yo!"

Everyone now seemed convinced that Swann could not possibly be Five-O. The train pulled out of the station and he felt that same backward tug of departure as when he played the vic. He now could remain open-eyed as the last car came alive.

Justice set the beat by clapping along with a cassette in the Walkman that was definitely not Barry Manilow. Tickle began sputtering along, as did Destiny and Gridlock. Reality tapped a three-finger ring against a steel pole.

"Party over here!" Reality said.

"Party over here!" Coleman said.

Coleman was sitting directly across from Swann and he figured he would not arouse the posse's suspicions if he looked at her as if he were giving her the eye, the once-over. She was definitely no beauty, and the time was not so distant when he had not considered her worthy of his attention.

Any shortcomings now seemed entirely his own, and he stifled a laugh at the message she had left with the boy on the stoop. He tossed the yo-yo and watched her strike her seat once with the knuckles of her right hand for every time she hit it with the open palm of her left. He felt the secret of their mission double with the secret of her.

"P-a-a-a-rty!" Coleman said.

"P-a-a-a-rty!" Truth said.

Swann's eyes went to Truth, of whom Knowledge had written *Kick her mostly in the face.* Truth was grinning as he slapped a white sneaker on the linoleum.

As the train neared Times Square, Swann slipped the yo-yo string from his finger and eased over to the emergency brake cord that hung by the door to the next car. He saw the whole posse still moving from beat to beat, seeming less like a wolfpack than youngsters in need of only a little good-hearted chaperoning. Both of Truth's sneakers were tapping, and even he seemed innocent of any desire other than to joke and laugh and keep the beat going.

Swann's hand closed on the red handle, the enameled wood feeling not completely inappropriately like a child's toy. He reflexively pulled right on the beat. The next beat was lost in the screech of the emergency brake.

The jarring force caused Truth and Reality and Pinnacle and the rest to tumble against one another. Only Swann and Coleman had known to prepare themselves, and they took position at the door to the next car while those in the posse regained their balance and looked about, momentarily dazed.

"Yo! Yo!" Coleman said again.

"Five-O!" Swann said.

Swann and Coleman held up their badges, and the surprise proved so complete that the posse forgot to go sullen. Truth and Reality and the rest stood gaping, as still as the train itself. They then began to shift their weight and swivel their heads. They were looking for an escape route, but these unlikely Five-O's blocked the only exit when the train was between stations. What made the last car a good place to party also made it a bad place to get caught.

* * *

Swann and Coleman instructed the teenagers not with the posse to go into the next car. Pinnacle moved to scoot out with them.

"Hold up, Pinnacle," Coleman said.

Pinnacle stopped as if his own private emergency brake had been tripped.

"Go back over there by Reality and Gridlock," Swann said.

The accurate use of the street names redoubled the posse's initial shock. Coleman announced that she and her partner knew all their names, street and actual, as well as addresses.

Swann took from the gym bag a pair of ten-foot daisy chains he had borrowed from District 1, each of which bore six single handcuff bracelets. He told the youngsters they had two choices: they could come along like gentlemen or they could act like criminals and put up a fuss.

Truth planted his sneakered feet wide.

"We ain't do nothing," Truth said.

Truth cocked his head to the side and loudly sucked his teeth. The faces of the other posse members began to harden. Swann's chest pounded at the possibility this standoff might explode out of control and end in another shooting.

"You keep saying that, people are going to have to stop calling you Truth and go back to calling you Milton," Coleman said.

Coleman might have just been seeking to further prove the futility of resisting, but she also might have guessed that some of the posse would not know Truth's real name. The resulting giggles made the posse again seem like only youngsters.

Swann spoke like a chaperon.

"Let's make sure we have the right address for Milton in case he gets away," Swann said.

Coleman read aloud Truth's address, complete with apartment number.

"Figure, we'd be at your house at four in the morning to drag you out of bed," Swann said.

"In front of your mother," Coleman said.

Swann stepped over with the daisy chain. Truth did not resist as one of the bracelets was snapped on his wrist.

"You're next, Theodore," Swann said.

The second cuff went on Menace, and Swann moved to put the third on Justice.

"I don't want to be next to him, I want to be with Gridlock," Justice said.

The rest of the posse began calling out.

"Yeah, and put me with Reality."

"No, I don't want Tickle. I want Destiny."

"Yeah, and Pinnacle on the other side."

At CCTV, a different cop was sitting before the fifty monitors. This cop was also doing a crossword puzzle.

"We're just gonna hold these kids here until we get some transportation," Swann said.

The cop peered through the Plexiglas partition to see Coleman and the eleven manacled youngsters.

"Be my guest," the cop said.

Swann returned to the front area and unstacked the benches that had once been in the Room.

"Have a seat, gentlemen," Swann said.

The front area had a telephone, and Swann called District 1 for transportation. The desk officer responded with the predictable howls and grumbles to news of an off-duty collar of eleven youngsters for an off-system robbery. He ended by saying that the lone functioning radio car already had a list of jobs.

Swann hung up and Coleman asked what the desk officer had said.

"What we figured," Swann said.

Swann and Coleman kept their voices as matter of fact as they had with the many Knowledges. The two of them once again had to mask any emotion, but he knew she was as jazzed as he was himself that their plan was working perfectly.

"What we here for?" Truth asked.

The time had come for the next step.

"Milton, you seem impatient," Coleman said. "Why don't I take you in the back and fill you in a little."

Coleman was still wearing the backpack in which she had a pad of paper. She took Truth down a hallway to a small vacant room.

The posse gazed through the partition at the monitors as Swann began notifying the families that the youngsters had been arrested for attacking and robbing a woman. Swann said that the youngsters would later be at District 1, but Justice's father insisted on coming immediately. Swann was giving him directions when the posse spotted some girls on a monitor. The posse hooted and howled.

"That's them I hear?" Justice's father asked.

Swann looked at Justice, who sat laughing, the Walkman earphones still around his neck.

"That's them," Swann said. "And, by the way, if he happens to have any cassette tapes lying around, you might bring them along. If what I'm looking for is there, you'll know what I mean."

Truth was swaggering when Coleman brought him back, but as Swann reapplied the handcuff he noticed an ink stain on the youngster's finger.

"Okay, Theodore, your turn," Coleman said.

Coleman took Menace in the back. Truth remained subdued, but the rest of the posse continued to joke and laugh. Swann had to strain to hear the dial tone when he picked up the phone to make the next call.

"Quiet, please," Swann said.

The posse ignored him.

"Quiet!"

The posse seemed to get only louder. Truth bellowed.

"He said, 'Quiet,'" Truth said.

The posse instantly hushed. Truth turned to Swann with his first unfought smile. He had shown his power.

"It's quiet," Truth said.

Destiny then loudly burped and the posse exploded into laughter. Swann remembered Danica saying that they had laughed on hearing her screams.

Coleman questioned one after another. She had just finished Gridlock when the posse erupted again on seeing something on the monitors.

"Look, Justice, your moms!"

"And father!"

Balance pointed at one of the eight-inch screens, and Swann saw a couple in their thirties crossing a mezzanine. They passed from that monitor's range and appeared on the next, this the one that showed the long passageway leading to CCTV.

Swann looked over at the door and saw the couple enter. Justice's mother was dressed as she might for church. The father was in work clothes, a splash of orange paint on the shoulder of his denim jacket, more on his construction boots. The arrival of parents caused the posse to hush as fast as it had at Truth's command.

Coleman looked as if she could use a break. Swann took the gold-nibbed pen and led Justice and his parents into the back. The posse's shouts and laughs became a murmur when he shut the door, and the small room filled with more immediate sounds. The mother's sigh. The creak of a chair under the father's weight. The beatless tap of Justice's fingers on the gray metal desk. The gentle, understanding tones of Police Officer Swann nudging Justice to waive his *Miranda* warnings and confess himself into jail.

"I wasn't really there," Justice said.

Swann prepared to give another nudge, but the father spoke first.

"What is it?" the father asked. "What is the problem? Why did they attack her?"

"Because they wanted to," Justice said.

"Are they angry at something?"

"I guess so."

"And you?"

"I wasn't angry at anything."

Justice and the father stared at each other.

"Is it me?" the father asked.

"No," Justice said.

"Your mother?"

"No."

"Why? What was the purpose?"

"Somebody said, 'Set it off.'"

"It. What's 'it'?"

"I don't know."

Justice tried his look of innocence on Swann and then his mother before he braved his father.

"I didn't do nothing," Justice said.

The mother began to cry and took a handkerchief from her handbag. The father laid a hand on Justice's shoulder much as Swann had done with Alvin and the Knowledges. His fingernails were rimmed by orange paint.

"Theodore, tell the officer what music you listen to," the father said.

"Public Enemy, Cool G Rap Polo," Justice said.

The father raised his hand from his son's shoulder and reached into his work jacket. A cassette clattered on the desk and Justice seemed to crumple. He was not even going to attempt a lie so enormous as to explain how he had come to possess a Barry Manilow tape.

When he had finished writing, Justice returned to the front. He squeezed between Menace and Tickle, who like most of the others did not have fathers at home.

"Say good night to your mother," Justice's father said.

"Good night," Justice said.

The father took the mother's hand and led her away. The posse that had claimed Justice as its own watched as his parents passed from monitor to monitor, finally boarding a train.

Swann took Reality into the back and had only to act fatherly. Another youngster confessed like a son and set gold nib to paper.

"*I rob . . .*"

Reality paused, but reluctance had nothing to do with crime or punishment.

"It's okay, it's not a quiz," Swann said. "Just spell the words the way they sound."

"*. . . ladee I wont monnuy. I still wont monnuy butt I sorre.*"

Gee Wiz was a juvenile, so he could not be questioned without his parents. That left only Pinnacle, and a surprise came when Swann asked what had happened to the watch. Swann nudged every way he could, and Pinnacle still clung to the weakest of lies.

"I don't know," Pinnacle said.

"You're not going to get in any more trouble for being the one who took the watch," Swann said. "What you will get in more trouble for is lying."

Pinnacle shrugged.

"Does your mother keep a nice house?" Swann asked.

"Of course she do," Pinnacle said.

"What's she going to say if we have to go tear up the place looking for that watch?"

"She going to ask why you tear up her house and don't find nothing," Pinnacle said.

Swann decided that Pinnacle here was speaking the truth.

"What, you sold it?" Swann asked.

"If I had sold it, I would have money," Pinnacle said. "You want to see what I got in my pockets?"

The posse had been patted down on the train, but Swann snapped alert as Pharaoh's hand dropped below the table. The hand reappeared holding two crumpled dollar bills.

"Look."

Pinnacle uttered that one syllable in a wistful tone, and suddenly Swann knew.

"Pinnacle, just tell me, how pretty is she?" Swann asked.

Pinnacle was recuffed to a posse gone drowsy, and Coleman asked Swann for her pen. Swann patted himself and turned to Pinnacle.

"Give," Swann said.

Pinnacle shrugged and his free hand held out the pen he had palmed after confessing. The posse erupted, but soon quieted of its own accord. Justice stared at the monitors that had shown his parents' departure. He grew as bleary as a cave cop as he watched the uneventful comings and goings of the underground.

"Can't you get real TV?" Justice asked.

Swann considered that the steel and concrete overhead blocked out not just radio transmissions, that the subway was the one place in the city beyond the reach of the invisible television beams that had so intrigued him when he was himself a youngster.

Justice lay on the floor with the other on his daisy chain and those on the second chain did the same. The absent Knowledge may have rightly called them considerate as they arranged their manacled arms so their possemates were comfortable. They were gentle with each other in a way that would have been remarkable for any group their age.

The youngsters drifted off to sleep, and Swann for a moment felt himself drifting with them. He looked over at Coleman, who was going through the statements he had collected. He still did not know if she had a father at home, but he was sure she came from a block similar to the one where they had watched the posse assemble. He puzzled at how she could be so unscathed by the street.

She looked up and he knew which statement she was reading.

"You don't have to say anything," he said.

"I don't need to," she said.

Coleman handed Swann the papers, and he saw he had been right. The last one she had read was Pinnacle's.

"*I giv wach to female name Nyesha.*"

Swann thought of Danica's face at the hospital. His eyes went to Pinnacle and all these other youngsters who lay snuggled before him like puppies.

A light shake of the youngster's shoulder brought the sort of little dream noise Jenny sometimes made.

"Reality," Swann said.

A second, slightly harder shake caused Reality to shift from his side to his stomach. Justice moved a leg to make room. Tickle drew in an arm to accommodate Justice's leg.

"Time to wake up, Reality."

The eyes opened and Swann watched Reality suffuse with self just as Danica had at the Plaza. The youngster seemed in these first instants to be only that softer, naive stuff that had made him confess to a deed for which Swann should hate him.

"Time to go to jail, pass it on,'" Swann said.

Reality lightly jostled Pinnacle. A snort came from one of the two uniformed cops who had finally arrived to take the first carload to District 1.

The desk officer, the transit detectives, and the city detectives all made noises about getting rid of this already closed case and setting the posse free. The problem was the written statements, which were on paper as real as any report and could not simply be made to disappear.

By general consensus, the situation was unusual enough that the district attorney's office should be notified. A city detective made the call and afterward gave Swann a look.

"Your name seems to mean something down there," the detective said.

The detective added that an ADA would be coming to the station-house, and Swann used the wait to make a notification of his own. Danica was sure to be asleep at this hour, but eight- or ten-year-old Pharaoh was certain to be up. Swann dialed the beeper number from the goom phone.

The phone rang minutes later. Swann heard the speakers of the jeep blasting in the background as he told Pharaoh that the posse had been grabbed. Pharaoh whooped and spoke in the comradely tone of one good guy addressing another.

"You fuck up a lady, it only right you go to jail, right?" Pharaoh said.

"Right," Swann said.

None other than ADA Curry arrived at District 1.

"Officer Swann, we meet again," she said.

Swann felt as much a good guy as Pharaoh believed him to be, which was too much to be intimidated. He gave an account that was not only accurate, but complete to the point of saying the victim was a friend.

"And, her being your 'friend,' you took it upon yourself to track down her assailants?" Curry asked.

"Nobody else was going to," Swann said. "The case was already closed out."

Curry could not argue with Swann on this point. She read the statements, but she remained skeptical about Swann. Whatever IAD had or had not told her about the Money Store, she still clearly believed he was a crook.

Curry asked the detectives to head for Brooklyn and recover what was described in the complaint as a "yellow metal watch." One of them checked his own watch, and he apparently had other plans. He suggested that there was already enough corroborating physical evidence.

"Anybody could have that cassette tape," Curry said. "It could be construed as racism to suggest that simply because a defendant is a black teenager he should not have a particular tape."

Coleman could not help but interrupt.

"You can take it from me," Coleman said. "No black person is going to be offended if you say they don't listen to Barry Manilow."

Curry shifted in her seat, clearly uncomfortable discussing racism with a black person.

"The law makes no distinction regarding Barry Manilow," Curry said.

Swann and Coleman managed to keep straight faces until they reached the prisoner processing area.

"We actually pulled it off," Swann said.

"Yes, I'd say we did," Coleman said.

Coleman looked at Swann and he looked at her and, had they not been in a police station, he might have gone ahead and given her a victory hug. He held out his hand and as she took it he puffed out his cheeks and crossed his eyes. They together began a routine that was the same as any other arrest save for one entry in the on-line booking sheet.

"Now, the complainant's name is spelled . . . ?" Coleman asked.

"D-a-n-i-c-a N-e-a-r-y," Swann said.

V

Seventeen

DANICA'S FACE was no longer swollen, but she still had bandages on her cheek and over her right eye. He had difficulty reading her reaction to seeing him at her front door.

"Hi," Swann said. "I just wanted you to know that the people who attacked you have been arrested. Every one of them."

Swann met the eyes that had always seemed to shine with her own splendor. She gazed at him from the center of what had been done to her, of what could not be undone.

"Who got them? You?"

Any interest the eyes might have held in this, her own case, was dimmed by tears.

"Me and my partner."

"Thank you."

Danica's distracted tone told Swann that she was thanking him for his efforts, not for any great comfort she could take in the arrests. She had no more questions.

"You look like you're healing fine," Swann said.

Danica's hand went to her wounded cheek. The nails looked freshly painted. They were bright red.

"That's what the doctor says," Danica said. "He keeps saying, 'Let's see that smile.'"

Danica's tone was flat, but anger was rising in her eyes.

"I keep thinking if only I hadn't read all that about being fit, then I wouldn't have gone on that walk . . ."

The eyes flickered and Swann sensed that her mind was aflash with images of what had followed.

"It wasn't anything that you did," Swann said. "It was what the did."

"Still, if I hadn't been in the park . . ."

Swann realized how wrong he had been not to tell her. He would have had to tell her now even if he had not known that IAD would hear about the arrests and deduce the Rolex must be the one he had purchased on Fifth Avenue. The next step would be to identify her as the pretty girl in the picture.

"Danica, that watch they took wasn't your watch," Swann said. "It was one I bought."

"What?"

"I bought a real Rolex and switched it with yours when you were in the bathroom that last day at the Plaza."

The eyes had steadied on Swann in one way he would have never wanted her to look at him.

"They knew it was real," Swann said. "That's why they attacked you."

Swann took the counterfeit Rolex from his pocket.

"This is yours," Swann said.

The watch lay there in his open palm, the second hand frozen as it had been when they joked about *getting late,* as it had when he picked it off the bed table in the Plaza.

"Why didn't you say something before?" Danica asked. "How could you let me not know?"

"I should have told you," Swann said. "I can only say I'm sorry."

"Well, that changes everything."

Danica took the watch. Swann dropped his empty hand.

"You'll probably be getting the other one back," Swann said. "And those guys who were following me, they'll probably be coming by to ask about it."

"Is that why you told me now? You figured they would tell me anyway."

"No."

Swann saw the unbandaged eyebrow knit.

"I really did borrow that money," Swann said. "All I'd been seeing in the papers was business guys borrowing millions, so I saw this commercial for the Money Store and I figured why not?"

"Did you think all that up just now?" Danica asked.

"It's the truth," Swann said.

Danica's eyes dropped to the counterfeit watch.

"I saw Ellen at the market," Danica said.

The eyes rose.

"I think she saw me. I think she knows."

"IAD told her," Swann said.

Swann paused.

"I'm out of the house," Swann said.

Danica just looked at him for a moment.

"I don't know what I'm supposed to say to you," Danica said.

"You're not supposed to say anything," Swann said.

Swann went down the stoop. He was a half-dozen strides up the block when he heard her door shut.

The yo-yo was beside his gun and shield on the dresser as Swann unpinned the boutonniere. The rosebud had wilted in the two days since its purchase, but he could still catch a fragrance when he raised it for a sniff.

Oooh.

Swann dropped the flower into the wastebasket and returned his suit to the closet. He had not slept in two days, but he lay awake wondering if IAD was even then on the way to Danica's house. He had no fear for himself whatever she might say. His worry was that Lieutenant Gentile would try to throw her off balance in hope she would say something damaging.

The guardian of cave cop virtue was entirely capable of producing the picture taken outside Eleanor's. "*Pretty girl,*" Lieutenant Gentile would say as Danica stood with her battered face. "*Is this you?*"

Swann was back in civil service attire as he returned to the life he had for a time escaped. The adventure with Coleman had not kept them from parting on the mezzanine where the way to Queens diverges from that to Brooklyn. He often heard her on the radio and he often thought of calling her, but he never had a good enough excuse for it not to seem as though he was asking her out. His regular fantasies nowadays involved the ODPD undertaking another case, he and she on a kind of police date.

Swann could foresee no such actual adventures and his on-duty department continued to post him at Sullivan's old desk. He again handed out the checks on payday. He fed his own into a cash machine.

Beep.

Swann punched in CAVE to prove again that he was him. He hit the button to deposit the check.

Beep.

Swann hit a button to withdraw his $50.

Beep.

Ellen answered the door in shorts and a T-shirt. Her face was flushed, her brow beaded with sweat. He decided that she must have been doing something more vigorous than mopping. He decided against making small talk about fitness and exercise. He handed her the check for the next two weeks.

"Jenny! Your father's here."

Jenny's clattering footsteps suggested she was glad to see him, though he could not be sure because her expression was obscured by the bill of her new baseball cap.

"She insisted on buying that," Ellen said.

The hat was leather, identical to the one Pharaoh had worn.

"It was my money," Jenny said. "I *saved* it."

Swann understood that she had financed the purchase with coins from her piggy bank, with the *clink, clink, clink* that had once inspired him.

"That doesn't mean you should throw it away," Ellen said.

"I didn't throw it away," Jenny said. "I *like* this hat."

Ellen gave Swann a look that was not dimmed by all the distance between them. He went down the steps after Jenny and she asked a question that should have been simple.

"You like my hat?"

Swann could only think to say what he thought.

"Yes."

Swann did not want to create any more conflict than already existed.

"Mommy just isn't sure that you need a hat," Swann said.

"You bought a hat," Jenny said.

Jenny was referring to the homburg.

"Mommy wasn't so sure I needed mine, either. And she was probably right."

Swann felt almost too sensible to be taking a yo-yo from his pocket. Jenny again declined a try. He gave a few tosses as they crossed into the park.

"We caught the bad guys, the ones who attacked the lady," Swann said.

Jenny peered from under her brim and asked a series of questions that he could actually answer. Each reply seemed to make her more pleased, and she gave him his turn to admire her when they reached the playground. She dashed from slide to tire swing to monkey bars, calling for him to witness her various feats and tricks.

"Watch me, Daddy! See? It's not that hard. Look!"

Jenny started across the balance beam and Swann thought of his ironworker grandfather. Joseph had once said that the trick to working the high steel was to walk with your middle, that all you had to do to have everybody think you must be an Indian was focus yourself at that spot right behind your belly button.

Whatever the secret, Jenny seemed to know it intuitively. She stopped at midbeam and raised a foot so that she stood on one leg.

"Beautiful!" Swann said.

Jenny set down her foot and continued across the beam. A breeze ruffled her hair, and Swann remembered his grandfather had died while leaning into a stiff wind that had suddenly slackened.

"Daddy, I want to see him," Jenny said.

Swann wondered for an instant if Jenny had somehow read his thoughts.

"Who?"

Jenny reached the end of the beam.

"That boy with the rings. The one who helped you."

Swann watched Jenny start backward along the beam. He thought he might take her and Pharaoh to the Empire State Building. He then considered that Ellen was angry enough about the visit to Times Square, not to mention the hat.

"We may have to wait a while," Swann said.

Jenny hopped off the end of the beam and was soon standing atop the jungle gym, both arms raised. Swann decided that in any event he would take her to the skyscraper her great-grandfather had died building. He again remembered the day Joseph had taken him, and again his keenest memory was not of the building's height nor of the eagle's view of the city but of his father's presence at his side.

"Watch me!" she said.

She did more feats of daring, and Swann thought of Pharaoh, whose father's address was *unkwn.* Swann decided he really should take Pharaoh somewhere as well, if for no other reason than to thank him for helping catch the posse.

"Look!"

She had hooked her knees over one of the upper bars. He caught his breath as she let herself fall back. Her hat dropped off as she dangled upside down, laughing.

"I'll get it," Swann said.

"It's okay," she said.

She did a neat little flip and retrieved the hat, pausing to place it on her head just so, just as she liked it. He was not so sure he had been all that sensible.

"Jenny, I gotta say, if you're gonna buy a hat, it might as well be one you really like," Swann said.

Swann passed from another night with Joseph to another day at District 1.

"Got a minute, Jack?"

Swann looked up from his desk to behold Police Officer Barney Fredricks. The expression was as distinctly friendly as the tone.

"I was just thinking I hadn't worn this since we marched last year . . . ," Fredricks said.

Fredricks held up the uniform he was carrying in a dry cleaning bag. He was harking back to the Saint Patrick's Day parade, when they had indeed gone up Fifth Avenue in lockstep.

". . . and that got me thinking about how things have been."

Fredricks went on to say that they had once been partners and they really ought to patch things up, forgive and forget.

"I mean, life's too short, you know?" Fredricks said.

Fredrick's smile was matched by a look so sincere that he must have put in extra time before the bathroom mirror.

"Hey, how come you stopped wearing those suits?" Fredricks asked.

"You noticed," Swann said.

"They must be expensive. What are they, two, three hundred?"

Swann could only think that IAD had caught Fredricks doing something like beating his wife or making obscene phone calls to a female officer or maybe taking free coffee from a diner. He must have then been offered a chance to escape punishment for informing on the Dark Side.

"Six."

"That's a lot of trips to the *bank*."

Fredricks meant Central Booking.

"Actually just one," Swan said.

Fredricks now seemed to be fighting a smile, for he no doubt thought Swann meant the arrest of the drug dealer.

"Oh yeah?" Fredricks said. "That must have been some trip."

Swann could see no telltale print, but he was certain that Fredricks was wearing a tape recorder. Swann spoke directly to Lieutenant Gentile, who had by this time confirmed the loan at the Money Store, who still could not accept that a cave cop would put up his house and go on a spree.

"Yes, it was some trip," Swann said.

Swann was now the one who was smiling. Fredricks seemed at a loss as to how to take the matter farther, and he shifted his uniform from one shoulder to the other.

"Anyway, uh, you marching Tuesday?" Fredricks said.

Swann was not going to let even the prospect of Fredricks's company keep him from the parade. He never missed the one day when an Irish transit cop could believe himself to be what he had imagined when he had first put on a uniform. The difficulty this year would be getting a uniform that fit.

That evening, Swann took his uniform to the neighborhood dry cleaner's. He was back to garments with patches on the shoulders, but he was still able to impress the man who chalked the waistband for alteration.

"This was you?" the man asked.

The morning of Saint Patrick's Day, Swann arrived at the assembly point in a uniform that fit as perfectly as had his blue pinstripe.

"Hey, Jack, glad you made it!" Fredricks said.

Fredricks was in his own uniform, identical to Swann's save for the numbers on their shields. The hidden tape recorder was no doubt rolling.

"Just like old times, hunh?" Fredricks said.

Mannering approached in the attire of the Emerald Society band: kilt, white spats, green tunic, cap with a cockade. A drum hung from a white leather strap around his neck.

"I see you two kissed and made up," Mannering asked.

"Hey, life's too short," Fredricks said.

Mannering laughed, and Swann knew that he had reached the same conclusion regarding Fredricks's unlikely friendliness.

"That's what they say," Mannering said.

Sullivan came over, also in band attire. Retirement had not precluded him from playing for the Emerald Society, and he was carrying what was likely the very bagpipe he had rushed off to practice that day Swann first saw the Room.

"I'm glad to see you guys are all talking again," Sullivan said.

"Why wouldn't we be?" Mannering asked.

Sullivan looked at Swann.

"Whatever you're doing, keep doing it," Sullivan said. "You look like you didn't put back on an ounce."

A shout caused everyone to turn. The band leader had donned his bearskin hat and was summoning Mannering and Sullivan. Swann watched them join other cop musicians who had gaped at his bow tie and homburg and were now preparing to parade before millions in what were only skirts by another name.

The firefighters marched by with the banner reading *The Bravest* and then the city cops passed with a banner reading *The Finest* and then it was time. Sullivan and the other pipers let out a first humming note. Mannering's drum was among a dozen that rattled a military beat as the New York transit police stepped from the shadows of the side street. Swann felt the sun on his face as he moved his triple E's in pace with a thousand other gleaming black shoes that were starting up Fifth Avenue. Fredricks fell in on his left.

Perhaps because nobody could come up with a single word to describe them, the transit police had no banner. They did have an American flag that flapped sharply in the wind. Their brass buttons glinted brightly in the sunshine and their uniforms had been delinted with Scotch tape and their cap visors had been shined with Windex and they suddenly looked proud and maybe brave and maybe even noble.

The transit police moved as one past Saint Patrick's Cathedral, and the cardinal stood on the steps, raising his gold-ringed hand in blessing. Swann continued the rare experience of being both in step and spirit with his fellow transit cops, moving in perfect pace with the others as they tramped on past the Gucci store and FAO Schwarz and the jeweler's where he had bought the Rolex and the Plaza hotel.

At Eighty-sixth Street, the drums stopped and the bagpipes gave a final hum. The transit police joined a great swarm of The Finest and The Bravest and other servants of the city. Each group had its own party to attend, and the transit police trooped crosstown to the subway gloom of a church basement.

A great happy babble filled the chamber beneath Our Lady of Perpetual Help. The heroes paid their $10 at the door and prepared to take advantage of the one day when you were allowed to drink and carry on in uniform.

"Hey, hey, what'll it be?" Fredricks asked.

"Club soda," Swann said.

"How could I forget," Fredricks said.

Fredricks fetched the first round, and Swann let him also get those that followed. Fredricks all the while pumped Swann about his suit and his money and the fun he must have had.

"You just got to go for the gusto," Fredricks said.

"That's what it says in the commercial," Swann said.

"No, really. I mean, who can blame you?"

Swann could not resist toying with him.

"For what?" Swann asked.

Fredricks fumbled for words.

"For anything," Fredericks said.

A piercing noise came from a stage at the back, and Swann saw that a portly cop was setting up a sound system. The cop was wearing an emerald green T-shirt and what hair he had was blow-dried straight back. He spoke into the microphone in a tone of a game show host.

The time had come to *pa-a-a-rty* transit-style, and a disco tune blasted from a set of speakers as big as those in the jeep driven by Pharaoh's employer. Some of the cops had brought their spouses, and a woman who was apparently Sergeant Quinn's wife began to nod her head in a way that suggested her dourness had less to do with her nature than her circumstance. Quinn took a slug of beer as if the music was just the roar of a passing train.

Fredricks eased closer to Swann, no doubt concerned that his tape recorder would pick up only the booming beat. He continued pumping, but then glanced at his watch and was only partly able to conceal his sudden alarm. He excused himself and he had no sooner dashed off than Mannering came over.

"I don't have to tell you . . ." Mannering said.

Swann understood that Mannering was warning him about Fredricks.

"No," Swann said. "Thanks."

Mannering leaned closer and said he had heard about Swann locking up a posse.

"With my partner," Swann said.

Mannering chose not to hear that.

"The victim, I figure it's got to be that one," Mannering said.

That one being Danica. Swann nodded.

"Nice move," Mannering said. "When you told her, she must have come in her pants."

Swann took a turn at not hearing.

"Speaking of which," Mannering said.

Mannering gave a shout and strode over to a pretty blond woman who stood by the door, appearing not entirely sure that a church basement full of cave cops was where she wanted to be. Swann knew he had seen her before, but he was not sure where until he suddenly pictured her in a white nurse's uniform with blood sprayed across the front. She was the nurse from that night he had shot Daryl Coombs, a night that still marked the start of what so easily might not have been.

The music stopped, and Swann watched Mannering step away from the nurse to fetch his drum. Sullivan got his bagpipe humming as the band formed a semicircle. They played a tune that Swann recognized only as Irish.

"Here you go, Jackie boy."

Fredricks had returned with an unsolicited club soda and no doubt a fresh tape. He sidled as close as before and mumbled about the line at the men's room. He then resumed his pumping.

"You know, Jack, there probably isn't anybody here who wouldn't have did what you did," Fredricks said.

Swann was watching Mannering; he worked the drum, seeming shed of all save the music, intent on keeping time with the others, yet intensely himself.

"You think?" Swann asked.

"Absolutely," Fredricks said.

Swann's eyes went to Sullivan, seeing all those nights of practice guide his fluttering fingers through the music of his forbearers.

"Really," Fredricks said. "No question."

"Then why don't they?" Swann asked.

Swann looked back at Mannering and again at Sullivan, who had spoken of the things he knew from the Room, whose face now shared with Mannering's a quality that was neither ancestry nor copness.

"It's not exactly an everyday opportunity," Fredricks said.

The music rose, and Sullivan and Mannering with it, both looking as pure as they ever pretended to be with an assistant district attorney.

"Especially if you're transit, you know what I mean?" Fredricks said.

Swann turned to Fredricks, who seemed to hear the music as only a noise to speak over.

"Fredricks, you want money, it's in the phone book under *M*," Swann said. "Even for us. Even for you."

The band played a final flourish, and the tune ended. Swann moved to join in the applause and realized that he had been holding the club soda.

"I'll remember that next time I need a few thousand," Fredricks said.

Swann took a sip, and he had the ordinary taste in his mouth as the musicians put down their instruments. He watched Mannering rejoin the nurse and say something. They laughed as they had that night at the emergency room.

"It must be some feeling walking around with that kind of money," Fredricks said.

Swann gazed about the hall. Evening had arrived and the feet that had marched proudly up Fifth Avenue were standing in puddles of spilled beer.

"Fredricks, I'm going somewhere for a drink," Swann said. "You want to come?"

Swann almost had to admire Fredricks for the cheerful front he maintained at the prospect of leaving the cave cop's equivalent of the last car.

"Sure, Jack. Whatever you say, Jack."

The walk downtown brought Swann and Fredricks past any number of bars crowded with cops and firemen. The only uniform in evidence in front of the entrance to the Plaza was the one worn by the doorman.

"What's the problem, Officers?" the doorman asked.

"Nothing at all," Swann said. "Come on, Fredricks."

Fredricks followed Swann through the shiny brass portal as if there might be some alarm that sounded at the intrusion of civil servants.

As they crossed the lobby, Fredricks stuck almost as close to Swann's side as Danica had in those first steps through the park. The Oak Bar hushed at the appearance of two uniformed officers and the maître d' gazed about for what might have caused the police to arrive. He looked back at Swann and Fredricks, clearly unable to guess what reason they might possibly have to be there.

"Yes?" the maître d' asked.

"Yes," Swann said.

Brass buttons and police shields gleamed among the diamonds and gold as Swann and Fredricks went over to a window table. The waiter had served Swann before, but seemed to see only the uniforms.

"Bud," Fredricks said.

"Pardon?" the waiter said.

Fredricks had to settle for Heineken, and he took his first sip giving no sign he even tasted it. Swann's club soda was not quite as miraculous as on his first visit, but still far superior to champagne.

Fredricks then seemed momentarily to forget his discomfort and indeed his mission. Swann was not surprised to see that the cause of this distraction was a pretty woman who had taken a seat at the bar.

"I might start hanging out here myself," Fredricks said. "Though I'm sure they ain't exactly giving these drinks away. But hey, you only live once. Right, Jackie boy?"

"Right," Swann said.

The waiter approached.

"Would you care for another round, Officers?"

Swann looked at the officer who was across from him.

"Just a check," Swann said.

The waiter put down a brown leather folder and Swann saw that Fredricks was waiting for him to reach for it. Swann snapped his fingers.

"I can't believe it," Swann said. "I forgot to go to the bank."

Fredricks could not even fake a smile.

"I'll get it the next time," Swann said.

Fredricks slowly opened the leather folder. He was as surprised as Swann had once been to discover that drinks at the Oak Bar cost only three dollars more than a Bud at Joey Farrell's.

Fredricks again glanced at his watch and said he needed to use the bathroom. Swann led the way downstairs and Fredricks ducked into a stall, no doubt to put in another new tape.

Swann splashed his face with water and took a towel from the attendant. Recognition and surprise flared in the man's eyes, but just as quickly vanished.

Swann would have felt that his police uniform had received its greatest honor of the day if the attendant had smiled. No smile came, only the same reserved expression as when Swann had put $20 in the tip dish. Swann put down the lone dollar bill he had in his pocket.

"Yes, sir, you have a good night now, sir," the attendant said.

Fredricks did not have to be invited to go first out the revolving door, but once he reached the street he turned boisterous for having been inside the Plaza.

"I thought they were gonna die when they saw the uniforms," Fredricks said. "But what're they gonna say, you can't come in?"

Swann watched a limousine roll past, but it was not the one he had taken on that rainy night with Danica.

"You know, I never really thought about it, but you're in uniform, you can go anywhere you want," Fredricks said.

Fredericks seemed suddenly to remember that he was wired. He caught himself, but not before he inspired Swann to think of just the place to go with the fresh tape.

A police uniform did prove to be the one outfit that guaranteed immediate admission through the velvet ropes at Eleanor's. Swann and Fredricks might have been movie stars the way Jonathan turned instantly solicitous.

"Is there some sort of problem, Officers?" Jonathan asked.

Swann knew that every word would later be heard by the man who had once showed him a picture of a rain-soaked Danica standing at these very ropes.

"Not at all, Jon," Swann now said. "Everything's perfect."

Jonathan just stood there as Swann led Fredricks through the unmarked doorway and into an alcove dimmer than any subway station. A tall man with weightlifter's muscles stood against a black wall.

"There's no trouble here," the man said.

"I should hope not," Swann said.

Swann then saw a pale woman with dark hair sitting behind a wood counter. He considered that there might be some trouble after all, for he had not known there was an entrance fee. He had only some change he had scrounged from his locker, and he was unsure that Fredericks would have enough to cover whatever it cost to enter this, the very hottest nightclub in the western world.

"Two, please," Swann said.

"It's five dollars each," the woman said.

Swann was surprised to find that Eleanor's offered a price break to uniformed cops like some Times Square hot dog stand. Fredricks, on his part, seemed to relax.

"I think I can handle that," Fredricks said.

Swann held up a hand. He was not about to get himself jammed up with IAD over something as petty as accepting a "discount."

"We appreciate it, but that's okay," Swann said.

The woman just stared at Swann and normally he would have simply put down what he knew to be the correct price. Only he was broke and he had no idea what that price might be.

"What's it for everybody?" Swann asked.

"Five dollars," the woman said. "Even for cops."

Beyond a black velvet curtain was a large, softly lit room with ornate chandeliers and mirrors in gilded frames and a small bandstand where a trio of elderly men were thumping jazz of an earlier time. Fredricks hung back, looking puzzled, no doubt trying to figure how the admission to such a place could be half what he had paid to get into a church basement.

The uniforms terminated one conversation after another as Swann started with Fredricks into a solid mass of hipsters who had gotten the right haircuts and donned the right clothes so they could sip imported beer with their elbows pressed to their sides. The bar area was about as long and every bit as packed as any subway car, but this In crowd proved generally easier to wiggle through than the humbler throngs to which Swann was accustomed. He encountered none of the slabs of laborer's brawn or hillocks of junk-food fat he would have met underground and the Swann of but a few months before could have stopped to spend a lifetime with any of the gorgeous women he squeezed past.

Just beyond a hundred-foot bar, a second set of velvet ropes marked off an area that was apparently for an In-in crowd. Swann's hours of sitting before a television enabled him to recognize two stars who had become famous by playing cops. He also spotted a half-dozen other actors, a talk show host, and a number of people who were definitely famous for something. Several were gawking at Swann and Fredricks in a way they surely would not at celebrities.

"They act like they never saw a cop before," Swann said.

Swann heard a beat coming from a dark stairwell off to the right, and he had the eyes of the In-in crowd on him as he led Fredricks over to the steps. The two of them descended as if they were a couple of transit cops going down a subway entrance.

The beat grew stronger as Swann and Fredricks reached what was in fact just about subway depth. Swann saw a second, smaller bar to the left and a modest-sized dance floor up ahead. The music was blasting from speakers that were not quite as powerful as those at the transit party. The tune was a rap song he had heard in the last car some weeks before.

Most of the dancers were white, and the sight of police uniforms caused some of them to go off beat and stare. Several then looked at what they clearly assumed to be the reason for the arrival of the police.

The three young black men at the center of the floor were in street attire, and Swann guessed they were part of the quota he had discerned while standing outside the ropes with Danica. He now speculated that their function was to impart some vigor the In crowd apparently lacked, and they were indeed moving with an energy right out of the last car.

On seeing the uniforms, the young men exchanged quick glances, and even they seemed to view themselves as the most likely object of police attention. Swann did not have his yo-yo, so he tried to put them at ease by tipping his hat.

Swann heard a grunt and looked to see Fredricks staring at a tall and beautiful young woman who was coming off the dance floor with a man in a tuxedo. She was wearing a black minidress similar to the one Danica had bought.

Fredricks grunted again as he followed the woman with his eyes. Swann thought not of Danica, but of Coleman. He spoke loudly enough so the hidden microphone would pick him up through the music.

"Fredricks, I'm not sure an officer in uniform should be staring at a girl's *behind*," Swann said.

Fredricks straightened.

"What are you talking about?" Fredricks said.

Swann nodded to the beat as he gazed about the room. He was turning back to the dancers when he happened to see that the woman in the minidress and her tuxedoed date were now standing with a young Hispanic man.

The young man had long, shiny black hair and wore a black T-shirt no doubt intended to show off the sort of well-designed physique that comes not from work but from working out. He could not have helped but notice the presence of two uniformed officers, and yet there he was, handing a small packet to the woman and her date. He then compounded an already intolerable affront by passing a second packet to a middle-aged man in a double-breasted suit.

Swann tugged Fredricks's sleeve.

"What?" Fredricks asked.

Swann started over, and Fredricks grabbed his arm as he never had when they strayed from the subway.

"No!" Fredricks said.

"Fredricks, what would you do if you were in the hole and somebody did that in front of you?" Swann asked.

"I'd break . . ."

Fredricks then must have again remembered his tape recorder.

"How're you gonna explain a collar here?" Fredricks asked.

"*We* will say it was a drug sale," Swann said.

Fredricks said nothing, but what he was no doubt thinking was that IAD would hang him if he got involved in something like this. Swann again spoke so Lieutenant Gentile would later hear every word.

"Officer Fredricks, the Patrol Guide quite clearly requires an officer to take proper police action whether on or off duty," Swann said.

The patrons of Eleanor's were apparently not familiar with the sound of handcuffs. No heads turned at the double click as Swann joined the drug dealer and the man in the double-breasted suit.

"Watch the prisoners, Fredricks," Swann said.

Swann charged into the women's room, the mixing of the sexes in public toilets apparently being in fashion. He found the woman in the minidress and her date squeezed together into a toilet stall.

"What's going on?" the woman asked.

Swann grabbed a foil packet from the date.

"I think we're being arrested," the date said.

Swann escorted the two into the main room.

"Cuff them while I call for a car," Swann said.

Fredricks had never hesitated to beat some derelict bloody, but he seemed to need all his nerve to approach such a woman.

"Sorry," Fredricks said. "It's just procedure."

* * *

The news of any cave cop making a collar at a hip nightclub would have been enough to make the desk officer apoplectic. The same man who had let Swann and Coleman sit with the posse now said he would dispatch forthwith whatever vehicle he could muster.

"Aren't you in enough trouble?" the desk officer asked.

"No, the ones with the drugs are the ones in trouble," Swann said.

Swann returned to Fredricks and they led their prisoners up the dark stairwell. The woman in the minidress spoke in a voice going juvenile with disbelief.

"Why are you doing this? We didn't do anything they didn't do."

The woman was speaking of the In-in crowd, and Swann noted that a good number of them seemed unusually animated for people of their age at this hour. He saw several take on an edgy look that was not entirely different from what he had received from crackheads.

At the coat check, the cops uncuffed the prisoners long enough for them to put on their coats. The woman slipped into a mink and her date buttoned up a dark gray wool overcoat. Swann suggested that an arrest was no reason to forget the coat check girl.

"I promise to tell the DA you tipped well," Swann said.

The paparazzi outside Eleanor's went into a frenzy, and camera flashes were firing from every direction as Swann and Fredericks climbed with their prisoners into a transit police truck. The truck pulled around the limousines at the curb. A uniformed cop in the front got on the radio.

"One-Adam to Central K, I got four perps, one female, en route to District One. Mileage three two one four six."

Transit communications were broadcast over underground antennae and were even worse on the street. Swann still had no trouble recognizing the voice of the dispatcher who responded. He realized how this moment would have been precisely perfect if Coleman had been with him.

"[Unintelligible] ten eighty-five," Coleman said.

The uniformed cop repeated the message thrice more before its gist got through the static. The woman wearing the minidress must have heard herself referred to as a perp on each occasion, and she seemed in a trance until they reached Columbus Circle. She jerked back from the steps leading down into the subway.

"I thought we were going to a police station," the woman said.

"We are," Swann said. "District One of the transit police."

"You work in the subway? What were you doing at Eleanor's?"

"Not what you were doing."

The silence at District 1 equaled anything Swann had caused before. The loudest sound seemed to be the click of the woman's high heels as he took her over to the front desk. She had tousled blond hair and long, shapely legs.

The desk officer grew flushed as he struggled to keep his attention on the details of the arrest. He seemed no less amazed to have this woman before him than she was to be there.

"Who's taking this?" the desk officer asked.

"Fredricks," Swann said.

Fredricks sputtered, no doubt at the prospect of having to explain this to Lieutenant Gentile.

"Since when do you give up a trip to the bank?" Swann asked.

Fredricks did not answer. Swann addressed the desk officer.

"IAD's gonna love it if you give the collar to me," Swann said.

"Good point," the desk officer said.

Fredricks could hardly say that IAD would go more crazy if he took it. He could only go along.

Swann and Fredricks took the prisoners over to the processing area. Marie was there, and she bobbed up and down as she pointed at the woman.

"I seen you!" Marie said. "I seen you in your picture!"

Swann began the booking sheet for the woman and had the novel experience of entering something other than "none" in the box marked Occupation. He instead wrote *model.*

The woman's date turned out to be an investment banker, and the man in the double-breasted suit was a book editor. The drug dealer was apparently only that, though his trade was a little different at Eleanor's.

"How many times you been arrested?" Swann asked.

"None," the dealer said.

Swann took the dealer over for fingerprinting and saw that Fredricks had started with the model. She was receiving sympathetic looks of such number as to set a record for a transit police facility. The kind words that Swann overheard included those from the female crackhead beside whom she was seated once the model was printed.

"All you got to do is do what they tell you and then you're done," the crackhead said.

The investment banker and the book editor were lodged in the holding cell with three sleeping black men. One of the trio opened his eyes to see that he had come to share the space with two prosperous-looking whites. His expression began as startled and ended as terrifically pleased.

Word of the bust at Eleanor's must have spread, for camera crews as well as reporters were waiting outside the district when Swann walked the male prisoners up to a waiting paddy wagon. Fredricks came behind with a prisoner he would have in almost any other circumstances have given anything to escort.

"Hey, Fredricks, it's only fair," Swann said.

Fredricks looked over, squinting against the television lights, for once looking not at all pleased to be cashing in a collar for dollars.

"After all, I took the last one," Swann said.

Eighteen

THE SHOOTING of Daryl Coombs had been reported in a single paragraph buried back with reports on the national debt, but the bust at Eleanor's was on page one of the tabloids. Swann rode into Manhattan gazing at a big photo of Police Officers Swann and Fredricks escorting their prisoners from the club.

At District 1, nobody actually came right out and greeted Swann, but the desk officer did nod, and a good number of other cops neither ignored him nor gave him hard looks. He appeared to have reached deeper than collars for dollars and necessary force and the rest. He had done something right out of the fantasies of adventure and glory that they had all brought to this job.

"You know who she is, don't you?" the desk officer asked. "She's on the cover of *Vogue* this month."

"You read *Vogue?*" Swann asked.

A big hand landed on Swann's shoulder. Mannering the swordsman was embracing someone who had become an even more esteemed personage. Swann was a *legend,* one of the very few cave cops whose renown had reached beyond the top of the subway steps.

"Hey, hey, Jackie boy," Mannering said. "All I did last night was get laid."

A voice other than Coleman's crackled from the portable radio on Mannering's belt. Swann sat down at his desk figuring she would see the newspaper and telephone from wherever she went on her day off when she was not hunting a posse.

The only calls were from wives and gooms and his favorite eight- or ten-year-old.

"You had to arrest that lady?" Pharaoh asked. "She was *nice.*"
"I guess you saw the paper," Swann said.
"Is there some reason why I wouldn't?" Pharaoh asked.

"Dad?"

Swann went from the living room to the kitchen to the bathroom to the bedroom.

"Dad?"

Joseph had been asleep when Swann returned from the Big Bust the night before and had been still abed when the time came to head for District 1 that morning. The unshipshape bed was empty, and Swann tried to think of where Joseph might be. This was not group therapy day, and Swann became afraid that his father had signed himself back into the hospital. That became less likely when he spied the duffel bag lying on the floor.

Swann also noticed some tissue paper and several pins on the dresser. Wherever Joseph had wandered, he seemed to have wandered in the white shirt from Fifth Avenue.

On the kitchen table, Swann found a note that he at first assumed would say where his father had gone. The handwriting he had last seen on the back of the hospital postcard instead reported that *Seemoan called.* Swann went to the telephone and dialed the number.

"Speak."

The same male voice had answered.

"Officer Coleman, please."

Swann heard the male voice call *Sis* and then say, *There's a white man on the phone.*

"Yes?" Coleman asked.

"It's me," Swann said.

Coleman said she had called that morning as soon as she saw the newspaper, but Swann had already left. She had gotten too busy running errands to try him at work.

"Anyway, I can only think of one reason why Fredricks would be with you."

Swann was sure Coleman was going to warn him again about Lieutenant Gentile, but she had apparently decided it was of no use.

"You just can't leave bad enough alone," Coleman said.

Coleman then laughed.

"But I wouldn't have minded being there."

Swann said that Pharaoh had called. He told her he had been thinking he should take his little helper somewhere.

"Like?"

"Empire State Building, Statue of Liberty, whatever," Swann said.

Swann realized that he had a pretext to see her so good it did not seem like one.

"You want to go?" Swann asked.

"Sure," Coleman said. "The question is, do he?"

They had both spoken as casually as if they were questioning a Knowledge. He heard a radio playing rap music in the background. He recalled the tune from the basement at Eleanor's.

"I just wish you were there last night," Swann said. "That you would have loved."

Swann hung up and went into the living room to await Joseph's return. His eye chanced upon the cassette player and he flipped a switch from Tape to Radio. A spin of the dial took him past talk shows and easy listening and heavy metal to the last notes of the rap tune that had been playing in Coleman's apartment.

Swann sat on the sofa, patting the cushion to the beat as more tunes came on. He closed his eyes as he had in the last car and he was in that decoy dark when he heard somebody bounding up the stoop.

The sound was livelier than the clump, clump, clump that had always signaled Joseph's arrival, and yet Joseph was the very one who appeared. He looked even better in the white shirt then Swann had anticipated.

"What's that?" Joseph asked.

Joseph meant the music on the radio. Swann hit the power switch and the usual quiet returned.

"I saw the paper," Joseph said.

Joseph smiled, and Swann felt a little as if he were up on stage, peering through the eyeholes of a papier-mâché beast's head.

"Can you believe it?" Swann said.

Joseph eyed Swann.

"Yes," Joseph said.

Joseph settled into his armchair. He seemed both proud and pleased as Swann filled the usual silence with the tale of the Big Bust at Eleanor's.

"The guy in the suit must have died," Joseph said. "Though I do feel a little bad for the girl. What a doll."

"Yes, I suppose she was," Swann said.

Swann had no more story to tell, but a mystery remained.

"So, where'd you go?" Swann asked.

"The bank," Joseph said. "My first check came."

Joseph now seemed proud and pleased with himself, more so than Swann could remember.

"We should celebrate," Swann said.

"That's okay," Joseph said.

"You ought to do something special."

"I am. I'm not going back to the sorting room."

Swann was struck by the thought that the bank had been closed for hours. Joseph must have been somewhere else, perhaps celebrating in his own way, though Swann could not have guessed what exactly that might be.

"So, where else did you go?" Swann asked.

"To see your mother," Joseph said.

Swann had not known Joseph to have visited the cemetery since the burial.

"Oh yeah?" Swann said. "I was there the other day."

"You didn't tell me."

"It was just something I did."

Swann and Joseph looked at each other as if across Celeste's grave.

"I'll tell you, she would have been thrilled seeing the paper," Joseph said.

Joesph seemed about to settle back in silence when he spoke again.

"Did you get the message?" he asked.

Swann thought for a moment that Joseph meant some deeper meaning, either to the bust at Eleanor's or the visit to the cemetery.

"About the woman that called," Joseph said.

Swann now understood. He also realized that Joseph would be curious about as to who this *Seemoan* might be.

“That was my partner,” Swann said.

“Oh yeah?” Joseph said.

Swann took this to mean *Really? You didn’t tell me your partner was a woman.* Joseph also might have surmised from Coleman’s voice that she was black. Swann could almost hear Joseph saying to himself, *There’s a colored woman on the phone.*

“Yeah,” Swann said.

Joseph sat until his finger began tapping on the arm of his chair. He rose and went to put a combat tape in the cassette player. He hit the power switch, but the selector was still on Radio and the result was a not at all subliminal rap tune.

Joseph looked at Swann and they laughed out loud together.

At eleven o’clock, Swann turned on the television for the first time since New Year’s Eve. The invisible beams brought the image of Fredricks escorting the model out of the subway. The effect was somewhere between the Ron Parker show and CCTV.

“Where are you?” Joseph asked.

“I came out before with the males,” Swann said.

Joseph looked at Swann.

“I was hoping I’d see you,” Joseph said.

Swann lay in his bed, the Big Bust forgotten as he pictured Joseph standing before Celeste’s headstone in the white shirt. Swann’s thoughts shifted to Celeste herself, and those rare moments in his childhood when she had spoken of her work in the Navy Yard. He imagined her perched on the ribs of the unfinished battleship, her mask down, her welding rod sending cascades of sparks, the air around her resounding with the rattle of rivet guns and the clang of steel.

Now Swann knew the air had also contained asbestos that Celeste had carried away in her lungs. The microscopic fibers had still been there thirty years later on the day Swann had found her standing in the kitchen, holding herself up with a mop handle, saying that she needed just a minute to rest before she finished the floor.

Celeste’s hair falling out, limbs going wooden, mouth filling with sores, ears going deaf. That recollection brought a rush of memories from the chemotherapy: The doctor saying, *None of that is unusual.*

The images stopped with the day Celeste returned from buying a wig. She had reached into the box with hands gone black and blue from needle punctures, and she had taken out a wig like her own brown hair. She had then grinned, her teeth tinted purple by some antifungal compound whose name he did not remember. What did come back to him were her words, *It was either this or become a redhead.*

Coleman was waiting outside the Department of Probation building in downtown Brooklyn. She had on the black car coat that Swann recognized as the one she had been wearing the day he chose her as a partner over Fredricks. He had at least made one wise decision in recent months.

"Didn't I see your picture in the newspaper?" Coleman asked. "Or was it in *Vogue?*"

Coleman made a show of appraising Swann's civil service attire.

"No, it wasn't *Vogue,*" Coleman said.

Swann held the door and Coleman seemed to like the small attention.

"He know we're coming?" Coleman asked.

"I thought we'd surprise him," Swann said.

"I would have thought he got all the surprises he needed the first time."

Swann and Coleman were in the waiting room when a crowd of youngsters emerged from a door at the back. They were accompanied by a tall black man who wore the kind of polyester suit typically seen on detectives and a foulard tie of the sort favored by businessmen. His face had a burdened look more profound than is often seen among either group. He clapped his hands in an attempt to summon some enthusiasm, and he seemed for all the world like a coach trying to rouse a team that was hopelessly behind at the half.

"That went very well today, guys," the probation officer said. "We all have some real things to think about between now and next week."

The youngsters continued silently toward the metal detector, their expressions blank as those of passengers escaping the underground. The sole exception was Pharaoh, who appeared smiling and sparkly-eyed from behind one of the biggest teenagers Swann had ever seen.

"Yo! Yo!" Pharaoh said.

The delight in the greeting was lost on the big teenager, who glared on making Swann and Coleman as Five-O.

"What he do?" the big teenager asked.

"You wouldn't believe what he did," Swann said.

The big teenager continued with the rest of the probationers through the metal detector and on to the elevator.

"That my AEG," Pharaoh said. "Adolescent Empowerment Group. It supposed to tell us how we think we got no power in our life."

Pharaoh lowered his voice.

"What's up with our case?"

Swann said that Danica's attackers would most likely plead guilty.

"That what I did," Pharaoh said. "You think they get probation?"

"I don't know," Swann said. "Maybe."

"What if they in my AEG?" Pharaoh asked.

Pharaoh seemed more amused than worried. He asked if Swann and Coleman were here with another case for him to work. Swann said they had come to take him on a day trip.

"The Empire State Building, maybe the Statue of Liberty," Swann said.

Pharaoh did not look wowed by either possibility.

"Or any place else you want to go," Swann said.

"I got to do my Easter shopping," Pharaoh said.

Swann had not anticipated that the youngster might have other plans. Pharaoh apparently sensed his disappointment.

"You know, if you wanted, you could come," Pharaoh said.

Swann showed his shield to the token clerk and held open the gate for Pharaoh.

"You're with us," Swann said.

They boarded the last car like a posse of three. Swann took out his yo-yo and executed a near perfect Around the World. He asked Pharaoh if he wanted to try.

"That for kids," Pharaoh said.

Swann was still tossing as they came out of the subway and rounded a corner to Orchard Street. He saw a narrow block of aged tenements and run-down little clothing shops. Coats and jackets hung on display from the awnings and fire escapes, and Swann had the sense of walking into one of those street scenes in movies about old New York. The big difference was that the shoppers who swarmed about him were not European immigrants, but black teenagers.

"It's not usually this crowded," Coleman said.

"You shop here, too?" Swann asked.

"Everybody do," Pharaoh said.

All around Swann swirled groups of young people from the city's toughest neighborhoods. Some of these kids no doubt got money from parents who rode the early morning trains to work. Others surely worked themselves. Others likely stole, risked jail, and maybe hurt somebody.

Yet Swann experienced none of the quickening that usually came when he saw a posse. He instead felt a vicarious jauntiness that reminded him of when he first had his hand on the lever. These kids on Orchard Street likely had with them every penny to their name and they had the air of being ready to spend it all. He was looking at a whole street full of people with that Money Store spring to their step.

"Got to get fresh for Easter," Pharaoh said.

Pharaoh turned with Swann and Coleman into a storefront. The tinkle of a bell over the door signaled entry into a long, dimly lit room. The walls were packed floor to ceiling with get-fresh clothes, and groups of young black people were trying on garments and calling out questions in sharp street voices. An elderly shopkeeper wearing a yarmulke and a frayed shirt answered in a thick Yiddish accent.

Pharaoh seemed guided by a particular taste as he quickly flipped through a rack of jackets. Swann saw two garments similar to those Coleman had worn at roll call, such items apparently as common in here as pinstripe suits at Brooks Brothers.

Pharaoh paused to examine a purple leather car coat, then continued until he came to a black leather jacket that had a pair of white dice on the front like a crest. He slipped it on and stepped before a mirror whose cracks had been patched with duct tape. He turned one way and the other and nodded to his dim image.

"Sweet," Pharaoh said.

The proprietor did not seem impressed by Pharaoh's bankroll, which was not quite in the league of the Money Store, but was definitely bigger than any civil servant's check, pay or disability.

* * *

Pharaoh still needed the rest of his outfit, and he led Swann and Coleman from one shop to another. He found a gray shirt he liked, but it did not have a polo player logo on the breast and he kept on until he found one that did. He then wavered on a pair of orange denims, finally deciding they were not quite right. He went on to another half-dozen places until he found a slightly brighter shade.

Swann had by then noted that the other youngsters also seemed to shop with a concentration unequaled by even such a champion redeemer as Ellen. Not that price appeared to be a consideration. The value they sought seemed to have little to do with cost.

In the next store, Swann watched Pharaoh try on several pairs of black sneakers. The youngster walked up and down, deeming one pair too tight, another too loose. He finally declared one to be just right.

"That'll save on socks," Swann said.

Pharaoh gave Swann a hooded look that made clear he saw no humor in that night at Spofford. They both turned when Coleman called out.

"Here you go," Coleman said.

She was holding up a two-tone wing tip, white and navy blue.

"That for church," Pharaoh said.

"Where *do* you go on Easter?" Swann asked.

Pharaoh responded as if not just Swann but the entire world should know the answer.

"Coney Island," Pharaoh said.

Swann posed what seemed an obvious question.

"Why?"

Pharaoh made a face as if Swann had asked why cops march up Fifth Avenue on Saint Patrick's Day.

"Come Easter, everybody go to Coney Island," Pharaoh said.

"It's what you might call a tradition," Coleman said.

Coleman held up the shoe that had begun the discussion.

"And anyway, I wasn't thinking about him so much as you."

You being Swann, who was still on a budget of $3.58 a day, and who probably would not have had the nerve to wear such a shoe to church or anywhere else.

"I'm a little short," Swann said.

Pharaoh pulled out his bankroll.

"I got you covered," Pharaoh said.

"No, it's on me," Coleman said.

"I can't do that," Swann said.

"Of course you can," Coleman said.

After Coleman bought herself a po-lice blue jumpsuit, the three of them returned to the subway all the more their own little posse. They then came to where the routes to Brooklyn and Queens diverge.

"You get another case, you can beep me," Pharaoh said.

Swann raised the shopping bag in his hand and thanked Coleman again for the shoes.

"You know you like them," Coleman said.

Coleman went down the steps and Pharaoh followed with his packages.

"Yo! Yo!" Swann said.

"Five . . ." Coleman said.

". . . O!" Pharaoh said.

In the morning, Swann went into the kitchen to see Joseph sitting with the newspaper spread before him.

"Whatever happens, deny everything," Joseph said.

Joseph pushed the paper across the table, and Swann saw a headline that hit him as none other had.

"*Eleanor's Cop Under Investigation.*"

The newspaper had run again the picture that had been taken of Swann and Fredricks coming out of the nightclub with their prisoners. The story reported that Transit Police Officer John Swann was suspected of skimming drug money.

"*A source close to the investigation says Swann went on a wild spree, spending thousands at swank Fifth Avenue shops, a luxury hotel, a trendy restaurant, and the very nightspot where he staged a drug bust.*"

Swann had no doubt as to the source's identity.

"Dad, I didn't do anything wrong," Swann said.

"Then you really better deny it," Joseph said.

Swann checked the byline on the story and pondered whether he should call the reporter. The problem was that everything in the story was technically true. He was under investigation. He had gone on a spree.

Swann could produce documents proving that he had borrowed the money. The "source" would then whisper to the reporter about money laundering, which would strike any reasonable person as unlikely. The problem here was that the truth was no less so.

Swann jumped when the phone rang.

"It's me."

The radio was playing in the background as before, only this time on an all-news station.

"You heard," Swann said.

"And read," Coleman said.

Coleman sounded as if she was still stunned. She might have warned Swann about IAD, but neither she nor he had imagined Lieutenant Gentile would seek revenge by calling reporters and becoming a "source."

"It's not like you really did anything," Coleman said.

Swann could hear his name being read over her radio.

"But it's close," Swann said.

"No, it's not," Coleman said.

Swann got off deciding that Coleman was right. He knew he was not a thief. She knew he was not a thief. Joseph at least seemed to know he was not a thief.

Jenny.

Swann reached for the phone and dialed. Ellen answered, her voice as clear and as neutral as that of a supermarket cashier, or maybe of a cop addressing a crook who was getting precisely what he deserved.

"I'm not going to say anything to Jenny unless she hears something," Ellen said.

"If she does?" Swann asked.

"I don't know. I guess that some people think her daddy stole some money."

"And?"

"And a person is innocent until he's proven guilty."

"Great."

"What do you want, Jack? 'No, honey, your daddy is father of the year'?"

"Maybe I should see her."

"She's still your daughter. You can see her Easter. If you're free."

Swann was getting dressed when he remembered the shoes that Coleman had bought him. He decided that this was one day he did not need to draw any extra attention to himself and he left them in the box. He rode into the city grateful that nobody seemed to notice him, much less recognize him as the cop whose picture was again in the paper.

When Swann arrived at District 1, Marie said nothing, and a fair number of his fellow officers suddenly became engrossed in filling out reports or making phone calls or adjusting their gunbelts. He had received acclaim from the world beyond the top of the steps, but with that had now come trouble of equal magnitude, more heat than had been generated by the combined misadventures of everyone who had ever served with the transit police.

The one cop in District 1 who seemed the least afraid approached on his way to patrol. Mannering appeared to welcome the prospect of more turmoil and therefore more excitement.

"That's the way, Jackie boy," Mannering said. "If you can't be good, be noticed."

Swann once more protested his innocence. Mannering gave him an appraising look.

"I'd work on the eye contact," Mannering said.

"It's the truth," Swann said.

"Jackie boy, all that matters is it looks like you're telling the truth," Mannering said.

Mannering laid a hand on Swann's shoulder and advised him that a little rehearsal in front of the mirror was always a good idea.

"Practice makes perfect," Mannering said.

Swann went into his office and did his paperwork and through the static on the portable radio came the voice of the woman who knew he was not a thief. He sat back with his coffee and absently scored his Styrofoam cup with his thumbnail. His next thought was of Pharaoh.

Swann dialed the beeper number once and again but got no reply. He decided that Pharaoh probably recognized the number and had no desire to talk to a cop who turned out not to be one of the good guys, after all.

* * *

Swann was going by the Plaza when he chanced to see a familiar limo driver standing at the curb. The driver saw Swann and turned away.

Swann took in a breath to say something but caught himself. He continued home thinking of the hotel men's room attendant, who had not been impressed by Swann in uniform even before the new stories of skimmed drug money.

The uniform Swann had worn that day had been blessed by the cardinal as the uniform of heroes who risked their lives and somctimes died fighting evil. The attendant had seemed to see only the uniform of those who dragged people into the Room and lied about it afterward.

Swann now turned angry, telling himself that he had done nothing wrong, that if anyone deserved to be branded bad, it was Fredricks and his kind. He passed into Holy Week feeling at one moment armored by his innocence, at the next forever branded guilty. He reassured himself that IAD would never be able to charge him. He resisted the thought that if he were never charged he could never be acquitted.

Swann's one cause for cheer was that Joseph had given up the combat tape for the radio. Joseph, like Ellen, favored music of his youth, and the subliminal sounds were replaced by gladsome tunes from the world before Swann.

On Easter morning, Swann rose early so he could see Jenny before work. He was dressing when his gaze fell upon the shopping bag from Orchard Street.

Swann opened the box and he was not entirely convinced that Coleman was right about his liking the shoes. He did decide that she would be pleased if he wore them on Easter. He also suspected that they might appeal to Jenny.

With every step to his former home, Swann's eye caught a blue-and-white wing tip advancing before his still slimmed middle. Ellen noticed the shoes as soon as she opened the door. Her expression suggested that she viewed them as footwear's equivalent to scattering birthday balloons around the living room.

"Jenny, it's your father," Ellen said.

Jenny had on her new hat, the brim pulled low, and Swann could not see her face until after she had noticed his shoes. She looked up at him, and he knew she did indeed like them.

"Cool, Daddy," she said.

Swann also deduced that Jenny had yet to hear of his latest troubles. She seemed if anything in slightly better spirits than at the last visit, and he might have let her stay that way had he not learned from Ellen and Danica to take greater care about what he refrained from telling. He did not want Jenny to be blindsided again, to feel that a sense of well-being was a form of ignorance.

"Jenny, I want you to know that some people think I took some money," Swann said.

Jenny again looked up, this time startled.

"I also want you to know that I didn't do it," Swann said.

Her expression changed to one Swann could not read.

"Do you have any questions?" Swann asked.

Jenny dropped her head. She was silent.

"Well, I have a question, and I want you to tell me the absolute truth," Swann said.

Swann stopped and tugged up his pant legs.

"What do you really think of my shoes?"

Jenny's voice was flat even when it came to two-tone wing tips.

"They're all right."

She tugged her cap brim lower. Swann noticed that her fingertips were stained several hues.

"One more question," Swann said. "What happened to your fingers?"

"Easter eggs," Jenny said.

"How'd they turn out?"

"All right."

Jenny seemed likely to mumble those same two words no matter what Swann inquired. He decided that she had not asked him any questions because she did not trust whatever he might say. He was reminded that being wrongly accused by IAD did not make him innocent.

At the playground, Jenny climbed onto a swing. Swann pulled her as far back as he could, raising her over his head.

"Bye-bye," Swann said.

Swann pushed and Jenny sailed away only to come swinging back.

"What!" Swann said. "I thought you were going away."

He gave her another push.

"Now, I don't want to see you hanging around," he said. "Get out of here!"

She again swung away and back.

"Hey!" he said. "What're you doing? I thought I told you to get out of here."

She was laughing now.

"Do that again," she said.

Jenny demanded that Swann keep up the game long after he would have expected her to tire of it. He finally stopped only because the time had come to take her home. The way back took them past several families that were most likely headed for mass.

"Daddy?"

"Yes, Jenny."

Swann prepared to answer fully whatever question she had about the money.

"Do you want to see the Easter eggs I made?"

Swann knew that Ellen would be angry, but he could give only one answer.

Jenny opened the door with the key that was now hers.

"Mommy, can Daddy come in and see the Easter eggs?"

Ellen stepped into the hall and glared at Swann, no doubt suspecting this was some scheme of his devising.

"It'll just take a minute," Jenny said.

Ellen was now the one who could only say yes.

"You can go get them and show them to him here," Ellen said.

Jenny dashed off and was back before Swann and Ellen were compelled to say anything to each other.

"Look!"

Jenny held up a basket of multicolored eggs sprinkled with glitter and festooned with feathers. Swann paid her each of the many compliments that came to him. He looked over to Ellen with the same smile he would have had if they had still been together.

"They really are great," Swann said.

Ellen did not return the smile, but her voice softened.
"They are," Ellen said.

District 1 was holiday quiet and became more so as one officer after another noticed Swann's two-tones. He sat at his desk with the portable radio and heard through the static that Coleman was also working.

Swann looked down at his shoes and decided he did in fact like them, that they were all right, as all right as Easter eggs. He felt as if he needed no excuse to reach for the radio and hit the transmit bar.

"So?"

Swann got the phone on the first ring. Coleman agreed to meet him for meal, and she arrived at the soda fountain in the new jumpsuit. Her shoes were of the police variety, whose color matched her tail, but she had replaced the laces with satin ribbons.

Coleman had the usual, as did Swann. He was not long in noticing something not at all usual about the citizens arriving in Times Square.

"No posses," Swann said.

"Easter," Coleman said.

Swann imagined all the posses seaside at Coney Island, parading in their Orchard Street clothes where his mother and father had met. He pictured Pharaoh among them in his black leather jacket with the white dice, gray shirt with the little polo player, denims of the slightly brighter shade of orange, and black sneakers that fit just right.

"It must be some sight," Swann said.

"That it is," Coleman said.

"You go?"

"Not in a couple years."

Swann sipped his coffee and imagined a younger Coleman at the Easter gathering. He then again pictured Pharaoh.

"I wouldn't mind seeing it sometime," Swann said.

"There's a train there every few minutes," Coleman said.

Swann was almost ready to hop the next train. He could find Pharaoh and explain that he really was one of the good guys.

"I'm due back," Swann said.

"The trains run after work, too," Coleman said.

The two-tone shoes and the yo-yo seemed to dispel any suspicion that Swann might be Five-O, and the last car was rollicking as the train crossed the Manhattan Bridge. He gazed out at the Brooklyn Bridge, which he had crossed on his solitary trek. He could see beyond to the Statue of Liberty and her *goal* torch.

The yo-yo thwapped into Swann's palm, and he looked at Coleman, who was popping her lips to the beat as the car returned to the tunnel. Each stop into Brooklyn brought at least one more posse in fresher-than-fresh gear, the youngsters on this night having less the air of criminals than of kids on their way to the prom. Or so Swann imagined, never having been to one.

A teenager boarded with a suitcase-sized boom box, and a girl to Swann's left began stamping and clapping her hands, not so much keeping the beat as summoning it. Her head started rotating one way while her hips ground the other and her bright green sneakers worked out intricate steps that would have been just so much scuffling had Swann been closed-eyed.

Other youngsters started dancing, and Coleman herself began to move. Swann watched her catch the beat with her feet and send it rippling up the entire lean length of her, bursting from her mouth as a shout.

Coleman's feet flashed one before the other and she seemed to pass into abandon only to give him a wink precisely on beat. The next beat had Coleman wiggling an index finger, and he understood she was summoning him to join in. A fear as elemental as that of heights kept his two-tones planted on the linoleum.

Coleman and the youngsters danced on until the train reached the next stop. The merriment ceased as always and Swann stared out at the platform, the windowpane dirt-streaked in the light of the station.

As the car rolled back into the tunnel, and the glass became aglimmer, Swann on this night saw his reflection standing motionless among those of Coleman and the other dancers. He watched their images flicker against the whooshing dark.

Coleman's face was shiny with sweat when she again summoned Swann to join in. He again declined. He would be revealing an aspect of himself that remained constant no matter what his waist size or his attire or his pocket print, whether he lived small, medium, or large.

The car rose onto elevated tracks and the steel wheels screeched as the train came to a long curve. Night had fallen and the pa-a-a-rty stopped as everybody gazed out the seaward windows at the lights of Coney Island. The Ferris wheel was a slowly turning blaze of red and orange and green.

The train braked for the last stop on the line, and everyone in the car crowded in silent wait at the doors. They poured onto the elevated platform, laughing and shouting, welcomed by a cool landward breeze that carried the smell of the sea.

Swann and Coleman and the various posses of the last car reached the street as a single happy bunch. Swann heard the *clank, clank, clank* of the roller coaster going up the big hill. Then came the delighted screams of people being scared but not too scared.

Swann started with Coleman along the arcades, thinking of Joseph and Celeste arriving here separately, not yet knowing of the other's existence, trooping with the crowds past the games of chance.

"Seven! Seven!"

Swann looked over to see a young woman standing before a wheel of fortune. The clacker went past the seven and on by the eight before stopping at the nine.

"No!" the young woman said.

Swann strolled on, absently noting several youngsters he had arrested in the past, keeping an eye out for one in particular.

"There's your man," Coleman said.

Pharaoh was standing at one of the games in the same Orchard Street jacket, pants, and shirt in which Swann had pictured him. He was up on the toes of his black sneakers as he prepared to toss a Ping-Pong ball at an array of goldfish bowls. He shifted his hand back and forth, waiting for instinct to direct his aim.

Pharaoh finally tossed the ball and it bounced off the rim of the chosen bowl only to plop into another. He cheered and stepped away from the counter holding a goldfish in a plastic bag of water. The sight of Swann and Coleman brought no smile.

"What, not even one 'yo'?" Swann asked.

Pharaoh stood mute, holding his fish to match his gold rings and chains and teeth.

"Pharaoh, did you ever get accused of doing something you didn't do?" Swann asked.

Pharaoh answered evenly.

"No, I always do everything they say I do," Pharaoh said.

Pharaoh's tone sharpened.

"You saying it's not true?" Pharaoh asked.

"I am under investigation, but I didn't do anything wrong," Swann said.

"Then why they investigating you?"

"Because they think I did."

"Why?"

"I had more money than they thought I should have, and I wouldn't tell them where I got it because it was none of their business," Swann said.

Pharaoh did not respond.

"I borrowed it," Swann said.

Pharaoh said nothing.

"Really," Swann said.

Pharaoh turned and strode off as tough as is possible for an eight- or ten-year-old who is carrying a goldfish.

A group of maybe twenty uniformed city cops stood by the end of the arcade, some of the younger ones bouncing on the balls of their feet as if they were out with a posse. The rest stood slack-faced and dull-eyed, not seeming even to hear the rap music that blasted from beyond where they slouched.

Swann and Coleman skirted past the cops and saw that the beat was coming from the Polar Express. This ride had cars similar to those on a roller coaster, only they did little more than go round and round. The effect appeared to be about as thrilling as riding a middle car on a Queens-bound local at moderate speed, and yet several hundred teenagers were waiting in line. Another thousand or so people were packed in the open area by the speakers bopping to the booming music that made this thrill-free ride the focus of the annual Easter gathering. The scene had the feel of some sort of pilgrimage, as if this were a kind of hip-hop Mecca, the source of the beat.

Over the music came the shout that people in a crowd make when they see an argument lead to somebody pulling a pistol. A gunshot followed, and the resulting stampede threatened to sweep Swann and Coleman with it.

The music went off and excited shouts filled the air as Swann and Coleman struggled in the direction of the shot. The uniformed cops were right behind them, and they all ended up standing with bruised limbs and heaving chests on a patch of deserted asphalt.

Nobody had been hit, and Swann saw that Coleman was as relieved as he was not to see another teenager lying shot. He joined her in surveying the crowd that had swallowed whoever had the gun. The young people now stood in a large ring, and they began to laugh and call to each other, as they might if they were coming off the most exhilarating roller coaster in the world.

The operator of the Polar Express rose from behind a wood partition as casually as if this were indeed all part of the ride. He switched the music to a slow, calming beat and the uniformed cops returned to where they had stood. The young people began to reassemble.

As the crowd closed in around Swann and Coleman, the operator switched back to a faster, harder beat. The two began working their way through the press of bodies, never able to see more than a couple of bopping teenagers ahead, getting no warning at all as they suddenly came face to face with Alvin from the space case.

Alvin had a cloud of cotton candy on a paper cone, and he tore off a clump with his teeth as he looked from Swann to Coleman. He drew the pink spun sugar into his mouth too calmly for an escapee, and he could not have made bail on a homicide charge. He seemed only happy to see them again.

"Hi," Alvin said.

"Aren't you supposed to be someplace else?" Swann asked.

"They let me out," Alvin said. "My lawyer say they got no case. He say all they got is you."

Swann realized what must have happened: the detectives had failed to secure any statements; the only identifying witness had been the victim herself and she had only been able to communicate by squeezing Swann's hand; the prosecutor did not like the idea of going to trial with nothing more than the testimony of a cop known to the whole city to be under investigation for corruption; thus, here was Alvin, nodding to the beat and taking another big bite of cotton candy.

"I see you on my TV," Alvin said. "They gonna put *you* in jail?"

A swell in the crowd brought Swann flush against Alvin.

"Where's the other guy?" Swann asked.

"He was out, too, but he got hisself in trouble."

"Where's the rest of the posse?"

"You standing right with them."

Swann looked at these young faces that nodded to the music. He tried to match them with those he had seen rushing from the scene of the space case. He knew he could do exactly nothing.

"I don't know about you, but I can think of company I'd rather keep," Coleman said.

The beat faded and the sea scent grew stronger as Swann went with Coleman up to the boardwalk. He stood beside her at the seaward edge, his hands on the steel railing. Lights shone faint and distant from the Rockaway Peninsula on the left and New Jersey on the right.

The Atlantic Ocean lay straight ahead, looking colder than the chilled steel under his palms, darker than the night, older than even the beat.

"She'll be asleep now," Coleman said. "We'll go tell her tomorrow."

Coleman was speaking of Estrella, the sister of the space case woman. He nodded and gazed out at what was always there, no matter what came to be.

"Let's walk," Coleman said.

Coleman moved more slowly along the boardwalk than she did underground, but Swann still had to walk a little faster than he would have alone. His eye then fell upon an electric sign whose working bulbs spelled *A la t s*.

Swann had pictured the Atlantis Bar as a dark little gin mill snug by a roller coaster. He now saw that it stood right on the boardwalk, the whole front open like a garage with the door raised.

"You mind stopping in?" Swann asked.

The landward breeze stayed at their backs as they entered. Swann stepped up to the long, deserted bar, surely the very one where Celeste had been able to stand with no objection. The bartender was too young to have been working back then, but old enough not to look out of place in this run-down saloon at Brooklyn's shore.

Swann had no idea what Coleman might order, though he was not surprised when she said she wanted a Drambuie. She was one cave cop who did not give him a look when he ordered club soda.

Coleman then crouched and took her money from her sock. She tossed a $10 bill onto the dark, scarred wood where Swann's mother had laid her last working wage.

Swann had just been standing there as if he were in a place that rang up a check. He quickly pulled out a bill of his own and slid it forward as the bartender came back.

"Out of here," Swann said.

Coleman pushed her bill forward.

"No, here," Coleman said.

The bartender shrugged and took Swann's bill, placing the change in front of him. Coleman's bill remained before her as they drank.

"This is where my mother and father met," Swann said.

"Yeah?" Coleman said.

Coleman looked around to give the place due appreciation. She started rummaging her pockets.

"I think you owe me a quarter," Coleman said.

Coleman took a quarter from Swann's change, and he watched her go over to a jukebox she had spied in the far corner. He wondered how her parents had met and what her early life had been like.

Music crackled through the jukebox only a little clearer than if it were being transmitted over the transit radio. Swann still recognized it as a tune right out of the last car and he watched Coleman begin to dance.

Once more, she summoned him with her index finger. His dread was just as strong, but he now turned reckless in this bar where his mother and father had chanced to come.

Celeste had been looking for nothing more than to be out, but her lipstick had drawn Joseph over and the moment had arrived when he told himself, *I'm in.* The eventual result was the Swann who four decades later walked over to the jukebox.

"So?" Coleman asked.

"So, yo!" Swann said.

Swann hunched over and threw up one hand and then the other as he began dancing the sole step he had learned in his teenage years, the Mashed Potato.

* * *

Swann left the Atlantis with Coleman, and each step was one step back to Alvin and Lieutenant Gentile and the rest. His eyes went to the darkened beach and the darker sea.

"Feel like a stroll?" Swann asked.

Swann went down the wooden steps with Coleman as they would into the underground. The lights of the boardwalk cast their shadows as big as Coleman sometimes seemed to consider herself, but the loose sand took the grown-up sureness from even a stride such as hers.

Swann scuffled along beside her and their twin shadows dissolved into the darkness at the water's edge. The sounds of Coney Island grew so faint as to be lost in the lapping of the waves.

The two walked along the hard sand just above the tide line, and they entered a dark, deserted zone where no regular citizen would venture for fear of being robbed and no robber would go for lack of anyone to rob. He stopped and they stood with the breeze coming off the cold, colossal sea. He looked at her to see that she was looking at him, and he was but a beat from leaning toward her.

Coleman dropped her eyes and yelped. She jumped back just in time, but Swann was too late. He stood at Brooklyn's shore with icy seawater seeping into his two-tones.

"Almost," Coleman said.

Nineteen

IN THE MORNING, Swann stepped into the kitchen to tell Joseph he was going out.

"What was that noise?" Joseph asked.

Swann realized that Joseph must have heard him banging his still-damp two-tones over the wastebasket.

"I had sand in my shoes," Swann said.

Joseph waited for Swann to explain.

"I was down at Coney Island with my partner," Swann said.

"Oh, yeah?" Joseph said.

Swann could hear Joseph thinking, *With the colored woman.*

"I found that bar, the one where you met Ma," Swann said.

"No kidding," Joseph said. "It's still there?"

"It's still there," Swann said.

The lookout at the corner of Estrella's block tossed an empty bottle high into the morning air. The sound of breaking glass sent the crackheads scattering from the nearby stoop, but the manager remained at his post above the chink between the third and fourth steps.

"Didn't you forget something?" Swann asked. "You know, like we're the police and you run away."

The manager stayed put, arms crossed.

"Let me rephrase that," Swann said. "Get the fuck out of here."

The manager's expression became smug.

"I'm supposed to call this number if I decide to tell the *truth* about you taking money from me," the manager said. "Even the TV say you took ten thousand."

The manager smiled.

"Who the one got trouble with the law?"

Swann and the manager both looked at Coleman when she laughed.

"You got to admit, it's a funny situation," Coleman said. "But I think we have more important business."

Swann and Coleman continued down the block to tell a woman her sister's killers had been freed.

Estrella's daughter was at her side, holding the Cabbage Patch doll.

"They just let them go?" Estrella asked.

"I'm the only witness to the identification and there have been some allegations regarding me," Swann said.

Her son toddled up to her other side.

"He's walking now," Coleman said.

"About two weeks," Estrella said.

The boy cried out and Estrella scooped him up.

"A couple days after you was here, some other po-lice came," Estrella said. "They don't say anything about my sister. They just ask do I know anything about some officer taking money. One of them give me this little white card, so I can call him if I hear anything. He says, 'This is a serious matter.'"

"For what it's worth, I didn't take any money," Swann said.

"I'm not saying you did," Estrella said.

The sound of footsteps passed down the hallway outside. The daughter sidled closer to her mother.

"And the whole time they're asking me questions, dope fiends are going by just like that, like it's Grand Central Crack House," Estrella said.

The boy on her hip began to fuss.

"Now, my boy's hungry," Estrella said.

"We're just leaving," Swann said.

The second raid on the crack house went much as the first, only Swann and Coleman required the addicts to lug down the mattresses and box springs from which they had been beaming up. These were stacked outside the building when Swann and Coleman started back up the block.

A crowd of crackheads had reassembled around the stoop near the corner, and Swann understood that the manager must have told them not to worry about these particular cops. One crackhead and then another bowed before the chink in the steps, buying drugs as openly as the In crowd at Eleanor's.

"What you want to bet Gentile gave him one of those little white cards, too," Swann said.

"It's definitely not as funny as it was," Coleman said.

The spot lay on the way to the subway, and neither Swann nor Coleman was about to go out of the way to avoid it. He watched the crackheads grow edgy as the two of them drew nearer.

"He can tell IAD whatever he wants, it would still be the kid's word against yours," Coleman said. "You're still a cop and he's still a drug dealer."

Coleman was speaking of the manager, who was now gesturing for the crackheads to relax. Five-O was still Five-O, and they began to scatter.

"Which means they probably wouldn't be able to lock you up," Coleman said.

Swann saw a girl of maybe thirteen remain by the stoop. She eyed the approaching pair of cops and turned back to the manager, holding up a stainless steel bread box.

"What they would do is try to take your job," Coleman said.

Swann knew that Coleman was right. He would almost have welcomed a chance to go to court and prove himself unjustly accused, but he was more likely to face nothing more stirring than a routine departmental proceeding. He would end up in some anonymous hearing room to have his fate decided by a referee hired by the very people who were prosecuting him. The question would not be anything so grand as whether he was guilty; only whether he would no longer be even a civil servant.

Swann felt a first real stab of fear just as he and Coleman came near enough to hear the girl trying to get a better price for the bread box.

"I can't do nothing with two dollars. You know I need three."

"What will you do for one more?" the manager asked.

"Not that," the girl said.

The manager's laugh was cut short when Swann arrived at the base of the stoop.

"Still here?" Swann asked.

"You got no cause to mess with me," the manager said. "You ain't even a real cop. You transit."

The manager took the bread box and made a show of admiring himself in the polished side before tossing it away. He pulled out a bankroll that was bigger than anything Pharaoh or, for that matter, Swann, had carried. He handed the girl a $20 bill.

"I don't have no singles," the manager said.

The girl glanced at Swann and Coleman and then took the bill.

"Don't worry about these cops," the manager said. "They won't do anything."

The girl hesitated, but hunger overcame caution and she slid the $20 into the slot. The manager called to whoever was under the stoop.

"You got the money. Go ahead. They do anything, I'm just gonna have to tell the truth."

The girl's hand came away with a half-dozen vials, and Swann faced a choice in which chance played no part. He understood that Coleman was going to let him alone decide.

The vials in his pocket as evidence, the manager and the girl in handcuffs, Swann waited while Coleman went to call for transportation.

"So, what's it to you? Niggers can't have money?" the manager asked.

Swann perceived that the manager was speaking to him the way he himself would address an ADA who wanted to know how a slob transit cop had come by so much cash.

"I don't know how to tell you this, but selling drugs is illegal," Swann said.

Swann heard shouts come from the vacant lot, and he saw that some youngsters had piled several of the mattresses and box springs beside a wrecked car. One of them leaped off the roof, hit the pile of bedding, and sailed upward, his arms straight out, his face tilted to the sun. He laughed when his sneakers hit the ground, and he scrambled to get another turn.

The youngsters were trying aerial somersaults by the time a transit radio car arrived to take the prisoners to a district in Brooklyn. The rest of the bust went essentially the same as the one at Eleanor's, until Swann emptied the manager's pockets at the front desk. Nestled in the bankroll was a white business card bearing the name and phone number of Lieutenant Gentile, IAD.

"I want you to call that number for me," the manager said. "I want to report a crime."

The desk officer did not want to be caught anywhere near the middle of this one.

"Why don't we take care of your crime first," the desk officer said.

The girl was released to her family, but the manager had just turned sixteen and that made him legally an adult. Coleman asked Swann if he wanted the collar.

"Or you can take the next one," Coleman said.

Coleman knew as well as Swann that he might not be making any more arrests.

"I might as well take it," Swann said. "I've gone this far."

"You most definitely have," Coleman said.

Coleman winked and left, needing to say no more. Swann proceeded to Brooklyn Central Booking and noted that his prisoner became markedly less smug in a holding pen of truly scary adult crooks. Swann had no doubt that the manager would be more than willing to tell any truth that IAD wanted if it would free him.

In the Brooklyn equivalent of ECAB, Swann had difficulty keeping his mind on the newspaper. He looked around the smoke-choked room, amazed that he could regret that this was possibly his last trip through what everybody called *the system*.

Several cops apparently recognized Swann from the papers and shot him glances as they whispered to each other. Their eyes lingered on his feet and he was reminded that he was wearing his two-tones. He decided that he liked them all the more.

Swann got home past midnight, and he awoke after Joseph had left for group therapy. He took his morning coffee into the living room and turned on the cassette player. The switch was still on Radio, and he worked the dial from the music of Joseph's youth to that of the last car.

Swann was tapping a two-tone and nodding his head as he put down his coffee cup. He was still doing the Mashed Potato at the end of the song, and he started up again with the next. He remembered a step of Coleman's that had been a sort of jumping jack with attitude.

Swann tried, but the move fell off the beat. He went back to what he knew, dancing without a worry until the time came to leave for work. He ended in a happier sweat than had ever come from jogging.

On payday, the first to collect their checks were the two young cops who had replaced Swann and Coleman in plainclothes. One was a Hispanic male, the other a white female who had been to college and was said to be gay. Both were brusque with Swann, as if they were the real cops and he was just some washed-up thief. He looked at them and mused that he had lately begun seeing more and more cops who did not fit the stereotype.

Fredricks then came in and his glower indicated just how miserable Lieutenant Gentile must have made him following the events of Saint Patrick's Day.

"You know, Officer Swann, when they take your gun and shield, they call it your *equipment*," Fredricks said. "That's because they think if they come out and ask for the gun, it'd be like asking for your cock."

Swann inferred that Fredricks must have heard IAD was preparing to act.

"Which shows how much IAD knows about my cock," Swann said.

Fredricks left Swann to quake. Swann instead fell to reflecting that *cock* had sounded like something with wattles, that he still had no name for the extremity that had charted so much of his life.

Swann had a cop's goom speaking in his ear and paperwork from a collar for dollars in his hand. Lieutenant Gentile walked in with the two men who had first shadowed him.

"Officer Swann, you are hereby notified as per the chief of the department that you are suspended forthwith," Gentile said.

Gentile's tone was solemn, but his eyes shone.

"You are ordered to surrender your equipment," he said.

Swann held his revolver out butt first. The barrel slipped from his fingers feeling not at all like his manhood, but very much like the weapon with which he had killed and that had almost killed him. He decided he had been right to imagine that he would be less pained by what he was losing than by who was doing the taking.

"The shield," Gentile said.

Swann handed over the shield and listened to it make a faint, dull click as it joined the revolver in Gentile's attaché case. The revolver was just a weapon that even a crook could get. The shield was authority, not only on duty but off duty as well, the power to grab robbers and track down posses, to live as he imagined himself living.

"There's still the other . . ." Gentile said.

"Gun?" Swann asked.

Gentile was speaking of the Walther PPK that would be listed on Swann's firearms card, the James Bond gun, the one that Swann had last seen on Christmas. Swann had since then found no compelling reason to remind Ellen that she had the gun in her possession.

"It's at my house," Swann said.

Gentile lowered the lid of the attaché case and snapped the twin latches shut.

"Let's go get it," he said.

Swann now considered that he might be open to an added charge if IAD discovered that he was keeping a weapon in a residence where he no longer lived.

"Let me just let my wife know in case she's running around in a negligee or something," Swann said.

Swann dialed the number and listened to the phone ring as he stood with the men from IAD. He noticed the first definite effect of losing his revolver, a slight slackening of the waistband such as had first signaled to him that he had begun to lose weight.

"Somebody would have answered by now," Gentile said.

Swann put down the receiver. Gentile took up the attaché case and led the way past the silent cops at the front desk. Even Marie seemed intimidated by IAD, though she did grin when Swann gave an unprompted look at his fly.

The gray unmarked car stood at the curb. Swann climbed into the back with one of his former shadows. The other one drove, and Lieutenant Gentile took the front passenger seat, lighting his pipe. The smoke was so bad that Swann was in one sense relieved when they pulled up to his former home.

The man next to Swann then spoke for the first time.

"We had you residing at another address," the man said.

"That's my father's," Swann said.

Swann stepped from the car, and the men from IAD were right behind him as he went up his stoop. He made a show of searching his pockets and then muttered that he must have forgotten his keys.

"Maybe somebody's home now," Gentile said.

Swann knocked and listened for footsteps approaching down the hall. He instead heard a shout come from behind.

"Daddy!"

Swann turned and saw Jenny running up the block, leather baseball hat cocked sideways. He met her at the bottom of the stoop and held her as Ellen approached, pushing a shopping cart loaded with groceries.

"You may remember Lieutenant Gentile of IAD," Swann said.

"How could I forget," Ellen said.

Ellen took one of the grocery bags from the cart as Swann explained that he had been suspended and that the men from IAD were there to take the other gun.

"I don't know why this doesn't make me happy," Ellen said.

"Let me help you here," Swann said.

Ellen let Swann take the grocery bags. He called to the IAD men.

"Hey, fellas, feel like giving a hand?" Swann asked.

Even the Dark Side could not refuse, and Swann went into the house with Ellen and had just enough lead time to quietly ask if she had returned the gun to the usual place.

"I don't even think it works," Ellen said.

The IAD men came in with the rest of the groceries.

"Maybe you could help her unload while I get what you want," Swann said.

Swann went back to the bedroom with Jenny scampering after him. He noticed that the bed was covered with a new spread of a hotter pink than he ever would have expected Ellen to pick. He opened the closet door to see that she had hung her few coats and dresses to fill the gap where his things had been. The gun was still in the back of the shelf overhead.

"Daddy, are you giving that to those men?" Jenny asked.

"Yes, baby, I am," Swann said.

"Why?" Jenny asked.

Swann popped out the clip in the butt.

"Because I don't need it anymore," he said.

Swann pointed the muzzle at the floor and yanked back the slide. The chamber was empty.

"I'm not going to be a policeman for a while," he said.

Swann started back across the room with Jenny at his heels.

"What if somebody needs help?" she asked.

Swann blurted the first response that came to him.

"I can still try to help them," he said.

Jenny's voice turned victorious, as it did when she had come up with a solution.

"And you could call the police!" she said.

In the kitchen, Ellen was putting the cash register tape from her latest redeeming on the refrigerator. Swann handed the gun to Gentile, who placed it in the attaché case.

"You are to call the operations desk before oh-nine-hundred tomorrow," Gentile said. "At which time, you will be notified of any further action."

The attaché case in hand, Gentile nodded to Ellen. She held a dozen bars of soap whose packaging would be mailed off for some gift or refund.

"I'll show these gentlemen out," Swann said.

Swann walked the IAD men to the front door and stood at the top of the stoop with Jenny as they climbed into the gray car.

"You're not going with them?" Jenny asked.

"No, sweetie," Swann said.

"Are you coming back in?"

The car drove away. Swann felt as small and tame as his father had seemed that night at the post office when he had to wait those four extra minutes to step off.

"No, sweetie," Swann said. "I have to go."

"Wait!" Jenny said.

She dashed inside and returned a moment later with her basket of multicolored Easter eggs.

"You can have one, Daddy," Jenny said. "Take any one you want."

Swann looked from egg to egg.

"They're all so beautiful," he said. "You better choose."

"No, you," Jenny said.

Swann selected one that had been crowned with glitter and ringed with yellow and white feathers. The yolk had been blown out through pinholes at the ends, and the shell lay almost weightless in his cupped hand as he went up the street.

Swann's fragile gift arrived at Joseph's house safe in his palm.

"Jenny made it," Swann said.

"I figured," Joseph said.

"I got suspended. I had to go by the house because they wanted a gun I had left there."

Joseph took a moment to ponder this latest development.

"That does not sound good," Joseph said.

Joseph looked back down at the egg with its feathers and glitter.

"You wonder where kids get it," Joseph said.

"And where it goes," Swann said.

Swann took the egg into his room and placed it on his dresser where he would have put his revolver and his shield.

Swann telephoned the operations desk and was told what he expected to hear, that he had been suspended without pay. His sole official duty until his departmental trial would be to call back every morning to be told that he was still suspended and should call back the following morning.

Swann hung up only to hear the phone ring.

"It's me."

Coleman had heard what happened.

"You'll beat it," Coleman said.

Swann said nothing, for Coleman knew as well as he did that nobody in recent memory had been acquitted in a departmental trial. The outcome was decided when the charges were lodged.

"Feel like meeting?" Coleman asked.

"I'm not really in the mood for Times Square," Swann said.

"Coney Island?"

That sounded better, but he was not ready to go anywhere, not even with Coleman.

"Maybe after I beat it," Swann said.

Joseph went grocery shopping in the afternoon. Swann stayed home and blasted the radio as he straightened and cleaned. He was making his room shipshape when he caught his image in the mirror affixed to the closet door. He remembered what Mannering had said about practice making perfect, and he faced the glass.

"I borrowed it."

Swann caught himself nodding his head to the music that had followed him into the room. He soon beheld Jack Swann dancing as if he were rolling through a tunnel. He again attempted Coleman's move, trying to match his image in the glass with his memory of her, practice making nowhere near perfect.

Swann stopped on hearing a knock at the door. He wondered for a moment if Joseph had paid his gas bill, but he decided to take a risk. He opened the door to see a short man whose most distinguishing feature was a bulbous nose.

"Mr. John J. Swann?" the man asked.

"Yes," Swann said.

The man held out a folded piece of paper. Swann returned to the living room with a subpoena commanding him to appear at a particular date and time before a Transit Authority hearing referee. He was to answer charges of egregious misconduct, in that he had violated Chapter 2, paragraph 6 of the rules and regulations of the Manual of the New York City Transit Police Department.

The time had come for Swann to telephone the lawyer held on retainer by his union. He made several attempts to reach David Meltzer, Esq., each of which led to the same initial response.

"I'll see if he's in," the secretary would say.

A minute or two would pass, and the secretary would then come back on with what sounded like a variation on *He's in the field.*

"I'm sorry, Mr. Meltzer is on a conference call."

Swann finally left his number, and Mr. Meltzer returned his call the next day. The lawyer had the same uninterested tone as on the night of the shooting, the tone of a *cave counsel.*

"I don't know if you saw what was in the newspapers," Swann said.

Meltzer only at this moment made the connection with the bust at Eleanor's. His voice became animated.

"Oh, yes, of course, why don't you come right on in and we'll talk," Meltzer said.

Swann hung up. He no longer had his gun and shield, but he did have the yo-yo, and he was not beyond the simple comfort of a few tosses as he headed out.

Meltzer's office proved to be no bigger than the anti-crime room at District 1, with his inner sanctum about five feet from the secretary's desk. The secretary could have simply leaned back in her chair to announce Swann's arrival, but she nonetheless used the intercom. Swann could clearly hear Meltzer speaking into his phone.

"Tell him I'll be right out," Meltzer said.

The secretary put down her phone.

"Mr. Meltzer says he'll be right out," the secretary said.

The phone rang and the secretary picked up.

"I'll see if he's in," the secretary said.

She put the caller on hold and buzzed Meltzer to say that an Officer something-or-other was on the line.

"Not now," Meltzer said.

The secretary took a sip of coffee, shifted in her seat, sighed, and then returned to the caller on hold.

"Mr. Meltzer is on a conference call," the secretary said.

Meltzer then appeared in the doorway, without the slouch Swann remembered from that night at Midtown North. Meltzer now was not some lumpish *cave counsel* handling another petty trespass by some transit cop. He was a *real* lawyer who had a *real* case, one that had made the front page.

"Glad to meet you," Meltzer said.

Swann took Meltzer's hand, and the grip was firm. Swann said that they had met before.

"I've lost some weight since then," Swann said.

"I'm sorry, I can't quite place it," Meltzer said.

"It was a shooting."

Meltzer squinted, as if straining to bring a vague recollection into focus.

"Well, that wasn't anything to worry about," Meltzer said. "*That* wasn't a problem."

Meltzer gestured for Swann to enter the inner office. Swann took a seat, his knees brushing against a wooden desk of such scale as to be appropriate for a room several times larger.

Meltzer sat on the other side in a high-backed black leather chair. He seemed to avoid inquiring as to the source of Swann's money. He asked only if Swann had a particular reason to have been carrying so much cash.

"To spend it," Swann said.

Meltzer nodded as if this was a completely reasonable response. He continued with what was not so much a line of questioning as a precise circle.

"You don't want to know if I did it?" Swann asked.

"It's a lot of pressure representing an innocent man," Meltzer said.

Meltzer smiled.

"But it almost never happens," Meltzer said.

"I didn't do it," Swann said.

"I'm not suggesting you did," Meltzer said. "I'm just saying I don't need to ask."

"And I suppose nobody can say you had a witness lie on the stand if you don't know what the truth is in the first place," Swann said.

"To knowingly have a witness testify falsely would be to suborn perjury," Meltzer said.

Meltzer and Swann then discussed who might be helpful as a defense witness. Swann suggested that his partner, Coleman, would corroborate much of his story.

"I would hope so," Meltzer said.

Meltzer recapped his pen and embarked on a general description of what to expect at the hearing. Swann would not be a defendant, but a *respondent*, and he would have not a judge, but one of the per diem *hearing officers* who sat one day a week. Whichever hearing officer they drew would reach not a verdict but a *finding*. The official rules of evidence permitted hearsay and would not require IAD to prove its case beyond a reasonable doubt, only to demonstrate that a preponderance of the evidence supported its theory.

"That means the weight of the evidence *substantiates* the allegations," Meltzer said.

Meltzer went on to explain that the real rules of evidence were that IAD did not need any evidence at all.

"There was one hearing officer who I would have to say was reasonable, maybe even fair," Meltzer said. "But his contract came up."

Meltzer checked Swann's notice for the date of the hearing and consulted his calendar.

"It's a Tuesday, so it's Judge Aronowitz," Meltzer said.

"I thought you said there isn't a judge," Swann said.

"He *was* a judge," Meltzer said. "But he retired years ago."

Meltzer then concluded his description of the proceeding that would determine Swann's future.

"Everybody says it's a kangaroo court," Meltzer said. "It's actually no kind of court at all."

"What do you mean they don't need proof?" Joseph asked.

"They don't need proof," Swann said.

Swann went to bed, and over the days that followed he came to appreciate the accuracy of the term "suspended." He was neither cop nor not cop, neither on nor off duty. He could still dance, and that continued to provide him with both exercise and escape.

At an instant when he was simultaneously extending his arms and legs, Swann felt the movement emanating not from his hips and shoulders, but from a single place at his middle. He decided that this was the very spot that had guided his grandfather across the high steel.

The telephone rang, and Swann picked up.

"You sound out of breath," Meltzer said.

"I was dancing," Swann said.

"I see," Meltzer said.

Meltzer proceeded to go over some discovery materials supplied by the Transit Authority. This included a list of probable witnesses.

"Simone Coleman is your partner, and I've spoken to her," Meltzer said. "Who's this Danica Neary?"

Swann fumbled for an appropriate way to describe what Danica had been to him, and he might as well have been trying to label his unnamed extremity. She had not really been a *lover* or a *girlfriend* and he would not have felt right calling her a *goom*.

"There should be a word for the girl you always wanted in high school," Swann said.

"Joan Atlas," Meltzer said.

Meltzer spoke as if he were saying it not to Swann, but to himself. He exhaled audibly and proceeded with the matter at hand. He reminded Swann that the hearing was the following morning.

"It won't make any difference, but you might wear a suit," Meltzer said. "It never hurts to make a good impression."

Twenty

AFTER A SLEEPLESS NIGHT, Swann took his suit from the closet to dress for the shabby fate Coleman had too rightly predicted as they approached the crack spot. He wrapped some cellophane tape around his hand and lifted stray specks of lint from the jacket as he would from a uniform in preparation for parading up Fifth Avenue. He reknotted his bow tie until it was exactly right.

The still trim Swann had no trouble bending over to tie his shoes. He decided he liked the two-tone wing tips even better with the suit.

Swann was complete with a fresh rosebud on his lapel when he arrived at the Transit Authority building in downtown Brooklyn. Coleman was standing by the entrance in a purple nylon pants suit. She eyed him from homburg to two-tones.

"You keep this up, you might have style someday," Coleman said.

The suspension had given Swann lots of opportunity to work on his yo-yo and he executed a double Around the World before entering. Coleman this time held the door for him.

On the fifth floor, Swann and Coleman stepped into a corridor as gloomy as anything in the underground. A number of figures were seated in a line outside the door to the hearing room, and both Swann and Coleman immediately recognized the one on the far right.

The manager of the crack spot sat wearing an orange shirt buttoned to the top and a black suit. The next chair over was occupied by one of the IAD shadows and beside him were a desk officer from District 1 and a clerk from the Plaza. The row ended with the Fifth

Avenue jeweler who had sold Swann the Rolex and the city detective who had later been dispatched to recover the watch from Pinnacle's lady friend.

All of them suddenly fixed their attention on something behind Swann. He turned to see that Danica had just stepped off the elevator. Her face had healed without obvious scars and the rest of her was as magnificent as always. She was wearing the same black dress whose tiny eyehook he had fastened in that last instant before he said he was going home.

Swann watched Danica come down the hallway as he had in high school, but what he imagined was not embracing her. He simply wondered what she was thinking.

"Hello, Jack," Danica said.

Her eyes gave him no hint.

"Hi, Danica," Swann said. "You've met my partner."

"Simone, right?" Danica asked.

"You have a good memory," Coleman said.

Danica ran a hand through her hair and Swann saw a watch on her wrist. He himself had no eye for real gold, but he was sure it was the counterfeit. The real Rolex was no doubt still being held as evidence against the posse as well as himself.

"See you inside," Danica said.

Danica walked over to the other witnesses. Swann noted that even the crack spot manager rose to offer her a seat. She remained standing.

"Here's our woman," Coleman said.

Swann saw that Estrella had arrived. She had on a white dress and a dark blue hat.

"I don't know what they think I would say against you," Estrella said.

Estrella went to join the rest of the witnesses. Nobody offered her a seat and she stood with Danica.

Meltzer strode up wearing a pinstripe suit nearly as nice as Swann's.

"You might have worn something a little less pricey," Meltzer said. "And I probably should have said something about shoes."

"Does it matter?" Swann asked.

"Probably not," Meltzer said.

Meltzer offered a lawyerly greeting to Coleman and looked over at the witnesses. He turned back to Swann as if to make a remark, but glanced at Coleman and checked himself.

"You can say anything in front of my partner," Swann said.

"I have no doubt," Meltzer said.

Meltzer did not continue with whatever he had been going to say. He instead announced that the hearing was due to begin.

"How about we go on in?" Meltzer asked.

The *we* did not include Coleman, who was herself a witness and was therefore required to wait outside until she was summoned to testify. She and Swann stood before each other and the moment would have called for a dramatic exchange had he been facing a real trial and not a foregone conclusion.

The line that did come to Swann was from the street photographer's banner before which Daryl Coombs had posed back on Liberty Weekend.

"As they say in Times Square, 'Go big or stay home,'" Swann said.

The hearing room was closer in size to the stage at Swann's grammar school than courtrooms where he had gone with even the pettiest arrests. He and Meltzer sat at a table to the left.

"Let me ask you something," Meltzer said.

Meltzer leaned close.

"There's this woman out there . . ."

Swann understood that this was what Meltzer had been reluctant to say in front of Coleman.

"Danica," Swann said.

Meltzer seemed to appraise Swann.

"I don't know if Joan Atlas ever looked like that," Meltzer said.

Meltzer pulled a yellow legal pad from his attaché case.

"Do you want a pad?" Meltzer asked. "Some clients like to take notes. I think it's because they see it on television."

Swann declined and glanced over at the table on the right. Lieutenant Gentile had arrived wearing a gray bargain-store suit that did not keep him, too, from the look of being on parade. He sat erect and remote all of six feet away.

A rasp Swann recognized as the rub of a fatso's thighs accompanied the appearance of a stout young man at Gentile's side. This had to be the lawyer for the Transit Authority, and though he was in danger of splitting the seams of his drab blue suit, the bigness he seemed to feel most keenly was his role as chief accuser in a case of *real* corruption. He sat with his head up, his plump hands on the table before him, his face as solemn as that of someone preparing to champion some higher authority than Transit.

A nondescript young woman took position at a stenographer's machine and a uniformed transit cop arrived to serve as a bailiff and then an elderly man shuffled through a door at the front of the room. His suit might have been from Brooks Brothers, but years before. His shoulders were stooped and his pink dome was splotched with liver spots. He hesitated before mounting the two-inch platform that raised a wooden table in an approximation of a judge's bench.

Judge Aronowitz gingerly lowered himself into the chair and gazed with milky eyes through a pair of oversized spectacles that had clear plastic frames. He had once been a real judge, but he now gave no sign of feeling himself to be anything but a per diem hearing officer.

"We might as well get started," Aronowitz said.

The TA lawyer rose.

"Your honor, the Authority calls Kharey Timmons to the stand," the TA lawyer said.

The crack spot manager entered and stepped up to the witness chair. He raised a right hand that had gold rings even on the thumb and solemnly swore to tell the truth, the whole truth, and nothing but the truth.

The TA lawyer asked his occupation.

"On the strength?" the manager asked.

"What did you say?" the stenographer asked.

"I had occasion earlier to ask him about that expression," the TA lawyer said. "It means 'to be honest' or 'to tell the truth.'"

"Right," the manager said.

"Moving on now, what do you do for a living?"

"Drug dealer."

The TA lawyer asked the manager to think back to an afternoon the previous year. The manager said he had just tallied the day's take and placed it in a plastic bag when he spied two plainclothes cops approaching.

"Do you see either of those officers in this room?"

The manager pointed a ringed finger at Swann.

"Him," the manager said.

"Indicating the respondent," the TA lawyer said.

The manager resumed his account, saying that he had tried to flee only to be tackled and beaten. He said that Swann had taken the bag and that the exact amount inside had been $66,300.

"But Officer Swann only vouchered fifty-six thousand, three hundred and twelve dollars."

"I got my dollars *clocked*," the manager said. "Word to mother."

The manager went on to testify that Swann had made a second visit to the crack spot, but had not been able to get any more cash.

"Thank you, Mr. Timmons," the TA lawyer said. "That will be all."

Meltzer rose for the cross-examination. His questions were quiet at first, but slowly grew louder, as if the answers were filling him with moral indignation. He strode back and forth in the eight square feet of open space.

"Were you not in the act of selling drugs when you were arrested?"

"I don't sell. I manage."

"At the time of your arrest, was somebody purchasing crack cocaine at the location you *manage?*"

"Yup."

"Would you be surprised if I told you the girl who was purchasing the crack is thirteen years old?"

"I didn't really look. I know she ugly."

Meltzer suddenly seemed to have had enough, and he hurled his next question in an angry, booming voice that was all the more startling for the witness stand being within arm's reach. The jury would no doubt have been mesmerized had there been one.

"What can be uglier than a death merchant?" Meltzer said.

The manager responded by sucking on his teeth. Meltzer boomed again.

"A death merchant who tries to stay out of jail by smearing the reputation of an upstanding police officer!"

Meltzer seemed to have hit exactly the right *beat,* and Swann was cheered until he noticed that Aronowitz's head had dropped. The hearing officer gave no sign of having heard a word of it.

The next witness Aronowitz might or might not have heard was Estrella. She reluctantly confirmed that Swann had twice visited the block and chased away the crackheads.

"Which is more than I can say about the other police," Estrella said.

"Perhaps Officer Swann was being better paid," the TA lawyer said.

Estrella stepped down, to be followed by the desk officer from District 1 and the IAD shadow and the clerk from the Plaza and the Fifth Avenue jeweler. The TA lawyer held up a clear plastic evidence bag.

"Your Honor, I would now like to enter into evidence a gold Rolex watch," the TA lawyer said.

The bailiff's weary, indifferent voice then called the Authority's final witness.

"Danica Neary."

The hearing room suddenly seemed to become even smaller, and the judge not only raised his head but straightened in his chair. The TA lawyer stuck out his chin. Meltzer seemed to puff up even a little more under his pinstripes.

Danica raised her right hand, the nails painted magenta, her wrist bearing the counterfeit watch. She swore to tell the truth and then demonstrated one reason her dress was not traditional court wear was that the hem rode a good six inches up her thigh.

"Ms. Neary, how are you today?" the TA lawyer asked.

"Hiya," Danica said.

The TA lawyer asked Danica if she had what he termed a "social relationship" with the respondent.

"More like we had a fling," Danica said.

The hearing officer seemed completely alert, the eyes behind his oversized glasses going from Danica to Swann to Danica, the lenses magnifying the same reaction shown by Meltzer. He appeared to take in every word as the questioning led her through her adventures with Jack Swann. She told of drinking champagne at the Oak Bar and staying in a room overlooking the park at the Plaza and having the table next to Ron Parker at Angkor What?.

"Would it be fair to say that all of this cost a great deal of money?" the TA lawyer asked.

"Certainly," Danica said.

The hearing officer again looked from Danica to Swann, the oversized lenses now magnifying a knowingness, as if the pieces had come together, as if he now understood not only why Swann had ripped off the death merchant, but the deeper mystery of what a woman like this was ever doing with a *cave cop*.

"Ms. Neary, did there come a time last January when you were the victim of a crime?" the TA lawyer asked.

Danica paused and bowed her head. The focus on her was such that the mood of the whole room seemed to shift.

"Yes," Danica said. "I was attacked."

"And, in the course of that attack, was something taken?" the TA lawyer asked.

Danica's head came up.

"A watch. And a Walkman."

"I direct your attention to the watch you are presently wearing. Is that the watch that was taken?"

"I thought it was, but it wasn't."

"I wonder if you might explain that."

Danica recrossed her legs and squared her shoulders. She had not missed the patronizing note that had slipped into the TA lawyer's tone.

"The one I have here, it's like you buy on the street," Danica said. "It's not real, and then it broke, so don't ask me why I kept wearing it. I just like the look."

"But you were not wearing it on the day of the attack."

"So I found out later. What had happened was, when we were in the hotel, I left it on a table and he made a switch while I wasn't looking."

"And he did not say anything to you?"

"If he had said anything, I wouldn't have thought it was my old watch."

"A simple yes or no, please."

"No."

The TA lawyer then presented Danica with the evidence bag containing the gold Rolex.

"Ms. Neary, I would now like to bring your attention to this gold Rolex watch," the TA lawyer said. "From what you can determine, is this the watch you were wearing at the time of the attack?"

Danica studied the watch through the clear plastic.

"It's still working," Danica said.

Danica's eyes flashed to Swann and returned to her questioner.

"I set it when we were in the hotel," Danica said. "I just thought my old watch had started working. I thought it was a sign of something good."

Danica again gazed down at the watch.

"Ms. Neary, I would ask you to stay with the questions," the TA lawyer said.

Danica looked up.

"I guess you're going to ask why he switched them," Danica said. "I figure he wanted me to come away with something, even if I didn't know it right then."

"Ms. Neary, please . . ."

"That was the same night he left me."

Her eyes snapped back to Swann and the years of being mesmerized by her ended with him having to force himself not to look away. He could feel the room poise with a single question, but the TA lawyer could hardly say, *A schmo like him left a tomata like you?*

"And how did you come to reacquire the watch you are presently wearing?" the TA lawyer asked.

"He came and gave it to me," Danica said. "After he and his partner caught the ones that attacked me. He gave me the watch and told me about switching it."

"Did he tell you why he had chosen that moment to inform you?"

"No."

"At one point did he say that someone might be coming to question you in the near future?"

"Yes. People that had been following him."

"Were you already aware of these people and why they had been following him?"

"They thought he had taken money."

"And were you in fact visited by anyone?"

"Some detectives. And the lieutenant right there."

Danica aimed a polished fingernail at Lieutenant Gentile. She kept her voice as neutral as if she were answering the phone at work.

"It wasn't about me being attacked. They really just wanted to know about the watch and the money."

Swann went empty at the thought of her standing with her battered face while IAD asked about everything but what had happened to her. He was certain that Gentile had shown her the picture taken of her outside Eleanor's.

"And what, if anything, had Officer Swann told you about the source of his money?" the TA lawyer asked.

"He borrowed it," Danica said. "When I told that to the lieutenant, he just said, 'I've heard enough about borrowing.'"

"I take it you believed what Officer Swann had told you about borrowing the money?"

"Sure."

Swann felt a lurch, for he was sure she had not.

"If you really want to know, it was my idea," Danica said.

Swann sat amazed. Danica's unbandaged face was composed as if a plastic surgeon had just said, *Now look truthful.* The room again poised with a single question and this was one the TA lawyer had no choice but to ask.

"Borrowing the money was at your suggestion?" the TA lawyer asked.

"Is this a yes or a no?" Danica asked.

"Yes."

"Then I'd have to say yes. But there's more to it."

The TA lawyer paused, as if to establish that he was in charge.

"At the time you say you made this suggestion, were you aware of the money Officer Swann had *found?*" the TA lawyer asked.

"If you want to know, that's what made me think of it," Danica said.

Danica glanced at Swann. He tried to detect if revenge lay behind her mask of honesty, if she was going to spell out the scheme that she had suspected.

"At what point did you become aware of the money in question?" the TA lawyer asked.

The TA lawyer's tone was going from patronizing to edgy. He was being compelled to do what lawyers abhor. He was having to ask questions to which he did not already know the answer.

"I was getting on the subway and I ran into Jack and we got talking and he asked me how work is," Danica said. "I tell him, 'Don't even ask me about work. I wouldn't even think of going back there if I didn't need money.' That starts me on money, which I don't usually talk about. You know, when I grew up, one thing that was never discussed in my house was money. It wasn't for children to hear, because we were kids."

"Please, Ms. Neary . . ."

"I know what you're thinking," Danica said. "You're thinking, 'What's this got to do with anything?' Right?"

"I'm the one who should be asking the questions," the TA lawyer said.

Danica sat silent, her hands folded in her lap.

"At some point in the conversation did Officer Swann discuss the money he had found?" the TA lawyer asked.

"I'm getting to that," Danica said. "We're on the train, and I'm telling him that I'm not a kid anymore and now it's all money, money, money. That's when he tells me about finding a whole bag full of money the day before. He says he chased this kid who was selling drugs and this kid dropped a whole bag full of money and said it wasn't his. I asked Jack what he did with it and he looked at me like I had asked a stupid question. He said, 'I turned it in.' I said, 'All of it?' and he said, 'Of course all of it.' I tell him, well, if it had been me that found that money, I would have kept some, like maybe ten thousand dollars. I said, 'I wouldn't be riding this train and going home to cook. I'd be eating out and I'd be drinking champagne and I'd be taking a limo home.'"

Danica gave the TA lawyer the slightly vacant look she would have given if he had been right to patronize her.

"I know what you're thinking now. 'What about the borrowing?' Right?" Danica asked.

The TA lawyer looked at this woman who he had apparently felt needed only a cursory interview before the hearing. He seemed to have brought her in not so much a witness as evidence, a jurisprudential piece of ass that would prove the respondent had a compelling motive to risk everything. Now he could summon only a nod.

"Since you want to know, I'll tell you," Danica said. "What happened was, I got to talking, and what I talked about was all those Wall Street types who borrow millions and drink champagne and ride around in limos with money that they don't really have. I look at Jack, and I say, 'Here's you, a cop who risks his life every day. You find a bag of money that nobody wants to say is theirs and you turn it all in and here you are riding the train.' And he's like, 'What are you gonna do?' And that's when I said what I wish I hadn't."

Swann saw that the TA lawyer had been about to cut Danica off, but he could only stand there as she rolled ahead as if she were talking of vacuuming or Santa Claus.

"Not that I really meant anything. I was only talking. I said, 'You know that commercial for the Money Store? Sometimes, I see that and I think, Why not? Why not just go in and borrow some money. You have to pay it back, but at least you had it to spend.' That must have got him thinking, because a couple days later I'm leaving work and I run into him, only I could tell he had been waiting for me. He's all dressed up and he tells me he'd done what I said. He'd gone to the Money Store."

Danica paused.

"I never thought that would happen, and after that there were all these other things I never thought would happen. But, we've already talked about that, so I won't waste everybody's time. And that's it, unless there's something else you want to know."

The TA lawyer no doubt had some questions, but that would have entailed Danica's answering them.

"I have nothing further, thank you," the TA lawyer said.

"You're welcome," Danica said.

Meltzer decided to leave well enough alone and said he saw no reason to subject Ms. Neary to cross-examination. Danica turned toward the hearing officer.

"Your Honor, now I'm done being a witness, am I allowed to stay and see what happens?" Danica asked.

"I don't see why not," the hearing officer said.

The hearing officer's gaze followed Danica as she took the seven steps from the witness chair to the spectators' section. He then looked once more at Swann. The eyes behind the magnifying lenses had become less knowing than intrigued.

"The Authority rests," the TA lawyer said.

The TA lawyer sat down as if he did indeed need a rest, and Swann had the wild sense that he just might have a chance.

"The respondent may proceed," the hearing officer said.

"The respondent calls Officer Coleman," Meltzer said.

The bailiff twice stole glances at Danica as he swore in Coleman. The hearing officer's magisterial air was no doubt more for the benefit of the woman in the spectators' section than the one who now assumed the witness chair.

Meltzer took Coleman quickly through an account of what had transpired on the crack block, and then the TA lawyer began his cross-examination. She kept to the simple truth that she would have noticed if Swann had taken fistfuls of cash from the bag.

"In other words, you can only tell us what you did *not* see," the TA lawyer said. "You really have no way of being *certain* of the respondent's actions at every moment."

The TA lawyer seemed almost to have recovered from his experience with Danica, and his voice once again had the ring of an accuser. He suggested that cops traditionally back up their partners.

"Do I look like somebody who would put up with a criminal?" Coleman asked.

The TA lawyer looked at Coleman in the latest offering from her closet.

"I have no further questions, Officer," he said.

Coleman stepped down, and Meltzer announced that the respondent also rested. The hearing officer said he would reserve decision, which was only usual in such proceedings. He sneaked a last look at Danica before rising with all the majesty he could muster.

The room filled with the scuffle of chairs and muttering voices. Meltzer whispered to Swann.

"I can't believe it, but we might be all right," Meltzer said.

Meltzer studied Swann as if seeking some final truth.

"She's a pretty girl," Meltzer said.

Swann nodded. Meltzer shook his head and stole a glance of his own at Danica.

"Anyway, we'll be notified by mail," Meltzer said. "It shouldn't be more than two weeks."

Coleman was waiting for Swann at the back of the room, and they approached the elevator just as Danica was stepping in. Danica kept a painted fingertip on the Open button as they boarded.

"Thanks," Swann said.

Swann caught those cat's green eyes.

"And thanks," Swann said.

Danica gave Swann a look of innocence that any transit cop would envy.

"I don't know what you mean," Danica said.

The common path to the subway took Swann and Coleman and Danica down into the underground together. Coleman flashed her shield to the clerk, and Swann reached for his own before he remembered it was still in a drawer at IAD. He turned with Danica to buy tokens.

"Whoa," Coleman said.

Coleman held open the gate.

"You're with me," Coleman said.

Swann followed Danica through the gate, and the three of them came to where passengers bound for Queens part with those headed deeper into Brooklyn. Coleman spoke to Danica.

"You know, you really did right," Coleman said.

"Whatever," Danica said.

Danica shot Swann a sidelong glance that suggested she had not forgotten those last moments at the Plaza when he had spoken of what was *right*.

"Be seeing you all," Coleman said.

Coleman was here addressing them both. Swann suspected that Danica might feel awkward riding off with him. He at the same time was not so ready to part with Coleman.

"Actually, I'm going out your way," Swann said.

Swann met Coleman's eyes, and what passed between them must have been apparent to Danica.

"*Oooh,*" Danica said.

Santa's Reindeer

Dasher

Dancer

Prancer

and

Vixen

Comet

Cupid

Doner

Blizen

and

Rudolph